TELL ME LIES

Also by Tony Strong

THE POISON TREE
THE DEATH PIT
THE DECOY

TELL ME LIES

TONY STRONG

BANTAM PRESS

LONDON · NEW YORK · TORONTO · SYDNEY · AUCKLAND

TRANSWORLD PUBLISHERS
61–63 Uxbridge Road, London W5 5SA
a division of The Random House Group Ltd

RANDOM HOUSE AUSTRALIA (PTY) LTD
20 Alfred Street, Milsons Point, Sydney,
New South Wales 2061, Australia

RANDOM HOUSE NEW ZEALAND LTD
18 Poland Road, Glenfield, Auckland 10, New Zealand

RANDOM HOUSE SOUTH AFRICA (PTY) LTD
Endulini, 5a Jubilee Road, Parktown 2193, South Africa

Published 2003 by Bantam Press
a division of Transworld Publishers

Extracts on pages 62, 130 and 166 are from, respectively, Rudyard Kipling's *Just So Stories*,
The Jungle Book and 'The Ladies', and are reprinted with the permission of A. P. Watt Ltd on
behalf of The National Trust for Places of Historical Interest or Natural Beauty.

A catalogue record for this book is available from the British Library.
ISBN 0593 050711

Typeset in 11/13pt Sabon by
Kestrel Data, Exeter, Devon.

Printed in Great Britain by
Mackays of Chatham plc, Chatham, Kent.

1 3 5 7 9 10 8 6 4 2

Some of this is true.
Ros Taylor is a real person, though this isn't her real name.
In retelling her story I have inevitably had to reshape it — without,
I hope, changing the bits that really matter.
As Picasso said, all art is a lie that tells a greater truth.

1
ROS

1

The needle hovers over the soft vulnerable skin in the crook of my elbow. I feel the tiny sting as it skewers me, then a deeper, subcutaneous ache as it pushes inside the vein.

'Almost done,' the doctor murmurs, loosening the tourniquet.

She's solid and professional, her grey hair pulled back in a bun. When she withdraws the needle, a tiny red berry swells from the puncture. She presses a pad of cotton wool on it and places my finger on top to hold it there while she tears a strip of tape from a dispenser.

This isn't happening.

She measures the blood from the syringe into three different phials. Their tops are colour-coded; purple, grey and red. On the red-topped tube are the words: 'ATTENTION. Serological samples only. This tube contains no anticoagulants. For DNA use purple jar.'

The doctor picks up her clipboard. 'Do you have any allergies, Ros?'

My mouth forms the word *No.* It must be almost inaudible but it seems to be enough.

'Are you currently taking any prescription drugs?'

No.

'Have you taken any non-prescription drugs in the last forty-eight hours?'

No.

'Is there any possibility that you might be pregnant?'

Oh God, no –

'If you're worried, Alice can take you to the clinic later to get a morning-after pill,' the doctor says gently. 'For now, I just need to know if you could have been pregnant before the assault.'

9

I shake my head.

'When was your last consensual sexual activity?' My confusion must show because she adds, 'We have to know this. It may affect the tests.'

'About six months ago,' I whisper.

'And your last period?'

A thick fog is gusting through my brain. 'I can't remember. Sorry. It'll come back to me.'

'Don't worry. You can let Alice know later.' She makes a note. 'Have you urinated, defecated, or rinsed your mouth or hands since the attack?'

'I think so. I can't remember. I went to the loo. That was when I found—' Images crash through the fog. I close my eyes and force myself to breathe.

'It's all right,' she says quietly. 'You don't have to talk about that yet.' She pulls out another form. 'I'd like to examine you now, Ros. My report will be used by the police as evidence, and it will also help me see what medical treatment you need. But I won't examine you unless you give your consent and you can ask me to stop, or to pause, at any time. If you're all right with that, I'll need you to sign this to say that you agree.'

She hands me the form. At the top are the words 'Declaration of Consent to Medical Examination for Non-treatment Purposes'. I have to sign twice, once where it says that I give my consent to examination and the taking of forensic samples, and once where it says that the doctor has explained what the form means. When I take the pen from her my hand shakes and my signature – a weird, unfamiliar calligraphy, like a loop of stray hair – veers erratically off the dotted lines. It belongs to someone else, some other Ros Taylor. Someone to whom nightmares happen. Not me.

The rape suite is on the seventh floor of a tall police station just off the Edgware Road. Its double-glazed windows look down at a queue of traffic, inching along the Westway flyover in the morning sunshine. The main part of the suite is like a hotel room, or perhaps the waiting room of a private osteopath. There are bland Scandinavian sofas, a cheap wooden coffee table and an incongruous stack of magazines. Beyond this are two other rooms. One is the doctor's, with an adjustable couch and shelves piled high with medical paraphernalia, where my examination is happening. The other door leads to a shower room. When the examination is over I will be allowed to help myself to towels, clean clothes and a range of toiletries. Alice has told me about the toiletries. They are a recent addition, one which Alice is rather proud of.

Alice is a sergeant, although she doesn't wear a uniform. According to the leaflet I have been given she is also my designated chaperone, whatever that means. If I had written it I would have tried to find a better word. 'Chaperone' conjures up visions of debutantes and dances, kisses snatched behind fluttering fans, men in breeches and girls in bonnets; not this cold, scientific drama of serological samples and blood tests. The leaflet also says, in the vague, soothing way that characterizes all of its fifty-four pages, 'Your chaperone has received special training to deal with this type of matter.' Sergeant Alice speaks very slowly and quietly, which is presumably what she was taught in her special training. She wears a knee-length straight skirt, as round as a barrel. In any other circumstances I would probably have had nothing in common with her at all, but as it is I find myself pathetically grateful for her presence.

The doctor has put on see-through plastic gloves and is cleaning under my fingernails with short wooden toothpicks, a different one for each nail. She asks me to open my mouth and she rubs my gums vigorously with a thing like a large cotton bud. Then she plucks half a dozen hairs from my scalp, gripping them with tweezers close to the skin.

'We have to get the root,' she explains when I wince. 'It's for the DNA tests.'

Everything – the cotton buds, spatulas and hairs – goes inside separate white envelopes with FORENSIC SPECIMEN – KEEP REFRIGERATED written across the front. Each time she seals an envelope she picks up a biro in her plastic-gloved hand and carefully writes out my name, her name, which is Dr Philippa Matthiesson, Forensic Medical Examiner, a crime number, a description of the contents and the date. It takes for ever, for which I am grateful. My whole body feels heavy, as if I am filled with glue, the way you feel after a ten-mile walk or a car crash.

She wants to know if I colour my hair.

'Um, sometimes, yes.'

'What with?'

I start to tell her, then stop, confused. For some reason I can't remember.

'It doesn't matter. The lab will know.'

I spit into yet another tube and blow my nose on a sterile tissue. The tissue is folded up, like something valuable, and put into a paper envelope. I give the doctor my shoes, which she puts into a large paper bag. Then she unfolds a square of brown paper and asks me to stand on it. She kneels down and draws an outline around my feet.

'Were these the clothes you were wearing?'

Standing up has made me dizzy and I reach out to the wall for support. 'No.'

'We'll need them anyway, I'm afraid.'

As if in a dream I start to undress. Alice tactfully withdraws. The doctor takes my clothes, folds them, and puts them into large paper bags. Like a shop assistant, I think. 'Just put the receipt in the bag.' Have I said that out loud? Evidently I have. She is looking at me with a quizzical expression on her face.

'Sorry,' I mutter. 'I don't know why I said that.'

'You're probably a bit confused. It's quite normal.'

'I've got the weirdest headache. Like I'm drunk and hungover at the same time.'

'Have you taken anything for it?'

'No.'

'I'll give you something. It'll have to be later, I'm afraid, when all the tests are done.'

I take everything else off and am given a towel in exchange.

'Have you been away?' she asks. I understand from the tone of voice she uses that this is not part of the medical questionnaire but small talk designed to put me at my ease, prompted by the contrast between my pale hips and the rest of me.

'Sardinia. We got back last week.'

'Sardinia's lovely. We went there two years ago.' She points at my stomach. 'I'd better have that, I think.'

I reach down and work the clip that holds the stud in my belly button. I want to tell her that I'm not really the kind of person

12

who pierces her navel. I suddenly feel irrationally guilty and embarrassed about it, as if a piece of metal in my midriff could somehow be to blame. Jo made me, I want to say – which is true: she'd decided we had to get matching ones done for our holiday, and before I could change my mind she'd found somewhere, a place behind Marshall Street run by a camp Australian with bleached hair who'd laughed at Jo's jokes and, when we almost got cold feet, offered to show us his own Prince Albert.

Jo. Trailing admirers and lovesick puppies in her wake. *Jo.* Oh God.

'Would you pop up on the couch for me, Ros?'

She examines me carefully, palpating my skin, occasionally asking me if a spot is tender. I can see faint bruises on my arms underneath my tan. The doctor marks the position of each one on a diagram fixed to her clipboard.

'Is there anywhere else that hurts?'

'On my back. I think there's a cut.'

'OK. Turn over and I'll take a look.'

I can feel her breath on my skin as she examines my shoulder blades. 'I'll mark it on the traumagram, but we'll need some photographs of this,' she says at last. She calls Alice and speaks to her quietly through the door.

There's a long wait while Sergeant Alice goes to find the photographer. I already know, because I've read it in the leaflet, that the police photographer has also received special training to deal with people like me. I rest my head on my arms. The doctor rearranges the towel over me. Bizarrely, I doze off. I dimly become aware that the photographer has arrived and is asking me politely if it's all right to take photographs. I don't answer. I know from the leaflet that they have to ask my permission at every stage. They want me to know that it is my body, that my consent matters to them. But I don't want to make decisions any more. I want to close my eyes and let it all wash over me without any of it touching my hammering brain.

'Go ahead,' I heard the doctor say quietly.

Flash-whirr. Flash-whirr. I open my eyes and see a Polaroid sticking out its tongue.

'Is it bad?' I ask.

The photographer starts to say something but the doctor interrupts. 'Let's get the exam over. Perhaps Alice can show you the photographs later.'

When the others have gone she puts a dressing on my back. Then she closes the blinds and examines me with an ultraviolet torch, like the Woods lights we use at work to examine the surface of paintings. In the strange purple half-light it is less hard for me to open my legs when she asks me to. She spends a lot of time peering between my thighs and around my breasts. When she has turned the overhead lights back on she takes a pad, moistens it with distilled water, and wipes it carefully and thoroughly over my thighs and crotch.

'I need to comb your pubis for forensic traces,' she says. 'It may be a little uncomfortable.' She presses a wooden comb against my stomach, just above my pubic hair. I can feel the teeth raking me, hard, the way a schoolgirl rakes a horse with hard steel combs and curry brushes. For a moment I drift off again into a sort of woozy fantasy in which I am somewhere else altogether. The doctor puts the comb into yet another envelope and seals it.

'I'll need to take some hairs as well. You can do it yourself if you'd rather.'

I just want to get this over with. 'You do it.'

She plucks six pubic hairs, holding each one up to the light to make sure it has a root.

'I'm going to give you an internal now. If it's too painful, just tell me and we'll stop until you feel better.'

There are portable stirrups on a trolley, which she wheels up to the couch. I put my feet where she wants them and try to stare at the ceiling as she gets to work.

'I'm afraid I can't use lubricant for this,' she says apologetically. 'It contaminates the swabs.' She tips some clear liquid from a bottle labelled Saline Solution BP into her gloved palm. 'This might help.'

Despite the saline solution her fingers hurt, pushing me this way and that. 'Try to breathe normally,' she instructs, putting her other hand on my stomach and pushing down gently. I force myself to exhale.

'I've nearly finished,' she says. And finally, 'That's done.'

Afterwards there's a similar procedure for my anus, which is mercifully briefer. 'That's the exam over,' she says at last. She rolls off her gloves.

'Did I pass?' Why am I making these terrible jokes?

The doctor says quietly, 'You did very well, Ros. You're a very brave young woman.' There's a pedal bin in the corner and she drops the used gloves into it. 'You can go and shower now.' She hands me another towel, and I swing my feet down onto the floor. For a moment, as I come upright, a sudden gust of dizziness makes me groan. The doctor quickly puts her arm round me and guides me back to a lying position. I close my eyes.

'I'll put a rush on those bloods,' I hear her mutter. 'Ros, stay there until you feel better.'

Eventually I force myself up. As I pass Alice in the sofa room she looks up from a magazine. 'All right?' I nod. 'Use anything you want in there. It's all provided. And help yourself to toiletries.'

Alice's toiletries are all from Superdrug. There is a fruit theme. Apple shampoo. Lemon skin scrub. Orange soap. There is no mirror. I shower quickly, the water stinging the cuts on my back. At one point in the examination the doctor used a blue dye on my bruises and I watch as it rinses off me onto the floor. I am not here, I think again. I am not in a rape suite. I am not in a shower washing saline solution out of my crotch. I can't be.

Then suddenly everything that has happened is crashing back into my brain, a loop of film on fast-forward, and this time I can't push the images away. I'd been holding them off for the examination because I'd had to, but now it's over I'm in free-fall. I stumble out of the shower, howling, crying so hard I can't actually breathe, sucking in great clots of air that stick in my throat, retching and crying and choking at the same time.

Alice comes and gets me out. She is gentle and reassuring and careful as she wraps me in a towel and leads me to one of the sofas.

'I'm sorry,' I say between bouts of crying.

'Don't be silly,' she says. 'Was it because of the shower?'

I nod. 'The shower. Yes. That was where I found Jo.'

*   *   *

Later, when I'm calm enough, Alice finds me a pair of tracksuit trousers and a T-shirt. The doctor comes out of her office.

'Ros, there are a couple of things I need to tell you. Don't worry if you can't take it all in now, Alice can explain it again later. First, from what I've seen I think it's very likely you've been drugged. I've asked the lab to be as quick as they can with the blood tests but in the meantime, don't drive a car and get plenty of rest until you're feeling more normal. I'd also suggest that you don't take any sleeping pills for a few days. Secondly, we'll test the bloods for sexually transmitted diseases, but that's to establish if any were present prior to the attack. Anything you picked up from the rape itself may not show up for several weeks. I'm sending you to a specialist clinic for some antibiotics, just in case. In the meantime, don't have unprotected sex. I know you probably won't be feeling like that anyway but I have to mention it. I'm also recommending a hepatitis vaccination. Even if he used protection, the cuts on your back could become infected from his sweat.'

My back. I remember the pictures. 'Can I see what he did now?'

She hesitates. 'It won't leave a scar, I'm pretty sure of that. The cuts aren't deep and they were done with a very sharp knife.'

She takes the Polaroids out of her pocket and hands them, not to me but to Alice, who says carefully, 'Ros, this may be upsetting for you.'

'I'm already upset.'

'I understand, but what I'm trying to say is . . . it's important to remember that you're not just a victim. You're a survivor.' She hands me the first Polaroid.

I don't recognize the person in the photograph at first. She is dark-skinned, her tanned back bisected by the faintest of bikini lines. Just above this line – almost as if it has been used as a guide – someone has written something on the surface of the photograph.

And then I look closer, and I see that the writing is not actually on the Polaroid: the writing is on my back, etched with the point of a knife in my skin. And it is not, strictly speaking, writing, but a series of numbers, separated by slashes.

11/7/1

16

'It's the date,' Alice says softly. 'It's yesterday's date.'

On my back, as casually as a bored teenager might carve graffiti into a tree, the man who raped me and killed my best friend has carved the date of his attack into my skin.

2

'So what's the damage?'

Jo, still in her pyjamas, her duvet pulled round her shoulders like a thick white cape, perched on our battle-scarred old sofa and yawned before she answered. I was already dressed for work, though I hadn't even thought about doing any clearing up.

'Natalie finally split up with Jedd. Lou split up with Ajay but got off with Paul. Some lovesick puppy took a dodgy e and put his fist through the bathroom mirror. On the plus side, Ian from upstairs came to complain about the noise and got off with one of Paula's South African friends.'

'Bless.'

Jo extricated a packet of Marlboro Lights from the debris on the floor and inspected it hopefully. It was empty. 'All in all, a pretty successful party. More relationships consummated than destroyed.' She yawned again. 'Do something for me?'

'Depends. I'm already late.'

'If I tidy up, will you phone the office?'

I made a face.

'Please? If I bring you the phone?' Still clutching the duvet round her, she crawled over to me and laid the cordless phone in my lap. 'Pretty please? Look, I'll dial the number for you . . .' She pushed some buttons and held the phone towards me.

'Oh, all right then,' I said, laughing despite myself. 'Now shush. I need to sound serious. Peter Longworth please,' I said into the phone. 'Any particular preference?' I asked Jo. 'Malaria? Dysentery? Nervous exhaustion?'

'Something gastric.'

'Peter Longworth speaking.'

'Oh Peter, hi. It's Ros – Ros Taylor. Jo's flatmate?'

'Oh, yes. How are you, Ros?' Jo's boss looked like Action Man – chiselled jaw, deep black eyebrows, beautiful chiaroscuro stubble – but was actually not very bright. He also took himself very, very seriously. The two facts were not unconnected.

'Well, that's it – *I'm* fine, but Jo isn't, I'm afraid. She must have picked up a stomach thing because she's been throwing up all night. She's asleep now but a few hours ago she asked me to phone you and explain that she may not be in today. She's projectile vomiting, so it's probably just a bug,' I added helpfully. 'I'm sure she'll be fine tomorrow.'

'Oh. Hang on. Let me grab her diary.' There was the sound of papers being moved around. 'Well, she's only got one meeting so I guess I can cover that for her,' he said grudgingly. 'Tell her from me I hope she feels better soon.'

'I'll definitely pass that on,' I promised. 'But don't worry, I'm sure it's nothing serious. I mean, I wouldn't send flowers or anything. Not yet.' There was a squawk of laughter beside me from Jo. She stuck the corner of the duvet into her mouth.

'Right. Well, thanks for letting me know.'

'Bye,' I said breezily and rang off. 'You so owe me,' I told Jo.

'Flowers – God, Ros, you are *evil*. What did he say when you mentioned flowers?' Jo's boss had been through a brief phase of pursuing her himself. For about a fortnight bunches of roses had turned up every time she sold an ad or made a presentation.

'He sort of went silent.'

'Think he believed you?'

'Of course.'

Jo took off the duvet and went to get dressed. 'There was a bloke in my bed last night,' I called after her.

'Lucky you. Who was he?'

'Some random friend of Paula's, I think. Sound asleep and snoring.'

Jo reappeared with her toothbrush in her mouth. 'Good body?' she said through a mouthful of foam, her eyes glinting.

'How should I know?'

'You mean you didn't check him out?'

'Er, no. I woke him up and chucked him out. It took forever, actually. He kept mumbling something about having to rescue the bears. I think he was still half-asleep.'

'Poor puppy.' She vanished again. I heard her voice calling, 'You won't believe this, but someone's stolen my mascara.'

'Why is it always the girls who steal things?'

'Ha. What makes you think it was a girl?' When she came back she was holding two cigarettes, one of which she gave to me. 'Here. I just remembered. I hid these last night. For emergencies.'

I was far too late to stop and have a cigarette. I put it in my mouth and leaned towards her lighter. 'Did Gerry turn up?'

'Uh-uh. But I wasn't expecting him to. Parties aren't really his thing.'

'What time did you get to bed?'

'Late. I got off with Leonardo DiCaprio.'

'Bloody hell.' I knew which young man she was talking about. He wasn't actually a dead ringer for the actor, but there had certainly been a resemblance. 'Define "got off with"?'

'More than a snog, less than a shag. Would I be unfaithful to Gerry?'

'It would hardly be unfair if you were,' I said tartly. 'Given that Gerry is, presumably, still sleeping with his wife.'

'Only in the middle of her menstrual cycle. It does something to her hormones, apparently.'

'I don't know why you're so chirpy,' I said. It had been 2 a.m. before I got to bed myself, and the pumping dance music had woken me up a couple of times after that. Our relentless partying was definitely incompatible with a nine-to-five job.

'Will you do something for me? Since you're going into work anyway?'

'Like what?'

'Drop these off at Boots.' She gave me two films. 'They're the holiday photos.'

'OK. I'll get them on same day and pick them up tonight.'

'Brill. And I'll get a video. Girls' night in?'

'Definitely. No booze, no fags, early night.'

'Better get some wine and ciggies as well then. But I do promise I'll have tidied up.'

I walked to Finchley Road tube station. The carriage I squeezed into was packed and silent and already too hot. Even with the windows open there was only a slight breeze, and the air that came in was still fetid from the day before. The metal poles were buttery from other people's hands but there was nothing else to hang on to. My face was jammed up against a grey suit that smelt of old newspapers. I tried to edge away but found my legs knocking against those of a seated passenger, a young man in shorts and a scruffy denim shirt. His own legs were spread wide apart, aggressively colonizing as much space as possible. Propped on his lap was some magazine, *FHM* or *Arena* or whatever. A TV bimbo was on all fours in her bra and knickers, apparently trying to smack her own bum. Without lifting his head from the magazine, he slid his eyes upwards to stare at the gap between my top and my skirt, which, as I was reaching up to hold on to the bar above my head, was exposing rather more flesh than usual. I felt a mixture of annoyance and appreciation. On the one hand, he was an odious little creep who had no right to ogle me just because I was forced to stand up. On the other hand, my stomach was tanned and flatter than usual after my holiday and it was nice to know that I was marginally more exciting than a self-flagellating Channel 5 starlet. For a brief moment I actually pictured myself as a pole dancer, twirling around the chrome bar at the end of the carriage. But only for a moment. The carriage was hot and sweaty and silent. I looked at the adverts and tried not to think.

According to an email that went round, a team of hygiene specialists recently removed a row of seats from a London Underground carriage for analysis. They had apparently found four types of hair sample (human, mouse, rat, dog); seven types of insect (mostly fleas, mostly alive); vomit; human urine; human excrement; rodent urine; rodent excrement; human semen and, when the seats were taken apart, the remains of six dead mice and a previously undiscovered fungus. The email was later shown to be a hoax but the point was that everyone believed it.

At Bond Street the carriage cleared and the young man got out. I sat down where he'd been. The seat was still hot with his body heat but at least I could stretch out my legs.

At Charing Cross I walked through the subway to St Martin's-in-the-Fields and then up the road to the staff entrance of the National Gallery. The lab where I worked was on the very top floor of the administration block, in Orange Street. The windows looked out over the top of the new Sainsbury extension towards South Africa House; if I stuck my head right up to the glass I could just see the back of Nelson's head, streaked with grey where pigeons had shat on him.

Seven of us worked in the department, but as the job involved checking archives, interviewing scholars and working with conservation specialists as well as lab work, it was rare for all of us to be there at any one time. The room was dominated by the lightbox, an enclosed booth with lights inside that could be switched from ultraviolet to daylight blue.

As no one else was in yet I took my shirt off before putting on my lab coat. It was made of polyester and clung to my skin but at least with no shirt I would stay reasonably cool. I turned on my computer and made a cup of Nescafé, more to postpone starting work than because I wanted one. Then I stepped inside the lightbox. At that time it held three paintings, all strangely small and naked-looking without their frames, like tortoises stripped of their shells. I started to fluoresce the surface of the one I was working on with a hand-held UV bar.

Under the intense ultraviolet the image on the canvas – a study of a Polynesian nude – vanished, replaced by a landscape in which tiny fibres and even individual brushstrokes stood out like glowing white-hot wires. Highlights jumping off the surface made the painting look as if it had been scoured with a fluorescent Brillo pad. I was looking for any foreign materials trapped in the paint, particularly fibres from the artist's brush. If I found some and they were synthetic rather than sable, it was a pretty sure bet that the painting wasn't a Gauguin. It seems incredible that a forger would be so stupid as to use a modern nylon-based brush to fake a painting meant to date from the nineteenth century, but in fact most forgers were usually careless. They relied on fooling the so-called experts, who rarely carried out detailed checks, rather than a scientist.

Officially I was the Laboratory Support Assistant to the Science and Conservation Department, but in practice I was part of a team known throughout the building as the Drewe Crew, after John Drewe, the most successful forger of the twentieth century. Drewe was remarkable, not least because he couldn't even paint.

He recruited an artist who was advertising his services in the small ads section of *Private Eye*, and paid him a hundred and fifty pounds a time to knock off paintings in the style of the Post-Impressionists and Modernists. Then he contacted several important institutions – the V&A, the Courtauld Institute, the Tate – and, posing as an academic with links to a mysterious but extremely generous art foundation, asked if he could come and do some research in their archives. Once inside, he added his fakes to the list of genuine works. When he wanted to sell the forgery, a prospective buyer would be invited to contact the institution directly to have it authenticated. Faced with a letter from the Courtauld testifying to a painting's provenance, even the country's foremost experts ignored the evidence of their own eyes and agreed. Deception is perception, as Drewe said somewhat smugly at his trial. He never spent much time or money on making his fakes stand up to scrutiny. He and his copyist just mixed together ordinary household emulsion with KY jelly to make a cheap and cheerful approximation of the 'slip' that genuine oil paints had. Because people wanted to believe the paintings were real, they ended up convincing themselves.

No one knew how many forgeries Drewe created, but it was certainly several hundreds. The scam had only been uncovered because his wife discovered he was having an affair and went to the police out of spite.

In scientific terms, my job was pretty undemanding. By the time a picture was brought up to the lab, the false papers would have already been uncovered and the painting pronounced suspect by a committee of art experts. All we had to do was to find some trace evidence which, when sent off for analysis by a specialist lab, would confirm or contradict their point of view. But it was more interesting than working for a manufacturing company or putting colours in processed food, which is what most of my contemporaries from Oxford were doing. I had one friend who was part of a sixteen-person team responsible for making sure that wherever it was made in the world, a certain fizzy drink was always exactly the same shade of black. Apparently when it comes out of the machines it's actually a lurid green, and in certain countries where they skimp on black dye you can occasionally still discern a faint green tinge to it. Too much dye, on the other hand, would stain the drinkers' teeth. She claimed it was actually rather fascinating.

As I had expected, there were dozens of brush fibres caught inside the paint. I prised three or four out with the tip of a scalpel and prepared a dry mount for the specialist lab in America that did our microscopics. Then I turned the overhead back on, my eyes aching from the UV light.

When I came out of the lightbox I found Alex, my boss, sitting at his table examining the back of a frame. He was wearing the LumiView, a head-mounted binocular microscope that made whoever wore it look like a cartoon vivisectionist. 'Hi, Al,' I said brightly.

He grunted a greeting. A lugubrious Hungarian, Alex liked to pretend that he was permanently depressed by his job. In fact, as I knew perfectly well, he liked nothing better than to take some masterpiece that had been praised by the art historians and prove that it was a fake. In this, I suppose, he was essentially on the side of the forgers, who often seemed to be motivated as much by a desire to get one up on the art establishment as by money.

'How was your holiday?' he wanted to know. I hadn't seen him since I'd got back.

'Great. Two weeks lying on a beach doing nothing. Perfect, in fact.'

He swung round and inspected me moodily over the top of the LumiView. 'If you were any browner, you'd look like her.' He gestured at the painting I was holding, where my fake Gauguin maiden bared her slim breasts to the viewer.

'So what's the gossip? Anything new?'

'Nothing ever happens here. It's a museum, and we are its exhibits.'

'You're cheerful, then. Must be the weather.' Outside, the sun sparkled on the huge fountains in Trafalgar Square.

'That's where we should be,' he said, following my gaze. 'Well, you, anyway. Out there. Being painted by great artists while you're still young and beautiful. Not helping to mummify the dead ones. Get out while you can, Ros.' He leaned forward conspiratorially and hissed, 'Don't let them curate you.'

'I'll bear it in mind,' I promised, and he laughed to show me that he hadn't really meant it. My phone rang, and I crossed to my desk to answer it.

'Is that, um, Ros?' The voice at the other end was male and hesitant.

'Yes.'

'It's Nathan.'

'Hello, Nathan,' I said, trying to remember who Nathan was.

'From the party. Friend of Jo's?'

'Oh – *Nathan*. Hi.' I remembered him now. He had cornered me in the kitchen and talked for half an hour about how superficial conversations at parties were. Unfortunately, in his own case he had been right.

'So I was wondering – uh, I was really interested in what you were saying.' Which was strange, because as far as I could recall I'd said nothing more interesting than 'yes', 'no', and 'hmm'. 'I was wondering if we could carry on the conversation over a drink sometime.'

A voice inside my head instantly said, 'No,' but for some reason I heard my real voice saying politely, 'Well, OK.'

'Great. Are you free tonight?'

Oh, God. I'd meant, maybe in two or three weeks' time, and then I'd find an excuse to bring along some other people too. I said cautiously, 'Actually, I'm busy this evening.'

'Another night, then. Tomorrow?'

I eased into reverse gear. 'I'm afraid tomorrow's not great either.'

'Well, I'll obviously have to work round you, then.' There was just the faintest hint of annoyance in his voice. 'Tell me a day, and I'll make sure I'm free.'

'I'm not sure. I haven't got my diary with me at the moment.'

There was a pause, and then he said doggedly, 'But this is your work number, isn't it? You must have a diary there somewhere.'

'I'm not at my desk. This call's been transferred to another room.' I was absolutely certain now that I didn't want to see Nathan for a drink. He was way too pushy.

'I'll pick a day, then, and you can phone me back and move it if you're busy.' Not *cancel it*, I noticed, but *move it*. 'Saturday? I'll book a table somewhere.'

Whoa, I thought. I'd half agreed to a drink, and now I was

being bullied into accepting dinner. 'That might be a bit difficult. I'm seeing my boyfriend on Saturday.' Which was probably not hugely tactful of me, because although it was the clearest possible way of saying that he was wasting his time, if he backed off now it would imply he'd only called me because he thought I was single.

Why was there no easy, acceptable way to say 'I'll happily meet up with you for a drink. But I'm sorry, I don't fancy you'?

'Oh, right.' There was a long pause. That's the end of it, I thought. Then he said, 'I was told you weren't going out with anyone at the moment.'

Oh, for God's sake. 'Maybe whoever told you didn't know.'

'Who is it?'

'Sorry?'

'Who's the lucky bloke?'

'Nathan, I have to go now. People are waiting for me.'

'Will you phone me back?'

'Maybe.' No, that was stupid. He'd already made it clear that he wasn't going to be fobbed off with maybes. 'I'll think about it. Perhaps later in the year.'

'Bitch.'

'*What?*'

'You heard.'

There was a short silence. Then I said, as politely as I could manage, 'Well, I'm glad we didn't go to the trouble of meeting up to have this conversation, Nathan. That would have really pissed me off. Goodbye.'

'No, wait. I'm sorry.'

He started to apologize at greater length, something about how I had to understand that it was very difficult for him making a phone call like this – 'cold calling', he called it, as if I was someone he was trying to sell a marketing plan to – but I cut him short. 'Forget it. Goodbye.' I put the phone down. 'Twat,' I said furiously to no one in particular.

Jo would have handled it better. She could be blunt to the point of rudeness with people she didn't want to see. But although she was better than me at saying no, she said it less often than I did. When the phone rang at two o'clock in the morning it was inevitably for her. 'Just one of my lovesick puppies,' she'd say,

26

taking the phone to bed with her, the puppy in question usually turning out to have been calling from some hotel bar in another time zone, drunk at his company's expense. I led a quiet and rather celibate life by comparison. I sighed.

Alex glanced in my direction but said nothing. I pulled out the Gauguin's file, though in fact I was too furious to work. Then the phone rang again.

'Ros Taylor,' I said cautiously, praying it wasn't Nathan.

'Ros, it's Gerry.'

'Hi, Gerry,' I said, relieved. 'How are you?'

'Good. How was the party?'

'It was fun. Shame you couldn't be there.'

'Couldn't get away, I'm afraid. Listen, I was just wondering if Jo's all right. Her office says she's ill and she's not answering her mobile.'

'Oh, she's fine. She's probably just got some music on. She decided to take a day off work and' – I shot a glance at Alex – 'she's run out of holiday, if you know what I mean.'

Gerry laughed. 'You mean she got you to pull a sickie for her?'

'That's it.'

'OK. Maybe I'll drop by and see her later.'

Which meant I'd better not get back to the flat too early, or I'd walk in on the two of them sprawled post-coitally across the living room.

I should explain about Gerry – aka the Mysterious Gerry, the Part-Time Boyfriend, the Elusive Gerry, etc., etc. Because Gerry was actually about fifteen years older than Jo and me, and married. With kids, a second home in Tuscany, the whole shebang. He was also good-looking, charming, self-assured; oh, and rich, not of course that it was ever a factor in Jo's decision to see him. It wasn't as if they went out together much, after all.

She actually met Gerry through me – amongst other things, he has a modern art collection which is worth a fortune, and when the National helped him win a court case against an unscrupulous dealer who was knowingly selling on fakes, he invited all of the lab staff to a celebration party at the Saatchi Gallery. I was the only one in my department who wanted to go, so I took Jo along too, and the next day he called her. I think at the time Jo just thought it was going to be a quick fling, but it rapidly became more than that, and soon I found myself in the slightly awkward position of living in the middle of a Grand Passion. I was, to say the least, a bit surprised by all this, but Jo is Jo and knew what she was doing. Coming home to the flat after the two of them had sneaked off for an afternoon was like coming back to a war zone – things would be broken, champagne bottles and ashtrays would be scattered around, bedclothes would be strewn in unlikely places, and the whole flat would reek of sex and Gerry's cigars. On one occasion drops of candlewax had been scattered around the bathroom, coagulating in the carpet like hard little burrs. Another time I came home and found Jo in a dressing gown, sprawled lethargically across the sofa, with one of Gerry's ties still fastened round her wrist like some exotic, trailing bracelet.

It soon became clear what the glue was that kept them together. She told me, quite early on, that the sex was absolutely fantastic. Then, a couple of weeks later, when I came back and found that the curtain rail in the living room was broken – the curtain rail, for God's sake; I mean, just how exactly do you break a curtain rail during sex? – she asked me, rather wistfully, whether I had ever had sex which was overwhelming, which was almost too much. I said I hadn't. In fact, that sort of sex didn't sound like something I could even imagine, let alone enjoy.

It had been going on for about five months – about as long as any of Jo's boyfriends had ever lasted. They had planned to go on holiday together, but then he couldn't get away at the last minute, so I went instead. When we were in Italy Jo told me that in some ways she was actually rather relieved. After all, you couldn't have sex all the time, and two whole weeks with Gerry might have been rather exhausting. I tried to drop gentle hints that it might be time to dump him and find a proper boyfriend, and she seemed to be agreeing with me. But I was careful not to push her. There was a side to Jo that didn't appreciate being given advice on men by me. All the time we'd known each other, it had been the other way round.

Jo and I met at Oxford – she was doing a two-year secretarial course and being pursued by a series of expensive young men who were inordinately serious about things like beagling and tractor-ploughing competitions. She'd already been a rep for a travel company and had worked in a bar; the secretarial course was her family's last-ditch attempt to establish her in some kind of career. I was just starting a doctorate in long-chain complex polymers, an area of organic chemistry so mind-numbingly obscure that even my supervisor couldn't be bothered to find out what I was meant to be doing. We met through Simon Cutter, an arrogant history postgraduate I'd gone out with a few times who unceremoniously dumped me because, he said, he'd met someone more interesting – by which I assumed, rightly as it turned out, he actually meant more attractive. That was Jo.

I subsequently got chatting to her at a party and the next day she turned up at my house with a bottle of vodka to continue the conversation. It turned out she'd just come from dumping Simon herself, partly because he was terrible in bed – she was refreshingly merciless with the details – and partly because she liked me more and realized that after what he'd said to me, she would have to choose between us. As she said, in Oxford men were two a penny but girlfriends were thin on the ground. It was the beginning of a friendship that had so far survived four years and God knows how many boyfriends.

We were very different – she was tall, blonde, curvy and extrovert, every man's *Playboy* fantasy; I was slight and dark and, I suppose, more serious. Her other friends were all arts graduates, by whom I was considered something of a freak. It was a universal truth amongst arts students at Oxford that all so-called Northern Chemists, as anyone doing a science degree was referred to, were spotty, unwashed and physically repugnant. I soon lost track of the number of times I heard the words, 'You don't look like a scientist,' or the even less original, 'What happened to the spots?'

When we first came to London we shared a house with two other girls in Putney and then, when the tenancy agreement collapsed in some strange quasi-legal row over who did what proportion of the cleaning, got a flat together in an area variously described as South Hampstead, Kilburn or Camden, depending on who was doing the describing. By this stage Jo had graduated from being a secretary in a trendy advertising agency to being a fully-fledged account executive, and I – the one with the degree and the doctorate – was a mere lab technician. On the other hand, I was handling Caravaggios and Titians on a daily basis, I worked in the heart of the West End, my work was undemanding, reasonably well paid and appreciated by my bosses, and life was too good the way it was to worry about what I'd be doing in five years' time.

I wrote out the form requesting analysis of the brush fibres I'd found, by which time it was one o'clock. There was a Pret a Manger on the Strand, so I put my shirt back on and walked across Trafalgar Square to get some lunch. It was baking hot. People were sitting on the edges of the fountains, eating their sandwiches with their legs dipped into the water. Tourists were buying bags of seed for the pigeons and taking pictures of each other with the birds festooned across their arms. Apparently the bird food contained a contraceptive to stop the birds breeding, but there were still hundreds of them strutting round the square.

I got a salad box and sat down on a bench to eat it. The flagstones acted like a giant sun reflector, bouncing heat and light in all directions. Exhaust fumes shimmered from the backs of buses as they crawled round the congested traffic lanes. Some girls nearby had taken off their tops and were sunning themselves in their bras. I didn't go quite that far, but I undid my shirt buttons and put my sunglasses on. My phone beeped but it was only a text message from Jo to remind me to bring back some wine.

As I walked back across the square I noticed two young black men moving diagonally across my path. They were overdressed for the weather – baggy jeans, sweat tops with hoods; one was actually wearing a parka. As they came closer one of them said, very politely, 'Excuse me, miss.'

You get a kind of radar, living in London, and if it had been later in the day or if it hadn't been such fantastic weather I would probably have pretended not to hear them. As it was I allowed my head to turn slightly, although I didn't stop or answer.

Big mistake. I should never have looked at them.

The one who had spoken said, 'Got the time, yeah?'

I wasn't wearing a watch. I said, 'Sorry. No watch.' I shrugged apologetically, as if to say it couldn't be helped, and kept on walking.

The second one said, 'Cool, cool. Got a phone?'

I hesitated and said, 'Nope.' Second mistake.

The first one gave a kind of roll of the shoulders, an exaggerated gesture of disappointment. 'But we seen it. We seen the phone, you know?'

'You want my number?' the second one demanded. 'Hey, put my number in yo' phone. Where's yo' phone? Show me the phone, come on.'

'Yeah, give us your phone,' the first one said, holding out his hand and grinning.

They seemed altogether too amiable to be mugging me. 'I'd rather not,' I said primly.

Suddenly they were up close, right in my face. 'Why you lie to me?' the first one said.

The second one dipped his hand into his parka and came out with a small knife, its blade already out. 'Don't report us, sister. We're just jacking the phone.'

I put my hand in my pocket and reluctantly took out my mobile. The first one grabbed it. 'Sweet.' He was smiling again. 'Don' get stressed now,' he said flirtatiously. 'People get jacked, you know what I'm saying?'

'I'm fine,' I said. For some bizarre reason we were all smiling at each other as the first guy inspected the phone before slipping it into a pocket.

'Got any money?' the second one wanted to know.

'You've already got my phone,' I pointed out.

'Yeah, allow her, man,' the first one said. 'Come on.' And they sauntered off happily without a backward glance. I looked around. Half a dozen people had been watching us incuriously.

'They stole my phone,' I said to no one in particular. 'Those bastards just stole my phone.' No one moved. They were all too busy sunning themselves, though one or two people looked vaguely concerned. The two thieves reached the road and stepped out into the traffic.

'Are you OK?' a girl sitting on one of the fountains wanted to know.

'I think so.'

She nodded, as if that meant everything was all right. I stood and watched the two young men disappear in the direction of Lower Regent Street. Then I went back to work.

I called the police from the office and eventually spoke to a bored voice at West End Central police station. He asked me the make and model number of the phone. I could remember the make, just, but I had no idea what model it was. The voice sighed. He told me I could come in and make a statement if I liked but if all I wanted was to claim the phone on my insurance he could give me a CAD number which would prove I had reported it as stolen. 'Fine,' I said, and hung up. I called Orange and told them not to charge me for any more calls. It was a funny thing but when I thought about it I had actually been more shaken up by Nathan calling me a bitch than I had been about being phone-jacked in broad daylight in the middle of Trafalgar Square.

'Why don't you call your own number?' Alex said. 'Maybe they'll answer, and you could offer them money for it.'

'Oh God. Would you do it for me?'

He dialled the number for me and listened for a while. 'No answer,' he said, shrugging. 'It's probably been sold on by now.'

'No one did anything,' I said. 'That's what's really freaking me. About a dozen people watched it all happen and no one did a thing.'

'There was a knife, though?'

'Well, yes. One of them had a knife. But it was tiny.'

He spread his arms. 'So someone should get stabbed for a phone? You're sensible, you did the right thing. Why don't you go home now and relax, try to forget it?'

He sounded like the phone-jackers. Just relax. But it was still a beautiful day and the sun was still shining. If I went home I could sit on our tiny patio with a cold drink in my hand. And I'd finish my tube journey before the hideous afternoon rush hour. 'Maybe I will,' I said.

He nodded. 'See you tomorrow then. And look, don't worry if you're late. Just come in when you feel like it.'

I put my stuff away and took the stairs down to the ground floor. I walked outside but instead of walking into the bright reflected glare of Trafalgar Square I'm walking into mist, a thick enveloping freezing fog, like something that had just rolled in off the sea, shrouding London in white.

Mist fills the tube. Mist fills the streets. Mist fills my head.

Mist rolls across my memory, blanking everything out. All I can see, for the rest of the day, is mist.

I can remember nothing after I walked out of the National Gallery at around 3 p.m. The rest of the day – the break-in, the rapes, the murder – is a blank.

Sorry.

3

The detective who took my statement had a crooked boxer's nose and soft, mournful eyes. If they chose him because they thought he had a sympathetic manner they had done a good job. His name was DI Thomson but he told me to call him Bill.

He started off by sending Alice to get us all tea while he told me how sorry he was about Jo and what had happened to me. He understood that I probably wasn't feeling much like giving a statement now but the first hours of an investigation were the most important. The quicker they talked to me, the quicker they could catch whoever did it. When Alice came back, he took off his jacket and hung it over the back of his chair. 'Hot, isn't it?' he said. Was it hot? I was shivering, but perhaps it was just delayed shock.

He wanted to know about the twenty-four hours leading up to the attack, so I told him about the party and about Nathan calling me a bitch and the phone-jackers. I had to keep stopping to cry. Then I hit the white mist. He tried to question me about it but he could see I was getting distressed again.

'OK. Don't worry. I'm sure it'll come back.'

I asked him if he thought either Nathan or the phone-jackers could have had anything to do with what happened.

'Well, we'll look at all the possibilities, of course. But I have to say I don't think it's likely. Was there any way the muggers could have got hold of your address?'

'I texted some people with it for the party. Could they have read my messages?'

He made a note. 'I'll check. Now, tell me what you remember about this morning.'

Just getting my thoughts in order was an effort. 'I remember waking up. I felt awful. I must have been sick in the night because it was all over the sheets. And I wasn't wearing anything in bed. I have to be really, really drunk to do that, but I thought perhaps I must have been – I must have got drunk and Jo had put me to bed. There was a horrible taste in my mouth.'

He was writing notes, and I stopped so he could catch up. 'What sort of taste?' he asked, still writing.

'Um – sick, mostly.' And a rubbery, plimsoll taste, I thought, like condoms, but I didn't say that yet.

Alice, sitting beside me, squeezed my hand. 'Ros, you're doing really well.'

'I needed to go to the loo. My head hurt too but I thought it was just some sort of terrible hangover. There was water all over the bathroom floor. Then I realized the shower was on. The curtain was closed, so I couldn't see if Jo was in there.' Our comedy shower curtain, with its outline of a naked woman painted on it. 'But I somehow knew she wasn't having a shower.' I thought for a moment. Steam, that was it. 'If the water had been hot, there would have been steam, and there wasn't any. When I could I got up off the toilet and – '

– *and nothing nothing nothing. None of this happened. Please please please, everything's fine* –

Through my gasps I said, 'And that's when I saw her. She was slumped down. You know, on the floor of the shower, with her knees pulled up. There was water running over her. No blood. But the side of her head was all – I mean, I couldn't really see because her hair was covering it, but the shape of her head was all wrong, I could tell it was sort of caved in, and her eyes were open. I need to stop.'

Alice put her hand on my shoulder.

Bill waited. I breathed. There was nothing to look at in the little room. I covered my eyes with my hand.

Eventually Bill said gently, 'Did you touch her?'

'Not then. I went and phoned 999. Then I – the man on the phone said was I sure she was dead, and of course I was, but I thought, just in case . . . So then I went back and turned the shower off and I touched her and that's when the blood came out. I touched her head and it moved sideways and all this blood gushed out onto the tiles. Oh God. Oh God.' I looked at the table and said in a tiny voice, 'I've been wondering whether I should have done mouth-to-mouth earlier. If I could have saved her.'

Bill stopped writing. He didn't tell me that I mustn't blame myself, or that I was a survivor not a victim, or any of that crap, for which I was grateful. He said gently, 'Mouth-to-mouth wouldn't have made any difference. The evidence suggests that Jo was already dead when her killer put her in the shower. Ros, I'm sorry.' He waited a few moments, then said, 'Tell me what you can remember about the evening before the attack.'

My mind was a blank.

'What did you eat, for example?'

Still nothing. I shook my head.

'There were two empty pizza boxes in the lounge.'

'I'm sorry. I can't remember.'

'They were from a restaurant called Spighetta, on West End Lane. They took the order at about nine thirty, by phone. They delivered them to your address just before ten. A neighbour, Mr Scott, saw Jo open the door. She was wearing a blue dressing gown.'

I shook my head. 'Sorry. Perhaps it'll come back to me later.'

'Can you remember going anywhere else last night?'

'We didn't go anywhere. At least, not that I remember.'

'There was a DVD in a rental box from Video City. *Sleepy Hollow*. You rented it at seven thirty.'

'Sorry,' I muttered. 'I don't remember that.'

'There were some photographs scattered round the living room,' he persisted. 'They show you and Miss McCourt – Jo – together on holiday. There's a till receipt showing that they were paid for yesterday at Boots in Finchley Road at seven fifty p.m. That branch of Boots closes at eight. Perhaps you were in a rush to get there before it closed.'

Just for a second, I had a sense that he was right – something about a rush made sense, but of the actual memory there was no trace at all.

He sighed. 'You said you thought you might have had a hangover. Can you remember what you'd been drinking?'

'White wine,' I said automatically. Jo and I always drank white wine when we stayed in.

36

He made a note. 'Do you remember where you got it?'

Something flickered in my brain. 'It might have been duty free. From our holiday.'

'Where did you go?'

'Sardinia. It's in Italy. We got back last week.'

Bill said, 'We think you bought two bottles of white wine from Oddbins in West End Lane last night. Their till's up the spout at the moment so we can't access the exact time but the manager remembers you. I'm afraid duty free allowances in Europe were abolished years ago.'

There had been no hint of impatience in his voice, but Alice said protectively, 'Perhaps Ros would like a rest.'

'Of course. Take as long as you like.'

I wanted to please him. It occurred to me that having that quality, being able to make people want to please you, must be very useful for a policeman. 'I don't want a rest,' I said. 'I want to help. I just can't remember.'

There was a short silence.

'Do you remember your holiday?' Bill asked curiously.

'Oh, yes. It was great.'

'Who did you book it through?'

'AirTours, in Swiss Cottage.'

Bill was writing again. 'How long ago?'

'Jo booked it. She'd been going to go with her boyfriend but at the last minute he couldn't get away.' Something occurred to me. 'Oh, God. I don't suppose he even knows. I don't suppose anyone knows. I mean, there's her family as well.'

'We've traced her brother. He's flying down from Scotland to identify the body.'

'Hector,' I said. 'Poor Hector. He adores her.' Poor Hector. The words looped round in my head like a nursery rhyme. *Poor Hector. He adores her. Poor Hector adores her. But Hector couldn't protect her . . .*

'What's her boyfriend's name?' Bill asked, his pen poised.

'Gerry. Gerry Henson.' I hesitated. 'There's something you should know. He's married.'

'Do you have his address?'

'It's somewhere in Hampstead. Will you have to tell his wife?'

'Probably not.' I saw him draw an asterisk next to his last note.

'Ros, sometimes it's hard when people are dead. Their lives are a bit messy or complicated and their friends sometimes don't like to tell us all the details in case we get the wrong impression about them. But all we're interested in is catching whoever killed them. Mostly that just means knowing who to talk to, so that we can eliminate them quickly.' He started a new section and wrote something at the top of it. I read my own name, Ros Taylor, upside down. 'How about you? Are you going out with anyone at the moment?'

'No.'

'Any relationships recently ended?'

'Not really. The last one was six months ago.'

'Can I have a name and address?'

'Peter. Peter . . .' I reached into the fog and came up with Peter's surname. 'Peter Carr. I don't know his address now. I'll have to look it up.'

'No one since?'

'No. I'm not very good at boyfriends.'

'I'll write that down, shall I?' he said seriously.

'It's not very . . .' I began, then I saw that he was teasing me.

It was a long time before I admitted it, even to myself. But looking back, I think I began to fancy him even then, in that windowless room, at the most inappropriate time imaginable. Which just shows how perverse, and how unlikely, the human heart can be.

Bill took my fingerprints so that the people searching my flat would be able to disregard the ones that were mine. He held my hand in his huge fist and rolled each finger for me carefully onto the ink pad. This little piggy went to market. This little piggy stayed at home. This little piggy got raped. This little piggy is dead.

'Ros, there are some standard questions I need to ask you so that the labs can make sense of the forensic evidence. Have you changed your sheets and bedclothes since the last time you had sex?'

What a strange question, I thought. Then I realized that they would be looking for DNA. 'I told you. It was six months ago. And I'm not that much of a slut.'

He smiled. 'Of course not. I didn't mean to suggest you were.' He ticked something off on a form.

Then I remembered. 'Ah. Hang on. After the party there was someone asleep in my bed.'

'A man or a woman?'

'A man.'

'Do you know his name?'

'Sorry.'

Bill wrote a short note next to the tick.

'I kicked him out, of course,' I added unnecessarily. But it got me another smile from Bill. He picked up a second form.

'And I need to ask you about the security arrangements at the flat. I noticed earlier that there are grilles on the windows, but they weren't fastened. Is that how they usually were?'

'Well, we unlock them when we stay in. You can't open the windows unless the grilles are unlocked.'

'And the paved bit just behind your flat. That's a communal area, is it?'

I nodded. 'Sort of. They keep the dustbins there.'

'Did you hear anyone out there last night?'

Mist again. Alice put a warning hand on Bill's arm.

This is all so wrong, I thought dizzily. At this time of day I should be at work, discussing brush strokes and polymer layers, not death and window locks. A thought struck me. 'Oh, God. I haven't told the gallery where I am. Has anyone phoned them?'

Alice said, 'I'll do it.'

'Don't,' I took a deep breath, 'don't go into details, will you?'

'Of course not. I'll just say there's been an incident.'

'Someone should phone Jo's office as well.' There were so many things to do, a huge mountain of organization that would have to be scaled. I started to cry.

Bill said, 'Would you like some more tea?' I nodded.

For a few minutes I was left alone. There was an empty ashtray on the table. I tried to move it away from me, but it was fastened down. I yawned a deep, shuddering, irresistible yawn. Someone had carved the word FUCK into the surface of the table. I thought about what was carved into my back. I wondered what I would do if it left a scar, and I was marked permanently. Then I remembered that the date cut into my back was also the date of

Jo's death. It would be the date on her headstone. I yawned again, and shivered. The clothes the rape suite had provided were pretty basic. I wondered if Bill would mind if I put on the jacket he'd left on the back of his chair. I decided that in the circumstances he probably wouldn't. It smelt very faintly of aftershave.

When Bill came back he was carrying a plastic cup in each hand, holding them by the rims to stop the tea burning his fingers. There was a document folder tucked under his arm. He put the cups down. 'Careful. It's hot.'

I lifted my arms in the sleeves of his jacket. 'I hope you don't mind. I was cold.'

When he smiled his eyes looked even more mournful. 'Wouldn't you like Alice to find something that fits?'

'This is fine. If you're sure it's all right.' There was actually something rather reassuring about swaddling myself in the over-sized garment. I pulled the lapels together.

'Can we talk about the attack again?' he asked softly.

I took a breath. 'Sure.'

'Tell me what you remember from the time you got home.'

I screwed up my eyes. 'I think I remember the pizza now,' I said slowly. 'But that might just be because you told me. I'm sort of pretty sure we were drinking and looking at our holiday photos. But again, you've told me all that. Otherwise, it's just a blank.'

'OK,' he said. He tapped the orange folder. 'I've just been given the doctor's report, and the first analysis of your blood. We won't know for sure until the forensic tests are done, but from what I'm reading, it does look as if someone had intercourse with you last night. There were no traces of sperm, though, which suggests that he used a condom. It makes our job harder, of course, but it's probably reassuring to you.'

I nodded numbly. I had been raped.

'Did either of you keep condoms in the flat?' he asked gently.

'Jo might have done. Well, probably did. I can't remember.'

'If you do remember, will you tell us? When we catch whoever did this, we'll want to prove premeditation, you see. Bringing condoms with him suggests that he planned it.'

'OK.'

40

'Also, the tests on your blood show traces of gamma-hydroxybutrate – GHB. Do you know what that is?'

I shook my head.

'Its street names are liquid ecstasy or easy lay. It used to be sold in health food stores as a sleeping aid. Then it became better known as a date rape drug. Taken in sufficient quantities, it makes you unconscious.'

'Like – what's it called – Rohypnol?'

'Yes, though Rohypnol now contains an additive which turns blue in alcohol, so it's used less often for this sort of thing. GHB, on the other hand, is colourless and very nearly tasteless. It can also cause vomiting, dizziness and temporary memory loss, which probably explains why you're having trouble remembering what happened.'

'*Temporary* memory loss? So it'll wear off?'

'Apparently. I'm not an expert on this sort of thing, but from what I've been told you can expect to recover your memory gradually over the next few days.'

'And I'll remember what happened,' I said numbly. Not remembering was bad enough, but what horrors might I suddenly recall when my memory returned?

'I've got to be honest, Ros, and say that it could be extremely useful for us if you do. I'm going to give you my phone number.' He pulled out a card and wrote something on it. 'And that's my mobile as well. Anything you remember, anything at all, I want you to phone me straight away.'

Alice came back and quietly took a seat.

'You had slightly higher levels of GHB in your bloodstream than Jo,' Bill was saying. I wondered how they knew, and then I realized that while I was being examined in the rape suite, with its low lights and comfortable sofas, Jo would have been going through a similar process in some mortuary suite somewhere, laid out on a slab under the harsh fluorescent glare of strip lights. Perhaps she had been cut open so that they could do their tests more easily. I had a sudden mental image of a pathologist standing over her, reaching into her stomach and pulling out her organs, like some horrible travesty of a Caesarean birth—

'Are you all right?' Bill was looking concerned.

'I'm OK,' I muttered. 'Go on.'

'We've also tested the remains of some liquid we found in two wine glasses at your flat. Both were positive for GHB, so that's probably how it was administered.'

'You mean he was *there*? In the flat? While we were eating our pizzas or whatever?'

'It looks that way, yes. He probably came in through the window, slipped the GHB into your wine when you were out of the room, then hid somewhere nearby while he waited for it to work. I don't suppose you can remember whether the wine had an unusually salty taste?'

I shook my head. I felt sick.

'Jo's blood was also positive for cocaine, and you'd both smoked cannabis in the forty-eight hours before the blood test, though in both cases we're talking about very small amounts. Is there anything you want to tell me about that?'

'There was some at the party. Cannabis, that is. I didn't see any cocaine but to be honest it wouldn't have been that unusual if there had been some around.'

'Was the cannabis yours, or did someone else provide it?'

'Someone else. I don't know who, honestly. It was just being passed around.'

'OK. Look, as I said earlier, our priority is finding the person who did this. If it's got nothing to do with it, we're not going to start going after your friends for a little bit of blow.'

'Thanks.'

'One other thing. The film you rented last night was on DVD. Presumably you have a DVD player?'

'Jo got one about a month ago.'

'Well, it's not in your flat now. We think there may be other items missing too. There's an empty wooden jewellery case on the floor of the back bedroom. It looks as if it's been emptied.'

'Is it red?'

He checked his notes. 'Yes. Yours?'

I started to cry again. Not because what was in the box was worth much, but because it was all my old life.

'It's likely that robbery was the primary motive,' Bill was saying. 'In which case, we may be able to trace him when he tries to sell what he's stolen. We'll need a list.'

'How did she die?' I said. 'Jo, I mean. What happened to her?'

'It may be too soon to—' Alice began.

'I want to know,' I said. I must have sounded determined, because Alice kept quiet.

'We haven't got the full results from the post-mortem yet,' Bill said slowly. 'But it seems fairly clear that, like you, Jo was sexually assaulted. There are scratches and bruises on her arms, too, which indicates that she woke up and struggled with her attacker. There's a blow to her head – we think she may have hit it on the table beside her bed in the struggle – but the cause of death was probably asphyxiation.'

The room swam. 'Did she suffer?' I managed to ask.

Again, he gave it to me straight. 'It varies a lot with asphyxiation. Sometimes you get a sensation called "air hunger" – struggling for breath. The defence wounds do suggest that she fought for her life. But not for very long.'

When I didn't say anything he went on, 'We think her killer dragged her body through to the shower, presumably to wash off any forensic traces that might identify him. We can't explain yet why he didn't do the same thing with you. It may be that the attack on you came later, after he'd searched for the jewellery. Or maybe Jo was just unlucky. We need to reconstruct what happened in much more detail before we can say.' He glanced at me. 'I'll need a list of everyone who's come to the flat in the last two or three weeks. Men and women. Particularly the people who came to the party. We'll need to eliminate their traces individually.'

For the first time I realized what a huge amount of work a police investigation is. 'Can I do it tomorrow?'

'Of course. Where will you be staying?'

'I don't know.'

'Is there someone you'd like to phone?'

I tried to force my blurry, clogged-up brain to think. My mother's house was hardly an option, since that was in deepest Yorkshire and I would need to stay in London to give the police all the information they'd asked for. Besides, I wasn't sure if I could face telling her about this yet. Since my father's death she had become increasingly frail and forgetful, and I wasn't sure how much of it she'd understand. My friend Anna was in South America, doing whatever she did for her company. Katie and Jim had a flat, but they also had a baby. Most of my friends lived in cramped communal flatshares. 'I'll ask Charlotte,' I said at last. Charlotte had married a banker. They owned a palatial residence in Maida Vale, and although she wouldn't have been my first choice they were the only friends I knew who had a spare room.

'Here, use this.' Bill took a mobile phone out of his pocket. 'It's more private in here than at the front desk. I need to go and write up this statement for you to sign, but I'll be back later.'

'Will I – will I be able to go back to the flat? I haven't got any overnight things.'

'If Alice goes with you. You'll have to log in with the crime-scene manager and make a list of everything you take. Bear in mind that we'll probably need the flat for a week or so.'

I took a deep breath. 'What about Jo? Will I be allowed to see her?'

The brown eyes looked thoughtful. 'Well,' he said, 'that's up to you. But not today. They won't have finished the post-mortem yet.'

He went outside. I called Charlotte, who was still at work, and told her as matter-of-factly as I could what had happened. She started to cry, which set me off again. She wanted to come and pick me up but I told her I was with the police and I didn't know how long I'd be.

Someone walked into the room, a big man of about fifty who looked at me briefly and spoke to Alice. When I had finished he extended a meaty hand. 'Ros Taylor? Superintendent Collier. Has my lad been looking after you?'

I must have looked blank, because he said, 'DI Thomson. He's taken a preliminary statement?'

I said that he had.

'I understand you're suffering from a lapse of memory,' Super-intendent Collier said. 'It often happens in these cases, but I'm sure that with a good night's sleep – beauty sleep, I would say, if it wasn't so clearly superfluous – you'll wake up refreshed and fully able to help us with our investigations. I'm sure you're aware that we're treating your friend's death as a murder inquiry.' He clanked a mint against his front teeth.

Alice bristled and murmured something to the effect that I was also a victim of a serious crime.

44

'Absolutely,' Collier breathed. As well as mint, he smelt of cigarettes and beer. 'A horrible business.' He looked at the phone in my hand. 'Is that Thomson's mobile? I've had to send him out, you see, and he asked me to make sure you didn't forget to leave it. So I said I'd set his mind at rest and introduce myself at the same time.' He held out his hand and I put the phone into it. His other hand came round my shoulder as if he were about to pat me. I flinched, and he thought better of it. 'We'll hope to see you very soon, then,' he said solicitously, his eyes gleaming. 'Toodle-oo.'

I muttered something and followed Alice out of the station. I could tell from the straightness of her back that she wasn't wild about Detective Superintendent Collier either.

4

Alice drove carefully, never exceeding the speed limit. I suppose that was part of the deal, when you joined the police: you had to take seriously all the rules that everyone else ignored.

To avoid a silence I asked her about her job. It was mostly schoolkids at the moment, she said, which made investigation difficult. 'Some of them want to keep the whole thing a secret. They're worried about how their families will react, whether people will think it's their fault. How old are you – twenty-five, twenty-six?' I nodded. 'And you're financially independent, single, well-educated – I'm not saying it's any easier on women like you, but it's easier for me to help you because by and large people like you want the person who did it to be caught. You'd be amazed how many times we know who the rapist is but the woman withdraws her statement before it comes to court.'

'That must be awful.'

'Not for me so much. My job's helping the victims, not investigating the crimes. It's more frustrating for the detectives.' She pulled up at an orange light. 'But once or twice I've had women in, and when they've described the man who raped them I know it's the same person a previous victim named but chose not to press charges against. Being in court can make me angry too, sometimes, when the defence throw some bullshit around and the jury believe it. I've heard the words "Just don't hurt me" or "Please wear a condom" accepted as evidence of consent. That makes me really mad.'

'Alice, there's something I want to tell you.'

She glanced across at me. 'Go on, then.'

In a small voice I said, 'I feel a bit of a fraud. I mean, I don't really feel *raped*. It's like it happened in my sleep – well, I suppose

46

in a way it did happen in my sleep – and I'm being given all this attention when I don't really deserve it. I feel as if tomorrow the doctor's going to phone you up and say, "I made a mistake, she wasn't raped at all," and then people like that superintendent are going to tell me that I was wasting their time when they had much more important things to think about, like who killed Jo.'

'That isn't going to happen,' Alice said gently. 'I saw the doctor's report. And I saw what he did to your back. Believe me, Ros, catching the man who did that is going to be a top priority for us.'

Broadhurst Terrace looked very different. The residents' parking bay had been suspended and was now occupied by three white vans, one of which had 'Metropolitan Police Tactical Support Vehicle' written on the side. A police car was parked up on the kerb. The entrance to our building was roped off with blue and white tape. A policewoman stood next to it, guarding the access. I saw Mr Scott from upstairs and a few other people I didn't know clustered round the edge of the taped-off area. A small yellow sign had been placed on the pavement: 'Witness Appeal – Fatal Assault – Can You Help?' The date, time and place had been filled in by hand. Someone had put a small cellophane-wrapped bunch of carnations on the ground next to it. The cellophane had filled with condensation in the heat and the flowers were already starting to wilt.

Alice led me to the larger van. In the back was a kind of mobile office, with a computer, fridge and telephones. A young Asian policeman was writing something in a file.

'Pesh, this is Miss Taylor,' Alice said. 'I've brought her to pick up some things.'

'No problem. The DI phoned earlier.' He handed us each a plastic bag in which something white was folded. 'I just need you to put these over your clothes and the plastic covers on your shoes. The SOCOs are still in there, but I can ask them to stop if you like.'

'I don't think that'll be necessary,' Alice said. 'Thanks, Pesh.'

The bag contained a white jumpsuit made of thin, papery material. There were elasticated bags, like the shower caps in hotel bathrooms, to go over our hair. When we had put them on

Alice took me through the entrance hall down to the front door of my flat, where a uniformed constable stood guard.

'Are you all right?'

'Nervous,' I said. She gave my arm a squeeze and we went inside.

It was as crowded as one of our parties – except that this was a fancy dress party. Everyone was wearing the white paper suits, and white masks as well. I pushed open the door to my bedroom. It still smelt faintly of vomit, but now there was something else as well, an acidic chemical smell, like Superglue. The wall was covered in purple blotches where some kind of dye had been sprayed over it. A figure in one of the white suits was crouching down beside the bed, scraping something off the floor. He stopped when he saw Alice and me and stood up respectfully.

I took some things out of the cupboard and put them in my sports bag. Jeans, a few shirts, a couple of smarter things in case I needed them. Bras and knickers. Some make-up from the table beside the bed. Deodorant. Chequebook. Trainers. Tampax. Shoes. Pyjamas. What else did I need?

Black. I'd need black for the funeral. My black cashmere sweater, my Russell & Bromley shoes, my black Jigsaw suit.

'OK,' I said at last. 'That's everything.'

The doorway to the bathroom had been closed off with a piece of transparent sheeting. Through it I could dimly make out a masked figure spraying something onto the shower curtain. In the living room, two more white-suited figures were crouched on the floor, holding a measuring tape. It took a moment before I realized that what they were measuring was a stain, or rather a series of stains, on the wooden floorboards. It looked like someone had taken a brush loaded with brown paint and swept it lightly along the wood, leaving a series of streaks and blotches.

I saw my cello, standing in the corner in its blue canvas case. I hadn't played it for months, but I suddenly needed to have it with me. I went and picked it up. The canvas felt slightly tacky to the touch.

'I was going to wipe it down,' one of the white-suited figures said apologetically through her mask. Until she spoke I hadn't realized it was a woman. 'The residue is just Toleduine – it'll come off with warm water.'

'Thanks,' I said. I gave the spider plant on the windowsill some water from the milk bottle we kept next to it. I turned to take one last look at the place where Jo and I had lived. Then I went outside.

'Message for you,' the policeman in the command vehicle said to Alice, handing her a note. 'It just came through on the squawk.'

She read it and said hesitantly, 'Ros, they want to know if I can go and help out at the suite. They've got three girls waiting to be examined and only one chaperone. But I can stay with you if you need me to.'

'No, you go ahead. I'll be fine.'

'I'll get a WPC to give Miss Taylor a lift,' the policeman said.

We stripped off our overalls. Alice handed me a card. 'Here's my number at work. And my home number. You can call me any time. And I'm giving you the number of a counselling service as well, just in case you can't get hold of me.'

'Thanks.' The card said 'Alice Turnbull. Sexual Offences Officer'. I put it in my pocket. 'You've been brilliant, Alice.'

'No,' she said, 'you have. You're strong, Ros. I know you're going to come through this.' She put her arms round me, gently so that she wouldn't hurt my back. As she drove away I felt bereft, standing there with my bag and my cello, a child abandoned by the school gates. I suddenly realized I was still wearing the detective's jacket, like an oversized school uniform I was waiting to grow into.

People who know you've been raped aren't quite sure how to deal with you physically. Charlotte, who would normally have kissed me delicately on both cheeks, gave me a sort of awkward embrace, and Johnny, who would ordinarily have wrapped me in a great big bear hug, didn't touch me at all. Perhaps he thought I wouldn't want to be touched by a man. Or perhaps I was in some way taboo now.

I went straight to bed. I was exhausted, and Charlotte's concerned horror was too much to cope with. I slept for three hours. When I woke up I could smell food, so I went downstairs to the kitchen where she was cooking pasta. We ate a slightly unreal meal, and I drank rather too much wine and chattered too brightly about anything that came into my head, everything except the murder and the rape – not because I was avoiding the subject but because after talking about it all day with the police I really had nothing left to say about it. And then finally I said something about Jo, so of course I had to explain what had happened, and what he'd done to my back, and Charlotte cried, and Johnny got up and said in a thick voice that if he personally ever got his hands on the bastard who did it, he'd tear him to pieces. 'Just ten minutes alone with him,' he kept saying. 'I'd rip his fucking balls off.' I must have flinched, because he said, 'Sorry.' But that led on to a discussion about what *would* happen if the police caught him, and how many years he'd actually get. Charlotte knew someone who had been raped by a boyfriend, and after the police had persuaded her to go to court and give evidence the judge had announced that there were mitigating circumstances, as she clearly wasn't very traumatized, so he was only going to impose a six-month sentence. Even murderers were sometimes out in six years, apparently.

I wasn't really agreeing or disagreeing, as it seemed to have nothing to do with my particular case, when Charlotte reached across and poured me some more wine and I suddenly had a moment of total clarity – a flashback, I suppose you'd call it, except that this was a sudden photographic recall of a moment I didn't even know had happened.

Twenty-four hours earlier – during the period I had told the police was a complete blank – I had reached across to where Jo's half-full glass stood next to my empty one and said, 'Aren't you going to drink that?'

And she'd said, 'No, you have it.'

So I'd picked up her glass – her half-full wine glass – and drunk what was in it.

'Oh, God,' I said across Charlotte and Johnny's voices. They stopped talking and looked at me.

'I've just realized,' I said slowly. 'I finished off Jo's drink last night.'

They looked blank.

'The GHB was in the wine glass,' I said. 'Don't you see? And I drank hers. That's why I had more of the drug in my blood than she did. I went to bed and collapsed – I was completely out of it, so later he . . . he did whatever he wanted with me. He even cut me and I didn't wake up. But Jo – Jo wasn't so out of it, because she'd had less than I had. So she woke up, and probably she struggled or fought or whatever, and that's why he killed her. That's why he killed her: because she let me drink her wine.' I could hear the rising note of panic in my voice. 'If I hadn't drunk that wine she wouldn't be dead. It all went wrong because of what I did. She wasn't drugged enough, so he killed her.'

'It's not your fault,' Charlotte said quickly.

'Of course it isn't,' Johnny agreed.

'I know, but don't you *see*? If I hadn't touched her wine, she would never have died. She'd be *alive*.'

'You can't think like that,' Johnny said. 'You'll just torture yourself. I mean, if you'd gone out to the pub it would never have happened either.'

'Exactly.' Suddenly, what had happened to Jo seemed grossly, almost ludicrously, unlikely – one outcome out of hundreds of possible alternatives, an obscure turning off a minor branch off the path of events. That she had actually died was as unfeasible as a lottery win. 'Do you see? It almost didn't happen, and then it did.' I stopped, aware that I was gabbling. 'Sorry,' I mumbled, and then I threw up.

There was a strange normality to the evening. The television schedules were still the same. The news was on at ten o'clock, my flatmate's death too unimportant to get a mention. Johnny announced that he was going to get an early night – I suppose he thought Charlotte and I would want to talk. Then the doorbell rang, and Charlotte went to see who it was.

I already knew it must be the police, and my first thought was, *they've caught him*. I heard Bill the detective's voice, and Charlotte say in response, 'She is, but she's pretty tired.' Then Bill himself came in.

'Any news?' I asked.

He shook his head. He looked exhausted. 'Sorry. I'm here because I need my keys. They're my only set.'

I must have looked puzzled because he added, 'They're in my jacket.'

'Oh – God, I'm so sorry.' I went and got his jacket from my

room and tried to explain that I'd been going to leave it with Alice but she'd had to rush away.

'It doesn't matter,' he said. He jangled the keys in his hand and looked around. 'I'm glad you're with friends, anyway.'

I suddenly saw the place through his eyes: the expensive furniture, the studied Conran-shop informality, the reek of money, and I cringed slightly. I'm not like this, I wanted to tell him. This isn't me.

'Do you want a glass of wine, Bill?' Charlotte said brightly.

'Um – well, I'd better get back.'

'Beer? Johnny's got loads in the fridge.'

'Well – a cold one would slip down,' he said. 'It's been a hell of a day.' Charlotte went to get it.

'Listen, I've remembered something,' I said. I told him about drinking from Jo's glass.

'That's very good,' he said. 'I'm sure the doctor's right and you'll remember more all the time. We'll get another statement from you sometime in the next few days.' He stifled a yawn. 'Sorry. I'm a bit tired.'

'How's it going?' I asked. It felt strange to be enquiring about the investigation as one might ask a banker how the markets were doing or a journalist if they had written any good articles recently.

Bill looked as if he was unsure how to answer. Then he said, 'This may not be the right time or place to ask this, but what sort of girl was Jo?'

'What do you mean?'

'Was she aware of the effect she had on people? Not that I'm accusing her of anything,' he added hastily. 'I'm just wondering if her manner, or her . . . lifestyle . . . may have put her particularly at risk.'

'She was good-looking,' I said, horribly aware of using the past tense. 'She liked to have fun. No more than lots of other people, though. Why?'

'Nothing, really. I was just thinking out loud.' He yawned. 'Look, I'd better leave that beer. We've got a team of thirty people searching the area first thing tomorrow, and I'll have to be up early to sort it all out.'

'Thanks for everything,' I said inadequately.

He let himself out, and Charlotte reappeared from the kitchen. 'Well? What did he say?'

I shrugged. 'They're going to search the area. And he wanted to know if Jo led a high-risk lifestyle, whatever that means.'

'So they don't think it was a burglar any more?'

'He didn't say that.'

'But that's the implication, isn't it? Think about it, Ros. Out of all the flats in the street he chose yours. Isn't it more likely that it's something to do with Jo?'

'What do you mean?'

'Let's face it, she could be a bit obvious sometimes,' Charlotte said primly. 'It would hardly be surprising if all that turned out to be a factor.'

'A factor in what? Are you saying it was somehow her *fault*?'

'No, of course not, but maybe someone misread the signals.'

'No one asks to get raped. God, I can't believe you're saying this.'

'Ros, listen. I'm not saying she shouldn't have dressed the way she did or anything like that. It's more – oh, I'm putting this badly – it's more the fact that she could be a bit *reckless*. And I'm not saying that excuses the man who did it, either,' she added quickly. 'Just that if she'd been a bit more careful, maybe she wouldn't have been singled out as a victim. And then you'd never have been attacked either.'

I suddenly realized how Charlotte and Johnny saw this. They had to blame someone. We all did, it was human nature. But while I'd been blaming myself for what happened to Jo, Charlotte and Johnny were blaming Jo for what had happened to *me*. I shook my head. 'It was a burglar,' I said. 'We left the windows open, which was stupid, admittedly, but it was hot and we were hardly going to sit there with them closed all evening. Someone came in. That's all. It could have been us, it could have been the people next door.'

But even as I said it I could see the obvious flaw – why were we drugged? I'd never heard of a burglar drugging people. And if he brought condoms with him – if, as Bill had suggested, the rape was premeditated – how big a coincidence was it that the burglar had chosen a flat with two young women living in it?

'Sorry,' Charlotte said. 'I didn't mean to upset you.' There was a short silence. 'That policeman's nice,' she said, which on the face of it was a non sequitur, but actually followed a very Charlotte-like train of thought.

'He's a policeman,' I said shortly. 'He's paid to be nice.'

'He's very young to be a detective inspector, isn't he?'

I was starting to wish I'd gone to someone else's flat and slept on a sofa. Charlotte was twenty-six going on forty. She'd rushed headlong into all the things Jo and I had avoided – a house, interior decorators, dinner parties with seating plans and a different wine for each course. She had never really liked being young and single. For her it had just been an unavoidable and rather perilous stepping stone to the next stage. As soon as she could, she'd found herself a nice wealthy young banker and turned into her mother. People like Jo – people who took risks – deserved what they got, if only because it proved that the Charlottes of this world had been right all along.

Jo had been a tall poppy, and tall poppies get cut down by nasty boys with sticks. It's the boy's fault, but the poppy should have been more careful.

5

I was already awake when Charlotte came in next morning with the phone.

'It's that policeman,' she said quietly. 'Do you want to take it?'

I nodded and pressed the handset to my ear.

'Good morning, Ros. Bill Thomson here.' He was on a mobile. I could hear the sounds of other people, as well as traffic noises and a distant siren. 'Can I come and see you? There's something you may be able to help us with.'

'Of course.'

'I'll be there in five minutes.'

'Fine. I'll get dressed.' But the line had already gone dead.

He was there even sooner than he'd said, with a policewoman he introduced as Detective Sergeant Grogan. Grogan was carrying a black bin liner. When I led them through into Charlotte's kitchen she put it on the table.

'Do you recognize any of these?' Bill asked. He produced some white gloves from his pocket, like the gloves the packers used at work to handle important paintings, and opened the bin liner. Inside was a sleek grey DVD player, a Walkman, some CDs and a heap of jewellery.

'I'm not sure.'

Bill picked up some of the jewellery to show me. Earrings, necklaces, a couple of rings.

'I'm sorry. It's another blank.'

'Is it definitely *not* your property?' Grogan asked me.

'No . . . I'm sorry, I just can't remember.'

'I recognize some of it,' Charlotte said suddenly. She pointed to a necklace. 'That's yours, Ros. You got it in Thailand two years ago. And that ring – that's Jo's.'

'Are you sure?' Bill asked her.

She nodded. 'Certain.'

'Look,' Grogan said to Bill. She had put on some gloves as well and had clicked open the front of the Walkman. Inside was a cassette tape with 'Compilation' written on the label.

'That's your writing, Ros,' Charlotte said.

Bill and Grogan both looked at me. 'It does look like it,' I said doubtfully. I reached for the tape, but Bill stopped me.

'Careful. It may have prints on.'

'Where did you find it?'

'In a rubbish bin in Belsize Road. We were lucky. If he'd dumped it any nearer, it would already have been collected. But Belsize Road is on a different schedule.'

'Why did he leave it, though?'

Bill shrugged. 'If it was a professional burglar, he'd know holding on to something that linked him to a murder was crazy.'

'But if it was a burglar,' Charlotte said slowly, 'why take it in the first place? I mean, if he was just going to dump it a few minutes later?'

'Good point,' Bill said, favouring her with a smile.

'Perhaps he panicked,' I suggested.

'People don't always behave rationally in these situations,' Bill agreed. 'That's generally why we catch them, to be honest. Not so much cleverness on our part as stupidity on theirs.' He looked at me. 'They've finished with Jo at the hospital, if you'd still like to see her.'

'Yes,' I said. 'Definitely.'

'What's this?' Charlotte said, looking from one of us to the other.

Bill said, 'Ros wants to spend some time with Jo.'

Charlotte looked appalled. 'Is that a good idea?'

'It is if Ros thinks it is,' Bill said quietly.

'Won't it upset her?'

'Perhaps, but if that's what Ros wants I think it's up to her, don't you?'

Thank you, Bill.

Charlotte drove us there in her Golf, following Bill's directions to a small staff car park round the back of the hospital. We walked past the laundry, heat and steam gusting through its open doors. From somewhere below came the smells of institutional cooking and the hot, chemical smell of dishwashers. Eventually we reached a fire escape where a group of nurses were leaning against the railings, smoking and chatting. A couple of them glanced at Bill as he passed. I wondered if he was pretending not to notice because he was with Charlotte and me, and we were going to see a murder victim.

He led us down a level and pushed open a door marked 'Pathology – Histology – Haematology'. It was suddenly much colder. There was a small waiting area with half a dozen chairs and, incongruously, some dog-eared copies of *Country Life*. Another nurse was sitting behind a desk. Bill spoke to her in a quiet voice, and she phoned through to someone. A few moments later a doctor in a blue surgical gown appeared.

'Miss Taylor?' he said, looking from Charlotte to me. I nodded. I felt a little light-headed.

'Your friend's just down here.'

I followed him down a corridor. There was an area on one side that had been curtained off and he opened the curtain a little to let me through.

Jo's body was on a trolley, covered with a sheet. The thinness of the sheet, and the way it draped over her, seemed somehow indecent. Then he folded back the sheet so that I could see her face. Her tan seemed to have faded, and her beautiful face was now quite white. All the bits that normally had colour in them – the lips, the ears, the crescents under her eyes, the tip of the nose – seemed especially pale. Her lips were white and wrinkled, set in a slightly sucked-in expression. A towel had been wrapped round the top of her head, as if she had just stepped out of the shower. Which in a way, of course, she had.

The sheet covering her was so thin I could see a line of stitches running down her stomach – huge stitches, like something in a sailcloth. I tried not to think about that and what it meant. They would have taken her navel stud out before they cut her, just as the doctor had taken mine before my examination. I wondered what had happened to them, whether they were both together in an evidence bag somewhere.

'Can I hold her hand?' I asked.

'Of course,' the pathologist said kindly. He took Jo's hand by the wrist, took my own hand, and put them together. It felt floppy in my grasp, as cold and loose-skinned as the carcass of a chicken. I noticed that her nails, which she'd always kept long, had been clipped down to the fingertips.

'I'll leave you now,' he said. 'Just call if you want anything.'

I talked to her. I told her about the police, and everything they were doing to catch the man who did it. I told her I couldn't remember what had happened, but that the police thought I would remember more soon. I told her about the doctor who had examined me, and Alice, and Charlotte's disapproval.

'I'm sorry,' I whispered to her. I bent down and touched my lips to her knuckles. 'I'm so sorry.'

I looked at her face one last time. A comma of blonde hair was sticking out from under the towel. I tried to tuck it back, but it came loose and fell to the floor. It had been shaved off. I picked it up and folded it into my fist, pressing it there until my nails dug into my skin.

There was quite a crowd in the little waiting room. I recognized Bill's boss, Superintendent Collier. Gerry was there too, immaculate in a linen jacket and a cotton polo neck. His face, though, was ashen.

'Gerry. Oh God,' I said.

'Are you all right?' he wanted to know.

'I'm OK. I've lost my memory, though. I can't remember anything. Are you OK?'

'I'm fine,' he said grimly. 'Look, if there's anything I can do . . .'

'There isn't. But thanks.'

Collier said to him, 'Come along, please. She's through here.'

He held the door open and waited for Gerry to follow him. Gerry hesitated, and turned to me. 'They say he was trying to rape her.'

I nodded.

'You really mustn't discuss the case,' Collier said. 'Please come this way, sir.'

'And you? Were you . . . ?'

''Fraid so,' I said, more bravely than I felt.

58

'Oh, Christ. Oh, Jesus. Ros, I'm so sorry.'

The door opened and two more people walked in. One of them was Jo's brother Hector. He looked terrible too. We hugged each other, and then I was crying again, and telling him what a mess it all was. Like Gerry, he wanted to know how I was.

'I'm all right,' I said. 'I was drugged, just like her. She wouldn't have suffered, Hector. She wouldn't have known a thing.'

They say the first lie is the hardest, don't they? But it wasn't. That lie was easy, as easy as a gift from me to him. As easy as a doctor writing a prescription for a pill that will take away the pain.

Hector was looking at Gerry with a puzzled expression. I realized they'd probably never met. 'Hector, this is Gerry Henson.'

Hector extended his hand. But he still looked puzzled. 'Are you with Ros?'

'I've come to pay my respects to Jo,' Gerry said. He was older than Hector by about a dozen years.

Hector looked at me for help. 'Jo's boyfriend,' I explained.

'I thought she didn't have a boyfriend,' Hector said slowly. 'How long had you been going out?'

'About five months,' Gerry said. He didn't offer any other explanation.

'She never mentioned you.'

I wanted to get out of there. 'I'll explain everything later,' I said to Hector. 'We need to have a conversation about this, but honestly, this isn't the time.'

Collier was looking from one to the other of us, expressionless. He pushed open the door to the mortuary again. 'Who wants to go next?' he enquired genially, almost as if it were a funfair ride.

'I will,' Hector said, his face dark. 'I don't know who this man is or what his relationship was with Jo, but I'm her brother and I want to see her.'

6

'Do you recognize any of these?'

'No. Should I?'

'They might have approached you in the video shop on the night of the attack.'

I looked again at the photographs Bill had placed on the table. The men ranged from about twenty to about forty. Two were wearing open-necked shirts, one a suit, and one a jogging top. 'Sorry. Why? Who are they?'

'The videos they took out were from the adult section.'

'Oh. I see.' I looked again at the photographs. 'No.'

'Fair enough,' Bill said. 'I don't think they had anything to do with it either, you understand. But we have to eliminate every possibility.' He rubbed his eyes. 'Someone's going through the films they got out, to see if there are any similarities to what happened.'

'Bet that's a popular job.'

His eyes crinkled. 'I've asked one of the female detectives to do it. I reckon she'll concentrate better.'

The cuts on my back were starting to itch under the dressing. 'What about that boy who phoned me at work? Did you talk to him?'

'Yes. I don't know if this is good news or not, Ros. Nathan was at home all evening. He says he was using the internet. We checked his phone records, and it all tallies.'

I nodded. I hadn't wanted it to be Nathan. Rapists were shadowy figures who came at you out of the night, not good-looking but rather over-intense boys of one's own age who got a bit upset when you knocked them back.

Bill put a thick file on the table. 'Would you look at these?'

'What is it?'

'These people are on our sexual offenders register.'

While I looked through the photographs he got us each a coffee. He set the plastic cup down on the table beside me, and I picked it up automatically and took a mouthful. I yelped. 'Hot,' I said, gulping air. 'Ow.' And then: 'Oh, *shit*.'

A split second after the pain on my tongue came a different sort of pain. A flicker of memory, zigzagging like lightning into my conscious mind. It was gone almost as quickly, but not before I had glimpsed what it lit up.

'He was wearing a mask,' I said slowly.

'What?'

'I've remembered. He was strong and – he held my face with one hand while he was doing it. He kept turning his face towards me and spitting in my face. He used spit – he used spit as well when he – oh God.'

'What kind of mask?' Bill said quietly.

'A – a—' I tried to picture it. 'A Homer Simpson mask. You know, like a fancy dress thing.'

'Anything else?'

'I – I think he was black. And he smelt of sweat.'

'What was he wearing?'

I paused, and he urged, 'Quickly. Before it goes again.'

'A grey sweatshirt. Jeans.'

'Anything else? Ros, what else can you remember?'

I felt sick. 'He kept spitting. All the time. And he slapped me when I wouldn't – when I didn't do it the way he wanted. He spat in my mouth. Oh, God. And my eyes.' I shut my eyes but the image wouldn't go away. The man was holding me, squeezing my jaw with his hand, forcing my mouth open so he could spit inside it again. I could smell the sour reek of him – sweat and stale booze – feel the hammering of his hips as he pushed at me—

'How long did all this last?'

I closed my eyes and concentrated on quelling the waves of nausea. 'For ever,' I said. 'How about that, Bill? It lasted for ever.'

*   *   *

He made me wait there while he went to fetch Superintendent Collier and Sergeant Alice. Collier made me go through everything again while he wrote notes. Then he sat back and looked at what he'd written. He recited under his breath:

> 'I keep six honest serving-men
> Who taught me all I knew.
> Their names are What and Why and When
> And How and Where and Who.'

I must have looked blank because he sighed and said, 'Kipling. Right, young lady. There are just a couple of things I need to double-check. You say he was wearing a mask?'

'A Homer Simpson mask.'

'And you're absolutely sure about that?'

'Um – pretty sure. I mean, it was dark and—'

'Ah.' Collier leaned forward. 'He attacked you in the dark?'

'There was light from outside,' I said defensively. Why was Alice letting him be so aggressive? I tried to catch her eye but she was looking at the floor.

'And this mask,' Collier said, writing something down. 'Did it cover the mouth?'

'Yes. There was a little hole to breathe through. You must have seen them. It's a face, and there's a little hole where the mouth should be.'

'That's what I'm wondering about.'

'What do you mean?'

'He spat at you?' Collier looked at his notes and read back what I'd said. ' "He spat in his hand and he used it to penetrate me. He spat in my mouth and in my eyes." That's right, isn't it?'

'Yes. I've told you.'

'Had he taken his mask off at that point?'

'Well, he . . .' I suddenly saw what he was getting at. I said limply, 'Well, he couldn't have spat through the mask, could he, so he must have taken it off.'

'What did he look like? His face, I mean.'

'I . . .' Now that I tried to picture it, the image that had seemed so vivid only minutes before – the image of a man levering himself up on me and holding my face so that he could spit into my mouth

– seemed to blur and dissolve, the way a dream does when you try to remember exactly how it worked. 'I'm not sure,' I said slowly.

'Which aren't you sure about, Ros? The mask or the spitting?'

'Both,' I said. I started to cry. 'I'm sorry,' I said. 'I must have got confused.'

Collier sat back and watched me. 'There, there,' he said without a trace of sympathy. He stood up. 'All yours,' he said quietly to Bill and Alice.

'I've fucked up, haven't I?' I said when he'd gone. The enormity of what had just happened was still sinking in.

'Don't worry,' Alice said awkwardly. 'It happens all the time. If we have four different witnesses we always get at least three different descriptions.'

That wasn't the same, and we all knew it. 'I wasn't making it up. Honestly.'

'It's our fault,' Alice insisted. 'We've put too much pressure on you to remember.'

Bill said, 'Of course you weren't making it up. You were telling the truth, I know you were. It's just that what you remember isn't what actually happened.'

They referred me to a doctor who worked with the police. Dr Griffin was small, dapper and full of barely suppressed excitement. He wore a yellow shirt and a blue bow tie.

He began by making me go through the day before the rape from breakfast onwards. Every so often he'd interrupt, 'And are you very sure, fairly sure or not at all sure that event took place?'

I still couldn't remember anything that had happened since lunchtime that day.

'What about the rape itself?'

'Nothing. I can't remember anything about it. Apart from this mask thing, but that doesn't seem to make any sense.'

He took a pack of cards out of his briefcase, separated the picture cards out so that I could see them, then turned them over so that the fronts were hidden. 'See if you can find a pair,' he instructed.

I turned over two jacks. 'Very good.' He reached across and removed the two I'd turned over. 'Again?' I turned over two queens. 'Excellent. What's your favourite book?'

63

'*Wuthering Heights*?' I said, wondering what Emily Brontë had to do with anything.

He wheeled his chair alongside mine and peered into my eyes with a small bright pen light. 'And your mother's maiden name?'

'Robinson.'

'Look up, look left, look right, look down. What time did you leave work the night before last?'

Blank. 'I'm sorry.'

'Any double vision? Headaches? Floppiness in any of your limbs?'

'I don't think so.'

He clicked the light off and pushed his chair back. 'Can you remember what the weather was like on Tuesday?'

I thought, then shook my head.

He turned to his desk and pulled a pad towards him. 'You have retrograde and anterograde amnesia,' he said as he wrote. 'It may be post-traumatic in origin, but I think it's more likely that it's a result of being drugged. There are no indications of neurological complications – if you'd had a blow to the head I'd be thinking of some further investigations, such as a CAT scan, but at this stage it's not really necessary. The most interesting thing, from my point of view, is this counterfeit memory. You say it was quite vivid?'

'Definitely.' I felt sick just thinking about it.

'Would you like me to explain what may have happened?'

I nodded.

'The brain is a very lazy organ. When asked to remember something, it doesn't actually bother to assemble every single detail. It generates patterns based on past experiences instead. It's a bit like when two people look at a cloud – you might see a bird, where I might see a butterfly. It all depends on which of the billions of patterns stored in your brain happens to get matched to it first.' He pointed his pen at me. 'The question is, what happens when the pattern is missing or damaged? When, for example, people have damaged their frontal lobes, the left part of their brain, where the language is, can't access the right part where the memories are. So the left part generates the missing information itself – makes an educated guess, if you like. That's why neurology wards are full of people who swear they're

64

doctors. It's the only explanation their brain can come up with to explain what they're doing there. The technical term for it is confabulation.'

'But I haven't damaged my brain, have I?'

'In your case, the confabulation was almost certainly caused by the memory loss. Under the pressure of questioning, your mind has simply supplied some of the missing answers itself.'

'It seemed so real.'

'It would do. Memory is an interesting area, actually. Every memory is made up of two memories – the memory itself, and a memory of how long you've had it. The fascinating thing about confabulation is that one even remembers how long ago the false event occurred.'

'Why did I . . . *confabulate* those particular memories?' I hesitated. 'I mean – the fact that he was black. Is that some kind of subconscious racism?'

'What were you doing just before the confabulation occurred?'

'I was looking at photographs of sex offenders.'

'Ah. Anything else?'

'We'd just been discussing adult videos. The fact that a police-woman was looking at them.'

'Have you ever watched anything similar yourself? Anything that might have triggered an association?'

I felt myself turn pink. 'I suppose so. Now I come to think of it.'

'Well, there you are.'

'How will I be able to tell when my memories are the real thing?'

'Ah. Now that is a tricky one.' Dr Griffin cocked one leg over the other, revealing an orange tartan sock. 'I suppose the short answer is that you won't, unless what you remember is corroborated by other evidence.' The doctor seemed to be losing interest in me now. He glanced at his briefcase, as if hoping to get on with whatever was inside it. He had squeezed me in between other patients as a favour to the police, and now I was taking up his time.

'Is there anything I can do?'

'Do you like playing games?'

'What sort of games?'

'Anything that uses your memory. Racing demon, Scrabble, even the little card game I played with you earlier. And you might keep a journal. Start with what you do remember, and add to it little by little. The more you use that part of your brain, the more likely it is the hidden memories will begin to emerge.' Dr Griffin clicked the top of his biro rapidly several times. 'I'd also suggest that you consider therapy. It's possible there's a psychogenic element in these deficits.'

'I'm sorry,' I said, shaking my head. 'You'll have to translate.'

'Sometimes the mind deliberately avoids remembering things which are traumatic. It's a sort of defence mechanism, to avoid exposing itself to something that will cause distress. Talking to a psychotherapist may help to loosen the blockage.'

'Are you a psychotherapist?'

'I'm a clinical psychologist, which is slightly different. But yes, I have used psychotherapy with some of my patients.'

'Could I come to you?'

He considered. 'Well, I don't see why not. If your GP's happy to refer you.'

'It's just that, since you work with the police, you'd know if the things I was remembering were useful.'

'I should stress that anything you tell me would be bound by doctor-patient confidentiality. It would be up to you if you chose to tell the investigating officers.'

I thought of Bill, exhausted and weary, following up every tiny lead in case it turned out to be of use. And I thought of Jo as I'd seen her in the morgue, all the colour drained from her body.

'I want to do whatever will help,' I said.

On my way home I went into a shop to buy a journal. It was quite an upmarket shop, and there were piles of leather-bound note-books containing blank pages of uncut vellum. I didn't want one of those. They were for poems or insipid beautiful thoughts. There was something narcissistic about them. I wanted something functional and unadorned. Eventually I bought a plain red cash ledger.

That evening was difficult. Charlotte had invited Hector to stay the night, which was reasonable enough, but his stricken face was a constant reminder of Jo. He seemed dazed by the discovery that

66

Jo had been seeing a married man. He was also appalled to have been told that Jo's body wouldn't be released for burial for several weeks, or until her killer had been caught, as his legal team would be entitled to have their own post-mortem. I helped Charlotte cook supper, but we kept getting in each other's way and I broke a salad bowl. She didn't say anything but I knew it was an old one that she treasured.

After we'd eaten I made an excuse and went up to my room. The red ledger was waiting on the bed. I got a pen. What had Dr Griffin said? Start with what you do remember.

I wrote for three hours. What I wrote was disjointed and out of sequence, a series of fragments. Griffin was right, though: it made me feel better. But it didn't trigger any memories.

I slept with the light on again. That night I had a dream that I was back in my own bed. In the dream I woke up and for some reason I knew I had to go down the corridor to Jo's room. I got out of bed and walked towards her door, which was closed. I tried it, but it wouldn't open properly. Then Dr Griffin opened the door from the inside, but just a little so that I couldn't see past him. He said mildly, 'You may not want to come in here, Ros.' He shut the door, and when I tried to open it again I found it was locked.

7

Over the next ten days I went back to the hospital five times for my follow-up appointments. I was given a battery of injections with big, military-sounding names. There was Ceftriaxone to protect against gonorrhoea, immune globulin to ward off hepatitis, Doxycycline to stop chlamydia, Metronidazole to repair the wall of my cervix, and Clomitrozole to prevent thrush. I had four counselling sessions and acquired a small library of leaflets. The cuts on my back healed quickly, just as the doctor had predicted. I thought, sometimes, about Bill the detective and his quiet, gentle eyes. In the afternoons I played Dr Griffin's memory games. I wrote my journal religiously.

It made no difference. The locked room remained locked.

The dazed lethargy I had felt in the immediate aftermath of the attack gave way to something that was almost its opposite. I became jittery and frightened and saw assailants everywhere. I thought that a man in the street who gave me a casual admiring look meant to follow me home. I couldn't sit still, even to watch television. I got up in the middle of the night and prowled round Charlotte's house, checking that all the windows were locked and the chain was fastened on the door.

Once, making idle conversation with Bill while we waited for a statement to be typed, I asked him something about himself and he said, 'I think I'll have to know you better before I tell you that.' It was a tiny remark, said with no significance, but at the thought of what it implied – future intimacy, closeness, sharing secrets – I felt myself blush.

*　　*　　*

Carl Howell was the 22-year-old who processed the film Jo and I collected from Boots on the night of the attack. Since then, he'd vanished. But what had really galvanized the police was the discovery that he had a conviction for sexual assault when he was fifteen.

'You think it's him?'

'Ros, I can't say that. We have to trace, interview and eliminate every possible suspect.' Bill already sounded as if he were in court. 'All I can say is that this is a very significant piece of evidence.'

We had started meeting in the Starbucks round the corner from Charlotte's place. I told him it was because I was going crazy, cooped up inside all day. That was true, but it was also because I didn't want Charlotte or Johnny around when I met Bill. I wanted to keep him to myself.

'And all because of a few photos we took on holiday? That seems crazy. It's just so . . . random.'

'Stranger things have happened. Don't forget, your address was on the processing envelope. And some of the photos were quite – well, to someone like that they might have seemed quite provocative.'

We had taken some pictures of each other by the pool, topless. Showing off. It seemed like another lifetime now.

'If you catch him, will it matter that I can't remember any-thing?'

'That depends. He may stick his hands up. If he doesn't it'll be up to us to build a case against him. But forensics will settle it, one way or the other.'

I nodded.

'There's something else I came to tell you,' he said carefully. 'We've finished with the flat.'

'Is it still—' I closed my eyes as a mental image of the six-foot bloodstain smeared across our living-room floor came back to me. 'Still messed up?'

He shook his head. 'Cleaned. All part of the service.'

'I must get my flatmate killed more often,' I said lightly. 'It saves so much housework.'

'Ros . . .'

I thought of that flat without Jo, and the fragile shell of normality I'd been developing so carefully fell apart. I began to cry. People looked at us curiously. An elderly woman next to us glared angrily at Bill. She leaned across and hissed, 'He isn't worth it, love. There's plenty better where that one came from.'

Bill took no notice of her. He put one hand reassuringly on mine and with his other hand he drank his coffee while I sobbed.

The flat still smelt of chemicals, but different ones – air freshener and powerful cleaning fluids, instead of the sticky blue fingerprint spray the scene-of-crime people had used. There was something else too – a peculiar stillness, an atmosphere. Or perhaps it just felt strange because Jo would never again come in here, kick her shoes off and reach for the TV remote control as she slumped in a chair. Never play Dido at full volume in the living-room so that she could hear it in the bathroom. Never eat tinned peaches in the shower. Never drape her clothes over the sofa while she changed to go out in front of the TV.

The brown bloodstain on the floor was gone too.

There was a pile of letters on the table. The cleaners must have put them there. Some of them were addressed to Jo.

'Should I open these?'

'Someone's got to,' Bill said.

I leafed through them quickly. Who would tell these people she was dead? I wondered. Who would get in touch with the foreign banks offering credit cards at preferential rates, the estate agents with urgent buyers for properties in our street, the mail-order lingerie companies and the Chinese restaurants, and tell them there was no point any more?

There was a postcard from Italy. 'Hi Jo! You said to drop you a line so I am doing that. I hope you are very well. I just wanted you to know I will not forget you. If you would like to come to Sardinia again some day, let me know. Your friend, Mele.'

'Who's Mele?' Bill said, reading it over my shoulder.

'Just an admirer.' One of many. 'I need a drink. Do you want one?'

'Just coffee.'

'There won't be any milk. Unless there's some long-life.' I opened the fridge. The police had left the contents untouched. An unopened carton of orange juice had inflated with gas and was nearly cylindrical. Satsumas in a net had gone squishy and split. A flaccid old potato had sprouted plump little arms, like an Indian god. There was a single bottle of wine. 'Looks like a drink after all,' I said, pulling it out. 'The bottle opener's in that drawer.' Strange how some things were absolutely clear, when others were covered in fog. 'And the glasses are in the cupboard.'

While he opened the wine, I played the messages on the answer machine. The tape was full of messages from friends who had heard what had happened but couldn't get hold of me. That cheered me up slightly. I had been feeling shunned as well as shocked.

I walked into Jo's room. The bed had been stripped and her duvet, without its cover, was folded neatly on the bare mattress. The bedside table was gone as well. But some things were still as she'd left them. There was a book lying on the floor. I picked it up. One of the pages had been turned over to mark her place. She'd got to page one hundred and forty-eight, and then she'd died. A magazine was open at a page about diets. Her deodorant was lying on its side, the top off.

'Who'll deal with all her stuff?' I asked Bill, who had followed me.

'Her family, in theory, but they'll probably be grateful if you packed it up for them. Just don't get rid of anything. You never know what may be useful for the investigation.'

I nodded.

'I'll help you, if you like,' he offered.

'That's rather above the call of duty, isn't it?'

'It's got nothing to do with duty.'

I tried to make a joke of it. 'Are all policemen as nice as you?' He didn't answer. I was suddenly very aware of his presence, of the fact that he was standing a fraction closer to me than he should have been. I didn't know what was going to happen. But I knew that something would, and I wanted it to. I put my hand on his arm. I thought he was going to kiss me but at the last moment he didn't. He stepped back.

'Sorry,' I said, horribly embarrassed. I turned away.

'Ros,' he said carefully. 'Wait. What happened to you . . . Everyone says it takes months, maybe years, to get over something like that.'

'Yes.'

'And I'm a policeman. There are very strict rules about who we – how we deal with witnesses. Who we socialize with.'

'Of course.'

'Perhaps when all this is over . . . But not now.'

'Well, of course,' I said. 'Not now.' Because what sort of woman, having been raped, would ask someone out just a couple of weeks later? It was clearly impossible.

But I needed someone, and Bill was there. I put my arms round him, and buried my head in his chest.

He could have taken it further if he wanted to. A bastard would have done. A bastard, or a rapist, would have taken that as all the invitation he needed.

But Bill wasn't a bastard. So he held me for a moment, and then he let me go, and that was as far as it went.

A few days later I went back to work. It was a relief to be back. When I put on the white lab coat and goggles I became a different person: calm, ordered, precise. I told the others I'd had flu.

Bill phoned me at the gallery to say Carl Howell had been arrested. A policeman had pulled over a white van for having no brake lights. Howell, who'd been driving, had produced his licence when asked to, and the policeman had recognized the name.

'Has he confessed?'

'No. He's asked for a lawyer. But don't read too much into that.'

'But if you had enough evidence to arrest him . . .'

'Ros, I'm afraid it's standard practice in a murder inquiry to arrest a suspect before they make a statement. It's to protect their rights, not ours. It means they can get legal representation.'

'Oh. I see.'

'The reason I'm calling is that we'd like you to do an identification parade.'

'But I won't know him from Adam.'

'Well, perhaps. But don't forget, he's got no idea you're suffering from amnesia. As far as he's concerned, you might be able to point the finger at him. So holding the parade will put him under pressure. And Dr Griffin thinks seeing him might just jog your memory as well.'

*　　*　　*

They sent a police car for me and drove me to the identification suite, which was a small, separate building on the outskirts of Kilburn. A door marked 'Witness Entrance ONLY' led from the car park directly into a small room with half a dozen chairs and some magazines. There were two posters on the wall. One said: 'If there are other witnesses present, DO NOT discuss your case. If you do, it may jeopardize criminal proceedings.' The other said: 'Why not become an Identification Parade volunteer? We pay £10 an hour and it will not affect your benefits.'

I waited for almost an hour. A policeman in a white shirt with a Metropolitan Police tie resting on the ledge of his beer belly came in and introduced himself as the identification officer. He told me the delay was because a solicitor was objecting to some of the volunteers. There was the inevitable form to fill – my name, my address, my date of birth. He asked if I knew my crime number. I didn't. I signed the form where he'd marked it with a cross.

Eventually a WPC came and took me to the identification room. It was long and narrow, not much more than a corridor. A window ran the whole length of one wall. There were blinds on the other side of the glass, and the glass itself was dark, like the glass in a pair of sunglasses. A notice stuck to the glass said, 'IMPORTANT. Do not stand near to viewing window. Dim all lights. Do not light cigarettes. You will not be visible to persons on the other side of the glass.' It reminded me of a picture I saw once of an execution chamber in America.

'All right?' the policewoman said.

'I'm fine, thanks.'

'Would you like a glass of water?'

I shook my head. The man with the beer belly came in and stood at a kind of lectern at one end of the room. He cleared his throat. 'Are you Ros Taylor, currently residing at 27 Broadhurst Terrace?'

I said I was.

'You are here because it is believed you may be able to assist the police by identifying an individual you have previously described, discussed with or named to an investigating officer. The person you saw may or may not be on the parade. If you cannot make a positive identification, you should say so, but

73

you should not make a decision before looking at each member of the parade at least twice.' He pressed a switch on his lectern and the lights dimmed. A buzzer sounded, and someone on the other side of the window pulled up the blinds.

There were nine men sitting on a bench built into the far wall. They were all black, and in their early twenties. The one at the end was quite good-looking. He had short stubby dreadlocks that stuck up from his head like cloves studded into an orange. In front of each man, on the floor, was a number.

'Do you want them to turn sideways?' the police officer asked.

'Can they stand up?'

'Sorry. That isn't allowed.'

I tried to imagine one of them on top of me, holding me down, and my mind recoiled from the thought. No pictures flashed into my brain. My memory was as lifeless as a dead battery.

I looked at them all again, but I already knew what I was going to have to say.

'I'm sorry. I don't recognize any of them.'

'No problem, love,' the officer said cheerfully. He pressed a button, and the blinds came down again. A little while later Bill came in.

'No luck?' he said quietly.

I shook my head.

'Don't worry. It was always a long shot.'

I did wonder, then, what would have happened if he'd come in a little earlier and just nodded surreptitiously at one of the men – at the end one, say, the good-looking one with the dreads. What would I have done?

But of course it wouldn't have been that easy. Bill, as an investigating officer, had probably only been allowed to come and talk to me after I'd said that I didn't recognize anyone. There were procedures for making sure that it was all done properly and above board. The police didn't want me to lie. What they wanted was witnesses who could identify their suspects truthfully.

One corner of the blind had caught on its way down. I watched the men file out, off to collect their ten pounds, with a feeling that once again I'd somehow let everyone down.

8

Dr Griffin read my journal in silence. Occasionally he stopped to make a note on the pad on his desk. As he read he rested one leg on the other and spun gently in his revolving chair, first to the left and then to the right.

'So,' he said, putting the journal down. 'Nothing more in the way of recovered memories.'

I shook my head.

'You know Carl Howell has been released?'

I hadn't.

'Not only was there no evidence linking him to the attacks, but I have to say that he was an unlikely match for your assailant.'

'Oh.'

'It's a technical issue. The latest studies show that rapists tend to fall into very distinct categories, depending on how they operate. The point is that even though they might become more prolific, more aggressive, take more risks or whatever, they tend to do so within those same categories of offence. The crime which Carl Howell was previously convicted of wasn't just different in degree to what happened to you, it was a completely different sort of offence. If he were to commit a rape, I'd expect it to be quick, opportunistic and disorganized – what one might think of as a typical rape. The person who raped you is a very different type of individual. His personality will undoubtedly be reflected in the way he arranges his life.'

'In what way?'

'It's a rather complex area, I'm afraid.'

'I'm not an idiot,' I said furiously. 'I have a doctorate in organic chemistry. I think I'm probably capable of understanding this.'

'Sorry. I didn't mean to imply otherwise. What I should have said was, I'm not sure it's the right moment for you to be steeping yourself in forensic detail. There's a danger of allowing your intellectual ability to understand to run ahead of your emotional ability to cope with what you know.' He sat back and watched me for a second. 'Which brings me to this,' he said, lifting my journal before setting it back on the desk. 'Ros, I appreciate how honest you're being with me. But I have to tell you that some of the things I've just read make me very, very concerned.'

'Such as?'

'Your feelings about Detective Inspector Thomson,' he said gently. 'In your journal, Ros, you pose the question, what sort of woman would contemplate starting a relationship only a short time after being raped? You're obviously concerned about the answer to that yourself.'

I shrugged.

'Well, let me suggest one possible answer, which is that it's more common than you think for victims of crime to form emotional attachments towards authority figures.'

I felt myself starting to go red. 'I don't like Bill because he's a policeman.'

Griffin's silence went on and on. A therapist's silence, I was beginning to realize, was the equivalent of an ordinary person saying, 'Bollocks.'

'Ros, you're an intelligent young woman. What does a policeman represent to someone in your situation?' he said at last. 'Security? Justice? Fairness? Retribution? It would hardly be surprising if that coloured your feelings about him.'

It was hard to disagree when he put it like that.

'He's also been trained to deal empathetically with traumatized people. It's easy to mistake empathy for something more. When someone's been through what you've been through . . .'

'If you're telling me,' I began, incoherent with embarrassment, 'that you think I'm behaving like some lovestruck schoolgirl—'

Griffin held up his hand. 'I'm not saying that at all. All I'm saying is that your emotions, and your judgement, may take a little while to settle down after what you've been through.'

Another long silence.

'There's also the procedural aspect to consider.' He handed the red cash book back to me. 'If you were to take these notions

76

about Thomson any further, it would put him in a very difficult position. It could jeopardize the whole investigation.'

Oh, the infinite condescension of that word 'notions'.

'I'm not going to *do* anything,' I said furiously. 'Neither is he. I like him, that's all. What's wrong with that?'

'Well, exactly. Nothing. And of course, from what you've written, DI Thomson seems to be behaving absolutely properly. I'm just sounding a note of caution, that's all.'

With Carl Howell no longer a suspect, the investigation started again from the beginning.

'I want you to make a list of every man who's come to your flat in the last six weeks,' Bill told me. 'Repair men, delivery drivers, friends, guests, even people who came to read the meters.'

I wrote the list and we went through it, with Bill questioning me about every name. How was that one? Was he agitated? Flirtatious? Surly? Strange in any way?

Bill himself was different, I thought: quieter, more distant somehow, even a bit wary. I wondered if Dr Griffin had said something.

I got up in the morning, dressed, ate, went to work, went through the motions. It wasn't me. It was someone on camera, playing the part of me, fooling almost everyone.

My friends organized a night out for me. We sat in the pub, about a dozen of us, getting pissed. Only a couple of them knew I'd been raped – just Anna, and Charlotte, and Johnny, unless any of them had been gossiping – but of course everyone knew about Jo. I wore my DKNY jeans and my favourite Morgan top, clothes I hadn't put on since before the attack. As the evening went on, and text messages were sent and received, the gravitational pull that any large group inevitably exerts attracted others, random clusters of couples and friends of friends, until we were a noisy knot of raucous good humour occupying the whole of one end of the pub. I suddenly found myself talking to a guy I'd never met before, Hugo or possibly Hugh, a friend of someone who worked with Anna, good-looking in a fairly conventional six-foot football-playing sort of way, a brand manager at some company I'd never heard of. We were having one of those inane pub conversations that has no structure to it but bounces along quite happily on its own, with just the occasional push to keep it going. Did I know that Alfred Hitchcock had no belly button? Yes, but did he know that Humphrey Bogart was Princess Diana's cousin? It had got to the stage where people were starting to say no thanks, got to be up early. Drinks coming back from the bar that other people decided they hadn't wanted after all were being pressed into our hands instead. 'So how do you know this lot?' he asked.

I thought, he doesn't know. A huge feeling of relief washed over me. 'I've known most of them for ages.'

'Got a boyfriend here?'

'No,' I said, smiling at his directness.

'Got a boyfriend somewhere else?'

'There's a couple stashed under my bed.'

'Can I call you sometime?'

'If you like,' I said tipsily.

He pulled out a pen and poised it over a cigarette packet. I said, 'Why d'you want to call me, anyway?'

He looked puzzled.

'Oh, yes. Stupid. To ask me out. Maybe we'll go to a film, then maybe you'll phone again and ask me out to dinner, and then there'll be a bit of a snog in the taxi, and the next date will be at your place and you'll cook me dinner, and then you'll ask me if I want to go to bed with you. The whole ritual. The palaver. The rigmarole.' I was just drunk enough for the difference between a palaver and a rigmarole to seem very important. 'Whatever. The point is, what you really want is a shag, but you don't think you should say so.'

'No, what I really want is a shag, but I think you'd run a mile if I said so.'

'I dare you.'

'Fancy a shag?'

'Why not?'

I looked round. Charlotte was trying to drag Johnny away from a drunken conversation about football. I didn't want to tell her what I was doing. I said to the person next to me, 'Will you tell Charlotte I'll be back later and I've got a key so don't wait for me?' She nodded. 'Come on,' I said to Hugo or possibly Hugh.

We went outside and I waited while he got a taxi. I snogged him in the taxi, because that was easier than talking to him. When we got to his flat he suggested a drink but I wasn't in the mood for that. I asked him where the bedroom was and he followed me in and I let him take my clothes off and have sex with me. I was upset that he almost ripped my pink Morgan top when he pulled it over my head and I said, 'Careful,' sharply. Afterwards I asked him to call me a cab. He asked for my number again, and I said, 'Why? You've shagged me, haven't you?' We didn't kiss each other goodbye.

So that's that, I thought in the cab. I've got back in the saddle. I stared out of the window. The cab driver had to ask me four times whereabouts in Maida Vale I wanted.

On Sunday I moved out of Charlotte's and back into the flat. Whatever had happened there, it was home. It was where I felt closest to Jo.

I talked to her all the time. I told her what had been going on, and about Bill. I told her what was going on at work. I even pointed out things in the paper I thought she'd like to know about.

I no longer had attacks of the jitters. Real life slowly resumed. But it was real life with the volume turned down, if that makes sense. Everything was muffled and strangely distant. When people spoke to me there was always a sort of timelag before the words meant anything, a bit like phoning America on a bad line.

The only time the volume went back up was when Simon gave me a flower. Simon was the IT guy at work. I called him up because my computer had developed a strange glitch which caused parts of my screen to disappear.

Shy Si was actually rather nice. He sat at my desk and chatted to me while he rebooted and reconfigured and reinstalled and made system disks and did all the other arcane stuff that IT people do. He was talking about a French rock circus troupe who were playing at the Roundhouse. They juggled chainsaws and performed ballets on bungee ropes. Si thought they were fantastic. He had seen them three times.

'I could go again, though,' he said enthusiastically. 'I could get some tickets if you like.'

'OK,' I said.

'Brilliant,' he said, surprised. 'Er – yeah. Brilliant.' He added significantly, 'I'd like that.'

Oh God, I thought, he surely doesn't think I meant a date.

'I'll get the tickets then. Saturday OK?'

'Shall we see if anyone else wants to come?' I said brightly. 'Alex, do you want to see a circus on Saturday?'

Alex shook his head. 'I'm too old for this kind of high jinks.'

'Tricia?'

Tricia, the other lab assistant, said, 'Nah. I saw them last time they were here. They're good, though.'

She was right, the circus was brilliant, and for two hours I forgot everything and just had a good time. And then on the way out there was a man selling flowers, and Si bought me a red rose, and presented it to me with a flourish.

I stood there, shaking. Everything went blurred. A horrible rage suddenly welled up in me – people talk about the taste of bile: it was true, I could actually taste my own fury. I hissed at him, 'You fucking little prick. What gives you the right—' and I crumpled the pathetic little flower in my fist and threw it on the ground.

He was staring at me, open-mouthed, with all the other punters still streaming out around us.

'Oh God,' I said. 'Oh God.' And then I was crying, and he walked off and came back again, because although he was hurt he could also see that there was something seriously wrong. We went to a café and got a bottle of wine and talked. All the stuff about the rape came pouring out, and he sat there listening and nodding and making sympathetic noises.

There were repercussions, though, because it turned out that shy Si rather fancied himself as my rescuer and confidant. He started sending me thoughtful emails about the nature of pain, complete with links to survivors' websites. After a while I stopped replying. I didn't want to be rescued, or at least not by him.

'I shagged a complete stranger. Didn't even know his name.' I stared at Griffin defiantly.

He said mildly, 'Did that make it worse or better? Not knowing his name, I mean.'

'Better, actually.'

He nodded.

'It must be a good sign, mustn't it?' I went on. 'A step in the right direction.'

'Well, it's certainly a step,' he murmured. He began doodling on his pad. I was confused. I suppose I'd been expecting more of a reaction.

'I found it quite easy,' I said. 'I mean, I'd been worrying about frigidity and so on. I read a thing in *Marie Claire* last year. Vaginismus, they call it. You just clamp up. But as it turned out, everything was in full working order.'

He nodded again. I stretched my neck to look at his doodle. 'What do you think?'

He looked surprised. 'About what?'

'About me shagging this bloke.'

'Ah.' He put down the pen. 'I think you're probably trying to provoke me.'

'Sorry?' I said. 'Are you really suggesting that I shagged Hugo or whatever his name is just so I could tell you about it?'

'That's an interesting way of rephrasing my question,' he murmured. 'Ros, let me put it this way. You're exploring a number of coping mechanisms. Some of them will turn out to be maladaptive, some won't. Some will be temporary, some may become permanent. I'm not here to tell you which are right and which are wrong.'

'You told me seeing Bill would be wrong.'

He opened his mouth, then closed it again. 'That's different. With my police hat on, I have to remind you that it would be against the rules. With my therapist's hat on, I have to be non-judgemental.'

I had a sudden image of Dr Griffin in a policeman's helmet. I wondered what his therapist's hat would look like. A tweedy deerstalker, perhaps.

'You're an intelligent woman, Ros, so I won't play games with you. One of the classic after-effects of rape is a kind of softening of pre-existing boundaries. You may feel a sense of dissociation for a while. But it is, as you suggest, a healthy sign – not because these responses aren't difficult and painful, but because they're an indication that you're moving on to the next phase of recovery. Whatever that may turn out to be.'

That weekend I began the task of going through Jo's things. Blouses that still smelt faintly of her. Her alarm clock, her toothbrush, a half-used box of Tampax. A hairbrush, matted with blonde hairs. In a box under her bed I found a vibrator, which I threw away despite what Bill had said about keeping everything. I didn't want her family finding anything that would embarrass them.

Much more surprising, though, was something I found in her wardrobe. At the very end, squashed up behind a Karen Millen coat, were half a dozen baby suits on tiny hangers. They were all new – some even had their price tags on. They weren't particularly expensive, just nice things from department stores, as if she'd been buying something else and had picked these up on impulse. Which was odd, because Jo had been the least maternal person I had ever met, always moaning about friends who started breeding and subsequently bored everyone around them with details of how wonderful and unique their snotty little offspring were.

I took one of the baby suits down and looked at it. Size birth to six months. I couldn't explain it.

Suddenly it felt too soon to be packing my friend's life away into boxes. I took all the dresses and put them back in the wardrobe, alongside the baby suits on their little plastic hangers. A queue of tiny mysteries, with question marks for heads.

9

Funerals aren't like weddings or christenings. There are no printed invitations, no months of planning and cross-checking diaries. The police finally released Jo's body on a Monday and the funeral took place four days later. She was buried in her parents' village, near Basingstoke, next to a little flint-built church where the service was held.

In his address the vicar called her Joanna, and talked about how he remembered seeing her riding her pony round the village on Saturday afternoons. It seemed wrong, somehow, as if the person in the coffin was not Jo but some previous, childhood version of her. As I sat there in my long black skirt and my black cashmere turtleneck, I suddenly caught a faint waft of CK One. Jo's scent. She must have been the last person to wear this pullover. I buried my nose in the woollen folds of the neck and inhaled her.

About twenty of her friends had come down for the service. Fewer than would have come to one of her parties. Of the dozen or so men she'd slept with, only two or three were there to see her buried. Gerry wasn't one of them. Had he just decided to erase her from his mind, I wondered, like something that never happened?

But of course, I realized with a sudden jolt, erasing her was exactly what I myself had done, with my amnesia.

It's strange how certain words seem to leap out at you when they have a particular significance. My word that day was 'memory'. The vicar kept talking about Jo's memory. Such an ordinary phrase, but of course he didn't really mean Jo's own memory, which had been wiped when she died, but our memories of her. 'And Jo's memory will continue to inspire us . . . she will live on in our memories . . .' Even the walls of the church were dotted with plaques bearing the words 'In loving memory'.

Because memory is love, and forgetting is neglect.

My black shoes slipped on the freshly dug mud around the grave. 'Forasmuch as it hath pleased Almighty God to take unto himself the soul of our dear sister here departed, we therefore commit her body to the earth,' the vicar intoned. He bent down and took a handful of soil. 'Earth to earth, ashes to ashes, dust to dust; in sure and certain hope of the Resurrection to eternal life, through our Lord Jesus Christ; who shall change our vile body.' He sprinkled the earth into the open grave, prissily, like someone crumbling an Oxo cube over a casserole. Jo's mother picked up a handful of earth, and tossed it onto the coffin. One by one the other mourners did the same. I flinched when it came to my turn: it felt as if we were throwing stones.

Afterwards there was tea in her parents' house. We drank sherry and ate walnut cake. As people started to drift away, Hector came up to me and asked if he could have a word. We went outside, and he fished a packet of cigarettes out of his suit pocket.

'I wanted to thank you for helping the police,' he said. 'They told me you've been putting in a lot of time with them.'

I muttered something to the effect that it was the least I could do.

He nodded. 'I know you want this bastard caught as much as we do, Ros.'

'Well, of course.'

'You still can't remember anything?'

'Bits and pieces. Nothing useful.'

'The thing is,' he said, 'Mum and Dad are taking this really hard. Dr Stockton's doped them up to the eyeballs, but I don't think they'll be able to cope if the police don't arrest someone soon.' He paused. 'All I'm saying, Ros, is – you will do everything you can, won't you? I mean, I'm not an expert, but there must be things – hypnosis or drugs, maybe . . .'

'The doctors say I mustn't force it.'

'Please, Ros. *Anything.*'

'Look, if I remembered anything, I'd tell them.'

'What about me?'

'What do you mean?'

'If there were things you weren't sure about,' he said slowly. 'You know, just half ideas, and the police didn't seem interested or didn't want to pursue it, would you tell me?'

'What are you saying, Hecks? You want me to tell you stuff so you can go and deal with this guy yourself? What are you going to do, kill him?'

He stared at the end of his cigarette and muttered, 'I don't know. I just wanted to check – there's nothing the police aren't telling me?'

'Like what?'

'This boyfriend of hers. Gerry. What was that all about?'

'It wasn't about anything. They were seeing each other, that's all.'

'Jo could be a fucking idiot sometimes.'

'You mean because he was married?'

He nodded grimly. 'It all sounds a bit strange to me. I'm thinking of getting a private detective involved.'

'*What?*'

'Let's face it, Ros. The police are just going through the motions now. Releasing the body means they're giving up. In a few weeks they'll mark the crime as unsolved and forget about it. I'm not going to let that happen.'

'Yes, but – Gerry? How can you possibly think it was him?'

'Maybe it was getting more serious than he wanted. Maybe he thought Jo was going to tell his wife. Married men don't always appreciate being jumped into divorce by their girlfriends. Particularly if they're wealthy.'

'She wasn't jumping—' I stopped. Because although it was true that Jo had always joked about Gerry rather dismissively, calling him her sugar daddy, her rich old man, that kind of thing, there were also the baby clothes to think about.

'What?' he said, his eyes narrowing.

And so I found myself lying to Hector for the second time, when I said, 'It's nothing, honestly. Look, Hector, the police are doing a brilliant job. I know they'll catch whoever did it. It just takes time.'

*　　*　　*

Next morning I phoned Bill and told him there was something I needed to talk to him about.

'OK. I'm busy now, but I could come to the gallery after work.'

'Great. About five thirty?'

'I said after work, not teatime. I'll come about eight.'

By six I was the only person left in the lab. The security guard came round and wished me good night as he turned most of the lights out. I went back to work.

'Hi.'

The bastard made me jump. I turned round. Bill was standing by the door. 'How did you get in?'

'Showed the guard my warrant card. He's an ex-copper, as it happens. He told me he makes more working here three nights a week than he used to make in a month in the force. Hello.'

We were on cheek-kissing terms now. I felt the sandpaper rasp of his stubble against my skin. 'Don't let me interrupt you.'

'It's all right,' I said. 'I was just clearing up.'

The Polynesian nude was propped upright on my desk. 'Nice,' he said approvingly, bending down to look. 'Now that's the sort of art I approve of. Bare nekkid ladies with their tits out for the lads.'

'That particular naked lady,' I said primly, 'is my job. She is, as you say, very nice, but she's also very wicked.'

'Really? In what way?'

'She claims she's a Gauguin. Actually she was probably knocked up a few years ago by a copyist in Hove, using Dulux emulsion mixed with KY jelly.'

He bent down to examine the picture more closely. 'How can you tell?'

'Iffy paperwork, initially. And a scattering of polyester fibres.'

'Ros,' he said, surprised, 'are you a detective?'

'Not really.' I thought about it. 'I suppose I'm a bit like your scene-of-crime people. When someone much more expert than me is fairly sure something's wrong, I have to find some physical evidence that a specialist lab can analyse. Of course, if it turns out that a crime has been committed, it's all handed straight over to the Art Fraud unit.'

'Ever been involved in a case yourself?' he said casually. 'Had to stand up in court, I mean?'

'Once. It was just chain-of-custody stuff. The defence barrister tried to claim that the paint the lab analysed might not have come from the painting his client had sold for several million dollars. But he didn't have much to go on. I was only in the witness box for ten minutes.'

'If we find whoever did this,' he said quietly, 'you know you might be in court a lot longer than that?'

I shrugged. 'Yes. It's got to be done, though, hasn't it?'

'Exactly. It's got to be done.'

But I couldn't help noticing that *if*.

'If Jo had been pregnant, would you have been able to tell from the autopsy?'

We were at the pub. Bill took a pull of beer while he thought about my question. 'Yes. There's a very simple test which would have been done as a matter of routine. Something like that would have been brought to my attention immediately.'

Damn. So much for the theory I'd been just about to expound. He saw my expression and said, 'Why do you ask?'

I told him about the baby clothes in Jo's wardrobe.

He looked thoughtful. 'She might not have been pregnant when she died, but that doesn't mean she wasn't trying. Or maybe she'd had a termination.'

'No. She'd have told me.'

He pulled out a notebook and wrote something in it. 'I'll follow it up, anyway.'

'How's everything else going? Is there any news?'

'I can't go into specific details about an investigation,' he said vaguely.

'Dr Griffin has said something, hasn't he?' I guessed.

'Like what?' he said, too casually.

'He's warned you off me.'

Bill looked at his glass. 'We did have a bit of chat.'

'And?'

'He wanted to know if my feelings for you were anything other than just professional.'

'Oh. I see. What did you tell him?'

'I told him the truth.' Bill's expression was suddenly serious. 'I told him I can't stand the girl.'

'Stop teasing me.'

'Actually, I told him I quite like you.'

Now it was my turn to take a sudden interest in my drink.

'At which point he reminded me that if it was going to be a problem for me, or for you for that matter, I should get myself taken off the investigation straight away.'

'Anything else?'

'Yes. He said that in his opinion you weren't really interested in me, you were just giving out confusing signals because of what happened. He said that if you seem to like me, it's because of my job, not me. He said that psychotherapists have to deal with that kind of thing all the time and that it would be tantamount to abuse if I took advantage of my position and your vulnerability and did anything about it. Oh, and he also implied that someone like you wouldn't look twice at someone like me if you weren't completely traumatized.'

'Blimey,' I said. 'He didn't pull any punches, did he?'

'Not many.'

'It's not true, Bill. I'd have liked you anyway. I know I would. It's just bad luck we didn't meet before.'

I put my hand on his. I noticed the black hairs covering his arm. I suddenly found myself wondering what Bill would look like naked. A jolt of – what? Lust? Curiosity? Anticipation? – shot from my brain to my groin. 'What do you want to do?' I asked. I thought, if he says 'I want to go to bed with you', I'll say yes.

'The right thing.' Bill looked searchingly into my eyes. 'Ros, I want to help you get over what's happened, and the best way to do that is to catch the man who did it. That's my job, and I'm going to do it as well as I can. Then, once that's over, we'll be able to do whatever we like about *us*.'

I nodded. If I was disappointed, I tried not to let Bill see it.

The following night, Gerry came round.

'What do you want?' I said cautiously into the intercom.

'I need to collect some things.'

I pressed the button that operated the street door and waited for him to come down to the flat. I kept the flat door double-locked too, these days. It was stupid, given that the attacker had almost certainly come in through the windows. On the other hand, how stupid would I look if it happened again?

'Hi, Ros.'

'Hello, Gerry.'

There was an awkward silence. He said, 'Are you all right? I meant to come sooner.'

'I'm OK,' I said warily.

'Have you really lost your memory?'

'Yes. What do you mean, really? Why would I make up something like that?'

He shrugged. 'I'm sorry. I didn't mean – is there anything I can do?'

'Well, you could have come to the funeral, for a start.'

'Ah. I thought it might embarrass her family.'

Or embarrass *you*, I thought.

'I went afterwards. I stood by her grave and said my own goodbye.' He rubbed his face. 'It's been hard for me, Ros. When someone you've been that close to dies – someone you're not supposed to be seeing – your grief has to be a secret too. That's not easy.'

'Your wife still doesn't know, then,' I said tartly.

He looked embarrassed. 'She knows something happened, I'm sure. She knows it's over. She doesn't know why.'

'How did you explain the police coming round?'

'I don't know. I made something up, I suppose.'

'So you lied about Jo's death in order to save your poxy marriage.'

He spread his hands. 'What was I meant to do? Jo's gone. Why cause Caroline unnecessary pain?'

I realized something I had never realized before: I disliked Gerry. I had hidden the fact from myself, the way you do with girlfriends' boyfriends, because otherwise life would have been difficult, and because he had a certain seedy glamour as a consequence of being older, and married, and rich. But actually he was just a lying, duplicitous prick.

'Maybe you should have thought about that before you started shagging Jo,' I muttered. I was being inconsistent, of course. Gerry had lied to his wife all along. Why should he suddenly start being honest with her now? For the first time it really struck me how appalling it must be to live in that kind of relationship.

As if reading my thoughts he said, 'Be angry with me, Ros, if it makes you feel better. But Jo knew what she was doing.'

Which was true, of course.

'You'd better get what you've come for,' I said.

He went into Jo's room and shut the door. I timed him. He was in there for exactly twelve minutes. When he came out he had a big carrier bag stuffed with clothes. On the top was one of Jo's dresses, the beautiful Italian green one. 'That's not yours,' I said angrily. 'It's hers. Put it back.'

'I bought it for her. I'd very much like to keep it.'

'So you can give it to your next girlfriend?' I said furiously. 'Or will your wife be wearing it to one of your business parties?'

'Ros,' he said. 'Please . . . Why are you so angry?'

'Because you're not,' I hissed. 'Because Jo's dead and your life is just going to carry on as normal.'

'No. You're wrong.' He looked down at the dress. 'I bought this in Venice. She wore it that night and we – that's when we talked about getting married.'

'If she hadn't died she'd have dumped you,' I said savagely. 'She was going to. She told me so on holiday.'

The phone rang. It was Charlotte. 'Hang on,' I told her. 'I'm just letting Gerry out.' I glared at him until he took the hint. He shrugged and left.

Later I went into Jo's room and checked to see what else he'd taken. That's when I discovered the baby clothes were gone.

Bill smelt of smoke and pubs. The first thing he said was, 'Why the fuck did you let him in?'

'Hello,' I said. 'Nice to see you. What was I meant to do, Bill? Restrain him by force? Dial 999?'

'Show me where they were,' he instructed.

I led him to Jo's room and pointed to the wardrobe. 'Right there.'

'I can't believe the SOCOs didn't bag them up,' he muttered.

'Is it important?'

'I don't know. We've got some new information, Ros, thanks to what you've told us. It seems that Jo did have a termination, on

June the fourteenth. We checked all the clinics near to where she worked. It was a lunchtime appointment, so she'd have been out an hour later, though it's unlikely she'd have been able to go straight back to work.'

I remembered Jo watching TV with a duvet wrapped round her, snuffling into a box of tissues. 'She told me she had flu.'

'There's something else. The lad who delivered the pizza now remembers seeing a silver Porsche parked just down the road. He doesn't remember the licence plate number, so in theory it could have been anyone's. But no one who lives in this road owns a Porsche. The only person connected with this investigation who drives a silver Porsche is—'

'Gerry Henson.'

'Yes. A silver Porsche Cabriolet.'

'Jesus.' I felt sick. 'Do you really think it could be him?'

'I honestly don't know, Ros. When we spoke to him the day after the murder, he said he'd been at home and his wife confirmed that. But sometimes wives say what their husbands tell them to. For the time being, he's back on the list of those who haven't been eliminated.'

'But Gerry . . .' This was a man who I had drunk countless bottles of wine with. I had chatted to him, joked with him, even cooked for him. The thought that someone I actually knew might be responsible for Jo's death was incomprehensible.

'If he approaches you again, better just say the police have asked you not to talk to other potential witnesses, or something like that. And don't, under any circumstances, let yourself be alone with him.'

'Why not?'

'I don't want you getting alarmed,' he said slowly, 'but if it was him, he'll be worrying that you could recover your memory. He might think it's worth making sure that can't happen.'

'The phone,' I said, remembering. 'Jesus. Charlotte called me. I told her to hang on while he went. If I hadn't done that no one would ever have known he'd been here. He could have killed me—'

'Whoa. Let's not jump ahead of the evidence here, shall we? I'm just saying you should be extra careful, that's all. With everybody, not just Henson.'

I was trembling, whether from fear or delayed shock I couldn't tell. 'Will you stay? I don't want to be on my own.'

'Isn't there anyone else?'

'Yeah. Sure. I'll phone Charlotte. She'll come over,' I said, turning away.

'No. Wait, Ros, I didn't mean that the way it sounded. I just wanted to be clear what you're asking.'

I took a deep breath. 'I'm asking you. Specifically. To stay here tonight. To be my big male protector. Obviously, not to do anything Dr Griffin would disapprove of. Is that clear enough?'

He smiled. 'Very clear. And very acceptable.'

I suppose that was one of the moments when everything might have changed, when a tiny decision made differently might have resulted in so much being different later on. Bad things don't only happen when you take a giant plunge into the dark. Bad things can happen when you edge forward, feeling your way, trying to do the right thing.

We walked with baby steps towards the abyss, Bill and I, inch by careful inch.

'Why did you become a copper?'

'Um. I suppose I thought I could make a difference.'

'And have you?'

'Dunno. Probably not.'

'What do you do the rest of the time?'

'Sleep,' he said simply.

'You know what I mean. What are your hobbies?'

'Drinking, mainly. With other coppers.'

'What about holidays?'

'I like to fish,' he said, almost shyly, as if he were admitting to doing needlework or wearing women's underwear.

'Where?'

'Ireland, mostly.' And he began to tell me about some of the rivers and lakes in County Mayo, where he'd lived as a child.

It was nice to talk. The attraction between us was there, but it wasn't a problem. We were just two adults being grown up about the fact that we fancied each other but weren't going to go to bed.

But at the back of my mind I heard Dr Griffin's voice saying,

'Of course. That's why you're attracted to him, Ros. He's safe. You can flirt without having to worry about the consequences.'

Fuck off, I told him.

I could also imagine Jo's voice, and what she was saying was more to the point. *So now you're prick-teasing the poor bastard.*

We're only drinking wine, for Christ's sake. Eating pizza. And talking. It isn't as if I've taken my clothes off.

It isn't as if you need to. Look at you both. You're lying on the floor, aren't you? Whose idea was that?

Mine, I admitted. But only so we could put the food between us.

And now you're asking him about his previous relationships. And telling him about yours. And I notice you're using the edited version.

Why not? Leave me alone, Jo. You're the one who had an affair with a married man.

That's different. He was up for it.

His wife wasn't.

She got the money, didn't she? And the nice house in Hampstead. If it hadn't been me, it would have been some other girl.

And you had an abortion.

Ah. So you know about that.

No thanks to you.

Want to know why I didn't tell you?

Of course.

Because it was no big deal, Ros. Horrible but true. For some girls it's a tragedy. For some it's just an inconvenience. That's the sort of person I am. You'd have wanted to make a fuss. And then I'd have felt guilty about it.

Don't bullshit me, Jo. I saw the baby clothes.

A long pause.

Hormones. They kick in and make you do the weirdest things. Just like drugs, really.

Jo?

Yes?

I've got to ask – did Gerry have anything to do with your death?

Of course not. Gerry loved me.

What about the baby? Where does that fit in all this?

I didn't tell you about the baby. What makes you think I told him?

'I've just imagined the strangest conversation with Jo,' I told Bill. 'Just now, while you were talking. A whole dialogue just popped into my head.'

We were still lying on our sides, facing each other. He stretched, and rested his head on the arm that was holding his wine glass. I noticed how reassuringly solid his muscles were, sleek and hard and fish-shaped where his arm came out of his T-shirt.

'What did she have to say?'

'She said that Gerry didn't know about the baby.'

'We might need a bit more corroboration than that,' he murmured. He rolled over onto his back and closed his eyes. 'I'm knackered, Ros. I'd better go to bed.'

I leaned over him and kissed him. He opened his eyes, but not his mouth.

'Night then,' I said, pulling back.

He smiled up at me. 'Well. Maybe in a minute.'

That reminded me. 'Jo also told me I was prick-teasing you,' I said seriously.

'Other way round, surely. It's me who's prick-teasing you. Or whatever the male equivalent is.'

'You're a cocky bastard, aren't you?'

He grinned. 'So I've been told.'

I leaned over him and kissed him again, and this time his mouth was already open.

Offered the choice of the sofa or Jo's room, he chose Jo's room. Which, I'm fairly sure, was as much because he wanted to exorcise any ghosts that might be lurking there for me as to get a good night's sleep.

Still, I couldn't help noticing that when he got up off the floor after we'd been kissing, there was a certain amount of trouser-rearranging.

'A *very* cocky bastard,' I murmured, watching him go.

*   *   *

I slept until around four. Then I got up and padded about. His door was shut.

I didn't want to wake him. I put some music on the CD player with the volume turned down low, curled up on the sofa, and hugged a cushion until the yellow and purple bruises of the sky above London began to fade to grey.

And then, quite suddenly, I remembered something. 'God,' I muttered. I charged into his room. 'Bill, wake up.'

He was awake instantly. 'What is it?'

'You know the pizza boxes that were here on the night of the murder – what kind were they?'

'I think, from memory, they were a Four Seasons and an American Hot. Why?'

'Jo and I used to share a pizza. A Four Seasons, usually.'

'So there was someone else here besides you two?'

'Exactly. Someone we were happy to share a pizza with.'

'Gerry?'

I hesitated. 'I can't actually remember that,' I admitted. 'But it fits, doesn't it?'

'It fits, yes. But it doesn't necessarily mean that he was here when the murder took place.'

I shivered.

'Are you cold?' he said softly.

I nodded. He pulled back the duvet and I slipped in next to him, next to that huge, hot body, and he wrapped his arms round me and held me safe until it was time to get up.

10

'So you've stopped writing your journal,' Griffin said. He placed his notes on the imitation-leather surface of his desk and swivelled his chair round, the better to fix me with an accusing stare.

'It didn't seem to be making any difference.'

'You'll never know if you stop, though, will you?'

I shrugged.

His eyes narrowed. 'It's not that you've written it but you don't want me to read it?'

'Of course not,' I lied.

'Good.' He leaned back. 'You've, ah, probably guessed that I had a word with Detective Inspector Thomson.'

I shrugged again.

'I didn't betray any confidences, Ros. I simply asked him a series of general questions. Any conclusions he came to were entirely his own.'

'Of course.' I didn't bother to tell him that Bill had told me otherwise.

'Good. So long as that's clear.' He laced his fingers over his right knee. Today he was wearing black cartoon socks. Tom on the right, Jerry on the left. 'What about the memory games?'

'I still do them. Nothing's happened, though.'

He considered me for a moment, swinging slightly from left to right on his chair. 'Ros, I think it may be time to look at some other ways of unlocking your amnesia. Frankly, I'd have expected it to have shifted of its own accord by now. I'm more and more convinced there must be an element of regression – of psychological block. I'm going to refer you to a clinic where they work specifically with post-traumatic stress disorder.'

'Do you mean hypnosis?'

Griffin shook his head. 'I'd very much like to hypnotise you, but we have to remember that you may be a witness in a court case. Unfortunately, juries tend to believe that hypnosis can make one a bit suggestible. It could mean your testimony becomes inadmissible. But it's an option we should probably keep up our sleeves.'

'I don't want to be inadmissible.'

'I also think it might be useful for you to take part in the police reconstruction. You were probably planning to do so anyway, but I have to say that it may help to jog your memory as well.'

I phoned Bill on his mobile. 'You didn't tell me you wanted to do a reconstruction.'

'Hang on,' he said. 'Let me just move somewhere more private.' I waited while the background noises shifted from busy workplace to street sounds. 'I was choosing my moment,' he said when he came back.

'Well, Griffin chose it for you.'

'The truth is, Ros, we're running out of options. If we shake the tree, maybe something will fall out.'

'What if it doesn't?'

More silence. Then, 'Have I ever mentioned the thirty-one-day rule?'

'Nope. Why?'

'It's a budget thing, mainly. If we don't have three pieces of usable evidence after thirty-one days, the case becomes what's called a sticker.'

'Meaning what, exactly?'

'A retired detective will be asked to come in and review the way the case has been handled, and to make some recommendations about the way similar investigations are carried out in the future.'

I didn't understand. 'How will that help catch whoever did it?'

'It won't.'

There was a pause while what he'd just said sank in. 'Are you telling me,' I said slowly, 'that if you don't catch whoever did it within a month you simply *give up*?'

'Well, the case won't be closed. But all the officers will be assigned to new, live cases as well.'

'Bill, how many cases are you on, as well as mine? How many stickers are you meant to be investigating?'

Another pause. 'Around fourteen,' he admitted.

'And how many of those are you actually working on?'

'None. Unless some new evidence turns up, there's nothing to investigate.'

Two thoughts cascaded simultaneously into my brain. The first was that Jo's killer was never going to be caught.

The second was that, if the case was abandoned, there would be nothing to stop Bill and me being together.

On top of both thoughts was a rush of guilt. She was dead, and I had to do what I could. 'Of course I'll do the reconstruction.'

He said, 'I was thinking, Ros. I've got some leave coming up, and I was planning a weekend fishing in Ireland. I was wondering if you'd like to come with me. Under, you know, under the same conditions as the other night. The same sleeping arrangements.'

I thought about it. 'I'd like that,' I said.

I thought, then, that my part in all this was nearly over. I just had to do the reconstruction, and wait a bit, then I could get on with my life. Either they'd catch whoever did it, or else the case would be abandoned. Either way I'd soon be able to see Bill properly.

That was what I thought.

I went up to a psychiatric hospital in a leafy suburb in North London to have my memories unblocked. The Trauma Unit was actually a couple of Portakabins, where a cheerful therapist called Susan told me to think of the most negative and upsetting part of not being able to remember.

'That's easy,' I said. 'I feel completely useless.'

'OK. Hold that thought and follow my hand with your eyes.'

She waved her hand rapidly from side to side in front of my face.

'Now think about something positive that would come about if you could remember.'

I thought to myself, *Jo's killer would be caught.*

She waved her hands in the opposite direction. 'That's the first session over,' she said cheerfully. 'We'll wait a few minutes and then do it again.'

'You mean that's it? That thing where you wiggled your fingers?'

''Fraid so.'

'What's that meant to do?'

'It's called EMDR – eye movement desensitization and re-processing. Basically, it replicates the rapid eye movements you make in your sleep, which is when you normally process traumatic information. We don't know how it works, but it does.' She was fitting some headphones over my ears as she spoke. 'OK, let's go again. Can you hear a pinging in your left ear?'

I nodded.

'Just look at my left or right hand whenever you hear a ping from that direction. Think of your negative thought.'

I flicked my eyes from side to side obediently.

'And now your positive.'

This time, I thought about going to bed with Bill.

'Well, something's making you smile, anyway,' the therapist commented as she took off the headphones.

I didn't pay much attention to Bill's suggestion that we'd be going to Ireland just as friends. I took that to be his way of saying that it was up to me, that there were no strings attached to his offer. But I wouldn't have agreed to go unless I'd been intending to sleep with him. It was just a question of waiting.

There were two parts to the TV reconstruction. First, I had to go and be interviewed in a darkened room with a bright light shining behind my head so that only my profile would be visible. Even so, I had to have a hair and make-up session so that my hair would look suitably traumatized. Then, a week later, there was the reconstruction itself, with actors playing Jo and myself. They wanted to film in the flat, for maximum authenticity. On the day of the shoot a location manager rang the bell at 7 a.m., with forms for me to sign. Then came the lighting people, unravelling thick cables that tangled all over the flat and led to a huge generator van parked in the street. A props man came next, followed by the make-up and wardrobe people. Sergeant Alice from the rape suite came too, to look after me.

The camera, after all that fuss, was tiny. It fitted on to a strange leather and steel harness that the cameraman wore strapped to his body, like a saxophone strap.

'We're shooting all this on the Steadycam,' the director said when he saw me looking at it. 'It's more real.' I nodded as if I knew what the hell he was talking about.

Finally, the actors turned up and went straight into make-up. The one playing me was petite and dark and rather continental looking. I was absurdly pleased to find that she was quite pretty. The one playing Jo was nothing like Jo, though, beyond being blonde and tall, so perhaps I shouldn't have taken my casting as any sort of compliment.

The man playing the killer wasn't supposed to look like anyone in particular, since the police had no description of their suspect. But I noticed that in build and dress he was just like Gerry Henson.

Each scene took about an hour to prepare. I had expected it to be difficult, watching a re-enactment of Jo's death, but in fact the whole process was so slow and so tedious that I felt nothing. I was just relieved when the director, having reviewed each take three or four times on a portable black and white monitor, finally pronounced himself satisfied and moved on to the next shot.

There was a storyboard taped to the side of the monitor which told the crew what form each shot would take. It was like a roughly drawn comic book. There was me in a drugged stupor on the sofa. Me struggling with the hands of my assailant as he pulled me towards the bedroom. Me on the bed, coming round, looking up at his blurred face before lapsing into unconsciousness.

I went to the bathroom. A wooden stool had been placed in front of the basin. On it sat the actress who was playing me, reading *Hello!* while the make-up girl applied blusher to her cheeks. The actress gave me a quick, professional smile. I wondered if she knew that she was meant to be me, or that this was the room where I had found Jo's body. 'Excuse me,' I said politely, 'I need to use the loo.'

Someone, presumably a man, or possibly more than one, had dribbled on the carpet around the loo. I wiped the seat before I used it. While I was peeing I noticed that someone had unscrewed the top of my moisturizer. I was getting a headache.

As I came out of the bathroom someone said, 'Excuse me, love, would you just come and stand in shot for a minute? We need to set the lights.'

'Of course,' I said, pleased to be doing something useful. I went and stood where he pointed, next to my bed. The actor was sitting in a fold-up chair, turning the pages of a book that I recognized as coming from my bookshelf.

'Would she lie on the bed?' the cameraman said, his eye fixed to the eyepiece.

'Lie on the bed, please,' someone said to me. I lay down obediently. I looked up at the lens of the camera, which waved in and out of my face.

'Martin, could you show me your first position?' the cameraman said without taking his eye from the eyepiece.

The actor got up and knelt on the bed.

'OK. That's great. Let's do it.'

'Quiet please,' someone thundered. 'Shooting sound. Lock it up.' The set went very quiet.

'Speed,' someone said behind me. In the periphery of my vision I saw a boom microphone being lowered towards my face, just out of shot.

'Hang on,' I began.

'And second position?' the cameraman said. The actor put his hands either side of my hips and leaned forward over me, his face contorted in a vicious, snarling leer. I hit him.

He jerked backwards, and his head hit the camera. The cameraman cried, 'Fuck!' and would have dropped the camera if it hadn't been strapped to his body. It swung sideways on its strap, and two assistants rushed to catch it. He put his fingers up to his eye and held it closed. The actor was hooting with pain, holding the back of his head with one hand and his chin with the other, as if he were about to twist his head right round on itself.

'Oh shit,' somebody said.

The cameraman ended up with a black eye where the camera eyepiece had bruised him. The actor first of all made an enormous fuss, and then made a big point of not making an enormous fuss and refusing all attention, until it looked as if he might genuinely not get any, at which point he reverted to making an enormous fuss again and took himself off to phone his agent. An ambulance was called for, and then cancelled when it emerged that Sergeant Alice had a perfectly adequate first aid qualification. I said 'Sorry' a thousand times. Everyone was very gracious and apologized to me in turn. The actress had looked so much like me that no one had realized that I was just standing in while the lights were set up. Then the ambulance came, despite having been cancelled, and took the actor off to hospital, just in case.

It was too late to cast a substitute, but eventually one of the crew was press-ganged to take the actor's place. He didn't look much like him, but it was agreed that it didn't matter very much as his role was to be blurry and half-glimpsed. Because of having a different actor they had to reshoot the earlier scenes, so they were in the flat for the rest of the day. I spent the time pumping Alice, as casually as I could, for information about Bill.

Over the next week he was busy arranging the showing of the reconstruction on TV, and then sifting through the hundreds of calls which followed. He called me late one night, sounding tired. I took the phone to bed with me and we had a long rambling conversation. Somehow we got on to the subject of Jo and Gerry and the kind of relationship they'd had.

He said, 'It must have been difficult for her. Being with someone who had to keep it a secret.'

I yawned. 'Not really. I think she just accepted it on its own terms. Some men like football, so you end up going to football matches with them. With Gerry, it was sex. But the sex was good, so the relationship worked.'

'I don't think you could ever have a relationship like that.'

I woke up then, because I knew that we weren't talking about Jo and Gerry any more.

'Not with someone who was married,' I said cautiously. 'But if there was another reason why it had to be kept secret – a good reason – then yes, that's what I'd do.'

He started talking about Ireland, about the hotel we'd be staying in. It was quite clear to me what he was offering. He was saying that when we slept together, it would have to be a secret. That was fine by me. I didn't want to show him off to my friends or go drinking with his CID mates. I wanted him in bed with me, with his arms round me and the door locked against the horrors that stalked outside.

I went to see Dr Griffin, who wanted to know if either the reconstruction or the EMDR had elicited any more memories. They hadn't.

'What happens next?' I wanted to know.

'I'll organize a CAT scan, just in case. But I'm certain there's nothing physical. Otherwise, the next stage would be things such as electric shock treatment – and to be perfectly honest, that's the psychiatric equivalent of banging a television because it isn't working to see what happens. I think we might just have to accept that your blockage will shift in its own good time.'

'Do you mean I should stop seeing you?'

'That's up to you. You can come back whenever you want to.' He looked thoughtful. 'May I give you a piece of advice, though?'

I shrugged.

'I'm sure you've read about the seven stages of grief – shock, denial, anger, acceptance and so on – but the truth is that it's not as neat as that. Grief is a very strange creature. It stalks us very patiently and pounces when we least expect it. People who've been through experiences like yours aren't always aware just how long it takes to get back to normal. I've even heard it argued that they never do – that they have to create a new normal to replace the one that was taken away. That may involve quite serious changes in your life, your outlook, maybe even your personality. You may find yourself making decisions, or judgements, that one day you'll look back on and feel almost as if they must have been made by someone else.'

Bill, I thought. He's still talking about Bill. 'Are you trying to say I'm unstable?' I joked.

'I'm saying you're fragile. You should take new situations very, very carefully.'

It was an odd warning. I couldn't help feeling that it sounded more like something out of a dodgy horoscope than the best a top psychiatrist could come up with.

11

It was three o'clock on Friday afternoon and I was waiting by the check-in desk at Terminal One for Bill, who was late. Horribly late. Last check-in was at ten past three. At three thirty they announced that the flight was boarding.

At three forty Bill ran in, gabbling apologies. We pushed our way to the front of the queue and put our tickets on the counter. The attendant glanced at her screen and said, 'I'm sorry, that flight's closed.'

'When's the next one?' Bill asked.

'Let's see.' Yet more waiting while she tapped at her keyboard. 'In an hour, but it's full. The earliest flight I can get you on is at half past ten this evening. Sorry – Friday afternoon and all that.'

'Isn't there anything else?'

She hesitated. 'Do you only have hand luggage?'

Bill slid his fishing bag out of sight. 'Yes.'

'You could try running to the gate. If they haven't pushed back yet, you might be able to talk your way on.'

We ran. The departure gates to Ireland were in a separate building, reached by a long series of walkways. We got to the gate just as two attendants were closing the doors. We thrust our tickets at them, but the elder of the two was already shaking her head.

'You're too late. Sorry. The plane doors have been closed and the captain won't miss his slot.'

'Shit.' Bill put his bag down.

I said to the attendant, 'The thing is, we're going back for my grandfather's funeral. There isn't another flight we can get on until half past ten, and if we wait until then we'll miss it.'

She hesitated, then said, 'What time's the funeral?'

104

'Six. In Mayo.'

'Ah, go on then.' She unhooked the barrier and we raced past.

As we got onto the plane, the captain was announcing to the other passengers that there'd be a ten-minute delay because they'd missed their take-off slot.

'How the *fuck* did you do that?'

I giggled. 'Easy.'

Bill shook his head in disbelief. 'You're trouble.'

Someone thrust two trays of cold economy-class food at us. I leaned into Bill and murmured, 'Fancy an upgrade?'

'What do you mean?'

'Jo had a friend who was a stewardess. She knew this trick that means they have to upgrade you to first class. Free champagne, decent food, beautiful flight attendants fawning all over you . . . Want to try?'

'Um – Jesus, Ros, I'm not sure I should be—'

'Give me a hair.'

'What?'

'Pubic preferably. I'm sure you can spare one. Oh, you're bashful. Never mind. One of these will do.' I put my hand on his forearm and tugged a hair off. I dropped it into the gluey mess that passed for food in economy. Then I rang for a passing stewardess.

'Can I help you?'

I pointed at my food. 'There's, uh, a hair in this.' I lifted it up so she could see. 'Look. It's disgusting.'

The stewardess lowered her voice. 'I'm sorry. Would you like another meal?'

'No,' I said firmly. 'I've lost my appetite. I'd like a complaint form, please.'

'One moment.' The stewardess hurried to the galley, where I saw her conferring urgently with her supervisor.

'Just wait,' I told Bill. 'They have regulations for everything. And for this, it's a free upgrade.'

The supervisor made her way down the plane to us. 'Hello,' she said brightly. 'I'm so sorry about the problem you're experiencing today. We do actually have some spare meals at the front of the plane. If you'd like to move down there, could I offer you one of those as a substitute?'

'Well, I suppose so,' I said grudgingly.

So we drank the free champagne, and ate the first-class food, and Bill told me that he could probably get used to a life of crime, if it was always like this.

But I felt sad, because it was Jo who had shown me the hair trick, and the last time we'd tried it was on our way out to Sardinia.

As Dr Griffin had said, grief crept up on you in the strangest places.

The hotel was an old manor house that had seen better days, but at least it was almost empty and the arthritic deerhounds out-numbered the guests. The elderly Irish aristocrats who owned the place tried to maintain a sad pretence that you were their guests, rather than paying customers, which meant that everyone had to gather in the freezing drawing room for drinks and chilly conversation, then sit round one big table for dinner. There was an American woman who described herself as a writer, whose job involved coming up with ideas for game shows. There was a couple from Manchester celebrating their golden wedding anniversary who barely spoke a word, to each other or anyone else. And there were two cheerful Dutchmen who avoided all mention of the fact that they were gay. I'd changed out of my old jeans into my favourite scoop-fronted black dress, which seemed to get Bill's attention, and though the meal lasted for ever, after-wards we managed to escape into the village and find a pub, where the Guinness was black and peaty and the air was full of smoke and music.

That first night, nothing happened – just a kiss in the corridor outside our bedrooms when we got back, and a slightly rueful smile from Bill when I said goodnight. I smiled to myself as I got into bed, thinking about it, thinking about what might happen tomorrow.

The next day he decided to teach me to fish. He stood behind me, working my arms for me while I held the rod, showing me how to flick it back and forth so that the line scribbled a huge figure of eight above us before shooting fifty feet or more out into the lake. On my own I was hopeless. But a part of me quite enjoyed being hopeless, because it meant I could lean back against his broad, Barbour-covered chest and surrender control of my limbs to him.

I thought: this is why they call it falling for someone. If I hadn't been leaning against Bill, I'd have been almost incapable of standing up.

And then there was a sudden tug on the line and the rod was arching down into the water, and Bill's hands, which had been holding my arms, were suddenly braced to take the strain. The fish zigzagged under the surface, tacking first to one side then the other, with Bill telling me to wind the reel in a little each time it turned. Eventually it got tired and we pulled it to the shore and out of the water.

'It's a big one,' Bill said. 'Lower it to the ground, but be careful.'

The fish trampolined frantically on the ground until Bill got hold of it and squeezed its mouth open to get the hook. Even when he had it firmly it thrashed its head and tail back and forth, a flickering fistful of muscle, mouth open in an O, gills working frantically like fans.

'Do you want to take it back to the hotel? They could probably cook it for us.'

'Not really. Do you?'

'No. Come here.'

I went and squatted beside him. Very carefully he transferred the fish to me. As my fingers closed on the hard flesh it erupted, writhing into an S shape, trying to hurl itself out of my grip.

'Got it?'

'Yes, got it,' I said. He let go. I stepped wellington-deep into the water and submerged my hands. Just for a moment I held on to it – a grenade with its pin out, an explosion waiting to happen. Then I opened my fingers, and the fish effortlessly dematerialized. I didn't even see it go.

Lunch, and another pub. More Guinness. 'I want to ask you something,' I said.

'OK.'

We were sitting at a small table, our legs companionably muddled together underneath.

'Is it only because of the rules that we haven't slept together? Or is there something else as well?'

He looked at me, his eyes cloudy. 'What do you mean?'

'Some men think that women who've been raped are damaged goods.'

'Christ, no. Of course not. I'm not that Neolithic.'

'Perhaps you're medieval, though,' I suggested. 'Perhaps you feel that a relationship that's unsullied by sex is somehow more chivalrous. Like a knight of the Round Table.'

He put his glass down. 'Jesus, Ros. What's brought this on?'

I shrugged. 'Lust,' I said succinctly.

'Oh.' He thought for a moment. 'Well, I suppose I do feel a certain amount of guilt by association. It was a man who did this to you. I want to prove that not all men are like that.'

'I don't need proof. I'm not a policeman.'

'Going to bed with you before you're really over it would make me as bad as him.'

'I don't think I'll ever get over it,' I said. I put my hand on his. 'Though being with you will help. Being with you properly, I mean. Sleeping with you. But if you really don't want to, that's all right too.'

'Want to? Christ, if only you knew. I think about nothing else.'

'Me too.'

He stared at the table. 'I can't believe we're having this conversation. I've got such a fucking hard-on,' he muttered.

'Me too. If you know what I mean. So, just to be clear, it's really only these police rules that are stopping us.'

'Fuck the rules,' he said suddenly. 'I mean it, Ros. Fuck them.'

'I'd much rather you fucked me, actually.'

We left our Guinness half finished on the table.

One of the arthritic deerhounds was asleep on my bed. We shooed it out and locked the door. And then we undressed each other, taking our time.

As he unclipped my bra he traced the cuts on my back with his fingers as if they were a kind of Braille.

'Is there a scar?' I wanted to know.

'No. They're hardly visible.' He reached round and cupped my breasts, one in each hand. 'So beautiful,' he murmured.

'Too small.'

'No. Perfect.'

I reached behind and slid my hand into his fly.

'Looks like I've caught a big one,' I said mischievously. 'Can I have it cooked for supper, or should I let it go?'

He gasped, and bit my ear, and I turned my head to find his lips before I pulled him forward with me onto the big, soft bed.

There was a moment, when he first slid inside me, when I felt a sudden clamp of panic. I said urgently, 'Stop.' He stopped, and the panic stopped too.

'What's wrong?' he said softly, not moving.

'Nothing,' I said. 'I think I just needed to know that you would.' And then I started moving underneath him, gently at first, and he held himself very still until I showed him with the pressure of my hands that I was ready for him again.

12

The silent anniversary couple had left, their room taken by two young lawyers on a fishing trip who kept the conversation at dinner going eagerly enough, talking to Bill about flies and currents and the merits of different kinds of rods. I felt wicked and post-coital and sluttish and they couldn't keep their eyes off me. It was almost as if what Bill and I had been doing had left some sort of chemical trace in the air, a sexual signature. I put my hand under the table and slipped it between his legs. He was hard instantly. I stroked the outline of his cock through his trouser leg, just once, then stopped. After a few minutes the conversation got his attention and I felt him soften. I moved my hand again, just a little. Another instant reaction. I kept him like that all through the meal, bringing him back to hardness with a tiny scrape of my nails or the briefest of squeezes.

When we finally got upstairs he thought he had to be slow but I was already halfway there myself. I wanted him inside me, fast.

That was the first time with him I came. We were fitting together very nicely.

The next morning we borrowed the boat from the hotel and set out onto the lake with a couple of rods. I was bored with fishing but it was nice to be out with Bill, and the sun suddenly came out and it was warm enough to take off the thick pullovers we'd come out in and bask in our T-shirts while the boat drifted lazily towards the middle of the lake. I watched him for a while, and then I started to think about sex again. Christ, I thought. Ros Taylor, you're turning into a nymphomaniac. I laughed. Bill turned and smiled at me. 'What's up?'

'Nothing. You keep fishing.'

He turned back to the water. I came up behind him and put my arms round him. 'I'll hold on to you,' I told him, 'in case a big fish comes and pulls you overboard.'

'If you like,' he said, casting again. I watched the line float away with the current. I rubbed my hands over his stomach and pushed them into his cords.

'Keep fishing,' I murmured. He was already hard. I unzipped him with one hand and pulled his cock out. 'There's a joke to be made here about rods,' I murmured, stroking him lazily. 'But I can't be bothered.'

He tried to turn round but I stopped him. 'Uh-uh. Just fish.'

He cast again, half-heartedly, while I gently milked him and bit his neck. I had intended to go on like that, to make him come into the water, but when he eventually turned round I was just too far gone to resist. I helped him get my jeans off and we made love in the bottom of the boat, with me on top crouching low over his chest so that the side of the boat hid us from the shore. While we were moving together I heard voices. It was the lawyers. They were still talking about spinner sizes and lines and eddies, their voices carrying across the water.

'Don't stop,' I muttered in his ear.

The lawyers were talking about the boat now, wondering aloud if there was anyone in it. I fastened my mouth on Bill's and bit his lip. We were close enough to them for me to hear the hiss of their lines as they cast.

When we'd both come I said into Bill's ear, 'If I sit up they'll see us.'

'We can't stay here all day.'

'Can.'

I held on to him and we went to sleep in the sun, with the sound of little waves slapping against the side of the boat and the autumn sun cool on my legs. It was childish in a way, but the fact that we had done it under the other people's noses had made it even better.

We flew back into a storm – literally: Heathrow was being lashed by gales and rain. But it also turned out that Bill's mobile, which he'd dutifully checked for messages every day, didn't work properly in Ireland. Back in the UK he discovered he had eight voicemails, all from Collier, summoning him urgently to Paddington.

That night, he phoned me at the flat.

'Ros, stay there. I'm coming round.'

'Great. I'll cook us something.'

There was a pause. 'That may not be a good idea. I'll have to get straight back.'

When he came he wasted no time. This was a different Bill – focused, unstoppable, almost frightening. 'There's been a call about the case. Someone who saw the TV programme.'

'Is it good news?'

'That depends. Ros, we've got a witness who saw Gerry Henson outside your flat on the night of the murder at three o'clock in the morning. He was carrying a black dustbin bag, just like the one that we found with your stuff in it.'

I was stunned. I'd never really believed it was Gerry. I'd thought he was just another person who would eventually be eliminated, like the men in the video shop or Carl Howell.

'You know what this means, don't you?' he said quietly. 'I can't stay.'

'Tonight or ever?'

He hesitated. 'Until the case is over. Ros, what happened between us could really fuck things up if anyone found out. Not because it actually makes any difference, but because clever lawyers would manipulate it so that the jury thought it did. Do you understand?'

'I'm not an idiot,' I said angrily.

'There's something else.'

'Just go,' I said. 'Go away. Talk to me when the bloody case is over.'

'It's about the case.' He looked awkward. 'This information – it comes from someone we can't put into a witness box.'

'Why not?'

'He has four previous convictions for burglary. Basically, he was out on a job when he saw Henson. It's sound evidence, but we'd get massacred if we tried to use it in court.'

The next day, the local news reported that one Gerald Henson had been questioned in connection with a double rape and murder. The footage showed police leaving his home with boxes of evidence and armfuls of clothes. The following day, an article in the *Standard* reported that Mr Henson had been released into the custody of his lawyer pending the outcome of forensic tests.

Bill left me several voicemails. I didn't call back. The messages got shorter and shorter. In various different ways, they all said the same thing. No news. Nothing to report. Investigations ongoing. Several promising leads but nothing conclusive.

Until finally he left one that said simply, 'It was him, Ros. We've got him. We've got some forensic.'

I mourned Jo all over again.

I'd mourned her the first time because she was dead, and I mourned her the second time because she had been killed by the man she trusted most. Because I thought I knew Gerry Henson, and would have said that he was no worse, and no more capable of evil, than any other man you meet.

Bill had said to me once that we're all capable of terrible things. Every murderer he met was just an ordinary bloke who'd surprised himself.

If I'm honest, I mourned Bill too. Because I had some idea now of just how long it took to bring a case as big as this to court, and I doubted whether we'd ever be able to pick up again where we'd left off.

I hated Henson now. I understood why men talked about getting hold of rapists and cutting their balls off. I found myself indulging in delicious fantasies in which he was in prison, and a group of other prisoners decided to torture him. I felt a kind of victorious thrill every time I imagined the scalding water from the kettles bleaching his hairy skin.

Collier left a message asking me to attend Paddington Green urgently, for an interview.

'Miss Taylor, I have to ask you some questions of a rather personal nature.'

Oh fuck, I thought, he knows.

'When you made your statement, you were kind enough to volunteer a list of your previous sexual partners. Were there any omissions from that list?'

I could feel myself going red. There was a policewoman in the room as well. I looked across at her but she was studying her feet. 'What do you mean?'

'Was the list of your partners completely accurate, with no omissions?' Collier pushed a piece of paper across the table. 'This is what you wrote, if you want to remind yourself.'

I knew I was going to have to say something. 'It was true at the time,' I began, 'but—'

He held up a hand. 'I'm not interested in anything that's happened since,' he said rapidly. Too rapidly. Was there the hint of a wink in the fleshy folds of his face? 'I just need to know whether, at the time of the attack, you had any sexual partners you haven't told us about.'

'No,' I said, mystified. 'Absolutely not.'

He made a note. 'I have to ask you this, specifically: have you ever had a sexual relationship, at any time, with Mr Gerry Henson?'

'Of course not. He was going out with Jo.'

'So there would be no truth at all in any suggestion that you slept with him?'

'Who on earth is suggesting that?'

Collier pulled a packet of TicTacs from his jacket pocket and tipped some into his palm before offering the packet to me. 'When we searched his house, one of the items we removed was a shirt. The labs found a hair wrapped round one of the buttons. The shirt had been washed, but the hair survived. It had been pulled out at the root, which suggests he was pulling away from the hair's owner with some force. In addition, there are three tiny spots of blood on the front of the shirt, and a small secretion of an intimate nature, if you'll pardon the expression, on the lower edge. They all contain the same person's DNA.' Collier's piggy eyes gleamed. 'Luckily Mr Henson's domestic arrangements include non-biological washing powder, a consequence of a skin sensitivity suffered by his wife. If it wasn't for that, the enzymes would have munched the evidence.'

'I'm not sure I'm following this,' I said faintly.

'The hair, the blood and the secretion all match to you.'

To you. To you. I heard it like an echo, bouncing around in my head. What did it mean? *To you.*

'Ergo,' Collier was saying, leaning back, 'chummy now has two options. Sexual contact having been established, he can either say he never went near you and run the considerable risk that he will be contradicted by the evidence in court, or he can say, yes, we did have sex but the lady was willing.'

'Oh Jesus.'

'I wasn't suggesting for a moment that you *had* been a willing partner, of course,' he added apologetically. 'But you can see why I had to ask.'

'Yes. Of course.'

'We think on the afternoon of the attack they argued – at a guess, she told him she was ending the relationship, on your advice. She may also have told him she'd terminated his child. He decided to teach you both a lesson, and came back that night with the GHB.' Collier was watching me in a strange way while he said all this. 'Is there anything in that sequence that rings any bells?'

'I'm sorry. I still can't remember anything.'

'That's a shame. Because, I don't mind admitting, it would be useful to have some corroboration from the other victim, namely yourself. Not having it is the one thing that makes this case just a little, shall we say, peculiar.'

'What will he get?'

'How many years, you mean?' Collier started packing his papers together. 'That all depends on what he's charged with, which of course is not up to us but to our learned friends in the CPS. But if he's found guilty, our friend Henson could be looking at twenty years, and that'll mostly be spent locked up in a nonces' block with other sex offenders.'

'How do the CPS decide?'

'In theory, they just have to assess whether a charge has a fifty per cent or greater chance of conviction.'

'And this has? Definitely?'

'Well, you can never entirely predict what the lawyers will say,' he said cheerfully, getting to his feet. 'But he did it all right. There's absolutely no doubt about that.'

But it wasn't to be that simple.

Ten days after Henson was arrested, my door buzzer rang. It was after midnight. I picked up the intercom handset.

'Yes?'

There was a long silence. 'It's Bill,' he said at last.

My heart soared. 'If you think you can just crawl round here for a furtive shag when the pubs close, Mr Thomson, you are absolutely right.'

'Ros—'

'Come on down.' I pressed the buzzer.

I knew as soon as I opened the door of the flat that something was wrong.

'Jesus, Bill, what is it?' I pulled him inside and he collapsed against me. I stroked his hair. 'What's happened?'

'This is so fucked up,' he muttered into my shoulder.

I felt a sense of dread. 'What is?'

'This. This case. It's fucked, Ros. I'm so sorry.'

'It wasn't him?'

'No. No, that's the worst fucking thing. It was Henson. We've got the evidence. We've built the case. Means, motive and opportunity, all there. A witness who puts him at the scene. Forensic too. And a bunch of fucking wet-arsed lawyers who say that none of it is conclusive enough to show a reasonable chance of conviction.'

'*What?*'

'It's all about money. There have been several large trials already this year and the CPS are way over budget. Plus there was a successful appeal in another case recently which hinged on our crime scene procedures, and now they're worried that could be used to undermine the evidence – how can we prove the tests were carried out properly, blah blah bloody blah.'

And me, I thought. He's too nice to say it, but Collier did. The fact that I can't remember is what's screwing our case up. 'Can't the police do anything?'

'The police don't give a shit. Our bit's over. It's a production line, Ros, just like building a Ford Fiesta. Everyone thinks, right, that's my bit done, I've slapped the windscreen on or whatever. Nobody cares if the wheels fall off.'

'Oh, Christ.' I was trying to get my head round this. 'So what happens now?'

'We'll leave it open and walk away. It's not even a sticker. It's a ghost case – no trial, no conviction, no sentence.'

I started to shake. After all I'd been through, after so long, it was just going to be left unresolved.

'Tell me something, Bill. Are you absolutely convinced it was Gerry?'

'Yes. There's no doubt whatsoever in my mind. He killed Jo, and he's going to get away with it.'

It wasn't Bill's idea. I want to make that absolutely clear. It was mine.

Because my friend had died.

Because I wanted it to be over.

Because of the people who did nothing when my phone was stolen.

Because it was my fault for not being able to remember.

Because the bad guys shouldn't be allowed to get away with it.

Because lying was my gift to Jo.

He stayed the night. He shouldn't have done, but neither of us knew when we'd be able to be together like this again. He was still asleep when I phoned the incident room the next morning and asked to be put through to Superintendent Collier. Finally, after being transferred to a dozen different people, I got hold of him.

'This is Ros Taylor,' I told him. 'I've got my memory back and I want to make a statement.'

There was a long pause. 'How much memory?'

'I've remembered everything. It was Gerry. Gerry Henson. I want to make a statement identifying Gerry Henson as the man who raped me.'

Another pause. 'Are you sure?'

'Absolutely.'

'Right. Don't say any more now. I'll meet you at Paddington Green in ten minutes.'

2
BILL

The restrictions – petty or otherwise – imposed on the off-duty private lives of policemen and policewomen are unknown in virtually any other occupation . . . Policemen are expected to continue to observe a nineteenth-century moral code while daily being vividly aware of its rejection by the rest of society.

– Ben Whitaker, *The Police in Society*

13

The victim's name was Merrily Brown. She was from the Harkur brothers' stable, out in Hackney, and what she did was lick-and-shine, which is street slang for buying a hit of crack and a blow job at the same time. Crack prices having fallen so much in the last six months – largely due to our inability to control people like the Harkurs – the brothers had hit on the idea of offering lick-and-shine at the same price as other dealers offered straight crack; in effect, throwing in the prostitute and her services for free. Since the girls were paid in drugs, which the Harkurs had coming out of their ears – not to mention various other orifices – it was yet another example of the brilliant horizontal integration that would have won them plaudits at any business school. It spun off nicely in all directions: the girls brought in new customers, the sort who maybe hadn't tried crack before, and the rush brought on by the combination of an orgasm and a potent cocktail of baked cocaine and sodium bicarbonate meant that a high proportion of those customers came back for more. The only additional resource it required was a supply of girls – not necessarily crack-addicted, since that could be taken care of; but plentiful, since one of the unfortunate side effects of being both a crack addict and a prostitute was a rather high mortality rate. The Harkurs solved that problem by finding the biggest pimp in South London, shooting him, and informing his girls that they were under new management. Some of them saw this as an opportunity to renegotiate their pay and conditions. The Harkur brothers gave the two ringleaders to their runners and told them to have some fun. When the party was over both girls were dead and the Harkur brothers had no more problems from the others.

Merrily Brown, however, had not been killed by drugs, or

disease, or a customer, or even by the brothers. Merrily Brown had been giving a very minor-league Yardie named Gusto Bart a blow job in his car – a Suzuki four-wheel drive with blacked-out windows, lowered suspension and gold-sprayed hubcaps – in a quiet road round the back of Euston Square, rendered slightly less quiet by the pulsing bass leaking from Gusto's sound system, when her left hand had encountered the nine-millimetre Glock he kept in the waistband of his trousers. Merrily waited until Gusto took another lick of crack, signalling that he was approaching orgasm and was thus at the moment of greatest distraction, then without stopping what she was doing she pulled the gun from its holster and shot herself, just below the ear. Although the bullet somehow passed through her mouth without touching his penis, her teeth and a large part of her jawbone did not. I saw the hospital pictures, before the surgeons had begun the lengthy process of reconstruction. It wasn't pretty. The last two inches of his manhood looked like a chef had very expertly cut it into strips, peeled back the skin and stuffed it with mince.

Minor-league Yardies do not generally talk to policemen, but Gusto Bart talked to us. He talked, or more accurately he screamed, even before the ambulance had arrived, while Merrily's blood was still dripping off the sun visor of his car. We were there pretty quickly, you see. We were there about twelve seconds after the shot was fired, running from our unmarked van in our baseball caps and our dark-coloured BPVs, shouting at him to get out of the car with his hands in the air and to leave the girl alone, because at that point we hadn't quite worked out who was shooting who or who the target was.

Gusto Bart was screaming back that the jiggy bitch had iced herself, or something similar. I wasn't paying him much attention, to tell the truth. By then I had wrenched open the car door and was staring at the corpse of Operation Mansion, which lay twitching in its death throes across Bart's leather seats. Twelve months' work obliterated in the time it had taken the bullet to travel four inches from the gun's chamber to Merrily Brown's brain.

Someone said, 'I'll tell you what, I'm not doing mouth-to-mouth. Not after that black bastard's had his cock in there.'

I reached forward and gingerly pulled Merrily's head off Bart's lap. Above her right ear her head had cracked open like a chocolate egg. Inside everything was shiny and wet. And that was just the exit wound.

Behind me a radio crackled. 'Ambulance on its way, sir,' someone said quietly. I nodded. Something semi-liquid and rubbery slithered out of Merrily Brown's mouth. At the time, I thought it was vomit. Later, when I read the reports, I discovered it was actually a mixture of Bart's shredded penis, blood and Merrily's own severed tongue.

They have good cabin lights, those big Suzukis. Bart looked down at himself, and that's when he started screaming. One of the many bits of shredded meat in his lap was pumping blood, which was the only thing that told me it was part of him rather than her.

'Better get a tourniquet on that,' Stretch suggested.

'Give me a shoelace, quick.'

He didn't argue. He handed his gun to the man next to him and pulled at his trainers.

'Come on. Hurry.'

He handed me the lace and with my other hand I carefully felt around in the liquid slop on Bart's lap for the source of the bleeding. He tried to hit me, a clumsy jab with his right.

'He thinks you are making an approach of an amorous nature, sir,' Falconer said lugubriously.

'Shut up and get him restrained.'

Two men reached into the car and held his arms. Unfortunately, Gusto Bart had just ingested twenty pounds' worth of crack and the armlocks might as well have been spider's webs for all the notice he took of them. As I scrabbled around the bloody stump of his penis, trying to get the shoelace as near to his testicles as possible to stop the flow of blood, he gave a thin, high scream and brought his head down on mine. The headbutt sent me sprawling against Merrily's corpse, inflicting further damage to her already precarious skull. But by that time I was unconscious.

Merrily Brown's autopsy was swift and cheap. The gun was still in her hand when they wheeled her into St Thomas's, and the needle tracks up her arms, together with the sunken eyes and the near-anorexic physique, all told their own story. Suicides, particularly the suicides of lick-and-shine whores, don't merit much of a post-mortem.

The post-mortem into the failure of Operation Mansion, on the other hand, was long, rigorous and increasingly bitter. Operation Mansion had probably cost more over the past twelve months than Merrily had earned in her lifetime. Operation Mansion was a very expensive fiasco indeed.

To be fair to Collier, he shielded me. He has many faults, but disloyalty to his men isn't one of them. He bollocked me to my face and the rest of the time he protected my back.

He couldn't protect me from having to attend an internal Incident Review, though. Two days after Merrily's death I found myself on the third floor of New Scotland Yard, answering questions from a roomful of senior brass, Collier among them.

'Tell us what you think went wrong,' the assistant commissioner suggested. He was a big, solid man called Grimes, known throughout the Met as Clean-up.

'We still don't know, sir. Merrily Brown had looked like a breakthrough – she was the first one of the Harkurs' stable to turn, and she'd offered to help us find another girl who'd do the same.' We'd needed two, of course. Defence lawyers have no problem making the testimony of a single drugged-up tom look ropy. Two drugged-up toms, each corroborating the other's story, is at least the beginnings of a case.

The AC nodded. 'And you'd registered her in the proper way?'

'Yes, sir.'

Evidently this point was a key one for the assembled top brass, who visibly relaxed. Thank God I hadn't listened to Collier's insinuations and left Merrily Brown off the Informants Register. 'Your own private snout,' he'd whispered sideways over the top of his pint. 'Why not keep this one between us?' I'd laughed and shrugged, and he'd laughed too, both of us pretending it had only been a joke.

'Presumably she had second thoughts about assisting us,' one of the brass suggested.

But not third, I thought to myself. Whatever passed through Merrily's head in the split second before the bullet did, she'd left no time for doubts. Whatever Merrily had been afraid of, she had

124

been so afraid that the opportunity to put a bullet in her own head had seemed like an unexpected stroke of luck.

'Well? Is there any evidence of that?' the AC demanded.

'It's possible she believed the girl she'd confided in, Sheena Mast, had told the Harkur brothers what was going on. Sheena hasn't been seen since Merrily's death, so we don't know for sure. What we do know is that about an hour before she died Merrily told one of the other girls that the brothers were after her.'

The AC said, 'But she didn't tell *you* that? Doesn't that strike you as rather strange?'

'Yes, sir. She knew we were in the van, waiting for her pimp to turn up with fresh supplies of crack – they don't trust the girls with a whole night's supply, in case they take it themselves. The plan was to wait until the pimp, Henry, appeared, and then arrest them all in the hope that we could persuade Henry to incriminate the brothers as well.'

'So why didn't she just come over and tell you she was frightened?'

'We've no idea, sir.' Other than the obvious one, that is. Merrily knew perfectly well that if we aborted the operation we'd leave her to swing anyway. There was no protection for people like her, not unless they were witnesses.

The AC dismissed Merrily Brown with a sigh. He picked a piece of paper off the desk in front of him. The desk was so clean and so polished that the paper clung to its surface, gluey with static, until he managed to peel it loose. 'And you're aware, Detective Inspector, of the allegations which the young man in the car is now making against the Metropolitan Police?'

'Yes, sir.'

'Augustus Bart,' the AC went on as if I hadn't spoken, 'says through his lawyers, first, that while he was injured and bleeding in the front seat of the car no attempt was made to give him first aid until efforts to resuscitate Miss Brown had been abandoned; second, that one of the officers present called him a black bastard, and thirdly, that while white officers were standing around the car they discussed the fact that they could easily have prevented the attack on him had they so wished. Hence his allegation of racism and his civil action for compensation.'

'Yes, sir.'

'Were you aware of any racist actions or omissions while you were present at the scene, Detective Inspector?'

I saw Collier's eyes on me. He was looking unusually thoughtful.

I said, 'Sir, Merrily Brown was black as well. It wasn't racism which prompted my men to attempt to revive her before we gave any attention to Bart.'

'Quite. You were concerned about your informant.'

'I was following procedure, sir. She was making no sound. It was reasonable to assume that she was in greater need of medical attention.'

'And how quickly did you ascertain that she was, in fact, dead?'

'My officers continued to attempt resuscitation until the ambulance crew arrived. She was pronounced dead on arrival at St Thomas's.' Not quite a lie. They'd checked her pulse again, after they'd pulled her out of the car. There was nothing to be done for her, but someone had gone through the motions anyway, pulling out a sterile dam from one of the portable medi-kits in order to give mouth-to-mouth. Even with me unconscious, they'd had the nous to realize there might be an inquiry into the events of that evening, and that everything had better be done by the book.

'And it was you who placed the tourniquet on Bart?'

'Yes, sir.'

'At considerable risk to yourself, I believe?' That was Collier's interjection.

'He knocked me out, yes. He'd been smoking crack while Merrily, ah,' I tried to think of the appropriate Met euphemism for a blow job, 'gave him what he'd paid for, and he was consequently rather unpredictable.'

' "He was in a highly malleable condition, and full of juice d'espree," ' murmured Collier.

'Yes, Superintendent?' the AC said, looking down the table at him. But Collier waved his hand, as if to say that he hadn't meant to interrupt.

The AC said tersely, 'According to the doctors, you probably saved his manhood, and possibly his life as well.'

'Shame,' Collier had said afterwards. 'If you hadn't done that, he wouldn't be suing us now.'

'And did you at any point,' the AC said, fixing me with a busy stare, 'hear any of the racist remarks which he alleges were made?'

A long pause. Collier's eyes rested on mine. Not worried but interested. Amused, even.

'Yes, sir,' I said at last. 'I did hear someone call him a black bastard.'

There was a general shifting around the room. Sideways glances. The AC didn't blink. 'Who said that?'

'I can't be sure, sir. There was too much going on.'

'And you don't want to name a brother officer.' That was Scratton, a wiry little man from Internal Investigations.

'It's not that, sir. I genuinely don't know who it was.'

Was it my imagination, or had one of Collier's eyes just briefly closed and opened again?

'And how long were you unconscious for, Detective Inspector?'

'About three minutes, I'm told.'

'Were you in any pain afterwards?' The question came from another man, someone I didn't know. He'd taken his jacket off, so it was impossible to guess at his rank.

'A little, sir.'

'But you chose not to go to hospital with the second ambulance. Why was that?'

'By that time Mr Bart had got out of the car and was involved in a struggle with four of my officers. I felt that I should stay and help to resolve the situation.'

Bart kicking off. He'd slammed Falconer against the door frame of the Suzuki, splitting the man's head open from the temple to the cheek. Two armed officers were pointing guns at him. He simply ignored them. The armed men unable to get a shot in because of the three others still trying to drag Bart to the ground. Little Kathy Grogan somehow, impossibly, getting a handcuff onto one of his wrists before being thrown clear like someone being thrown off a bucking bronco. Stebbings seeing an opening, extending his telescopic truncheon with one fluid upwards swipe, then clubbing Bart with the downstroke. And all the time that lacerated cock spraying blood everywhere Bart turned . . .

'The situation seemed quite fluid, sir,' I added. 'I wanted to stay and get it under control.'

'In your opinion, could Miss Brown's death have been prevented?'

'No, sir. We'd had no reason whatever to suppose that Bart was armed, or that Merrily was suicidal.'

'Very well. There are no more questions.' The AC turned and started conferring with his neighbour in a whisper. As I got to my feet Collier raised his eyebrows at me, as if to say, 'Well? What did you expect?'

'What happens now?'

Detective Superintendent Collier drank deep before replying. He set the half-empty pint glass down on the bar counter before he said, 'There are three sorts of people in this job, Bill. There are those who would look at this pint and say, that glass is half full. And there are those who would say, no, that glass is half empty. And there are a few, a very few, who would say, that half-empty, half-full glass is the glass of my senior investigating officer. Would you like that filled up, sir, possibly with a chaser to accompany it?'

I sighed and waved some money at the barmaid. 'What happens about Bart?'

'A deal. If he'll drop his case, we'll drop the crack charges and possession of a handgun.'

'Will he take it?'

'That depends on his lawyer. Chances are it's a no-win no-fee job, in which case a nice tidy deal like that isn't going to leave anything for the brief. We may need to up the compensation just to buy off the lawyer.'

'You don't think I should have said anything, do you?'

'About the black bastard comment? Don't fret yourself, lad. That was of no great consequence.'

'What?' I'd lain awake nights wondering what I'd say if they asked me that question.

'Remember Rogers asking if you were in any pain after you were knocked unconscious, and you said you might have been?'

I nodded.

'What you actually said was, you were concussed and in no fit state to make accurate recollections about anything that happened.'

'I did?'

'By the time the report's written, that's how it'll read.'

'Oh. I see.'

'All that you've succeeded in doing,' Collier said kindly, 'is in fucking up your own hitherto unblemished career. Yesterday, you were a rising star. Tomorrow, a – what's the opposite of a star? You know, when it explodes in a great ball of white heat?'

'A supernova?'

'Exactly. Ah, the wonders of a college education. It doesn't make you any smarter, but it gives you the vocabulary to describe your ignorance.' Collier poured the chaser down his throat and clucked disapprovingly. 'No ice next time, lad. It impedes the smooth progress of malt between gob and gullet. Fuck.' The last word was addressed not to me but to his pager, which had started beeping. He pulled it out of his trouser pocket and looked at it. 'No rest for the wicked. Drink up, lad, we're wanted.'

In the taxi Collier pulled out the tin of extra-strong mints he kept in his top pocket and returned seamlessly to the theme he'd been addressing in the pub. 'So now you've been noticed. Believe me, you didn't want to be noticed. Paul Scratton stood alongside me in the urinals after. ' "Interesting young man, your Mr Thomson," he said. "Very good at drawing straight lines, I expect." He hath no lower praise.'

'Meaning what?'

'Meaning that in this job a little discretion goes a long way. Of course, if you hadn't put Merrily on the register, none of this would have happened.'

'Maybe not, but I'd be guilty of not registering an informant.'

'I think you may be confusing a clean nose with clean hands,' Collier murmured. We turned sharply as the taxi went round Marble Arch. His surprisingly heavy shoulder leaned against me. 'The point is, Bill, a number of people will feel that you should be taking rather more responsibility for what happened the other night. Some of the canteen cowboys may even insinuate that accusing your fellow officers of racism is a cynical attempt to pass the buck.'

'Let them,' I said. 'What's the case?' I wanted to change the subject. I liked Collier, but his generation did things differently.

'Hmm?'

'What are we going back to?'

Collier pulled the pager out of his pocket and made a show of re-reading it. 'Aggravated burglary. One fatality. West Hampstead.'

As the taxi crawled up Regent Street he murmured, only half to himself:

> 'Now this is the law of the jungle – as old and true as the sky;
> And the wolf that shall keep it may prosper, but the wolf
>   that shall break it must die.
> As the creeper that girdles the tree-trunk the Law runneth
>   forward and back –
> For the strength of the Pack is the Wolf, and the strength of the
>   Wolf is the Pack.'

14

I didn't want the Broadhurst Terrace case. I wanted to find Sheena Mast, Merrily's friend and the only person who could tell me why Merrily had suddenly got so scared she killed herself rather than go on with the operation. Broadhurst Terrace was a slap on the wrist, a pre-emptive strike from Collier so that people like Scratton and Rogers could see that his grip was as firm as ever.

Not that he put it to me in those terms. What he said to me, when we were back at Paddington, was, 'You've done Advanced Interviewing, haven't you?'

'Yes. Last year, at Hendon.'

'And SOIT?'

'That too.' Sexual offence interview techniques were now considered worthy of a separate course, and qualification, for officers wanting to become detectives.

'Good. The survivor's up in the rape suite and she'll need sensitive handling.' Just the hint of a sneer, behind that word 'sensitive'. *You go and chat to the victims, Bill. Leave the sharp end to those of us with fewer scruples.*

I sighed. 'What's the story?'

He handed me some papers. It was the CAD report – the transcript of the 999 call – and a one-page Decision Log, detailing what action had been taken so far. I looked at the dec.log first:

0812 Crime Reported (CAD Trans. 786 J422, attached).
0820 2 officers on scene. PS Roberts, DC Horner. 1 fat.,
    1 possible ass., ?sexual. Ref. rape suite. Forensic Support called.
0922 Ambulance 1. Rape suite, Pad Grn. Serg. Turnbull, Dr
    Matthiesson.

0948 FSS arrives. SOCOs in attendance. CSM Anwar secures scene.
0952 Ambulance 2. Fat. to St Mary's. Accomp. Roberts. Professor
     Collins receiving. Post mortem 2PM (approx).
1048 D.Sup Collier SIO.

By the end of the week, I knew, this list of decisions made by
the investigating team – each one meticulously logged in case of
future disputes about whether proper procedures had been carried
out – would run to several volumes. I turned to the CAD
transcript.

CAD 786 J422
>>*Emergency, which service do you require?*
>>*I don't know. I think she's dead but I'm not sure.*
>>*I'm sending an ambulance and a police car. Would you confirm
    your address for me please?*
>>*[sobbing]*
>>*Caller, are you at Basement Flat, 27 Broadhurst Terrace?*
>>*Yes. I think my friend's been killed. She's in the shower.*
>>*Is she breathing?*
>>*I don't know. Oh shit. Just come, will you? Come quickly.*
>>*They'll be with you in a few minutes, caller. Can you check your
    friend's breathing? I'll stay on the line. Check her breathing
    and come back to me.*
[Elapsed Time: 4 mins.]
[Caller hysterical]
>>*Is she breathing?*
[No reply]
>>*Caller, could you tell me your name?*
[No reply]
>>*Caller? Who are you please? Are you the householder?*
>>*Ros Taylor. I'm Ros Taylor and it's Jo McCourt who's dead.
    She's dead. She's not breathing and she's cold.*
>>*Ros, I'm going to tell you how to breathe for her. Listen
    carefully . . .*

Nothing unusual there. It was a shame that the body had been
disturbed by the attempts to revive the victim, but understandable
in the circumstances.

I looked at the single statement clipped to the CAD. PS Roberts' initial report, faxed over from the hospital when he went in with the body:

At 0812 DC Horner and myself attended Basement Flat, 27 Broadhurst Terrace, in response to a 999 call. At 0820 we were admitted by an IC1 woman who identified herself to us as Rosalind Taylor, age twenty-six. She was in a hysterical state. She indicated that we should look in the shower, where we found one fatality, female, IC1, unclothed. Miss Taylor confirmed that she had touched the body in order to ascertain death and had turned the water off at that time. An ambulance arrived and the crew commenced paramedic action. After approx. four minutes they confirmed that further intervention was unlikely to be effective. Pathologist called to certify death. RT seemed incoherent and her speech was slurred. I asked if she had taken anything which might have caused this. She said not. I asked whether she had sustained any injuries herself. She suggested she might have been attacked too, 'in my sleep', and mentioned having pains of a sexual nature. Called second ambulance, alerted Rape Suite. Called Forensic Science Support Unit. Examined scene. No sign of forced entry. No sign of weapon. Large number of bloodstained footprints on bathroom floor from naked foot, probably RT's. Some contamination by ambulance crew (boot sizes 8 and 11). Sketch of scene attached. In lounge, partial bloodstain found on floor, approx 7 ft x 2 ft. Number of photographs strewn around, also photograph packet and developing receipt from Boots, Finchley Road branch, dated 11/7/01 and timed 19.51. Also DVD box from Video City, Finchley Road. Two pizza boxes marked Ristorante Spighetta containing some food remains, quite fresh. Red wooden box, of the type used to store jewellery, found open and empty on floor. 9.22 1st ambulance took RT to Paddington Green Rape Suite. DC Horner phoned ahead to alert them. I waited with the 2nd ambulance until FSS and duty pathologist arrived at 9.48, then accompanied the body to St Mary's. DC Horner remained to secure the crime scene. I alerted the Duty Sergeant by radio to the possibility of speaking to the shops indicated.

I couldn't go the crime scene myself until it had been declared sterile. Yet another of the endless precautions against defence lawyers, in case fibres found their way onto my clothing and thus into the homes of any suspects I interviewed. That wasn't going to happen in a million years, of course; the point was that we had to be able to *prove* it hadn't. I spent the dead time organizing my team, first calling the resources director to ask which incident rooms and incident room supervisors were free.

'Cathy Harris is next on the list. Room three.'

'Thanks.'

I unplugged my laptop and carried it up to the incident room she'd given me, actually a whole set of interconnecting rooms on the eighth floor that still smelt of smoke and stale booze from the wrap party of the last case to be run from there. The portaboards still had police photographs pinned to them. Victims? Villains? There was no way of knowing. I took them down and chose a desk by the window. Then I opened the thick A4 file I had brought upstairs with me. It had the Met logo and the words 'Murder Investigation Manual' on the front.

People are sometimes surprised to learn that a murder investigation follows a completely standardized procedure. The image of the detective is of someone who breaks rules, subverts procedures, follows his instincts. Actually, the reverse is true. When you have up to a hundred people working on a case – when personnel change as quickly as the night shift follows the day, and people take leave, or get promoted, or go sick, or simply get caught up in another investigation – and when you know that every single detail will eventually be scrutinized by very clever people who are paid a lot of money just to pick holes in it, the most important thing is to follow an agreed process, or chaos ensues. At Hendon they used to say that if you dropped dead, another officer should be able to come in and pick up your investigation without losing more than an hour.

The Murder Investigation Manual told me that my next task was to appoint a deputy and an administrative officer. I was required to estimate manpower requirements, allocate duty rosters and suggest a budget. I had to appoint a receiver, who would look at every piece of information that came into the incident room and decide what to do with it. I had to set the parameters of the material I personally wanted to see – policy directives? Telephone messages? Officers' reports? Witness statements? Exhibits? – decide how many statement readers we would need, and nominate an allocator who would make sure that every single task was given an action number before being passed to a detective. I was even required to determine how many computer files the case would require. There would be an indexer who would constantly go through the files looking for connections, cross-referencing them, and a researcher who would trawl through the HOLMES database looking for information from other cases.

Like most police work it was a mundane, methodical, administration-heavy process, and although like all the other coppers I bitched about the amount of time it took, like the rest of them I loved it. I loved the way the random chaos created by an act of violence or stupidity or greed would gradually be ordered into statements and actions and matters arising and finally charges. I loved the way every procedure was itself broken down into sets of smaller procedures, each with its own acronym, so that to instigate a MIRSAP – a major incident room standard administrative procedure – you first had to sort out your CRIS, or crime reporting information system, which in turn required that you follow the IIMAC, and so on. I loved the way the process took over, no matter how confusing or inexplicable a crime seemed initially, guiding you towards a result that had seemed impossible when you began.

By the time I had done all this Cathy Harris had turned up. I heard her talking to the switchboard, activating the incident room phone lines and ordering stationery and office supplies. She had already sent DCs Price and Morgan down to the scene to interview neighbours. The surviving victim was still in the rape suite, so I went to join Roberts at the post-mortem.

Strictly speaking, there was no need for me to attend the autopsy. The chain of evidence was being maintained by having Roberts there. However, there was a general supposition that the acting SIO would always attend a cut-up. You didn't ask your men to do anything you wouldn't do yourself.

When I got there Professor Collins was completing his external examination, while one of his assistants filmed him. Roberts was there, making notes. He looked pretty grim. After children, the autopsies of attractive women are the ones policemen hate most.

The pathology suite at St Mary's doubles as a teaching room, with banked rows of seats arranged round the autopsy units. Bright directional lights, like those above a dentist's chair, add to the impression that you're in some kind of theatre. I took a seat next to Roberts, who nodded at me. Below us the victim's body was laid face upwards, her arms turned out and hanging over the edges of the table. Her hair, which was blonde and quite long, hung straight down towards the floor. One of the assistants was retying the plastic bags which had been fastened round her hands. I kept my voice low so that it wouldn't disturb the pathologist, who was speaking his findings aloud to a microphone hanging from the ceiling. 'What's the story?'

Like most uniformed policemen, Roberts carried two note-books: the official one, which could be requested as evidence in a trial by either side and was thus only used as a fair copy, and the one he actually scribbled in. I read over his shoulder: '2 broken nails on rt hand – suggest ?resisting attacker. ?poss. broken bone in little fngr rt hnd (boxer's fracture) – X-ray requested.'

I nodded. Boxer's fractures, as they were called, were common in assault victims. They usually took the form of small breaks in the little finger or the knuckles, resulting from hitting someone a glancing blow. The pathologist would probably wait to have the X-rays done in the middle of the night, when it was quiet. Live patients, waiting seven hours or more in casualty, tended not to be too happy if they saw dead ones jumping the queue.

Collins was examining the girl's neck now. 'There are a number of surface scratches on the neck, perpendicular to the larynx and along the line of the carotids,' he was saying. 'I count approximately five on the left and four on the right, with those on the right being slightly deeper. They are consistent with the broken nails on the victim's hands.'

Even with my limited knowledge of pathology, I knew what that meant. It was probably asphyxia. She had tried to prise the killer's hands, or whatever he had strangled her with, away from her neck, scratching her own skin in the process.

'The lower lip is swollen and has two abrasions corresponding to the incisors,' Collins said.

In other words, the killer had put his hand over the girl's mouth while she struggled, forcing her lips hard against her teeth.

'There are petechial haemorrhages under the eyes – '

Asphyxia, for sure. The pressure had burst tiny blood vessels in her cheeks.

' – and a haematoma, approximately circular in shape, measuring twenty-five millimetres, just above the larynx, which has collapsed.'

Roberts looked at me, pen poised over his notepad. 'Search me,' I muttered.

As if aware of our confusion, Professor Collins raised his voice slightly. 'From its position and size, I would suggest that this may have been caused by the assailant's wristwatch.'

I felt a quickening of interest.

'In other words, when she started struggling he may have leant on her neck with his left forearm and wrist. His watch went into her neck, causing the mark we see here.' Collins placed his arms in the appropriate positions, demonstrating his words as he spoke. He glanced up at us to make sure we had understood. 'This is not uncommon in assaults of this type, I believe.'

Well, maybe. In crimes of anger, that is. I had never heard of a burglar strangling anyone. And a professional wouldn't even consider wearing a watch on a job. All the evidence was pointing to an opportunist – a junkie, out looking for car radios or an empty flat to service his next fix, had seen the open windows and decided to try his luck.

Then again, you didn't usually meet a junkie who hadn't sold his watch to feed his habit.

Collins was examining the wound on the girl's head. Her hair was in the way. He said something to one of the assistants, who plugged in a razor and began to shave the back of her scalp. Her hair dropped to the floor in thick clumps. When the wound was exposed Collins stepped back to the body.

'There is a contusion to the cerebellum. This may have been sufficient to cause unconsciousness but is unlikely to have been the cause of death.'

He worked his way down the body. When he pushed apart the girl's thighs I looked away. I heard him say, 'Small moon-shaped indentations on both inner thighs. Possibly a thumbnail mark.' I pictured the killer gripping her legs and trying to force them open, digging his thumbs into the soft white skin while she kicked and tried to fight him. It was not a pleasant thought.

Next to me Roberts, too, had gone very pale. Collins moved on to the rape kit protocols, taking various blood samples and swabs. I kept my gaze fastened as much as possible on the lights. I thought: this is what the rapist did to her. He didn't just screw her, or kill her. He had stripped her and pushed her naked in front of me, her body defenceless against the indignities that were now being done to her in the name of science. A part of me always wanted to stand up and intervene, to stop people like Collins, to beat them off her and help her to her feet and tell her that it was all right now, the police were here. Except of course it wasn't all right, and Collins was only doing his job. In the periphery of my vision, I saw him reaching inside her like a vet reaching into a cow.

I was thankful when I got a text message to say that the survivor was ready to make her statement and I was able to slip away. I'd be lying if I said I wasn't looking forward to this part of the investigation. As Collier had pointed out, I'd done a cognitive interviewing module three months before at Hendon, and I was curious to see if the techniques I'd learned would be useful.

She was in room twelve, with Alice Turnbull. Alice and I went way back. We'd been detective constables together, before she'd decided to concentrate on victims rather than villains. It was an unusual job being a SOOF, a sexual offences officer, a bit of a career cul-de-sac, but Alice had obviously decided it was worthwhile because she'd stuck with it for three years. I sent a text message back to her phone and she slipped out of the room to brief me.

'The FME's report should be here any moment. According to her, there's a strong possibility Ros may have been drugged, so she's put a rush on the bloods.'

I nodded. Date rape drugs break down in the body after a few hours, so speed is essential. 'Good. Make sure the pathologist knows to do the same.'

'There's something else you should see, Bill. He did this to her back.' She handed me a Polaroid. 'The doctor says it was done with a very sharp knife, maybe a scalpel or a craft knife. It's yesterday's date.'

I didn't understand why anyone would do such a thing. If it was a junkie and he was high, it was possible that he'd done it on the spur of the moment. But junkies tend not to commit crimes when they're high. When they're high they just sit around happily enjoying themselves. It's when they come down – when they're clucking, in street talk – that they start to worry how they're going to pay for the next fix. Besides, most of the junkies I met didn't know what month it was, let alone the date.

'How is she?' I asked.

Alice shrugged. 'Like you'd expect.'

15

She was dressed in tracksuit bottoms and one of the plain T-shirts the rape suite provided, and she was sitting up very straight. Later, I was to discover that she always held herself like this, her shoulders pulled back and her spine upright, the legacy of a childhood filled with ballet lessons. In the crook of each elbow there were small pads of cotton wool taped to her skin where the FME had taken blood samples. She had black rings under her eyes, no make-up, and her straight dark hair was cut short, emphasizing the slightness of her neck. She looked bruised and wary and fragile and desperately beautiful.

Cognitive interviewing is basically a package of techniques developed by psychologists to help us get more from interviews, particularly interviews where the interviewee might be traumatized. One of the ideas is that you split the interview into three distinct parts. In the first part, your objective is simply to gain the subject's trust. So you let them tell the story at their own pace, rather than interrupting all the time to hammer out the details. You might echo their answers back to them, so if a subject says, 'And then the big man with the gun came and hit me,' rather than ask, 'How big was the gun?' you just say, 'So he hit you.' Then you go through it again, trying to get a clearer picture. This is when you try to get the information you'll use in the statement. But as well as asking them for the facts, you also let them talk about what happened, and how they feel about it. And then you go through it all a third time, only now you try to get them to tell the whole story in a completely different way – backwards, say, or from someone else's perspective: 'When the big man with the gun came round the corner, what would he have seen?'

A lot of detectives think this is just psychobabble. But studies have shown that it not only produces more information, it also helps build up a rapport between the interviewee and the detective which makes it easier to *use* the information. Particularly in sexual offences, where a victim will often be able to supply a good description of an offender to the investigating officer, but suffer from cold feet when it comes to repeating the description in court.

Ros Taylor wanted to co-operate, but she was also deeply traumatized. Several times she broke down when I asked her to describe what had happened. It also became apparent that she couldn't remember anything about the attack, or even the hours preceding it. No matter what I asked her, no matter how I rephrased the questions, she kept repeating that she couldn't remember.

After an hour or so I called a break and went to get us both some tea. The blood results were in, and I scanned them quickly while I waited. Both girls had tested positive for GHB.

Collier stuck his head round the door. 'How are you getting on?'

Something in his voice told me that this wasn't a casual enquiry. 'Fine. Why?'

'Sheena Mast's been seen down at the Ramp with a dealer called Azad Karim. Want to have a crack at her, pardon the pun?'

The Ramp was street slang for Old Montague Street, the centre of Whitechapel's sex industry. It was run by a loose affiliation of Bengali gangsters and white pimps, the detritus who got pushed out of King's Cross by bigger, harder gunmen or, in the case of the girls, marginally more attractive whores. They slopped east along the route of the Great Eastern Canal until, like all the rest of London's sewage, they fetched up in the wharves and docks east of the City.

'Of course.'

'Better get rid of your interview, then.'

'Give me twenty minutes.'

I went back into the interview room and tried not to let Ros Taylor know that I was rushing her. There was nothing more that could be done, anyway. She'd seen nothing, heard nothing, done nothing. Or nothing that she could remember. She gave me a few names – people who'd come to the flat, the dead girl's married boyfriend, a lad who'd used abusive language on the phone when she'd knocked him back – but nothing that seemed likely to have any bearing on the investigation. Eventually I lent her my phone so she could call a girlfriend to arrange somewhere to stay, and left her with Alice.

The address we'd got for Azad Karim was at the top of an old council block just behind Brick Lane. I told one of the PCs to stay with the vehicle. Round there, even police cars get nicked. They didn't smash the windows, they hacked the remote-control locks.

'Funny, I don't remember leaving Dover,' Stebbings murmured behind me, glancing up at the street sign. It was in Bengali first and English second.

'Any remarks like that, keep them to yourself,' I said sharply.

'I've got nothing against the Pakis. Great curry place at the end of this road. Best biriyanis in London.'

'They're not Pakistanis. They're Bengalis.'

'Yeah, whatever. I was forgetting your well-known affinity with the immigrant population.'

I stopped short. 'What's that supposed to mean?' Collier had been right. News travelled fast. Stebbings clearly knew all about what I'd told the Incident Review Board. I shook my head. 'Oh, forget it. We've got work to do.'

A group of American tourists on a Jack the Ripper walking tour looked at us curiously as we pushed past them. Their guide – dressed rather improbably in a Sherlock Holmes deerstalker and a tweed cape – was talking loudly about a prostitute called Dark Annie who'd been murdered here in eighteen something or other when it was known as Gin Lane.

'*Plus ça change*,' Stebbings said. 'Pardon my French. Or do I mean Spanish, sir?'

'All right, give it a rest,' I said wearily. The staircase up to the top flat stank of old curry. The wall was looped with graffiti, some teenager's tag so stylized with repetition it had become as unreadable as a doctor's signature. As we got higher, the stairwell increasingly smelt of urine as well as food.

'That's the one,' Stebbings said, pointing. 'Number twenty-two.'

The door was unlocked. Inside, the stench was augmented by

the acrid smell of stale crack. A woman was lying face down on the sofa. A pipe improvised out of a Coke bottle with a plastic biro jammed into it lay beside her. Stebbings looked at me questioningly. I shook my head. 'That's not Sheena.'

The table was littered with used syringes and discarded wraps. Stebbings squatted down and gingerly poked the detritus with a finger. 'Looks like they're doing brown as well as white.'

I nodded. If Sheena was injecting heroin she'd make an unreliable witness, even if she survived long enough to walk into the witness box.

I pushed open a door at the far end of the room. It led into a bedroom. There was a mattress on the floor, surrounded by empty takeaway cartons and pieces of silver chocolate wrapper. A sari had been pinned up over the window, but it didn't keep out much light. Three people were asleep in the bed, two dark-skinned men and a white woman. As I walked in, one of the men woke up and immediately swung his feet onto the floor. He was a short, tubby Bengali. 'I'm going,' he said, even before I'd shown him my card. He started to pull on some trousers that were lying beside the bed.

'Azad Karim?'

'Not me.' He indicated the other man, asleep on the other side of the bed. 'That's Azad. I'm just a customer.' He scuttled out. I didn't try to stop him.

The girl in the bed opened her eyes, saw me and said wearily, 'Oh, fuck.'

'Hello, Sheena.'

Sheena sat up in bed and coughed, clutching her arms round her skinny ribs. After a few moments the coughing turned into dry retching.

'Get dressed. We need to talk to you.'

I went back into the other room and waited. The girl on the sofa didn't stir. After a few minutes I went across and checked her pulse. She wasn't dead, just out of it. Stebbings began to search the flat, muttering expletives at the foulness of it. He found what he was looking for in the kitchen: a shoebox containing a clutch of syringes, a few wraps of heroin and three small rocks of crack twisted inside a chewing-gum wrapper. There was a crack pipe made out of an empty Evian bottle. 'That's nice,' he murmured.

'Mineral water. She'll be one of those classy birds, then. Into her health and that.'

Sheena came out of the bedroom. She was dressed now, though it wasn't much of an improvement.

'What you want, then?' She had a little girl's whining lisp. 'Then' came out as 'ven'. She went to the table and found a packet of cigarettes amidst the detritus.

'We need to talk. Down at the station.'

'I need a coffee first.' She moved listlessly towards the kitchen.

Stebbings held up the shoebox. 'Your gear's here, Sheena.'

'Give me that, you bastard. I need to fix. I'm clucking like a bitch.' She started to rub her arms frantically. 'Come on, give it me.'

Stebbings looked at me. 'Sir?'

That was all I needed: a skag queen. On the other hand, she wasn't going to be much good to me like this. Reluctantly I said, 'All right, Sheena. One fix. But make it a small one, will you? I don't want you too stoned to talk.'

'No fucking chance of that. This stuff's weak as piss.' She grabbed the shoebox and sat down on the floor to prepare her gear, calmer now she'd got her own way.

'How long have you been on brown, Sheena?' I asked as I watched her.

'I don't fucking know. I'm not really on it, am I?'

'It's looking that way to us, Sheena,' Stebbings said as she sucked the murky liquid up into the syringe.

'I do it while I'm working. I'm going to stop, aren't I?'

'Stop working or stop shooting up?'

'Both.' She picked a length of electric flex off the floor, pulled it round her arm as a tourniquet and inspected the result critically. Her skin was covered in what looked like tiny burns, the little red sores of infected injection sites. She flicked at herself with her fingers, trying to raise a vein. 'Oh, fuck it,' she muttered. She pulled her bare foot into her lap and stuck the needle between her toes. When the syringe was empty she pulled the plunger back again, filling it with blood, then re-injected the blood back into herself. She did this twice more before she was satisfied that she'd flushed every last speck of heroin into her body.

'I bet you roll up toothpaste tubes as well,' Stebbings said.

'You what?'

'Nothing. Come on, let's go.'

The girl on the sofa stirred and opened her eyes. Seeing Sheena shooting up, she started screaming. Sheena screamed something back. Stebbings reached into the shoebox and tossed the second girl a wrap. The screaming stopped.

'Anything for a bit of peace and quiet,' he murmured.

We took Sheena up to Old Street and commandeered a room. The brown must have been as weak as she'd said, because it was already wearing off. She was biting her fingernails and tapping her foot manically. As I sorted out a tape she lit a cigarette and immediately started to pick the filter apart with her nails.

I did the usual introductions. 'Sheena, do you know why you're here?'

She shrugged.

'We want to talk to you about Merrily Brown.'

The life of a crack prostitute is not a healthy one. Under the bright lights of the interview room I could see that Sheena had cheekbones any woman would have died for. Unfortunately, the rest of her looked as if she already had. Her face was a skull. There was a scabby cold sore by the corner of her mouth, probably the result of supplementing her crack and heroin habits with solvent abuse. I thought, incredulously, that there were men who were actually prepared to put their dicks into that mouth. But then, the places where Sheena worked were never going to be brightly lit.

'What about Merrily?'

'You know she's dead?'

She didn't look at me. 'Yeah, I heard.'

'She killed herself. The brothers were after her and she decided to beat them to it. I'm sorry, Sheena.'

Sheena shrugged. 'Too bad.' She started to rub herself again.

'She was a friend of yours, wasn't she?'

'Sort of. Yeah. We started the same time.'

I reached into my pocket and pulled out a bar of Galaxy I'd got from the Old Street canteen. Junkies eat a lot of chocolate. I snapped it in half. I hadn't had any lunch myself. I started to

145

unwrap one of the halves. 'Did she talk to you about the brothers?'

'Sometimes.'

'I mean recently? Did she talk to you about the brothers and the police?'

'She might have done.'

I started to eat my half of the chocolate. She eyed the other piece. 'Is that for me?'

'Go ahead.' As she picked at the wrapping paper with a talon-like nail I said, 'Did she ask you if you'd be prepared to make a statement?'

'That. Yeah. She talked about that.'

'What did you say?'

'I said you must be fucking mad, girl.'

'But you agreed to help her?'

'I might have done.' She pushed the chocolate into her mouth. She began to pick, absent-mindedly, at the sore on her lip with her fingernail.

'You don't sound very sure, Sheena.'

'I said I might. That's all. I said if she wanted to talk I might come with her. I dunno. I never meant it. I was on the pipe, wasn't I?'

I sighed. This was what investigations like Operation Mansion came down to in the end: a couple of crackheads' chit-chat, dressed up as evidence. 'But you told someone else, didn't you? Who did you tell that Merrily was going to talk to us?'

'No one. I'm not fucking stupid.'

'Well, you must have told someone. Because the brothers came after her.'

'I never told no one.'

'Sheena, you've just told me you were on the pipe. You could have told half of London.'

'I don't talk when I'm up,' she said doggedly. 'Not about the brothers. I'm not fucking stupid. They'd kill me too.'

I considered what she was saying. Sheena Mast might be an addict but she'd also been on the street long enough to know the ground rules. But if she hadn't talked about Merrily's plans, who had?

'I'm starting to cluck,' she said abruptly. 'That brown's like water. I need another fix.'

'Sheena, you're in a custody suite. Just try and concentrate. You'll be out in a little while.'

'I want some brown,' she whined. 'You've got it, haven't you? It's mine. Give it me.'

'I can't do that, Sheena.'

'Bastard.'

'I need someone else to tell me about the brothers, Sheena. Someone who can take Merrily's place now she's dead.'

'Not me. They'll fucking kill me.'

'We can always arrest you. Remand you in custody until the trial. You know what that means, don't you? You'll be sent up to Holloway. Nice warm cell, friendly people. No drugs, but then you were saying you wanted to come off. No punters either. No one to beat you up.'

It was a long shot, but to my amazement she actually seemed to consider it. 'How long for?'

'Until the trial. Longer, if you want. We can do you for soliciting and possessing. You'll probably get at least six months. That should sort you out.' What sort of crazy world was it where a policeman held out the promise of prison to a prostitute like some kind of bribe?

'I liked Holloway. I liked the singing.' She stared at me. 'No fucking men in there, neither.'

I heard myself say, 'We could probably manage a parole violation too.'

'I only do the drugs because of the work,' she said abruptly. 'You need the brown to stop you clucking, so you do that first, then you need some white to get you out the door. You don't care who you go with, once you've had the white. But you need the brown to come down again, after. And the brown costs so much you got to go out next day to earn your money again.'

I nodded with what I hoped looked like sympathy.

'Sixteen times I've been raped. I don't know how many beatings I've had. I fucking hate this work. And all I have to do is talk up the brothers?'

'Absolutely. Just make a statement.'

'All right then.'

I tried to keep the surprise out of my voice. 'Good girl.'

'I just need a fix first.'

'Sheena, I can't let you have drugs in here. It would jeopardize your statement. People might say you made it up while you were high.'

'I've gotta have my fix,' she said stubbornly. 'I can't talk unless I stop clucking, can I? Besides, you let me before.'

'We weren't in a custody suite before.'

'Forget it then.' She took the cigarette end out of the ashtray and started peeling it apart. 'Take me home.'

I considered my options. I could get an FME to examine her, register her as an addict and prescribe some methadone, but that could take all day.

Stebbings said, 'I think we could all use a cup of tea.'

'For the benefit of the tape,' I said wearily, 'DS Stebbings is leaving the room.' Sheena lit another cigarette and scratched herself. I closed my eyes.

Stebbings came back a few minutes later. 'Here you go, Sheena,' he said cheerfully. 'Nice cup of tea.' In his hand was a wrap, a teaspoon and a syringe. Her eyes lit up.

'What are you fucking doing?' I hissed into his ear.

'Relax,' he whispered. 'The custody officer is a mate. It's fine.'

I watched aghast as he reached into his pocket for a lighter. Like a gentleman lighting a lady's cigarette, he even held the flame steady so she could heat up her spoonful of junk. 'Thanks, love,' she said, favouring him with a death's-head smile.

'Do you take milk, Sheena?' Stebbings said for the benefit of the microphones. 'Or just a little brown sugar?' He's actually enjoying this, I thought. Sheena tried to squeeze a vein out of her scrawny arm. When none appeared she said, 'Oh, fuck this.' She stood up and undid her jeans. Her thighs, like her arms, were covered in red sores. The texture of her skin was like cottage cheese. I didn't want to see where she was injecting this time. I wondered what laws we were breaking. At the very least, we were supplying class A drugs. On the other hand, if it was the only way of getting her into protective custody, we might also be saving her life.

Sheena closed her eyes. For a moment, as the brown hit her blood, all the tension left her face and she looked almost normal. It was like a glimpse into a parallel reality. You could see the woman she might have been, if the drugs and the pimps hadn't got hold of her soul.

I thought of the other girl I'd interviewed that day, Ros Taylor, with her fragile, shocked beauty. I thought how little separated the two women, just a few simple twists of fate.

'All right,' Sheena said dreamily. 'Let's talk about the Harkurs.'

16

In my absence Collier had delegated various tasks relating to Broadhurst Terrace. Falconer and Grogan had statemented the pizza driver. Morgan and Price had questioned the neighbours. The SOCOs report had been inputted into HOLMES. An area search had been organized for seven thirty the following morning, at shift changeover time, to maximize the number of bodies available. Collier himself had tracked down next-of-kin and arranged an identification.

Everywhere I could feel people glancing at me. Word of the Review was clearly all over the nick. It didn't worry me. It was just the way the police service was. All the same, it was a relief to get out of the place to go and statement the boyfriend.

Gerry Henson lived in a huge house at the top of Frognal Lane, its front drive cluttered with cars. There was a silver Porsche, the obligatory four-wheel-drive BMW without a speck of mud on it, a Mercedes, and then a triad of staff cars – a Polo and two Fiestas. I was in an unmarked Vectra. I parked it next to the Polo.

The woman who answered the door was in her forties, well-groomed and effortlessly well-bred. 'Can I help you?' she said in a voice that made it clear she didn't expect she could.

'Mrs Henson?'

'No. Caroline's upstairs. I'm Mr Henson's assistant.'

I produced my warrant card. 'Is he in?'

She took the card and scrutinized it for a few minutes before giving it back to me. 'I'll see. Come in.'

I followed her. She pointed to a door and said, 'You can wait in there. Would you like some coffee?'

'No thanks.'

Henson's sitting room was larger than my entire flat. The walls were crowded with pictures – or rather artworks, since there was nothing pictorial about most of them. They were modern and garish and, it seemed to me, deliberately ugly. The exception was an oil painting showing a group of men standing accusingly over a young woman with a bowed head. It seemed strangely out of place, and I walked over to it to get a closer look.

'You like that?'

The voice had come from behind me. I turned round.

Gerry Henson was much younger than I would have expected from the big house and the personal assistant. I reckoned he was in his late thirties. He was wearing a rollneck shirt and a linen jacket, and on his good-looking face was a pair of fashionable thick-rimmed glasses which gave him an intellectual appearance. His upper body carried the slightly disproportionate muscle you get from gym weights.

'Gerry Henson.' He extended his hand and I shook it. I felt the rough surface of a sticking plaster on his palm.

'Detective Inspector Thomson.'

He indicated the painting. 'How old do you think it is?'

'Mr Henson—'

'Please. Humour me. Take a guess.'

'I've really no idea. Old, obviously.'

'Sixteenth century? Fourteenth?'

'I couldn't say.'

'Try.'

I shook my head firmly. He seemed disappointed that I wouldn't play his game. 'Well, you're wrong, anyway. It's a forgery, painted in nineteen forty-one. It fooled Goering himself, briefly.' Henson touched the canvas with the back of his finger. 'Worthless, of course, compared to my YBAs. But in its own way just as interesting, and possibly just as valid. Anyway, where would you like to start?'

'Mr Henson, I'm afraid I'm here on a very serious matter.'

He stared at me. 'Not the security?'

'Not the security, no.'

'The station said—' He stopped as what I'd said sunk in. 'How serious?'

'Is your wife here?'

'Yes. She's upstairs.'

'I think you'd better shut the door. It's about Jo McCourt.'

He quickly went and shut the door that led to the hall. 'What about her?'

'You do know Miss McCourt?'

'Yes, of course,' he said impatiently. 'What's happened?'

'We've been informed that you were having a relationship with her. Is that correct?'

'Ah. Who told you that?'

'Is it true?'

'We see each other from time to time, yes.'

'There's no easy way to say this. I'm afraid she's dead.'

'Oh Christ.' He stared at me. 'How?'

'We're not sure yet. It's possible that it was a burglary that went wrong.'

'Jesus.' He shook his head. 'What about Ros? Is she all right?'

'Well, we believe she may have been assaulted. And she's lost her memory.'

'But why? They had nothing to steal. Nothing worth killing for. Not like . . .' His eyes travelled over his paintings.

'Mr Henson,' I said gently, 'we think whoever broke in may have tried to rape Jo, and when she fought him off he became violent.'

'Oh, Jesus. *Jesus*. So if she'd – if she'd just let him – he wouldn't have killed her?'

'Well, it's a possibility.'

'But why didn't she just go along with it? It's not as if rape – I mean, she was hardly – rape wouldn't have been so terrible, would it? Compared to being killed.' He sat down and rubbed his face. 'Sorry. Earlier I thought – the local police have been promising to send someone round to talk about security.'

'That's all right.' I got out a statement form. 'I need to ask you some questions, though.'

'Of course. God, what a mess. Will you need to talk to my wife?'

'Our job is to investigate crimes. If you've been unfaithful, that isn't against the law. I can't see any reason at this stage why she'll have to know. But I'll need to confirm your movements over the last forty-eight hours.'

'Mine?' He looked shocked.

152

'We're trying to build a picture of Jo's last hours. It would help to know when you last saw her.'

'Oh. Of course. I saw her yesterday, in fact. Yesterday afternoon.'

'At her flat?'

'Yes.'

'I'm afraid I need to know whether you had sex.'

'Is that really necessary?'

'It'll affect the forensic tests.'

He sighed. 'Yes. We had sex.' He glanced at the door.

'How long were you there for?'

'Not long. An hour or two. I had to get back.'

'So you were here by . . . ?'

'Well, about six.'

'And is there anyone who could confirm that? Your assistant, perhaps?'

'No. She'd gone by then. It was just me and Caroline.'

'That's your wife?'

He nodded.

'I will have to speak to her, then. But I'll try to be discreet.' I made another note. 'How long had you been seeing Jo?'

He shrugged. 'Since January.'

'How did you meet?'

'Through her flatmate. Ros works for a lab which had done some work for us on a picture – there was a dealer who was trying to rip us off, and the scientists were able to prove it. I threw a party, and Ros brought Jo along.' He sighed. 'I suppose it seems crazy to you. Why I would risk all this for a girl like her.'

Without looking up from what I was writing I said, 'I don't really know what sort of girl she was.'

'Well, she was great. A lot of fun. And, ah . . . undeniably very attractive.'

'Was it a serious relationship? I'm just trying to build up a picture of what her life was like.'

'No. Christ, I'm glad they didn't send a woman. It's easier to explain to a man, isn't it? There's some you bed and some you wed. Jo was definitely the former. You will be discreet, won't you?'

I thought: twenty-four hours ago you were in bed with her.

Now she's dead and all you care about is making sure no one but me knows you fucked her. Aloud I said, 'I'll talk to your wife now, sir.'

Henson showed me into a large bedroom which had been filled with canvas drapes. Two young men were fussing about with lights and Polaroids. There was a board set up on an easel and they were sticking the Polaroids onto it one by one to build up a sort of composite picture. Caroline Henson was sitting on the bed dressed in a feathered black see-through thing. She looked tired.

'Ian, Kurt, I'm afraid we need five minutes,' Henson said.

'Will it take long?' one of them wanted to know. 'The light is changing, and we have to finish—'

'It'll take as long as it takes,' I said firmly. The young men reluctantly removed themselves.

'And I'll need to talk to your wife alone,' I said to Henson.

'Of course,' he said nervously. As he left us he shot me a conspiratorial look, which I tried not to acknowledge.

'Hello,' I said.

'Hello.' She had a quiet, nervous voice.

'It's nothing very complicated, really. Someone your husband knows was assaulted last night and he can't remember what time he came home. He thought you might.'

She picked up a glass that was on the floor. There was nothing left in it except some ice cubes, but she held it in her hand anyway. 'I think it was about five. Between five and six, that's right.'

'Good,' I said encouragingly. 'And then you both stayed in all evening?'

'I think so.'

'But you're not sure?'

'No – sorry – I'm trying to think. Yes, we were definitely here,' she said nervously.

'What did you do?'

'Do?' She seemed surprised by the question.

'Can you remember?'

'Oh. Well, we ate supper. And watched TV. Nothing special.'

'OK. I'm just going to write that down on a statement form for you to sign, and then you can get back to your picture.'

'It's not my picture,' she said quickly. 'It's a commission. They're Gerry's latest find.' She waved the glass, and I realized that she was just a little drunk. I noticed, too, that although the glass was empty, the ice cubes had barely had time to start melting.

I wrote out the statement by hand and gave it to her to sign. She scribbled her signature on it quickly.

'You're meant to read it before you sign. To make sure I haven't made anything up.'

'Sorry.' She scanned the statement. 'Yes, that's fine.'

I put the statement back in the folder and left her to it. I didn't think it particularly odd that she was nervous. People are often anxious when they talk to the police, whether they've done anything wrong or not. I thought that she probably guessed her husband wasn't telling her something and she struck me as being the sort of person who wouldn't confront him if she thought he was having an affair. It was no concern of mine.

'By the way,' I said as I put the statement away. 'Does your husband normally wear a wristwatch?'

'A what?'

'I noticed earlier that he isn't wearing a watch. Does he usually wear one?'

'I gave him a Rolex for his birthday two years ago.'

'One of the heavy ones?'

'Yes. But he takes it off when he goes swimming. It's probably by the pool.'

'Of course.'

I didn't attach any particular significance to that either, at the time. Plenty of men wear big watches. You couldn't say someone was a suspect just because they'd taken off their watch.

On the other hand, Henson had been wearing a polo neck, which might have concealed defence wounds. And there was that sticking plaster on his palm. I made a note to call the local station to see if he really had requested any advice on security.

When I got back to Paddington I discovered that Ros had walked off with my jacket and my house keys.

'Tell you what,' Collier said, 'why don't you tell her you're actually her boyfriend? She'd probably get into bed with you before she realized her awful mistake.'

'Thanks a lot.'

'Here. Don't knock it till you've seen what you're missing.' He pulled out some photographs in clear plastic scene-of-crime sleeves. They showed the two girls by a pool. In one of them both girls were topless. Jo, the blonde one, was sitting up, laughing at the camera, deliberately cupping her hands under her large breasts in a jokey parody of a Page Three pose. Behind her, on a sunlounger, Ros was looking up from her book and smiling, slighter and smaller-breasted than her friend.

'Christ. What I wouldn't give for some of that,' Collier said jovially, rubbing his stomach.

I went round to where she was staying and got my keys back. It was difficult. She was wearing a bathrobe. I kept thinking of her friend's body, stretched out voluptuously on the mortuary table, and of Ros's breasts as they'd been in the photograph. I turned down the beer they offered me and left as soon as I could.

17

The next morning the search team found a bag of stolen items in a dustbin in Belsize Road. I took it back to Ros to see if she could identify them. The memory loss didn't help things, but there was no doubt they were hers.

It was looking less and less like a burglary. It sometimes happened that professional burglars raped and even killed their victims, but any burglar who was smart enough to know he shouldn't keep items linking him to a murder was also too smart to take them and then dump them in the next street.

Which posed an interesting question. If the point of the attack had been rape, why bother to try to make it look like rape and robbery? What advantage would it give the criminal if we believed it?

One possible answer was that the rapist thought we'd never consider him if we were looking for a burglar.

In other words, it might be someone who was known to the victim.

I phoned Hampstead nick. No one had any record of a request by Gerry Henson to talk about security. The CID officer I spoke to said I shouldn't read too much into that, though. 'Round here, everyone's a millionaire,' he said cheerfully. 'We get twenty requests a day for security visits. Maybe we just lost it.'

Maybe. I decided to arrange a meeting between Ros and Gerry Henson, with police officers present – what's called a contrived identification, an encounter that appears to be accidental but isn't. I thought that if they bumped into each other at the autopsy suite, for example, there was just a chance it might help her to remember something. I also thought it might be useful to consult someone who knew a bit more than I did about this area.

Steve Griffin was a forensic psychologist who did a bit of part-time work for the Met as a profiler. Most of us distrusted him on principle, not because he was a psychologist, but because like all profilers he was unpaid. There's something faintly creepy about people who choose to hang around murder investigations. On the other hand, until the Met establishes a professional profiling service, enthusiastic part-timers like Griffin are all we have.

Griffin suggested we look at other reported incidents of girls being drugged, whether they'd resulted in a rape or not.

'He'll have rehearsed this over months. To begin with, when he was planning it, he'll have been getting sexual satisfaction out of the fantasy alone. Getting a bottle of GHB and carrying it around with him would have given him a sexual kick, a feeling of power, comparable to carrying around a knife. Then, as the fantasy started to wear thin, he'll have taken it a step further. Maybe he'll have drugged someone in a pub, slipping the GHB into their drink to see what effect it had, working out the right dose, watching to see how incapacitated his victims became. But he wouldn't actually have touched them yet. He's very careful – that's the attraction of GHB for him, it gives him control.'

'So there's no chance he was wandering round West Hampstead, saw an open window and decided to try his luck?'

Griffin shook his head. 'I doubt it. It can't be a coincidence that he climbed into a flat occupied by two young women. It's much more likely that he came across one or both of them in some other capacity and planned his attack from there. He may even have followed them home on a previous occasion, saw them through the open windows, and began to fantasize about what he might do if he gained access.'

'So – just so that I'm clear – there's nothing in the evidence that makes you think it could have been a jilted boyfriend, for example?'

Griffin's eyes narrowed. 'You've got someone in mind, haven't you?'

As Collier would have said, Griffin might be a twat but he wasn't a fool. I explained about Henson.

'Interesting. Would you like me to draw up a full report?'

I hesitated. I knew the other detectives would think I was going over the top. On the other hand, I was getting strong signals that this wasn't just some random attack.

'Yeah. Would you? And the sooner the better, really.'

Later that day, Ros Taylor thought she'd remembered something new – a masked man raping her. Unfortunately, the details didn't hang together. She thought she recalled him spitting at her repeatedly as he raped her. I didn't see how he could have done that if he was wearing a mask.

Remembering what Griffin had said, I went to see Collier.

'Did you challenge her?' he wanted to know.

I shook my head. 'I've been trying to build a rapport with her. My feeling is that she'll be less likely to give me information if she thinks I'm simply waiting to tear it apart.'

Collier picked up a pad and got to his feet. 'Leave her to me.'

I said quickly, 'What about Steve Griffin?'.

'What about him?'

'Maybe he can do something to help her remember. Maybe we should go easy on her until he's had a chance to try, anyway.'

He smirked at me. 'Aha. You *do* fancy her. Don't worry, I'll be gentle.'

The van smelt like a changing room after a rugby match – the same reek of testosterone, sweat and male bodies pressed too close together. We had been in it for three hours, which was about an hour too much. There's only so long you want to keep a van full of coppers in combat gear cooped up in a small space. We had a stash of empty milk bottles for emergencies, but we were all hoping it wouldn't come to that.

We were waiting for the Harkur brothers to arrive at their factory, a rundown warehouse at the very end of the estate. Apart from the heavy steel doors and the steel shutters that had been welded to the inside of the windows, it appeared to be derelict – an empty commercial property that had been secured against vandals. In fact, our information was that there were a dozen people working here round the clock, baking the little grey crystals which the brothers' dealers knocked out all over north London.

Further back down the road, some men were working on a hole

in the ground under portable floodlights. A sign apologized for essential cable installation. It was a pretext to have a JCB standing by with the engine running. If the hand-held rams couldn't take the steel doors, the digger would.

The operation was being run by a superintendent from Clapham, parked in a mobile C&C unit half a mile away. Three armoured riot vans waited in another industrial building nearby, ready to appear as soon as we gave the order.

SO10, the undercover unit, had arranged for one of their people to pose as a businessman with a large order. Delivery was tonight. We figured the brothers wouldn't entrust half a million pounds' worth of drugs to a courier. They'd come to the factory themselves to pick up the goods. If we were wrong, we'd be here until the milk bottles were full.

The radio in the front of our van squawked softly. 'All units.' A pause. 'They're on their way. Repeat, target on way. Maintain position.'

We waited. This was the hard part. Whatever was pumping through me then was just as potent, and just as addictive, as the stuff Sheena shot up.

Another squawk. 'Car approaching. One black Mercedes. Also one black Landcruiser.' The brothers had brought an escort.

We saw the headlights turning into the road. Light raked briefly across the back of the van and moved on. We heard three long pumps of a horn.

'Two men getting out of Landcruiser. Building doors open. Mercedes driving through doors. All units, go go go. Repeat, all units go . . .'

Tumbling out of the back of the van one after another like parachutists out of a plane. Barely aware of the fact I was running. My BPV cutting into my chest. The riot vans screaming up the road. Shouting. The doors closing. The JCB coming up behind me, fast. Amazing how those machines can shift. Get out of the way. The bucket swinging lethally from side to side. It hit the doors at about forty. The doors crumpled and were gone. The JCB immediately reversed at high speed, followed by the Mercedes, also reversing but with less control. The first shot cracked out – one of ours, I thought: a marksman trying to take out the tyres. I heard the ping of a ricochet, which meant he'd missed. Another police van was hurtling towards us, moving to block the Mercedes' exit. The car cannoned into it, shunting it sideways about six feet, and stopped. Instantly there were a dozen officers round it. The driver got out and threw himself down on the ground. The officers pulled open the back doors. The Merc was empty.

Which meant the brothers were still inside the factory.

Men were filing out of the warehouse now, hands above their heads. I pushed past them. I caught a glimpse of a long table made out of scaffolding bars. The lights had gone out. The armed officers had torches on the end of their weapons, and the JCB had come back in with its headlights on, but everything was confused. Then there was a huge flash of light, followed a moment later by an almighty bang and a pressure wave that knocked me to the ground. The place filled with smoke. All around me I heard the rattle and patter of falling brick dust.

When it cleared, several minutes later, there was a large hole in the back wall. Of Sammy and Joshua Harkur, there was no sign at all.

It turned out that the brothers had kept an explosive device in the factory for just such an eventuality. The hole they'd blown led into the building next door, where they'd stored a four-wheel drive with a full tank of petrol. We found it later in Shepherd's Bush, full of forensic but unfortunately nothing that could link it, or the brothers, back to the factory.

The feeling among the top brass was that it didn't really matter. We had put one of London's biggest crack factories out of business. We had arrested the brothers' main chemist. One of their gunmen was dead, and two others were in custody. Without their crack and their muscle, the brothers would lose their turf anyway. Someone else would move into the vacuum.

Overnight, the price of crack doubled. It's a futures market, out there on the streets. If dealers know supplies are going to be limited, they hike their prices and start to stockpile. Petty crime also doubled as addicts stole more car radios and carried out more muggings to pay for their supply.

That's just the way it goes. Most of the younger officers will tell you that drugs should be legalized. If people want to kill themselves, let them. The older ones – well, they've mostly given up trying to make sense of what they do. They just get on with the job.

For what it's worth, I thought it did matter that we hadn't got the Harkur brothers. I thought about Merrily Brown, and it seemed to me that the brothers were determined enough, and vicious enough, to do just about anything. But what I thought wasn't listened to. Since giving evidence to the Incident Review Board about Gusto Bart, I'd been sidelined. A report had come out, making it clear that my concussion meant it was unlikely I had heard what I claimed to have heard, particularly as none of the other officers present had the same recollections as I did. Gusto Bart was quietly paid off, and the foot soldiers closed ranks. I made an application to re-interview Sheena Mast, and was told to concentrate my energies on Broadhurst Terrace. With the brothers out of the picture, Sheena was no longer of any importance.

The following day the cross-indexers came up with a name.

'The manager at Boots in Finchley Road mentioned in his statement that one of his staff hadn't turned up that morning – a man called Carl Howell,' Cathy Harris explained. 'It turns out he was the one who worked the developing machine which processed the girls' photographs. It's all automated, but someone has to check them as they're going through and bag them up at the other end. Anyway, he's an RSO.'

The Index of Registered Sexual Offenders was a list of everyone in the country who had been convicted of any sexual crime. If our investigation came across someone who was on it, there was a high likelihood we'd found our man.

'That'll be it, then,' Collier said. 'Find the little bastard, Bill. Drag him out from whichever stone he's hiding under. Overtime, more men, whatever it takes.'

'How did he know the girls' address?' I said to Cathy.

'It's written on the film docket, in case no one comes to collect the photographs.'

'There you are, then,' Collier said. 'Chummy saw the photos as they were going through the machine and decided he'd found his playmates.'

I still wasn't sure. The way the body had been put in the shower to wash off forensic, the cuts on Ros's back, the dumped stolen goods – to me these things seemed to indicate someone brighter than the kind of person who pushed buttons on a Kodak machine. But until I had Griffin's profile I decided to keep my opinions to myself.

Strictly speaking, taking Ros back to her flat once the FSS had finished with it was a job for Alice Turnbull, but I was curious to find out if Ros's memory was coming back.

She was looking better, but it quickly became apparent that her composure was only superficial. She broke down several times, and I found myself wishing that Alice had been there after all. I did what I could for her, but it was clear that I couldn't just hand over the keys and drive off.

They do warn you, when you do the cognitive interviewing course, that building up a rapport with your interviewee is a double-edged sword. It may create an impression of intimacy. Several times she clutched me for support – physical, but also emotional. Once or twice I let her have my shoulder to cry on.

I'm not sure when I first suspected there might be anything more than that. It seemed, on the face of it, so unlikely that she'd be interested in me. It wasn't just what she looked like. It was her whole lifestyle, the kind of people she hung out with, the way she dressed and spoke. But when she rested her head on my chest I thought: she wouldn't have done that with Alice Turnbull.

They teach you, on the course, what to do when something like this happens. Let them down gently, is the official advice. Re-establish your professional boundaries gently but clearly. Make it clear it's nothing personal, but that rules are rules. It's easier said than done. I stammered something along the recommended lines. I think I succeeded in being clear. I'm not so sure about the gentle part. I saw the hurt in her big dark eyes before she turned away and pretended that nothing had happened.

18

Steve Griffin wrote us a good profile, carefully constructed with one eye on the officers who would need to use it and the other on the lawyers who would eventually try to discredit it in court. Nowhere did he actually say that Henson should be our prime suspect, but if you read between the lines the message was clear. He had pulled out some research which divided rapists into five different personality types, and from the evidence left behind at Broadhurst Terrace – the cuts, the use of drugs, the attempt to conceal DNA and make it look like a robbery – he was sure we were looking for a highly intelligent predatory rapist with no pressing need for money, Caucasian, in a relationship, extremely competitive with other men, the owner of at least one status-symbol car, who had a history of short-term relationships and sexual conquests, and who was probably a collector of some sort of trophies. It didn't give us anything we could use to march into Henson's house with a search warrant, but it gave us a series of very good reasons to eliminate Carl Howell.

I called Griffin to thank him.

'My pleasure. I just hope it helps.' He hesitated. 'Actually, there was something else I wanted to mention to you.'

'Yes?'

'As you know, I've been working with Ros on her memory deficits.'

'No improvement yet, I understand.'

'No. But in the course of our sessions, it's become apparent that one of the effects of the rape has been to intensify a mild fixation with authority figures. Her father's dead, which may go some way to explain it. I think it's possible she's looking to the police to fill the vacuum.'

'I'm not with you,' I said, although I already knew what he was trying to say.

'I'm just warning you, in general terms, that she could develop an interest in one of your officers. It might be as well to remind everyone she comes into contact with to be on their guard against any lapse of professional standards.'

I thought: *she's told him what happened in the flat.* And my next thought was: *damn.*

'I noticed it first in relation with myself, actually,' Griffin was saying. 'She asked me if I'd give her some psychotherapy. It seemed a reasonable request. It was only later that I realized I'd allowed myself to wander into a slightly untenable position.'

I said nothing. I was wondering how a position could be slightly untenable, or indeed how one could just wander there.

'In hindsight, I'm sure the reason she wanted me rather than another therapist is because she's become over-attached to the investigation. The police – or even someone like myself, only tangentially associated with the police – seem to represent the security and protection she craves.'

'She must be the last person in the country who holds that view,' I muttered.

'Of course, as her doctor now, anything she says to me is confidential, which is why it's slightly difficult. I've managed to ensure that she doesn't fixate on me, by dint of careful therapeutic handling. But I'm concerned that she'll try to find a substitute amongst your lot.'

Me as Griffin's substitute? It was hardly an appealing thought.

As if he was reading my mind, Griffin said, 'It could be anyone. In fact, she's likely to set her sights a lot lower than she normally would. She won't want to risk rejection, you see.'

I said curtly, 'The only officers she's spent time with are Alice Turnbull and myself. And I think we're both experienced enough to deal with anything like that.'

'Well, quite. But forewarned, as they say, is forearmed.'

There was an air of frustration about the investigation now. Even though we hadn't reached the thirty-one-day cut-off, we were leaking officers in ones and twos to other, more pressing cases.

In the pub that night, I felt duty-bound to tell Collier what

Griffin had said. He laughed. 'Fancies you too, does she? I'm sure you'll be very happy together.'

'Don't worry, sir. I won't forget that she's a witness.'

Collier took a long pull of his pint. 'Ah. Well, that's not strictly true, is it? She won't be a witness, not unless she starts remembering what she witnessed. Maybe you can shag some sense into the silly cow. She might even remember what happened the previous time she was on her back with her legs open.'

'You don't mean that.'

'There's only the one rule, William, and it's the same for coppers as it is for villains. Don't get caught.'

'Which, as we always say to villains, you invariably will be in the end.'

'Your integrity,' Collier said, bowing slightly, 'is an inspiration to us all.' I realized he was ahead of me by several pints. And after that I got no sense at all out of him, because he started quoting that poetry of his, which is what he does when he can't be bothered to have a conversation.

> 'Now I ain't no 'and with the ladies,
> For, taking 'em all along,
> You never can say till you've tried 'em,
> An' then you are like to be wrong.'

But he was not so drunk that he didn't return to the subject later, as I was getting up to leave. I was drunk myself by then, but I do remember that he looked at me sideways and said, 'It's a shame, Bill. Because unless you tell her what to remember, the chances are she'll remember completely the wrong thing.'

The Harkur brothers' comeback was characteristically brilliant, both in the simplicity of its strategy and the savagery of its execution. Reasoning that they would now be competing on an uneven playing field – they had few weapons, while their rivals had many; they were low in their supplies, while their rivals were not – they decided to rearrange the field before they re-entered the game.

So it was that on a wet Thursday night in August fires were reported in four separate locations across London. On closer investigation, they turned out to be arson attacks on four separate crack factories, each owned by a different drug baron. Simultaneously, we heard that a vast new factory had opened up in Hackney. The brothers were back in business.

Once again, I was amazed by the sheer efficiency of their methods. Your average gangster is a small-minded creature. If he's attacked by a rival, he goes after the rival. If he's shut down by the police, he takes it out on whoever he thinks talked to the police. It takes a very special type of villain to be shut down by the police but to retaliate against his rivals.

Your average gangster, too, makes a fortune and spends a fortune. He doesn't keep some back to set up a new factory when the need arises. The brothers were either unusually frugal, or—

Or they had access to a network of backers. People like Gerry Henson.

I don't mean that literally, of course. There was no actual link between Henson and the brothers. But someone, somewhere, was bankrolling the brothers, and if we ever found that person it would turn out to be someone like Henson. Wealthy, middle-class, and arrogant.

The longer I did this job, the more I realized that everything was ultimately connected. Every crime had its roots in another crime. Cut down on kerb-crawling, and muggings went up. Solve a bank robbery, and somebody somewhere was murdered in retaliation for information received. Clamp down on illegal immigrants, and the smugglers switched to girls or drugs. We were like kids on a beach, building a dam out of sand. The more successful we were, the more the pressure built up until it made itself a new outlet somewhere else.

Broadhurst Terrace was related, in some way I hadn't figured out yet, to every other crime in London. It was just a question of letting the pattern make itself known. Preferably before thirty-one days were up, and the screens went blank.

Sheena Mast never went to Holloway. Instead, she was sent to a secure hostel in Uxbridge on an experimental detoxification programme. She knew, because I made sure she knew, that the brothers were resurgent and that she should continue to keep her head down. She said she wanted to go to Bristol, where she had friends. We figured she'd be safe in Bristol.

But Sheena was a junkie, and junkies lie. As soon as she was moved on to the next phase of the programme – a halfway house involving some limited freedom – she got on a bus to King's Cross, where she scored a lick of crack with what was left of her sweet money. It felt so good that she decided to get another. Having no money left, she approached a car, an early kerb-crawler trawling the Caledonian Road. Five minutes later she had the wherewithal for another lick. That, in turn, soon led to the desire for another, which in turn led to another kerb-crawler. By then it was evening, and the punters were coming thick and fast, if you'll excuse the pun.

Sheena never did get to Bristol. While she tottered around King's Cross, alternately stuffing her face with cocks and crack, the grapevine was carrying news of her presence across London to her former employers. Soon after eleven a car with blacked-out windows cruised down the Cally Road and slowed down next to her. She asked if the driver wanted business. When she got in, the doors were locked and the car drove off at speed.

We found her body three days later in a derelict flat in North London. Forensic analysis of the sperm in her stomach indicated that she had had sex with at least a dozen men, probably more. I say 'men', but I mean that only in the biological sense. A fourteen-year-old schoolboy called Daniel Mazola later told his teacher that he had done a bad thing. It turned out that word had spread around the estate that there was a free-for-all going on. Daniel's gang was one of several that had set aside boyish rivalries to share in the largesse. Free drugs were being handed out like party snacks, courtesy of the brothers. Someone brought in an old sound system. A queuing system evolved. In the middle of it, on an old mattress soggy with the DNA of those who had gone before, Daniel lost his virginity to Sheena Mast while his fellow gang members cheered him on and waited their own turns.

The cause of death, we established, was a crack overdose. From what Daniel told us, it was probably self-inflicted. Throughout the party, Sheena had been suckling on the pipe whenever it was left within her reach. An experienced addict, she would have known when she'd reached her limit, but I think she willingly went beyond it in order to blot out the pain.

I thought about Sheena a lot over the next few days. She had been a whore and a junkie and the system had failed her, just as it failed Merrily Brown. She would have died anyway, sooner or later, but she should not have died in that way, at that time. It was not my fault, but it was partly my responsibility. I felt angry and sick with self-loathing.

I thought about Ros, too. I thought about the hurt in her sweet bruised eyes, but I also thought about the way she had put her arms round me when I took her to her flat. She had wanted comfort, but she had also, unwittingly, been offering it too.

I wanted to lose my anger in the wonderful oblivion of her body. I wanted to fuck her and I wanted her to love me and to make me feel forgiven and the terrible thing was that, thanks to Griffin and his warning, it was tantalizingly possible.

I didn't do it, of course. I got drunk, staggered into my own bed, and did the lonely thing with my hands while her image floated above me like a ghost. Got up, went in to work, got drunk again. More handiwork. More drinking.

It seemed, at the time, like the professional thing to do.

19

I went to Sheena's funeral. I thought one of us should be there. I wouldn't miss her and she wouldn't miss us, but she had been a human being and she had died.

It was a depressing affair, held in the municipal crematorium up in Finchley. No one from Social Services turned up. There was just the undertaker, the priest, and, to my surprise, Alice Turnbull.

I went over and stood next to her. 'I didn't realize you knew her.'

'Oh, yes.' She smiled bleakly. 'Sheena was one of my regulars.'

Sheena had said something about being raped – how many times? I couldn't remember. It hadn't occurred to me that she'd have reported them. I said so to Alice.

'Oh, she just liked to come in for a chat and a cup of tea. She wanted sympathy, not justice. Plus any drugs she could persuade the FME to dish out, of course.'

'Did she ever press charges?'

Alice shook her head. 'Never. Once she even had the punter's business card with his phone number on it, but she still didn't want us to go after him. "If I let you hassle him, he won't pay me next time," was her attitude. And this towards a man who'd broken her jaw. Guess how old Sheena was?'

'Hard to say. Twenty-eight? Thirty?'

'Nineteen.'

'Jesus.' She'd even looked haggard for thirty. 'What a fucking waste.'

The priest looked up and frowned. That struck me as pretty funny. Here was a girl who had died a squalid death in a crack squat, on the orders of her dealer, a stranger's cock in every orifice, taking hits of a pipe whenever she could get her mouth free. And the priest didn't want me to swear at her funeral. What, did he think God would be offended? Because if so, God had a pretty fucked-up set of priorities.

'I'll see you later,' I said to Alice. I went outside.

That night I stayed with Ros.

I stayed the night because she asked me to. I stayed the night because she said she was scared and she wanted someone there. I stayed the night because Gerry Henson had come round and taken some things from Jo's room, and Ros had panicked.

No. None of those things made me stay the night. I could have arranged for a patrol car to drive past every hour. I could have arranged for one of her friends to come over. I could have phoned for a WPC.

The real reason I stayed with Ros was because I wanted something I couldn't describe, even to myself.

We sat on the floor and ate some food, and I tried to explain to her what it was like at work.

I remember, when I was a kid, reading how the worst thing for soldiers fighting in the trenches wasn't the mustard gas or the shelling. It was when they came home on leave and found that back in England life was going on pretty much as it had always done. Theatres were open, restaurants still had food, people slept in beds. Those people couldn't comprehend what the troops had been going through, crouching in their muddy water-filled dugouts night after night, shot at by snipers, eaten alive by lice and fleas, the bodies of their comrades lying in pieces all around them, let alone having to climb out of those hellholes at the sound of a whistle and march forward into shelling and machine-gun fire. So more soldiers cracked up on leave than when they were actually in the trenches.

That's what being a policeman felt like, sometimes. You were fighting a war, and ordinary people – civilians – just couldn't imagine how brutal and bloody and never-ending it was. What made it even stranger was that your war, your trenches, were in the same happy city where the civilians were going about their daily business. Like two worlds, each invisible to the other. Until a stray bullet from my war flicked out and killed a civilian.

I tried to tell Ros what it felt like, and when I had finished she said, 'I was talking to Jo. Just now, while you were talking to me. Isn't that odd? It was as if I could hear her, in my head.'

And I felt bad, because after all she had been through, the last thing she needed was to hear me whining. I lay back. She nestled against my chest and then she turned her head and kissed me.

I told myself it was all right. That so long as nothing serious happened, no rule had been broken. So long as I didn't sleep with her, everything was fine.

'There are three sorts of detectives in this job,' Collier said to me once. It was my first day on his team, and he'd been showing me the ropes, culminating in a mammoth drinking session across the road at the Swan. Neither of us was drunk, though. For my part, the adrenalin and excitement were counteracting the alcohol. In Collier's case, he was just more used to it than I was. 'There are those who obey the rules, those who bend the rules, and those who make their own rules. You can't change which sort you are. The important thing is to know, and then to stick with it.'

He pretended to be disappointed when he discovered that I fell into the first category. But I think that, secretly, he was rather pleased. He was the second kind, and he quite liked having me around as his foil.

I knew that kissing Ros was wrong. But I told myself that the comfort I could give her outweighed that. Because after all, nothing was going to happen.

Eventually I disentangled myself as gently as I could and went to bed, alone. Where I lay for an hour, face down, pressing my aching hard-on into the mattress until sleep came.

I made my own rules.

Number one: don't sleep with her.

Number two: don't let her see how much you want to sleep with her.

Number three: no one else must know.

I was like a junkie who tells himself that smoking smack instead of shooting it will make the craving go away; only to find that when you feed the monster anything at all you simply make it stronger.

I kept the photographs from the crime scene, the ones in which Ros and Jo were topless. I kept them in my desk, in the bottom drawer, where an alcoholic keeps his vodka and his mouthwash. I looked at her sweet body a dozen times a day, and after a while I didn't even see her. It was just something I did, as automatic and as meaningless as a genuflection in church.

Barristers in court are fond of talking about the jigsaw of evidence, of the pieces that slowly build up to make a complete picture. Maybe, with the benefit of hindsight, it can be made to look like that. At the time, it's more chaotic. It's more like a blizzard – an information blizzard – with no clue as to which tiny flake out of the thousands swirling around you will turn out to be the one that's really significant. What did it mean that on the night Jo was killed two other women were attacked, in different parts of London, but managed to fight off their attackers? Well, statistically, two attempted sex attacks in a city of five million wasn't unusual, so it probably meant nothing at all. But the possibility of a link still had to be investigated and eliminated. What did it mean that there were only five wine glasses instead of six in Jo and Ros's flat? Probably nothing. We all break wine glasses and don't replace them. On the other hand, it might indicate that their attacker took a glass away with him – in which case, we might be looking at someone they knew well enough to offer a drink to. What did it mean that, on the night in question, a known sex offender living in a halfway hostel at a North London psychiatric unit had stormed off into the night and not been seen for four hours? What did it mean that the cuts on Ros's back were so small and so controlled? What did it mean that the Forensic Science Service had distinguished DNA traces from at least eighteen different men in the Broadhurst Terrace flat, of whom eight were still unaccounted for?

And all the time, the clock is ticking. For thirty-one days, you can throw money at an investigation. You can order searches and initiate forensic analyses and commission expert opinions. After thirty-one days, the received wisdom is that you're probably throwing good money after bad.

After a while, the blizzard stops anyway. There are just a few flakes now, falling randomly out of the sky. They're easier to catch, these single flakes, but that doesn't mean they're any more or less significant than those that fell before, during the deluge.

So, after a while, you stop catching snowflakes and you start going backwards, digging through all the information you've already got, looking for the bits you missed first time around. But it still isn't a jigsaw. It's just a mess of facts and loose ends.

And still, sometimes, none of it fits.

Gradually, though, tiny fragments of evidence were starting to accumulate around Gerry Henson. The lad who delivered the pizza remembered seeing a car like Henson's parked near the flat. He couldn't remember the number, but of the five hundred or so silver Porsches registered to London addresses, none was registered to Broadhurst Terrace. A lead from Ros led to the discovery that Jo had undergone a termination earlier that year. Had the relationship between Jo and Henson been going through a difficult patch? Had Ros persuaded Jo to dump him? Is that what triggered the attack?

Henson had no previous convictions for violence, but his company had lost a case two years previously for unfair dismissal. We went to talk to the employee, a woman called Jill Fresca. She told us that Henson had made a pass at her, and fired her when she'd made it clear she wasn't interested. She described him as a flash bastard, a bully, who ruled his company through fear and preyed on attractive women.

We decided it was time to rattle Mr Henson's cage. So we invited him, by letter, to attend Paddington Green to give an urgent forensic sample. No explanation was given.

As I'd expected, we got a phone call from a brief. A very expensive brief, from a firm of solicitors in Lincolns Inn Fields who were so damn upmarket their phone number was ex-directory. The brief wanted to confirm that the sample was purely for elimination purposes. I said it was, but that we would also be questioning Mr Henson further about his movements.

I gave instructions that he was to be given the whole forensic circus. He was taken to an examination suite and asked to remove his clothes. Swabs were taken from his mouth, blood from his arm, hairs from his head and his groin. Finally, he was asked to provide a sample of sperm. He refused, as I had anticipated he would, but it was an angry and humiliated man who faced me across the interview table afterwards.

'Three weeks ago you were visited by myself and asked to make a statement about your movements on the night of the eleventh of July,' I said. 'And that statement was accurate, full and truthful.' I paused, waiting for him to agree. It's the oldest trick in the book when you're about to confront a suspect with a discrepancy in their statement. First of all, you get them to defend the lie they've already told.

But Henson, or his brief, was cleverer than that. He simply waited.

His brief said, 'That isn't a question, Detective Inspector.'

'Was the statement you made accurate?'

'No,' Henson said.

The solicitor opened her briefcase. 'My client has prepared a revised statement.'

'Wait a minute. Are you telling me that you lied to me when I came to your house?'

'My client has subsequently remembered more details and is volunteering them in an effort to assist the investigation.'

I took the statement and read it. Henson now admitted that as well as being at the girls' flat in the afternoon, he had stayed there until the evening. But he had left them well before midnight and returned to his car, going straight home.

'And the reason you didn't tell me this at the time was . . . ?'

'As you know, my client had been having an affair with one of the girls in the flat,' the solicitor said smoothly. She was a well-dressed, elegant woman who looked as if she would be more at home discussing skiing trips and opera than her client's sex life. 'The prospect of having to tell his wife made him anxious to remove himself from the investigation as quickly as possible. He accepts that he made a mistake.'

'Why did your wife confirm that you were there when you weren't?'

'She was mistaken.' It was the longest sentence he'd spoken since the beginning of the interview.

'Really? Or did you go home, collect the things you needed for the assault, and then go back to the flat?'

'That's ridiculous,' he said coldly.

'Did you know that Jo had had a termination?'

'No.'

'She had a termination at the Pregnancy Advisory Service in Montagu Street at twelve forty-five on the fourteenth of June.'

He stared at me.

'You must have known,' I said, 'because you visited the flat after her death and removed, among various other items, a quantity of baby clothes.'

'They were a present for my godson. Jo chose them for me.'

'What's this godson's name?'

'Joshua Elias Richards. His father is one of my best customers.'

'We've been told that you asked Jo to marry you. Is that true?'

'That's hearsay,' interjected the solicitor.

'Perhaps, but as we're not in court your client surely won't mind answering the question.'

The brief said to him, 'You don't have to.'

Henson leaned back in his chair and stared at me arrogantly. 'It's all right. The answer is no. I never asked Jo to marry me.'

'Did you tell Ros Taylor that you had?'

'No. If she says I did, she's making it up.'

I looked into his eyes. We both knew he was lying.

I said, 'I don't have any more questions. You've told me everything I need to know.'

He smiled, and stood up. As the two of them left the interview room I saw Henson reach his arm around the solicitor's back to indicate that she should go first. His fingers brushed the small of her back, casually, just above her bottom. She didn't react. It was the kind of familiar gesture a lover makes, and it was made for my benefit. But it occurred to me that Henson had not been wise if he was mixing business with pleasure. Soon he was going to be very dependent on that solicitor.

20

The second oldest trick in the policeman's armoury is misdirection. We had never expected that the interview with Henson would produce any evidence. What it did do, however, was get him out of the house so that we could interview his wife again. I'd wanted to do it myself, but Collier had pulled rank.

'There's a time for charm and sympathy,' he said, 'and there's a time for scaring the shit out of someone. This is the latter.'

He came back in a jubilant mood. 'The god of small things is starting to smile on us.' He tossed the statement on my desk. 'Take a look at page two.' He stabbed a finger on the paragraph he wanted me to read:

> Earlier in the evening I had consumed several gin and tonics. It is possible that I fell asleep. When I woke up it was dark. I went upstairs to bed. I was awoken by my husband coming to bed much later. When I first spoke to an investigating officer I may inadvertently have given the impression that I was more definite about the time my husband returned than is actually the case. He could have returned any time between midnight and five a.m.

I looked down at the signatures. It was all kosher, signed by Caroline Henson and DS Collier on each page. 'How the hell did you get her to say all that?'

'Read on. It gets better.'

> I knew that my husband was seeing someone. He has a high sex drive and I believe there have been many occasions during our marriage when he has been unfaithful. He also goes to prostitutes. I know this from his credit card statement, which is sent to him here

and which I sometimes open without his knowledge. I do not recognize the name Jo McCourt but all the usual signs were there. Sometimes I smelt her perfume on his hair. The only thing that surprised me was that it was the same perfume on more than one occasion. My husband is not usually interested in relationships.

'You told her about Jo,' I said. It was the obvious way to shake her, of course. 'How did she take it?'

'Rather well. She cried, of course, and then she talked.' Collier smacked his fat hands together. 'And now I need a celebratory drink. I think I might even be buying.'

We had removed all the obstacles which said it couldn't be Henson. But we were a long way from saying that it *was* him. I was reluctant to put Ros through a reconstruction, but there's no doubt that when your biggest problem is one of identification, a public appeal often produces leads. Griffin also thought re-enacting the events of that night might help Ros recover her memory.

'Frankly,' he said to me, 'it's a bit of a puzzle that she hasn't remembered more. The effects of the GHB will have worn off long ago, and the memories should have started returning soon after. I'm starting to wonder if there's a deliberate repression – if she's not remembering because deep down she doesn't want to remember.'

'Is there a chance the memories will never come back?'

'Hard to say. I'd imagine that something, some day, will trigger at least a partial flashback, either because it's a similar set of circumstances, like this reconstruction, or because she's under stress of some kind.'

'She's already under stress.'

'She's tougher than she looks. A lot of people who'd been through what she has would simply fall apart. She's coping remarkably well.'

I nodded. Griffin picked up a pen and said casually, 'And how about you?'

'What?'

'How are you coping?'

I stared at him. 'What do you mean?'

'It's just that one or two people have mentioned to me that you're under quite a lot of pressure yourself at the moment.'

I felt a red flash of anger, though I held myself rigid. 'Who?'

He waved the pen dismissively. 'That doesn't really matter, does it?'

'Well, I'm fine.'

'Can I ask you a question?'

I shrugged.

'Are you as good at your job as you used to be?'

I hadn't expected that to be the question. I didn't answer.

'Please understand, I'm not making any comment on whether you are good at your job or not,' he said quickly. 'I just want to know what *you* think.'

'Well,' I said reluctantly, 'it's been difficult lately. We've had some stickers. Some people think I let them down over the Merrily Brown thing.' I rubbed my hand over my face. 'I broke ranks, I suppose. Now everyone's watching me. And Collier – he thinks I've lost it.' The words came out without my meaning them to, surprising me. But I knew as I said them that it was true. 'Whenever there's any real police work to be done, he keeps me away from it.' Like interviewing Caroline Henson. 'He thinks I'm too soft.'

'Or perhaps he thinks you're good. So good that he wants to make sure he still gets some of the glory himself.'

I shook my head. 'No. I'm not like the rest of them – not as hard. That's what they all think.'

'What do *you* think?' Griffin asked gently.

I didn't answer for a moment. Then I said, 'I carry the badge. But deep down, I'm not really one of them.'

'You got a commendation last year, I understand.'

'That's right,' I said reluctantly.

'How did that happen?'

'I shot someone. An armed man who had a hostage.'

'That was a brave thing to do.'

'Not really.' I struggled to explain. 'When the adrenalin's pumping, you do things you'd never do normally. You don't think. You just react.'

He said gently, 'Are you familiar with the term "burn-out", Bill?'

179

I shrugged.

'People will tell you that there's no such thing. But I've been around the police for seven years now, and I've seen countless cases. And it always starts the same way – a vague feeling that you're faking it, while everyone else is the real thing. A feeling that sooner or later, you're going to be found out.' He paused. 'And the more you doubt yourself, the more you compensate by trying to live up to the image other people have of you. Which just widens the gap even further.'

'So you think I'm too soft.'

He sighed. 'I didn't say that. What I am saying, though, is that you might need to stop pushing yourself to be perfect.'

Oh, I thought, if only you knew. If only you knew.

When I asked Ros to come away with me I made it absolutely clear that this wasn't to be a dirty weekend. Quite the opposite: I thought that if I could spend some time with her, get to know her as a person, she might stop being the pliant, pornographic cipher of my fantasies. I made it clear to her that I could never have the sort of furtive, duplicitous relationship Gerry Henson had tried to have with Jo. What we had was more like friendship. Even if I hadn't been a copper, she was a rape victim and needed me to be in control of my baser instincts. I was actually quite proud of the fact that I was succeeding. My relationship with Ros seemed like the one pure, untainted thing I had achieved.

They came for little Daniel Mazola one Monday after school. Three men, one white and two black – the witnesses were clear on that point, though there was little else they agreed on. They pulled up next to him in a white builder's van, slid open the side door, and bundled him into the back before anyone realized what was happening. Daniel had been moved to a new school, and a new home, on an estate out in Barking. He hadn't had time to make new friends and as a consequence he was walking home alone. From the absence of a crime scene we think, although we can't be sure, that what happened to him next probably took place inside the van, possibly while they drove up the motorway, so that the sound of other cars would have drowned out the noise – the white van shows up on several traffic cameras along the route. There wouldn't have been much room to swing their baseball bats. I imagine three men, in that confined space, gripping the bats halfway down their length in order to make the blows short and accurate. At some point a belt was placed round his neck and tightened, presumably to restrain him. And finally, they laid him down and knelt on his arms while they crushed his windpipe with one of the bats. Then they turned round and drove back to the Macclesfield estate where Sheena had died, and they dragged his body onto a rubbish dump before they torched the van. And the Macclesfield estate – which like all estates normally emits a constant quiet chorus of whispers and mutterings, low-level intelligence passed on in pubs or offered up to constables by friendly miscreants – suddenly went as silent as a broken television set.

'They've got a copper,' I told Collier. 'It's the only explanation. Finding Merrily or Sheena was one thing – they were their girls, they knew where they worked. This kid was under our protection, for Christ's sake. Only a copper could have told them where to find him.'

'That is not a conclusion we may yet allow ourselves to leap at,' Collier intoned. 'Daniel may have got lonely and phoned one of his old mates for a natter. He may have been careless in an internet chat room. His new school might have requested a report from his old one. It may even have been a random attack by one of the marauding gangs of child molesters our tabloid papers are warning us of.'

'You know I'm right. It was you who told me not to put Merrily Brown on the register.'

Collier scratched his nose. 'True. But it's not as simple as bent coppers, Bill. Sixty per cent of the people who work in this station aren't even police officers. Maybe one of the secretaries has a boyfriend who likes a recreational toot at weekends. Maybe one of the cleaners came across a file that hadn't been locked away. Maybe Daniel's social worker had her handbag stolen. Just because the system leaks like a sieve, it doesn't mean it's corrupt. When choosing between cock-up and conspiracy, go for cock-up every time. Besides, it's not your investigation now. You've got enough on your plate.'

But I was not so detached from Operation Mansion that I

didn't hear how it finished. The word came down from on high: forget the brothers. Too many unsolved murders makes us look incompetent. It is not an efficient use of our resources. If it isn't the brothers selling crack it'll be someone else, so why not let them get on with it? Why harass them further if it causes the deaths of yet more innocent citizens?

I argued with that decision. I may have raised my voice. I may have picked up a telephone and hurled it across the room. And Collier sat there very patiently and explained the Real World to me without raising his own voice once, which was good of him because we both knew that no matter how much I shouted at him, the decision was not his to make or unmake and he could have just said, 'Live with it.'

As a consequence of all that, I almost missed the plane to Ireland. I made it to the airport by the skin of my teeth. Ros talked us onto the flight and she did some silly game with a hair that got us upgraded, and I could see that for once she was bubbling with excitement and happiness at the prospect of going away. I pretended nothing was wrong and as soon as I could I took off my horrible police-issue tie and I stuffed it down the back of the seat pocket, between the in-flight magazine and the instructions for an emergency landing.

And then there was Ireland.

A different country, and a different world. We were staying in a country hotel, and the old boy who owned it was a wonderful Irish rogue, who despite being at least sixty and under the watchful eye of his wife flirted outrageously with Ros over dinner, telling her what a lovely young thing she was and how if he was forty years younger he'd be giving me a run for my money – 'Jaysus, what am I saying? If I was only four years younger I'd have a damn good try.' And Ros loved the old bastard and his bogus charm, and basked in the attention. I'd only ever seen her in casual clothes, jeans and T-shirts and her lab coat and the awful shapeless sportswear the rape suite dished out, but that night she was wearing a black dress with a scoop neck that hung forward from her shoulders as if she was half-undressed already, and a chain necklace that fell into the dip between her little breasts like a plumbline. By the end of the meal even the two awful old queers who were our fellow guests were starting to make eyes at her. I felt a sudden hot flash of jealousy. The thought of her in her underwear was like a dirty video, powerful and shocking and forbidden. The way her breasts moved in my imagination as she took off her dress for me gave me a hard-on under the table. As soon as I could I dragged her away, down to the pub at the other end of the village, where I drank too much in an effort to calm myself down. If she had given me any sign, any encouragement at all, I would have made a pass, but she didn't and eventually I managed to get myself under control. Apart from anything else, the return flights were booked and we'd have to stay together all weekend however awkward it became. I told myself we were having a good time and it would be stupid to spoil it.

When we finally went back to the hotel I managed to get into my own room without falling on her, though the touch of her lips on my cheek when she kissed me goodnight seemed to throb for minutes afterwards. I couldn't sleep. I waited half an hour and then I thought, fuck this, I just need to talk to her. I went out into the corridor in my pyjamas and knocked softly on her door. There was no reply. I knocked a little louder, but either she was asleep or she knew better than to let drunken coppers into her room in the middle of the night.

The next day the weather was perfect and the fish were biting. At lunchtime I took her to another pub and sat quietly with her while she talked. She told me about her family, and her dead father, the first time she'd ever done that, and I tried to explain about the Harkur brothers and how all the women I'd been meant to protect had died. I was just thinking that we had done it, that I was over the worst and that a good friendship like this was better than any amount of bad sex, when she told me that she wanted to go to bed with me.

There was never any question of saying no. Everything I'd told myself beforehand suddenly counted for nothing.

When we went to bed it was nothing like I had imagined it, of course. Ros naked was beautiful in different ways from those I had expected. Her body, whiter now than it was in the photographs in my desk. The imprint her walking socks had left on her ankles, a bracelet of ridges that I traced with my fingertips. The faint taste of fish scales when I sucked her fingers. The kisses I planted on her belly, like a series of tiny flags. And then, finally, when I could bear it no longer, the sweet warmth inside her.

'Stop for a moment,' she said, and for perhaps half a minute we lay there, not moving, until I couldn't bear it any longer and I started to move again, tentatively at first and then with more and more urgency. I reminded myself that I was the first man to be inside her since the rapist, and I tried to hold back. I waited until she started to come herself, and then I finally hurled myself over the cliff.

Afterwards she lay nestled into me, her back against my front, and I found myself looking at the cuts on her back. They had faded now, a tiny series of white almost-scars. Her shoulder blades were as flat as a butterfly's wings. I traced the scars with my fingers, and kissed them, and then we did it all again.

That weekend we crammed a year's worth of lovemaking into a couple of days. Unspoken between us was the knowledge that one weekend might be all we had; that when we got back to England everything could be back to the way it was before.

21

The breakthrough was a description to *Crimewatch* from a caller who had been in Broadhurst Terrace in the small hours of the morning, several hours after Henson said he had been at home. The man he saw matched Henson's description and had been carrying a black bin liner over his shoulder. Unfortunately the caller, a man named Billy Mallows, was – as they say in court – known to the police; so well known, in fact, as a consequence of his many convictions for 'going equipped', that he exchanged Christmas cards with the local CID. It was precisely because Billy had suspected that the man he saw on the opposite side of the street was a fellow housebreaker that he had scrutinized him so carefully.

Billy was a congenial villain of the old school – no guns, no drugs, no violence unless absolutely necessary – but he was also one of the blunter tools in the box and there was no way we were going to put up a case based on his testimony alone. It meant, however, that we were able to arrange an ID parade and, when Billy picked Henson out, arrest him and organize a forensic search of Henson's house.

The two-week wait for lab results was agonizing. By now we were pretty sure we'd got our man, a suspicion that was confirmed when Henson's arrest finally propelled the case into the papers and a young artist called Kate Blake got in touch with us. Kate was initially a hesitant, nervous voice on the phone, saying that she wasn't sure how relevant it was but did we know that this wasn't the first time Henson had been involved in something like this. I assured her that it was extremely relevant and persuaded her to come in for a chat. She was a scruffy, pretty young woman, very quietly spoken but very clear about what had happened. Five years previously she had been at Goldsmiths College, showing her work in her degree show. Henson had visited, which had caused quite a buzz as he was known as one of the handful of really serious collectors who, simply by purchasing a work, could make a young artist's reputation. She had been flattered to discover that he was apparently interested in her exhibits, and accepted an invitation to go to dinner at Claridge's to discuss it. She hadn't thought it odd that he had booked a bedroom as well as a table, and accepted an invitation to have a drink there before dinner. As she was telling me all this I was thinking that she had probably been quite naive at that age – even now she had a rather innocent quality. But Henson had taken it for granted that she would have sex with him. He had forced himself on her, and she hadn't been able to stop him. Unfortunately she hadn't reported it to the police at the time, but, taken together with the employee who had already come forward, a pattern was definitely starting to emerge.

When Ros's blood and DNA were found on one of the shirts taken from Henson's house, the investigation entered a new phase. Now we were tying up loose ends, ruling out scenarios, however bizarre, that the defence might suggest to the jury. It was hard work. But we made good progress and for the first time since the death of Merrily Brown I began to feel that what I was doing was not a complete waste of time.

Not long after Henson was arrested I got a call from Ros. I had been holed up in the incident room for over five hours, going through statements and paperwork, arguing about budgets, fending off raiding parties from other investigating officers in search of man hours, spare overtime, unused budgets. They say that a detective spends sixty per cent of his time doing paperwork. That day it seemed like an underestimate.

She said without preamble, 'I think someone's been going through my rubbish.'

'How do you know?'

'The contractors send someone round to put the bags out on the pavement before the van comes. This morning I saw that one of the bags had been opened. It was definitely mine. It had some stuff in that I recognized.'

'Maybe it was just an accident. The bag might have ripped when it was picked up.'

'It wasn't ripped. The knot had been unpicked.'

'Are you quite sure you knotted it?'

'Quite sure. Bill, I think Henson may have got someone spying on me.'

'Why do you say that? Apart from the rubbish, I mean.'

There was a long pause. 'I don't know,' she admitted. 'I just feel it.'

Alarm suddenly trickled down my spine. 'Ros, what phone are you calling me on?'

'Not my mobile, if that's what you're thinking.'

'Good. Look, if Henson has got a private detective going through your rubbish he'll be looking for drugs paraphernalia, condoms, anything they can use to discredit you. If there's anything like that, take it to work and get rid of it there instead.'

'There's nothing like that.'

I tried to think. Had I left anything at the flat? I didn't think so. Thank God we'd been careful.

'I need to see you again,' she said softly.

'That's not possible. If there's someone watching—'

'We could go to a hotel.'

Instantly I felt myself react. Blood surged into my groin. Chemicals surged into my brain. 'It's too risky,' I said weakly.

'We could go to Heathrow. There are dozens of hotels, and no one in them except international businessmen. I'll book a room for this evening.'

Scenes from Ireland flashed in front of my eyes.

'I can be there by three,' I said.

She was sitting in the lobby, reading a newspaper and having coffee. I slipped into the chair opposite her. She looked at me. 'Yes? Can I help you?'

For a moment I actually thought she'd lost her memory again. Then her eyes glinted, and I saw it was just a game.

'You looked as if you might need company,' I said, trying to play along.

She shrugged. 'I've got nine hours before my flight. So yes, I suppose some company would be acceptable. If you think you can be more interesting than my newspaper.'

'Are you on your own?' I said.

'Not any more.' She picked up her coffee cup and did something filthy with the tip of her tongue and the cappuccino froth, all the time keeping her eyes fixed on me. My throat went dry.

'Do that again.'

'Do what?'

I tried a different tack. 'Ros—'

'My name's Natasha. Who's Ros?'

I was never any good at this kind of thing. 'Would you like to go upstairs with me, Natasha?'

She signalled to a waiter. 'Maybe. When I've had some lunch.'

'What can I get you?' the waiter asked as he came over.

She slipped a foot out of her shoe and slid it up my thigh under the table. 'I suddenly feel quite ravenous,' she told him. 'What do you suggest?'

'Could you give us a few minutes?' I said to the waiter. And to Ros, as soon as he had gone, I said, 'Upstairs. Come on. Right now.'

Something strange happened, in that anonymous hotel bedroom. Ros didn't want to stop playing her game. All the time I was undressing her she was still talking away, pretending to be this businesswoman waiting for a flight. And when she was finally naked, and I wanted nothing more than to start fucking her properly, she suddenly pulled away from me and said, 'I'm afraid I've changed my mind.'

'Oh,' I said, deflated.

And she smiled that same weird wicked smile she'd smiled in the lobby and, coming close so that the hard tips of her breasts pressed against my chest, she put her mouth against my ear, and whispered in her normal voice, 'It's OK. I don't really want to stop.' Her tongue, wet and thunderous, bathed my ear before she pulled away. In the hard businesswoman's voice she said, 'So you'd better go now, hadn't you?' She unzipped me and held me with both hands. 'Because I really don't feel like doing this.' She lifted up one leg and pulled the head of my cock inside her, just for a second, before she pulled away again and said, 'And that's all you're going to get.'

'Ros,' I said. 'I don't understand. What is this?'

'Natasha. My name's Natasha. Who's Ros? That's so rude, talking to me about your girlfriend.'

Her eyes laughed at me as she stood up and danced away around the bed. I understood now. She wanted me to chase her. And when I'd caught her, and pulled her onto the bed, she lay supine, and I thought the game was finally over until I found her legs rigid, closed together, and she whispered, *Force me.* All the connotations and the implications of that phrase suddenly meant nothing. I did what she wanted. I held her down with one hand and with the other I pushed one knee up against her chest to let me into her. I fucked her savagely, shunting her up on the bed with every push. She laughed delightedly, and then she closed her eyes and screwed her face up so that I couldn't tell if she was getting any pleasure out of it or not.

'What was all that about?' I asked afterwards.

'It was only a game,' she said. She rolled over so that I couldn't see her face. 'Don't take everything so seriously. It was just a game.'

But we both knew that she was lying.

The meeting with the CPS took place at their offices in Harding Street. From our side there was Collier and myself and Cathy, to go through the evidence. From theirs there was a whole gang of eager, bright-eyed civil servants, fast track written all over them, which should have alerted me that something was up. They'd taken the precaution of bringing along counsel, Nick Hawthorne, a young barrister grown sleek and plump on CPS fees.

They listened without comment as we went through the case against Henson. At last we had finished, and there was an awkward silence. Hawthorne was the first to speak.

'What is his motive?'

Collier and I exchanged glances. We had just spent the best part of fifty minutes explaining exactly why we thought Henson had done it.

'Rejection,' I said simply. 'He couldn't take no for an answer.'

The CPS solicitor, a career civil servant called Derek Berry, said, 'So he's not a danger to the public.'

'In the sense that he's not about to go on a serial raping spree, no,' I said evenly. 'In the sense that he *is* a threat to any woman who says no to him in the future, then yes, he's undoubtedly a danger to the public.' I was beginning to suspect now where this was heading. 'A prosecution is definitely in the public interest.'

Hawthorne shrugged and made a note on his pad. 'Then let us consider whether it's likely to succeed.' He pulled his notes towards him. 'We have evidence from a friendly burglar, who the defence will obviously claim has been offered inducements by the police. We have unsubstantiated allegations from a past employee, Miss Fresca, who profited handsomely from her allegations and who in any case will probably be excluded under the similar fact rules. We have another girl, Miss Blake, who now alleges an assault she didn't think worth reporting at the time. We have evidence from the wife, but it simply places the accused away from home at some point on the evening of the murder, and by her own admission she had been drinking heavily and is therefore hardly reliable. We have forensic evidence which suggests intercourse between one victim and the accused, although the victim herself is unable to explain what happened as she is suffering from amnesia. We have evidence that suggests both victims were hardly paragons of virtue – we have drugs, we have affairs with married men, we have wild parties, we have topless photographs. The one thing we don't have, it seems to me, is a reasonable chance of conviction.'

They looked at me.

'Cases have come to court on less evidence than this,' I said doggedly.

'And been lost,' Berry said, smoothing his tie. 'We have a target, Detective Inspector, as I'm sure you know. We are committed to winning sixty per cent of our cases.'

'You've got a good chance of winning this one, surely.'

'Ah, but unfortunately, our batting average is running a bit lower than sixty. Around forty per cent, in fact. So we need to be – well, what's the maths? About eighty, is it? Eighty per cent, something like that?' No one helped him. 'Anyway, we need to be pretty damn sure we're going to win any cases we put up between now and the end of the fiscal year,' he finished.

I felt myself getting angry. 'I thought your job was to prosecute, for God's sake, not to find reasons to give up.'

'Actually, our job is to get convictions,' one of the bright-eyed graduates said.

'We're also seven point two million over budget,' Berry said apologetically. 'Not that it's about money, of course.'

'And Henson has the resources to drag this out into a marathon,' the graduate said. 'It'll be a high-profile case, and if we lose it our reputation scores will go down even more.'

There was a pause. 'So that's it,' I said flatly. 'It's because he's rich and you don't think you can beat him.' Beside me, Collier put a warning hand on my arm.

'Of course not,' Berry said. 'But we have a duty to take all the factors into consideration.'

'All right,' I said, lifting my hands off the table, acknowledging defeat. 'Let the bastard go. Just don't dial 999 if it's your wife he rapes next time.'

In the lift I said to Collier, 'I notice you're not saying much.'

He sighed. 'It's all a question of expectations, William. I've never expected them to be any damn use, so I've never been disappointed. It's different for you. You could have been one of them, so you're that much more pissed off when they let you down. Come on, let's find a pub.'

By nine o'clock I was staggering out of a taxi into the corner shop below my flat. Old Ranjiv was behind the counter. Probably giving his son a night off with his family. I nodded to him and he smiled back happily. He gave me small gifts occasionally, once he'd discovered I was police: Indian sweets, pistachio nuts, chocolate. Mind you, I was probably one of his best customers. Proper supermarkets were closed by the time I got back from work.

As I rummaged through the freezer cabinet for something to microwave I had a brief mental picture of how different my life could be if I was living with Ros. There would be food that didn't come out of a box. Talk that didn't come out of a television. Sex that didn't come out of a magazine or one of Ranjiv's top-shelf videos.

I had absolutely no idea how I was going to tell her about Henson.

I heard a crash from the front of the shop and looked to see what was happening. Two teenage girls had come into the shop and were now trying it on. One of them had pushed the rack of lottery cards off the counter onto the floor, so that the old man was more or less penned in, while her mate grabbed as many bottles of vodka as she could, which wasn't many. She got one in each hand and a third one shattered on the floor. Old Ranjiv was shouting and the girls took off up the road with me after them. They were young and surprisingly fast but they kept looking at each other, trying to work out where the other one was going, which slowed them down a bit. I shouted, 'Police – stop,' which had about as much effect as I'd expected it to have. After a hundred yards or so they did the sensible thing and split up. I followed the girl with the bottles. No point in getting a body but no evidence. There was an estate further up the road, a typical sixties mess of dirty tower blocks, and I knew that once she got in there I'd have to give up. Not because I wouldn't be able to catch her, but because I had no idea who might be waiting for her and what they might be armed with. But either the girl was more panicked than she'd looked or she didn't know the estate as well as her friend. She turned up an alleyway which turned out to be exactly that – an alley that led to some garages, with no way out. She only had one bottle now, I noticed. She must have chucked the other one. She stopped, and turned to me, bending over and leaning her free hand on her knee, for all the world like a jogger who was out of breath and had stopped for a rest. She tried to smile at me. I was too tired and breathless to recite a caution straight away so I stopped too, a few yards away.

'You're not really filth, are you?' she gasped.

''Fraid so.'

'Shit. Fancy a blow job?' She moved towards me and at the last moment swung the bottle at my face. It was a pathetic attempt. I caught it in my hand. She laughed nervously, as if to say she'd only been joking.

I thought, if I let her go, that old Indian will never forgive me.

But if I took her in, I'd be at the station all night. She was probably under sixteen. I'd have to book her in, fill in all the forms, then wait at least two hours for an appropriate adult to turn up. I'd statement her, charge her, eventually appear in court, all for a bottle of vodka.

I twisted the bottle out of her hand and threw it as far as I could off to my right. I heard it shatter on the concrete.

She misunderstood. She laughed breathlessly and reached for my trousers. I felt her hands groping me, squeezing my hips, rubbing the front of my crotch. I pulled her towards me by the shoulders and brought my knee up, hard, into her stomach. She sagged in my arms with a sound like air coming out of a tyre valve. I punched her in the same place and spun her round by her neck. As she fell to the ground I kicked her, hard, up the backside, with another one in her ribs for good measure.

'Don't go back to that shop,' I told her. 'And if I ever see you again, I'll nick you.'

She lay on the ground, gasping for breath. She was trying to cry but she was too winded. All that came out was a little mewing sound.

I turned round. Old Ranjiv was standing at the end of the alleyway, watching me. I walked straight past him. He didn't say anything.

It was me who was responsible for the lie. I want to make that absolutely clear.

I went to Ros and told her about Henson.

She said, 'But are you certain he did it?'

'Totally certain. Ros, it's true that sometimes there are charges you're not sure about, suspects who are suspects simply because they were hanging around at the time of the crime, or they have a previous conviction for a similar offence. This isn't like that. It has to be someone who knew you. Henson was there and he had a motive. The clincher is the forensic evidence.'

She was silent for a moment. 'What if there was a way of getting the forensic evidence in front of a jury?'

'What do you mean?'

'I could tell the CPS that I remember him being there. And I could say that he got angry with Jo when she dumped him.'

'Ros, you can't—'

'And then, once the trial is under way, I could refuse to give evidence. They couldn't back out then, it would be too late. The jury could make up their own minds.'

I said, 'It's a good plan. But it won't work. The defence would say that you'd pulled out because you knew he didn't do it. It would look worse than if you'd never come forward.'

'It's unfair, isn't it? We have to tell the truth, and they're allowed to tell as many lies as they like.'

'Yes. It's very unfair.'

She said, 'So I'd have to tell the court I remember Henson raping me. That wouldn't be a lie, would it? He did rape me. It'll be the truth. It's just that I can't remember it.'

I felt everything slipping away from me. 'Ros. Think what would happen – if you just got tripped up on some tiny point, some discrepancy between what you said and the forensic evidence.'

'But you can tell me what to say. You can show me all the forensic evidence. There'd be nothing to trip me up on.'

I rubbed my face in my hands. 'It's dangerous. If you were caught, you'd go to prison. Think of that, Ros. Henson would be a free man, and you'd be in prison.'

'But I owe it to Jo,' she said simply.

I said nothing. I didn't care about Jo, not really.

'Don't you see,' she was saying, and her eyes had that same shining intensity they'd had when she was pretending to be someone else in the hotel that time. 'I've been so frustrated because I couldn't *do* anything. I've been a pathetic little victim. Now I can actually do something to help. I've always been good at keeping a straight face. No one will ever know.'

I thought, she needs to close this. If Henson does get put away, she'll have a chance to put it all behind her.

And, if I'm honest, I thought about me as well. If she lied, and Henson went down, I'd have won. I'd have beaten the pen-pushers at the CPS, and the people who caused the deaths of Merrily Brown and Sheena Mast and Daniel Mazola. And, though they'd never know it, I'd have beaten the station whisperers and the canteen cowboys who thought I was useless because I'd told an Incident Review Board that someone had called Augustus Bart a black bastard.

She said, 'It's up to you. If you tell me to do it, I'll do it. If you think it's wrong, I won't.'

'Let's sleep on it,' I said.

That night we made love slowly and gently and tenderly, and it was Ros again, the real Ros, not Natasha. But in the dark, where these conversations are easier, I whispered something to her, and when I woke up in the morning she was gone, and the sheet was dotted with brown stains, the colour of a bitten apple left in the sun.

3

ROS

There are no truths, only interpretations.

– Nietzsche

22

'Ros Taylor?'

'Yes.'

'They're ready for you now.'

The usher held the door open and waited for me to follow her. Her shoes clacked on the wooden floor. I wanted her to walk faster, but she seemed determined to proceed with ceremonial slowness and I could hardly overtake her.

At last she held open the door to the courtroom, where a second usher was waiting for me. Heads turned to look at me as I made my way towards the witness box. Like a bride making an entrance at her wedding, I thought, with the usher as my bridesmaid and the judge on his raised platform waiting for me like a priest.

As I mounted the steps I felt a little dizzy. Then before I knew it the usher was telling me to hold the Bible and did I swear to tell the whole truth and nothing but the truth.

I did.

One of the QCs got to his feet. He was wearing a black robe and an old grey wig the colour of cooked cauliflower. That would be Nick Hawthorne, the prosecuting counsel. Across from him I saw an elegant-looking woman sitting at a table covered in bundles of paper tied up with pink ribbons. I guessed that must be Elizabeth Bishop, Henson's QC. Her wig was smaller than the male lawyers'. It made her look pert and feisty, like a girl playing a boy's part in a pantomime. It was clever of Henson's legal team, I thought, to choose a female barrister. The jury might think a woman couldn't possibly represent a man accused of rape unless she thought he was innocent.

Court number seven resembled a larger, sleepier version of the anonymous hotel room near Heathrow where Bill and I had sneaked off occasionally during the investigation to make love: pale wooden furniture, padded seats in institutional blue, a somnolent air of dust and furniture polish. The only distraction from the oppressive blandness was the brightly coloured plaque of the lion and the unicorn that dominated one wall. It looked out of place, as if a Travelodge had decided to brighten up its reception with a gaudy knick-knack from an antique shop. But perhaps the neutral colours and soothing civic furniture were deliberate: an attempt to leach the drama out of the cases that were tried here, to reduce horrific crimes to something more manageable.

The jury stared at me curiously. No doubt they were looking forward to hearing all the gory details, even if they hadn't yet decided whether Henson had done it or not. They looked stupid and unimpressive, the sort of random disconnected group you might find hanging around a bus stop. A couple of men were wearing cheap grey suits. Another, a thin intense-looking young man with glasses, was in a T-shirt. There were a pair of cycle clips on the ledge in front of him. A very broad man who looked like a builder sat in an open-necked red shirt with the sleeves rolled up, exposing huge forearms which he had crossed over his chest. There was a middle-aged woman with a brooch pinned to her cashmere sweater who looked as if the toughest decision she'd ever had to make was whether she'd left her cats enough food. There was an Indian woman in a bright red sari. I didn't have time to look at the others.

'Would you state your name please?' Hawthorne was saying. He smiled at me reassuringly. He had a very pronounced upper lip: it folded over his lower lip in a fleshy W, like a soft beak. Together with his tubby face, it made him look like a naughty overgrown choirboy.

'My name is Ros Taylor.'

'And your occupation?'

'I'm a laboratory assistant.'

'What are your qualifications, Miss Taylor?'

'I have an DPhil in organic chemistry.'

'So you are in fact a highly qualified scientist.' He emphasized the word *scientist*, just a little, and turned to look at the jury to make sure that they had noted that I was an objective, dis-passionate truth-teller by profession, and not some screaming, neurotic arts graduate.

'Yes.' For the first time I sneaked a glance at the dock. I was shocked by how handsome Gerry looked. He didn't look like a rapist. He was wearing an impeccable Italian suit, and he seemed relaxed and interested in what I was saying.

'Prior to the events of last July, did you have any history of amnesia or any other medical problems, Miss Taylor?'

'None whatsoever.'

'And how long had you known Jo McCourt?'

'We had been friends for five years.'

'You shared a flat together, at 27 Broadhurst Terrace?'

'That's right.'

'And did a man regularly visit her at that address between the months of February and July?'

'Yes.'

'Who was that?'

'Gerry Henson.'

'Did she know that he was married?'

'Objection, my lord.' That was Henson's QC, who had risen to her feet and was bowing to the judge.

Hawthorne inclined his head politely in her direction. To me he said, 'I should have said, did *you* know he was married?'

'Yes. He never made a secret of it.'

'Was their relationship a casual affair or something more serious?'

'Quite serious. I think he—'

Henson's QC had got to her feet again. 'My lord, the witness is being asked for her opinion. My learned friend will have ample opportunity to put questions about my client's relationship with Miss McCourt to him in person.'

'Quite right, Mrs Bishop.' The judge looked over his reading glasses at Hawthorne. He had a larger wig than the other legal people: it gave him the air of an amiable old sheep. 'Proceed, Mr Hawthorne, but kindly confine your questions to matters of fact.'

'My lord.'

I did not understand this game of tennis. Did Mrs Bishop's objections mean that we were doing badly, or the reverse? Was she objecting in order to limit the impact Hawthorne's questions were having? Hawthorne himself did not seem disconcerted in the least. He said, 'Did you observe them together on many occasions?'

'Yes. He was often at the flat when I got back from work.'

'Doing what?'

'Getting dressed, usually.'

There was a faint ripple of amusement around the courtroom. I stopped, surprised. I hadn't meant to be funny. Perhaps they were just bored.

Hawthorne went on, 'Were you aware of anything unusual about that side of things?'

The question hung in the air for a few moments. I was very aware that every person in the courtroom was looking at me. Hawthorne prompted, 'Did you see any signs of violence, for example?'

'My lord.' Mrs Bishop was on her feet again. She said with some exasperation, 'My learned friend is leading the witness.'

'I am seeking to establish the deceased's state of mind, my lord.'

The judge said mildly, 'Rephrase your question please, Mr Hawthorne.'

Hawthorne nodded. I got the impression that he felt he had done well, because he said quickly to me, 'Did you observe anything about their relationship which disturbed you?'

'Yes.' I explained about the curtain rail, and the candlewax, and the marks on Jo's arms. As I spoke I could see one or two members of the jury – the man with the big forearms, who I had mentally christened the Builder, and the thin intense one with the T-shirt, who I had dubbed the Cyclist – turn their heads to look at Henson. Were they thinking, you lucky bastard, I wondered? Or were they thinking that he might have done it after all?

'In the weeks before the murder you and Miss McCourt – Jo – went on holiday together, I believe?' Hawthorne was saying.

'That's right. She had been going to go with Gerry, but at the last minute he dropped out and she asked me instead.'

'I refer the court to the travel documents on page thirty-six of your bundle.' Hawthorne waited while the jury found the place. 'These confirm that Mr Gerry Henson was originally to be Miss

McCourt's travelling companion.' Then he said to me, 'How did she react when she found he couldn't go?'

'Well, she was upset at first. But later she told me that she'd been quite relieved. She thought it might have been a bit difficult.'

'And why was that?'

'I took it to mean that the relationship was coming to an end.'

'She had decided to dump him?'

'My lord.' Henson's QC was on her feet again, and this time she looked icily angry. 'The question is inviting the witness to repeat hearsay.'

'It goes to state of mind, my lord.'

'Even if it does, my learned friend is leading.'

'So he is,' the judge said drily. To Hawthorne he said, 'Perhaps the witness, rather than you, might tell the court what happened.'

Hawthorne nodded and said to me, 'How did Jo seem to you, on that holiday?'

'She seemed uneasy.'

'In what way?'

'She wasn't sure how to tell Gerry that she wanted to end it.'

'She was frightened of him?'

'My lord.' Mrs Bishop was on her feet.

'Quite right,' the judge agreed. He turned to the jury. 'Mr Hawthorne has asked a question which is clearly intended to prejudice your feelings about the defendant. I am therefore instructing you to ignore both the question and the implication behind it. For the purpose of clarity, I will repeat that there is no evidence before this court that the deceased was ever in fear of the defendant.' He glanced coolly at Hawthorne, who seemed not in the least perturbed by this ticking off. 'Proceed, Mr Hawthorne, but not with this line of questioning, if you please.'

Which was presumably what Hawthorne had intended all along, because as he must have known perfectly well, the answer to his question was actually no, and now the jury would think I had been about to say yes.

'So on the afternoon of the murder, what time did you get back to the flat?'

'About half past three.'

'Was that earlier or later than usual?'

'Earlier.'

'Was the accused there?'

For a moment the grey mist that filled my mind whenever I thought about that afternoon swirled around me. I stepped into the fog and said, 'No. Jo told me that he had phoned, and she'd finally told him—'

'Objection!' Mrs Bishop snapped.

'Miss Taylor, you may not repeat what the defendant is reported to have said,' Hawthorne said gently.

'Sorry. Gerry wasn't there, no. We got some wine and a film and had a girls' night in, just the two of us.'

'How much did you have to drink?'

'Not much. A couple of glasses each.'

'On what floor is your flat?'

'The lower ground floor. The windows look on to a paved area at the back.'

'How could someone gain access to that area?'

'From the street, if you knew how to get to it. There are steps at the side.'

'Did you ever leave the wine unattended?'

'Yes, several times, when we moved around the flat. For example, the bottle was in the kitchen while we were watching the film.'

'And of the two of you, who drank most?'

'Jo had slightly less than I did, because I finished off what was in her glass. That's when I began to feel sick.'

'You were intoxicated?'

'Yes, but not from the alcohol. I'd only had one or two glasses. I felt – out of it. Very, very tired. I went to bed and just collapsed.'

'Do you remember what happened next?'

'Not at first. The next thing I can remember is when I woke up. It was hours later – it was dark, but some of the lights were on. I felt terrible. I couldn't move. I heard someone moving. Then I realized he was in my room.'

'Who was?'

Bill and I had practised with a lie detector from a gadget shop, one you plugged into a computer. It measured stresses in the voice and tiny changes in electrical activity in the skin caused by changes in perspiration. We reasoned that if we could teach ourselves to lie to the computer, we would at least be able to lie with more confidence in court. What the machine couldn't measure, of course, were the tiny gestures or tics or nervous glances that betray us silently. That took much more practice.

The courtroom had gone very quiet. Hawthorne glanced at me, waiting for me to answer.

'Gerry,' I said calmly.

'The defendant?'

'Yes. Gerry Henson.'

It should have been a significant moment, but the truth was that I barely noticed it. I had rehearsed it and planned it for so long that it was just another version of events. And Hawthorne was pushing on with his questions, establishing a quiet, urgent rhythm.

'What did he do?'

'He pulled my clothes off and he – he got on top of me. I felt him raping me.'

'Did you move or cry out?'

'I tried to but I was completely paralysed.'

Mrs Bishop appeared to consider getting up, then changed her mind. Hawthorne pressed on.

'How could you be sure it was him?'

'I saw his face quite clearly.'

'You say he raped you. What do you mean by that?'

'I felt him penetrate me.'

'Would you like a glass of water, Miss Taylor?'

'No, I'm all right.'

'What was his manner during the rape?'

'He was violent. Very violent. He yanked me around as he did it. And afterwards he cut me.'

'The following morning, were you taken by an ambulance to a rape suite at Paddington Green police station?'

'Yes.'

'Were some of your injuries photographed by a police photographer?'

'Yes.'

'I refer the court to exhibit F12,' Hawthorne said. There was a long pause while the jury fumbled through their bundle of papers and found the photograph of my back. Mrs Brooch shot me a horrified look.

'Are these wounds that the defendant inflicted on you during the rape?' Hawthorne asked me.

'Yes.'

'What happened after he cut you?'

'I must have become unconscious again. I woke up and it was morning. I went into the bathroom and that's when I found – that's when I found Jo's body in the shower.'

'You found your flatmate murdered in the shower,' he repeated slowly.

'Yes. Then I phoned the police.'

'Did you attempt to revive her?'

I said, 'Yes. It was too late. She was completely dead. I'd like that water now, please.'

Hawthorne brought up the subject of my memory loss himself, rather than leave it to the defence.

'When did you tell the police that it was Gerry Henson who had raped you?'

'Not for some time. I had amnesia for about three weeks after the rape.'

'When you did recover your memory, how soon did you tell the police?'

'Immediately.'

'And when you reported it, were you in any doubt about the identity of the man who raped you?'

'None whatsoever.'

'Despite the interval of time, you were quite sure?'

'Yes. It was definitely him.'

'Thank you. No further questions.'

And so I lied on oath. Or rather – to use the sort of fine distinction that Nick Hawthorne might have used – I did not lie: I described a set of events which I knew to have happened. I simply omitted to tell the court that I couldn't actually remember them.

Derek Berry, one of the CPS solicitors, had taken me out to dinner, ostensibly to explain the legal procedures but actually to make a series of increasingly desperate passes. Towards the end of the dinner, when we were well into our second bottle of wine, he'd said, suddenly serious, 'You know that you will be cross-examined by Henson's QC?'

'Well, of course.'

'In theory, there are more safeguards these days – certain lines of questioning they're not allowed to take. But you should be aware that it can get quite messy. Henson's silk can only do two things, if she's going for an acquittal. She can either destroy your evidence, or she can destroy your credibility. She may even try to do both.'

'But how can she do that?'

He'd shrugged, and swirled his red wine round his glass. 'I don't know. They really don't have much of a defence, on the face of it. On the other hand, she's got nothing to lose, so she might as well try to undermine you in the cross.'

'I wish you wouldn't keep calling it the cross,' I said, half joking. 'You make it sound like a crucifixion.'

He looked at me shrewdly over his glass. 'Well, you may find the comparison rather an apt one,' he said. 'Let's hope not.' He sniffed the wine appreciatively. 'Ah. *Ça sent la merde.* Literally, a faint whiff of shit. All the best Burgundy has it. Without it, it's just a rather insipid pinot noir.' He put the glass down. 'And there's absolutely nothing you want to tell me? Nothing you'd like the chance to rehearse with me off the record, as it were?' His smooth, fleshy hand reached out and grasped my forearm.

I was quite drunk, but I wasn't that drunk. 'No,' I said, discreetly pulling my arm away. 'There's nothing.'

Now, as the regal figure of Mrs Bishop rose to begin her questioning, I felt less sure of myself.

'You've given the court an account of the day Jo McCourt was murdered,' she began. 'We'll come to that later, but first I want to take you back a little further, to the holiday – the holiday you went on in place of my client.' She picked up something from the table. 'Jo wasn't short of male company on that holiday, was she?'

'In what way?'

'I'm referring to this postcard, which arrived after her death.' She held up the card and read aloud, ' "I just wanted you to know

I will not forget you. If you would like to come to Sardinia again some day, let me know. Your friend, Mele." This was an admirer she met, I take it?'

'Yes.'

'A holiday romance?'

'Not a romance, no.'

'A flirtation, then.'

'Well, *he* flirted with *her*, yes.'

'And she allowed him to?'

'It was harmless.'

'Harmless?' she repeated. 'On that occasion, perhaps. Your friend, after all, is dead.' She placed the card back on the table. 'Miss McCourt was clearly a woman to whom men were attracted.'

'Yes. She was extremely good-looking.'

'And who in turn enjoyed men's attention.'

'She was certainly used to getting a lot of it.'

'What did you and Miss McCourt do on the night of Tuesday the tenth of July?'

'We had a party.'

'At your flat?'

'That's right.'

'Were there many people present?'

'About forty.'

'And were you able to provide the police with a list of all their names and addresses, for elimination purposes?'

'Not all of them.'

'Why not?'

'Well, I didn't know all of them.'

'There was nothing so formal as a guest list, then?' This drew one or two wry smiles from around the court.

I said shortly, 'No.'

'Some of those present were in fact complete strangers?'

'They were friends of friends, yes.'

'Two attractive young women, newly back from foreign parts, apparently happy to welcome all comers into their house. Your parties must have been very popular.'

'My lord.' Hawthorne got to his feet. 'My learned friend is indulging in comment.'

'I agree,' the judge said. 'Do you have a question, Mrs Bishop?'

'Was the defendant present at this party?' she asked me.

'No.'

'But he had been invited?'

'Yes. It was sometimes difficult for him to get away from his wife.'

'Or he didn't want to come,' Mrs Bishop said coolly. 'In fact, there were many occasions, weren't there, when my client left Jo to her own devices? The holiday, the party, to name but two.'

'I suppose so.'

'It's hardly the picture of a grand passion, is it?' Before I could answer she went on, 'Isn't the truth that, for my client, this was nothing but a casual dalliance? Regrettable, perhaps; reprehensible, even, but hardly the first time that a rich and successful man has allowed himself to be carried away by the flattering attentions of a younger woman. Particularly when, as in this case, the younger woman was attractive, uninhibited and, as you told the court earlier, sexually adventurous.'

'He told me—'

Mrs Bishop said smoothly, 'We'll come to what he told you later. At the moment we are seeking to establish certain facts. And the facts are that, first, Miss McCourt was more than happy to attach herself to a married man, and secondly, in his absence she was not slow to find a substitute.' She gave me a long stare. 'What was she wearing that evening?'

'A T-shirt and a skirt.'

'She was showing off her holiday tan, I expect?'

'I suppose so.'

'So a short T-shirt and a short skirt?'

'Yes.'

'She must have looked even more attractive than usual.'

'Jo always looked good.'

'And particularly so when she was dressed to kill?'

'My lord,' Hawthorne began with an expression of distaste, but Mrs Bishop had already continued.

'Was there a great deal of sexual activity at this particular party?' She put the emphasis on *great*.

'My lord,' Hawthorne said again.

'It goes to the forensic evidence,' Mrs Bishop said crisply.

'Very well,' the judge said. 'Miss Taylor, you may answer the question.'

I said reluctantly, 'I think a few people got off with each other.'

' "A few people got off with each other," ' Mrs Bishop repeated. 'Would you tell the court exactly what you mean by that?'

'Flirting, kissing, that sort of thing.'

'But it's possible that some went further?'

'I suppose it's possible. I didn't go around checking, if that's what you're asking.' That got me a faint chuckle from the back of the courtroom and the public gallery. I thought: these people don't like Mrs Bishop. They want me to win, not her.

Mrs Bishop waited until the last laugh had died away, then said sternly, 'What I'm asking, Miss Taylor, is whether Miss McCourt was one of those who "got off" with someone.'

'She kissed someone. It wasn't anything serious.'

'Who did she kiss? Not the defendant. He wasn't there.'

'Just someone she was dancing with.'

'Did you see this someone leave?'

'No. I'd gone to bed.'

'Ah, yes.' Mrs Bishop consulted her notes. 'A bed which was itself already occupied by another young man.'

'He was asleep. I asked him to go.'

'What time was this?'

'Soon after midnight.'

'The party was otherwise still in full swing?'

'Yes.'

'And Miss McCourt was still kissing her new friend.'

'I suppose so.'

'So for all you know, Miss McCourt might have had intercourse with this other man.'

'She'd have told me if she had.'

'Did she usually tell you about her one-night stands?'

'Yes. I mean—' I felt stupid. I had walked into a verbal trap. 'She didn't have one-night stands, not while she was going out with Gerry. But if she had, she would have told me.'

'Had she told you that a few weeks earlier she'd got pregnant and had an abortion in her lunch break?'

'No,' I admitted.

There was a ripple of disquiet around the room. 'So she didn't

210

tell you quite everything,' Mrs Bishop said calmly. 'Had she had many lovers?'

I glanced at Hawthorne, wondering if he would be able to stop this, but he nodded fractionally to indicate that I had to answer the question. 'I think about a dozen in all the time I knew her.'

'About a dozen. And she was – what? Twenty-four? Some of them must have been quite brief liaisons.'

'Some of them.'

'One-night stands, in fact.'

'You're trying to make her sound like a slut,' I said angrily. 'She wasn't.'

Mrs Bishop's eyes widened. 'Whether she was, to use your terminology, a *slut* is beside the point. The forensic evidence shows that she had had intercourse during the forty-eight hours preceding her death. We have several witness statements indicating that she was enthusiastically kissing a young man during that period. It seems quite possible, doesn't it, that the person with whom she had sex was the same person she was kissing? Or, if not, that there was at least one person besides the defendant who was in a position to feel that she had led him on?'

'My lord,' Hawthorne said, getting up, 'this is speculation.'

'Your question please, Mrs Bishop,' the judge said.

'Can you say with absolute certainty that she did not have sex on the night of the party?' she asked me.

'Of course I can't.'

She made a note. 'At the party, were there any drugs on offer?'

'My lord,' Hawthorne said. 'The witness is once again being led.'

'Allow me to rephrase the question,' Mrs Bishop said. 'The police found traces of cocaine in your bathroom. How did they come to be there?'

The judge said, 'I should remind you that you don't have to answer that question, Miss Taylor, if you feel the answer might incriminate you.'

'That's all right. I assume someone brought it to the party. I didn't know about it at the time.'

'Would that be normal, to have drugs available at one of your parties?'

'If you throw a party, people sometimes bring drugs.'

'And you turn a blind eye.'

I said wearily, 'You can't exactly stop people.'

'The police also found traces of cannabis in your own blood, I believe.'

I hesitated. 'Yes. I took a few puffs of a joint that was going around.'

'Are you a regular drug abuser, Miss Taylor?'

'Not like that.'

'Not like what?'

'Well – I suppose like most people I've tried them. That's all. It's not something I make a habit of.'

'When do you suppose you last tried ecstasy?'

'You don't have to answer that either,' the judge interjected. 'Though if you do decide to say nothing, the jury are entitled to draw certain inferences from that.'

I said impatiently, 'I haven't taken ecstasy more than three or four times in my life. The last time was probably a year ago.'

'That's not quite true, is it?' Mrs Bishop consulted her notes. 'You had gamma-hydroxybutrate, also known as GHB or liquid ecstasy, in your blood at the time of the forensic tests.'

I stared at her. 'That's different.'

'Is it? For the benefit of those of us who don't have your detailed knowledge of class A drugs, would you please tell the court what the difference is?'

I felt myself flushing. 'Well, firstly I didn't take it voluntarily. And secondly, GHB is a date rape drug.'

'And how do you know that?'

I didn't understand where this was leading. 'The police told me.'

'But *before* you spoke to the police – before your friend was killed – were you aware that GHB, also known as liquid ecstasy, is a dangerous narcotic with side effects that include unconsciousness, nausea and memory loss?'

'No.'

Mrs Bishop said calmly, 'So you might have been offered liquid ecstasy at that party and thought it was a relatively harmless variant of a drug which you had taken on several occasions before.'

I had gone bright red. 'I wasn't offered any.'

'Perhaps you found some the next day, when you were clearing up,' Mrs Bishop suggested. 'Or perhaps your flatmate did.'

'No.'

'You are absolutely sure on that point?'

Just for a second, something twitched at the sheets of white mist in my mind. But there was no point in being anything less than certain. This Rottweiler would seize on any hint of uncertainty and turn it to Henson's advantage.

'Absolutely sure,' I said.

Mrs Bishop regarded me almost pityingly. 'You had memory loss after the incident, I believe.'

'That's right.'

'Did your memory return all at once, or gradually?'

'Gradually.'

'So in fact you can't be certain whether or not there are things you haven't yet recalled.'

'No, I'm certain that I've remembered everything.'

'For example,' she said, ignoring me, 'you might one day remember finding that liquid ecstasy and taking it voluntarily.'

'No. Absolutely not.'

'But you don't *know* that,' she insisted. 'That's the simple truth, isn't it, Miss Taylor? It's quite possible that you might leave this court and tomorrow remember something else, some detail which at the moment has evaded your recollection.'

'I don't think so.'

'But it is possible.'

'I suppose it could be. But I don't think it's likely.'

'It could be possible,' she repeated. She busied herself with her court papers, letting my words sink in. Then, 'You were examined by a psychologist, Dr Griffin, I believe.'

'That's right.'

'Who referred you to him?'

'The police.'

'Can you tell the court why?'

'They thought he could help with my amnesia.'

'And did he?'

'Yes.'

'He encouraged you to remember things which would help the police build a case against Mr Henson?'

'No. It wasn't like that.'

'Wasn't like what?'

'He didn't suggest anything to me.'

'My lord,' Hawthorne said, rising, 'Dr Griffin will be giving expert evidence to this point shortly.'

'Oh, I shall have several questions for Dr Griffin,' Mrs Bishop said. 'But first, I should like to ask Miss Taylor this: how do *you* know that the things Dr Griffin helped you to remember weren't influenced by him?'

'It wasn't like that. We didn't talk about the police case at all. He was just as interested in the things I got wrong.'

Mrs Bishop's head came up. 'So some of your memories *weren't* true?'

My head swam. 'I had some flashbacks – things like flashbacks – hallucinations.'

She pounced. 'And how do you know that your memory of my client attacking you wasn't a hallucination?'

'I–' I stopped.

'You were confused.'

'No.'

'Come, Miss Taylor. You must have been confused, or why see Dr Griffin?'

'I was just trying to help.'

'Help who? The police?'

'Well, yes.'

'Who had already decided that my client was guilty, and lacked only the evidence to prove it.'

'They never suggested anything like that to me.'

'Miss Taylor, by your own admission you gave the police two versions of what you saw that night. In the first version your memories are a blank, or at best a blur, full of confused hallucinations. Yes?'

'Yes.'

'Yet after several visits to a police psychiatrist, there is a second version of events. In this second version, you have changed your story and – lo! – it becomes remarkably consistent with what the police need to hear in order to prosecute my client. Yes?'

'Yes,' I said reluctantly.

'So which are we to believe, version one or version two?'

Another long pause. 'Version two.'

'And why?'

I said wearily, 'It's the truth.'

'The truth, Miss Taylor, is for the court to determine,' she said sharply. She turned over a page of notes. God, it looked as if there were still another dozen or so pages to get through. 'I want to turn now to the morning after the party – that is, the morning before the attack. Only one of you went to work that day, I believe.'

'Yes. Me.'

'You told Miss McCourt's boss that she was suffering from a stomach bug.' She looked up at me as if puzzled. 'But as I'm sure you're aware, that was not consistent with the findings from the post-mortem.'

'Jo was tired after the party. She asked me to phone in sick for her.'

'But how were you able to convince Miss McCourt's employer that she was seriously sick when in fact she was suffering from nothing worse than substance abuse and lack of sleep?'

'I . . .' I ground to a halt.

'Did you lie?'

'No. Not exactly.'

Mrs Bishop looked at me quizzically, and like an idiot I blundered on, 'She *was* feeling rough. I just exaggerated a bit.'

Mrs Bishop's eyes widened. 'Do you exaggerate very often?'

'Well, no, of course not.'

'But you've exaggerated what you've told this court.'

'No.'

'You've told the court that you remember my client raping you. The truth is you remember no such thing.'

'I know what happened,' I said weakly.

'You had passed out. You woke up briefly and something unpleasant was happening. Almost immediately you lapsed into unconsciousness again. That's correct, isn't it?'

'Yes.'

'So you were, at best, only half awake.'

'I suppose so.'

'Which means that you were also half asleep.' I opened my

215

mouth, but she went on, 'You might have been dreaming, or hallucinating, or both.'

'I'm sure I wasn't.'

'In fact, you were so heavily drugged that when you came round you remembered nothing. For several weeks you continued to remember nothing. And then you decided that the hazy figure whom you now recalled attacking you might have been my client. You told the police – who, as we shall see, were getting nowhere with their own attempts at an investigation. No doubt they said to you, are you sure? Because you have to be sure if we are to make an arrest. So, for the best of reasons, you exaggerated what you thought you might have remembered. I'm sure, you say. Before you know where you are, your drug-blurred recollections are the basis of an entire prosecution.'

'I know what happened,' I said wearily. 'It was Gerry Henson who raped me.'

'So you keep saying. But how can you be sure? You were in the middle of a drug trip.'

'I think the point is made, Mrs Bishop,' the judge said gently.

Henson's QC sighed faintly, like an eager torturer denied the opportunity to administer a favourite combination.

'I think this might be a good moment to adjourn for lunch,' the judge said. 'Mrs Bishop?'

'Certainly, my lord.'

'In that case, we will meet back here at two o'clock. I would remind the jury that you are on no account to discuss the case or anything connected with it with anyone outside your number, or to allow anyone to discuss it with you. The only place for discussion is in the privacy of the jury room when you are all together.'

When I had finished throwing up in the toilets I went out for some air. It seemed extraordinary that all these people bustling down Ludgate Hill, getting their sandwiches and crowding into the pubs, should be going about their ordinary days when I was being flayed alive by Mrs Bishop. I wondered if Third World torturers took two hours off for lunch. I tried to imagine where she was. Tucked up in some cosy lawyer's pub somewhere with a shepherd's pie and a glass of wine? No, I decided, she was the sort to have a low-fat sandwich at her desk while she rehearsed her questions for this afternoon. I imagined her smiling mirthlessly as she dreamt up some particularly devastating character assassination masquerading as a question.

I turned on my mobile and called Bill. 'It's me.'

'Jesus, Ros.' He sounded alarmed. 'Where are you?'

'Outside the Old Bailey. Where are you?'

'You'd better ring off. If this call's ever traced—'

'Since you asked, it's hell.'

A pause, then, 'Are you OK?'

'Not really. I need to see you.'

'Ros,' he whispered, 'are you crazy?'

'I'm not sure I can do this if you aren't there at the end of it.'

Another pause. 'Phone me when you're finished. I'll see what I can do.'

23

As I made my way back into the courtroom, Derek Berry intercepted me. 'You're doing very well,' he murmured.

'Am I? I feel awful.'

'It's all smoke and mirrors. Don't worry, she hasn't done any damage.' He squeezed my shoulder. And with that I was being led to the witness stand again.

'Let's go back to the day before the attack,' Mrs Bishop began, flicking through her notes. 'Did you stay at work all day?'

'No. I was mugged – well, my phone was stolen. I took the afternoon off.'

'According to your personnel file, you were off sick.'

'I was just a bit shaken up.'

'Another exaggeration,' she muttered. But her manner had changed over the lunch break. Before, she had been stern and vengeful, remorselessly hammering me over and over again on the same point. Now she seemed brisk and almost cheerful as she asked me, 'When you got home, what did you do?'

'How do you mean?'

'It's a simple enough question, isn't it? How did you occupy the hours between returning from work at about – let's see – three o'clock and the attack, which took place at about eleven at the earliest?'

'I don't really know. I suppose we chatted, we watched a film, we drank wine.'

'Which film was that?'

I opened my mouth and closed it again. 'I don't remember.'

'So there *are* some things you don't remember. Do you recall what either of you was wearing?'

I thought. 'No.'

'Was Miss McCourt roughly the same size as you?'

'Yes. Roughly.'

'Did you ever borrow each other's clothes?'

'Sometimes.'

'Have you had your navel pierced, Miss Taylor?'

I glanced at the jury. They seemed as bemused as I was by these sudden changes of tack. 'Yes.'

'When was that?' Mrs Bishop persisted.

'About a week before we went on holiday. We both got them done at the same time.'

I saw Hawthorne being tapped on his shoulder by his junior, who whispered something in his ear.

'Since Miss McCourt's death, has there been any contact between yourself and the defendant?'

'Yes, I've seen him a couple of times. Once at the mortuary, with the police. And he came to the flat once.'

'Why did he come to your flat?'

'To get some of his things.'

'Did you not think that was rather curious?' Mrs Bishop said mildly.

'In what way?'

'Why would a guilty man risk a confrontation with you?'

'I hadn't realized then that it was him.'

'So his behaviour at that time was completely normal?'

'Well – yes.'

'He behaved towards you, in fact, like a man who was completely innocent of the crime you subsequently accused him of?'

'I suppose so.'

'Thank you,' Mrs Bishop said. 'I have no further questions.'

And with that, quite suddenly, it was over. The judge asked if either counsel foresaw any further use for me. They did not. I was released, spat out of Mrs Bishop's elegant jaws like a lump of gristle that had been thoroughly chewed over but only half digested.

By the time I made my way to the public gallery someone else was in the witness box. It took me a moment to recognize the doctor from the rape suite. As I sat down she was saying, 'I took three blood samples, in accordance with the standard protocol, and performed a physical examination of the victim's skin. There were a number of surface cuts to her back, which were photographed.'

'What did you do then?' Hawthorne asked.

'Three genital swabs moistened with distilled water were taken and air dried before being marked for analysis. I also performed a visual and bimanual inspection of the victim's vaginal canal and cervix with the aid of a narrow Pedersen speculum. This caused the victim some discomfort so I lubricated with saline before reinsertion. I marked each of the swabs accordingly.'

A man sitting near me in the gallery with a notebook open on his lap had turned his head to look at me. I stared straight ahead. I felt his gaze travelling up and down my body. I got up abruptly and went and hid in the toilets. I was getting to know those toilets quite well.

When I eventually plucked up the courage to return, Mrs Bishop was cross-examining.

'So the difference is that the blood taken for DNA analysis contains no preservatives, whereas that taken for serological analysis contains chelating agents to keep the samples fresh?'

'That's correct.'

'Dr Matthiesson. You must see some very serious injuries in your clinic at the rape centre.'

'Yes, that's right.'

'Could you describe for us some of the wounds that are associated with a violent sexual assault?'

'Well – bruising around the genital area, obviously. Abrasions or lacerations to the cervix and anus. And then there are other wounds which are common, such as bruises to the face and arms caused by the man gripping his victim to subdue her. Bite marks, genital tears, skin gouges – that kind of thing.'

'Were any of those present in this case?'

The doctor hesitated. 'Not to any severe degree.'

'In fact, what wounds led you to say definitely that the woman you examined had been raped?'

'Well, I didn't say she had been.'

Mrs Bishop did her quizzical look. 'Really?'

'It's not my job to say whether someone's been raped or not. I simply collect the evidence.'

'And the evidence in this case, if I have understood you correctly, is less like that of a rape and more like that of consensual intercourse.'

'Drug-rape cases are different. You're less likely to see violence, because less is needed to subdue the victim.'

'And what was it that made you suspect that in this particular instance the alleged victim had been drugged?'

'Well, it was a combination of things. Firstly, she was having dizzy spells. And secondly, there was the relative lack of any wounds, as you mentioned.'

'In other words,' Mrs Bishop said, 'what led you to suspect that the victim had been drugged was the *absence* of any of the normal signs of a rape, coupled with her obvious intoxication.'

'Well, yes.'

'Thank you, doctor. No further questions.'

'I performed an autopsy on a body of a white female aged approximately twenty-four years. The body had been accompanied by a policeman, Sergeant Tom Roberts, from the place where it was discovered. The body was brought to me unclothed and Sergeant Roberts confirmed that this was the state in which it had been found.'

'Thank you, Professor Collins. What form did the autopsy take?' Hawthorne had left the examination of the pathologist to his junior, a younger and less flabby version of himself. I wondered why this was. Some kind of work experience scheme? Was Hawthorne so confident he was leaving the case to trainees? Or was the examination of pathologists considered a speciality, one that could be safely left to less experienced barristers, like medieval stonemasons making their apprentices carve animals before they were allowed on to human faces?

Professor Collins said, 'I initially inspected the outside of the body for surface markings, of which there were several. There was a large wound to the left side of the head, which would have bled profusely, but which would not in my opinion have been fatal. There were also a number of surface wounds to the skin, as detailed in my report. These fall into two distinct categories: wounds inflicted on the victim by her attacker as he handled her, and self-inflicted or defence wounds, probably caused by the victim's own fingernails as she struggled to free herself from her attacker's grip.'

'As a result of your examination, can you tell the court how Miss McCourt died?'

'Yes. She died from asphyxia as a consequence of simultaneous compression of both the jugular vein and the carotid artery.'

'And how did you determine that this was the cause of death?'

'There was bruising to the larynx, notably to the superior horns of the thyroid cartilage, and the greater horns of the hyoid bone. In addition, there were numerous petechial haemorrhages around the face, due to raised venous pressure.'

'How long would it have taken for her to die?'

'It's surprisingly fast – much faster than if just the jugular is affected. From compression to loss of consciousness would be only about ten seconds. Irreversible brain damage would take place after about twenty seconds, and death would occur from around thirty seconds to a minute.'

There followed a long discussion about the medical evidence, including the difference between strangulation, suffocation and asphyxiation.

'Did you determine whether asphyxiation in this case was caused manually?'

'My hypothesis is that it was probably caused by the killer bearing down on Miss McCourt's neck with his forearm. This would additionally explain a small circular bruise to the right of the laryngeal prominence, which may have been caused by a wristwatch or other jewellery digging into the skin.'

More technical discussion. Even with my scientific background, I was finding it hard to follow. I glanced over at the jury. Brooch Woman and the Cyclist were riveted, looking from the pathologist to the barrister as if they were following a game of tennis. The Builder was staring fixedly at the floor in the middle of the courtroom. It was impossible to tell if he was doing this in order to concentrate all the harder on what was being said, or because he was just bored. He was breathing very deeply and rhythmically, so I suspected it was the latter.

At last Mrs Bishop stood up to cross-examine. 'Professor,' she said brightly, 'was Miss McCourt killed deliberately?'

'There is certainly evidence that supports such a view,' the professor said cautiously. 'The interval between unconsciousness and death would, as I said earlier, have been around thirty seconds. If her assailant was simply trying to subdue her, he would presumably have stopped as soon as she was unconscious.'

'What if he was distracted by the fact that he was able to penetrate her?'

Professor Collins looked wary. 'What do you mean?'

'Let me help you to picture what I'm suggesting.' She leaned forward over the pile of papers on her table, with her left arm crooked over an imaginary neck. 'I am the assailant, intent on having sex with Miss McCourt. I crouch over her with my arm held so. Correct?'

Professor Collins nodded. 'Yes, I think that would be right.'

'She has been struggling with me, thwarting me in my attempts. But now she is unconscious. Is that still correct?'

'I think so, yes.'

'When she is unconscious, I immediately seize the opportunity to penetrate her.' Mrs Bishop put her right hand on her groin and pushed her hips at the table to illustrate her point. I glanced across at the jury box. They were transfixed. Even the Builder was staring at her, his mouth wide open. 'But I do not take my elbow off her neck,' she continued. 'In fact, my forearm is now taking all my weight – not to mention any force I am now exerting as I have violent sex with Miss McCourt.' More pelvic thrusts. Then, suddenly, the show was over. Mrs Bishop stood up, smoothing her skirt. 'Might that have been enough to kill her?'

'It might,' Professor Collins agreed. He looked a little dazed himself.

'In other words, Professor, the *purpose* of the arm across the neck might not have been murder. The purpose of the arm across the neck might have been restraint.'

'I suppose it might, yes.'

'The kind of restraint, in fact, which we already know Miss McCourt had a taste for.'

'My lord.' Hawthorne was on his feet. For the first time since the trial began, I thought he looked worried. 'This is comment.'

'Indeed it is, Mr Hawthorne.'

'I apologize, my lord,' Mrs Bishop said. 'Professor Collins, let me ask you this: what is it about the death of Miss McCourt which makes you believe that she, rather than Miss Taylor, was the particular focus of the killer's assault?'

'I'm not sure I do believe that.'

'Oh?' Mrs Bishop said. 'But the police have singled out as a suspect a man who barely knew Ros Taylor. They are assuming, on the basis of her death, that Jo McCourt must have been their attacker's principal target. Yet you've just stated that her death might well have been an accident.'

The professor hesitated. 'Yes. Well, in all honesty, I think either one of them could have died. I don't think the evidence shows that he treated either of them more brutally than the other.'

'Thank you.'

I thought: and the purpose of that little sex show of yours was to get our attention back, so we wouldn't miss the point you just made.

'Do you wear a watch, professor?'

'Well, yes.' The professor held up his left hand, where a large silver watch clanked on his wrist.

'Are you left-handed?'

'No, right-handed.'

'That's usual, isn't it? A left-handed person generally keeps his wristwatch on his right arm, and vice versa.'

'Yes.'

'And in this case, the indentation you mention would have been caused by a wristwatch worn on the left wrist.'

'Yes.'

'And can you explain, Professor,' Mrs Bishop said, 'why a right-handed killer should have used his left arm to asphyxiate Miss McCourt, when his other arm would have been stronger?'

Professor Collins blinked. 'I – uh – it's not something I've given any thought to.'

'Would you give some thought to it now?' Mrs Bishop said sweetly.

The professor blew out his cheeks. 'Well. I suppose one explanation is that it supports the suggestion you made earlier – that death was accidental.'

'The left hand was doing the restraining, because the right

hand was doing something more important, such as aiding in penetration?'

'Well, yes.'

'One final point. Would the wound to Miss McCourt's head have covered her assailant's clothes with blood?'

'It's hard to say. Head wounds tend to seep, rather than to spray. He could have avoided the blood if he was careful.'

'But it would have been extremely difficult?'

'It's always difficult to manhandle a bleeding body without getting blood on oneself, yes.'

'Thank you, Professor. I have no further questions for you.'

I suddenly realized who Mrs Bishop reminded me of. She was from a different world, of course, but in some ways she wasn't unlike Jo.

Emily Pearson was an inspector with the scene-of-crime support unit.

'We entered the premises on the morning of July the twelfth in response to a request to attend a crime scene. Under the direction of Sergeant Anwar, the crime-scene manager, I then deployed five specialist officers in sterile clothing with instructions to search the scene and mark significant items for further analysis.'

'And at that time, Inspector, did you find any significant items?' Hawthorne asked.

'Yes. In a bedroom, which we subsequently designated bedroom one, there was a small table beside the bed with splashes of blood along the foreside edge, affixed to which were several human hairs. There was also a quantity of bloodstained bed linen, which was sent for analysis, and a large bloodstain on one of the floors.'

'I understand you have prepared a diagram to show us the location of the various bloodstains.'

'Yes.'

Hawthorne went to his table and produced a large diagram on white card, which he handed up to Inspector Pearson in the witness box. 'Would you talk us through your findings?'

A long explanation of the layout of the flat followed. It was strange, but I felt increasingly disconnected from the events she was describing. It was no longer something that had happened to me. When Inspector Pearson described the articles of soiled under-clothing she had removed from the crime scene, it wasn't my dirty underwear any more. It was just stuff.

I was in the witness box again. Mrs Bishop was saying, 'For the benefit of the court, would you remove your clothes so we can get a better look at you?'

'Of course.' I took off my clothes and handed them one by one to Dr Matthiesson, who had been recalled to help me.

'Now then. Doctor, I believe you inspected the victim with a narrow Pedersen speculum lubricated with saline?'

'That is correct.'

'Perhaps you would assist the witness into the correct position.' Mrs Bishop snapped her fingers and the ushers came running in with a surgical trolley and some wheeled stirrups.

I walked naked down the steps into the well of the court.

'Just a moment,' Mrs Bishop said icily. 'I can see I'm going to have to demonstrate the correct procedure myself.' She took a speculum off the trolley to make room for me to lie down. Then she put her mouth very close to my ear and whispered, 'This will tell us the truth.'

I woke up with a start. God, I had dozed off. I looked around to see if anyone had noticed. I didn't think anyone had, unless I had done something terrible like snoring. I straightened up.

Mrs Bishop was saying, 'Did you make an inventory of all the articles in the flat?'

Inspector Pearson shook her head. 'That would have taken weeks. Our normal practice is to establish the parameters of the search with the investigating officers, and to proceed on that basis.'

'In other words, you look for what you're told to look for.'

'That's simplifying it somewhat. But yes, that's roughly what happens.'

'And in this case, what were you told to look for?'

'Well, anything that might relate to unlawful entry, unlawful killing, rape, or sexual assault.'

'In other words, the police had already decided what had happened, and asked you to find the evidence to back up their suppositions?'

Inspector Pearson hesitated. 'Those were the priorities, based on the way the crime scene presented. But that's not to say we would have ignored any other evidence.'

'Presumably that depends on whether or not you realized it was evidence,' Mrs Bishop said enigmatically. 'No further questions.'

The next witness was a representative from the forensic laboratory. Clearly very used to giving evidence, he rattled off his answers to Hawthorne's questions with brisk authority. He had been asked to examine a number of items which had been delivered to the laboratory in sealed and labelled packages, including a rape kit. Various items, as specified by the police, had been subjected to DNA analysis with a Polymarker machine, which he described as being 'less informationally rich than an STR machine but more accurate when the amounts to be tested are very small or fragmentary'. From this they had established DNA profiles for a number of individuals connected with the investigation, who were not known to the laboratory by name but designated person A, person B and so on. Materials from the two alleged victims were labelled victim 1 and victim 2. At a later date a second batch of materials had been delivered from the home of a suspect, including a raspberry-coloured linen shirt of Italian origin. A hair caught in the third button of the shirt matched the DNA of victim 2. Four tiny spots of blood, almost invisible to the naked eye, likewise. In both cases there was a less than 1 in 500,000 possibility of error. Ditto a small dried secretion on the front of the shirt. He could confirm that the shape and size of the spots of blood were consistent with the cloth coming into momentary contact with fresh wounds on the victim's skin. The dried secretion also contained victim 2's DNA. The specific mix of proteins and acidic antigens matched the vaginal swab preserved in the rape kit.

I wondered how on earth Mrs Bishop was going to undermine this. But in the event she didn't even try. She stood up, bowed, and said, 'My lord, I have no questions for this witness,' leafing through some documents as she did so, as if the cornerstone of the prosecution case was no more than an inconvenience.

'In that case, as it is now four o'clock, I think that concludes matters for today,' the judge said. 'I would remind the jury, once again, that you are on no account to discuss this case with anyone. I will see you all here tomorrow morning at nine o'clock.'

We stood up as the judge retired, like children in a particularly well-run school.

'I thought for a moment she was going to trip me up.'

'But she didn't.'

'But she didn't,' I agree.

'You did well.'

'I don't know how the jury will have seen it.'

We are in Bill's bath, entwined around each other like Gemini. Two thick candles stand on the toilet seat, their flames twisting and dancing in endless courtship.

Here, all is calm. A womb. Darkness and water and fire and love. I scoop water in my palm and let it run over his back. 'Let me wash you.'

He has a tub of liquid soap, functional stuff in a green plastic pump dispenser, like something a mechanic might use to get grease off. I fill my hands with it and work a lather on his chest. The dark hairs make soapy rosettes of curls, like a bull's forehead.

Broad shoulders, smooth under my soapy hands, but tight and knotted with stress. I massage them with my thumbs, digging in hard, then gradually work my way down his more sensitive ribs. He groans. I dip my hand in the water to clean it of soap and put two fingers in his mouth. He sucks them. Under the soapy surface of the bath, two of his own fingers open me and slide inside. It feels strange – the water on his fingers less slick than my own lubricant.

'Keep them inside me,' I say.

I reach for the shampoo, tip some onto his head and slowly knead his scalp. Our faces are very close, his eyes barely an inch from mine.

'Slowly,' I whisper, when the pleasure from his fingers threatens to be too much.

His head is periwigged with foam like a judge's. I kiss him. His fingers twist inside me, burrowing, like a maggot. I bite his lip, in the corner, with my sharp back teeth.

With his free hand he scoops water over my breasts.

'Here,' I say. I pick up the nearest candle and offer it to him. With my other hand I offer him a breast.

He strokes the nipple gently, considering.

'Go on,' I whisper.

He tips the candle. A thin rivulet of transparent wax falls towards my nipple. I gasp.

When I look down the wax has hardened, a white cap around the aureole.

I put my other hand under the other breast so he can reach that too. Under the water his forefinger and thumb find my clitoris and pinch it, hard.

Afterwards I say, 'I'd better go.'

'Don't. Stay.'

'I can't.' I struggle up. 'Think how it would look if I turn up at court in the same clothes as today.'

'Who'd notice?'

'Only a man would say a thing like that.' I sit on the edge of the bath and look around for my underwear.

Bill catches my wrist with his hand. He grips it. I try to pull away but it's impossible.

'Bill, no,' I say. 'Game over.'

For a long moment he says nothing. Then, abruptly, he releases me.

I get dressed in silence.

Just before I go he says, 'When all this is over, Ros . . .'

'Yes?'

'Let's not play these games any more. Let's close the door and lock it.'

I don't reply. I leave. I close the door of his flat as I walk out. But I don't pretend that's what he was referring to.

On the other side of the road, the man with the telephoto lens gets several fine shots of me hesitating, turning round, and almost going back inside before finally moving off again.

The next morning the prosecution called Jill Fresca. Mrs Bishop immediately asked for the jury to be sent out. There then followed a long legal debate about the admissibility of Jill Fresca's evidence.

I sent a text message to Bill. *Hu Jill F?*

He replied: *Worker – Henson – harassmnt.*

I sent back: *Where U?*

Outside crt. Waiting. Then, a few minutes later: *I cn still smell u on my fngrs.*

I smiled and sent back: *Gd lck.*

Eventually the judge ruled that Jill Fresca's testimony was inadmissible because it was not 'similar fact', whatever that meant. Hawthorne accepted this with a shrug.

And then the jury were back, and Hawthorne was calling Detective Inspector Bill Thomson.

He walked confidently to the witness stand, looking more like a musician than a policeman, with his dark hair lapping the collar of his suit. I glanced at the jury, and I could see they were impressed as well. Brooch Lady was actually smiling.

He gave his answers in a clear, confident voice. He described how the investigation had begun by considering all the possibilities, and how the methodical gathering of evidence had gradually come to implicate Henson. He mentioned that Henson and his wife had both changed their statements several times. He said that Henson had removed items from the crime scene several weeks after the attack, 'which were relevant to his relationship with Miss McCourt'. He described how the police had already had sufficient evidence to arrest Henson, and get a search warrant, even before I had made my own statement.

By the end there was only one conclusion that the jury could draw: Henson was guilty.

Mrs Bishop got to her feet and regarded Bill wearily.

'Detective Inspector. Traces of cannabis and cocaine were found at the crime scene, I believe?'

'That's right.'

'Did you ever trace the source of those drugs?'

'No.'

'Did you try?'

'To some extent. But we had other priorities to investigate, such as unlawful killing and rape.'

'It didn't occur to you that the taking of a drug and the taking of a life might be linked?'

Bill said cautiously, 'We had no evidence linking the two.'

'Because you didn't look for any.'

Bill opened his mouth to reply as she went on, 'The link, surely, is obvious. Cocaine and gamma-hydroxybutrate are both class A drugs.'

'Unfortunately, drug use is now so common that it is rare to find a crime which does not involve them.'

'Does the defendant have any history of drug abuse?'

'Not so far as I am aware.'

'In that respect, a model citizen, then.'

Bill said drily, 'In that respect, yes.'

'And these other people, the ones who attended the party Miss Taylor and Miss McCourt gave. Were they all model citizens as well?'

'Unfortunately, we weren't able to trace them all. Around a dozen remain unidentified.'

'Despite, I understand, an appeal on the programme *Crimewatch*?'

'That's correct.'

'One might almost say, they seem not to want to talk to the police?'

'We can speculate, but the truth is we don't know why they haven't come forward.'

'What is the cause of most break-ins, Detective Inspector?'

'Most crimes against property are drug related.'

'And how many break-ins are solved?'

'I believe the clear-up rate is about fifteen per cent.'

'Quite a hard crime to bring to a successful conclusion, then?'

'I suppose so.'

'What is your clear-up target in the Metropolitan area?'

'We aim to solve thirty per cent of all crimes.'

'A modest enough target. And are you achieving that quota this year?'

'I believe we are slightly under.'

'So there must be considerable pressure on you to secure convictions.'

He said gently, 'It doesn't take a target to make a policeman do his job.'

'Detective Inspector, here we have a property in which a party has been held, a party attended by a number of drug users.

They would have had ample opportunity to notice that the windows opened on to a paved area at the back, providing easy access. They would also have an opportunity to notice the two young women who shared the flat. One of them is kissing a young man she'd never met before, and is so drunk that she fails to go to work the next day. The other goes into a bedroom from which another young man later emerges. Both women are attractive, and have dressed to show themselves off to their best advantage. Is it really beyond the bounds of possibility that the following night one of these shadowy figures returns, with evil intent?'

'There was no evidence to suggest that was the case.'

'Doesn't that rather depend on how you read the evidence?'

Bill didn't answer.

'The truth is, Detective Inspector, that the most logical scenario was also the one which gave you the least chance of getting a conviction. So you turned your attentions to my client and tried to re-shape the evidence to fit him up.'

'Absolutely not. We had clear statements from Miss Taylor, amongst others, which pointed to Mr Henson's involvement. This was confirmed by the forensic evidence.'

She kept trying to shake him, to throw dust in the jury's eyes, but try as she might, this was the sticking point she couldn't get round.

She had an easier time of it when she came to cross-examine Dr Griffin.

'Tell us, Dr Griffin, your psychological profile was based on exactly how many cases?'

'The study I based my profile on was the result of analysis of over forty cases.'

'And in how many of those were the victims cut on their backs, as in this case?'

'None. This kind of very controlled cutting is unique, so far as I am aware.'

'In other words, this was not a textbook offence.'

'That's exactly right.'

'Which suggests, in fact, that the textbook is likely to be of limited use in providing an explanation.'

Griffin said cautiously, 'It's always difficult to generalize about these things. But I hope that I provided some useful pointers.'

'Well, let's see.' Mrs Bishop flicked through the pages of the court bundle. 'You said that the offender probably drove a sports car or a four-wheel drive and attended a gym. What proportion of the population would you say that describes?'

'I couldn't say. A significant proportion, obviously.'

'You also say that he probably has a history of poor relationships and is rude to women. If the police had listened to you, they could have arrested almost any one of my learned colleagues at the bar.'

Chuckles all round the courtroom. The ice maiden has shown that she has a sense of humour.

'A profile isn't intended to help the police find suspects,' Griffin said mildly. 'It's to help eliminate them.'

'Would you agree,' she said, 'that there are many thousands of perfectly innocent people who wouldn't be eliminated by this?'

'Of course.'

'Would you also agree that there is in fact nothing in this profile which incriminates the defendant?'

He hesitated.

'Yes or no, Dr Griffin?'

'I can't give a yes or no answer, I'm afraid. It's much more complicated than that.'

'Dr Griffin,' she said, 'I have asked a straight question. It deserves a straight answer. Does your psychological profile incriminate my client – yes or no?'

Griffin said pompously, 'I'm under oath to tell the whole truth. Neither yes nor no is the whole truth.'

'There is, then, an element of doubt?'

'Of course, but—'

'Thank you,' she said pertly, turning away from him. 'No further questions.'

Hawthorne rose again. 'In case my learned friend has inadvertently confused the jury, would you clarify what the psychological profile is for?'

'Yes. It's simply an aid to identification, based on past experience. Just as we can say that muggers tend to be young and fit and in need of ready cash, and that they prefer to rob people with plenty of valuables on them, so we can make a series of observations about rapists and their choice of victims. A psychological profile can't incriminate anyone. All it can do is say that they're the right sort of person to have committed a particular crime.'

'Dr Griffin, thank you.' He turned to the judge. 'My lord, that concludes the case for the prosecution.'

The judge peered at the clock. 'That being so, we shall pause there until tomorrow morning. Members of the jury, the instruction not to discuss the trial outside this court still applies.'

24

'And on the night in question,' Mrs Bishop was saying, 'did you deliver two pizzas to an address in Broadhurst Terrace?'

'That's right.'

'What name was given for the order?'

'McCourt.'

The first defence witness was a young man – very young, about eighteen or so, and very nervous. He was wearing a shiny grey suit and his hair was slicked back with gel. His acne-marked face glinted with sweat.

'So you rang the doorbell?'

'Yes.'

'What happened next?'

'This woman opened the door.' Gel boy was getting more confident now.

'Can you describe her?'

'She had blonde hair. And she was well fit.'

'You subsequently identified this woman from a police photograph as the deceased, Miss McCourt.'

'Yeah.'

'What was she wearing?'

'A sort of dressing gown thing.'

'Which was fastened how?'

'She was sort of holding it closed.'

'What happened then?'

'I gave her the pizzas and the delivery chit. You have to sign, right, to show we've delivered them.'

'Go on.'

'Well, she sort of – like, she put one hand under the pizza boxes and took the pen with her other hand, and she signed the chit like that.'

'What happened to the dressing gown?'

'It sort of fell open.'

'What was she wearing underneath?'

'Nuffing.'

Mrs Bishop did her best to look shocked. 'She exposed herself to you?'

'Well – just the top.' Gel boy couldn't resist a smirk at the recollection.

'Did she seem embarrassed?'

'Nah. She was – it was like she thought it was funny. She said something like, "Whoops, I don't need to give *you* a tip now, do I?" '

'My lord.' That was Hawthorne. There was a brief legal debate I couldn't follow. Mrs Bishop evidently won it, because she turned back to the witness and asked, 'How would you describe Miss McCourt's manner?'

'She was pretty happy. I thought she was a bit pissed or whatever.'

'She seemed to be intoxicated?'

'That's what I thought.'

More legal bluster from Hawthorne. But the point was made. Jo could have been high already when she answered the door.

'Would you state your name, please?'

'Peter Longworth.'

'Where do you work, Mr Longworth?'

'At Leo Burnett. It's the sixth largest advertising agency in London.'

'And what was the nature of your relationship with Miss McCourt?'

'I was her boss.'

'Is that all?' Mrs Bishop asked.

'I – briefly – had a physical relationship with her.'

'You were lovers?'

'Sort of.' Jo's boss fiddled with his cufflinks. 'It was a one-off.'

'By mutual agreement?'

'Not exactly. I wanted – I hoped it would be more than that. But she made it clear she wasn't interested.'

'Were you surprised?'

'Well, yes. I was a bit.'

Mrs Bishop shot a knowing glance at the jury. 'Why don't you tell us what happened,' she suggested.

Soon Peter was giving a blow-by-blow account of his fling with Jo, culminating in the night he took her out after work and got her drunk.

'She became increasingly flirtatious,' he said seriously, sticking out his jaw. 'It became pretty clear that she was game.'

'What happened then?'

'I suggested we go back to my place in Barnes.'

'Did she agree?'

'She said that the office might be a more exciting venue. Plus it was nearer.' A hint of a snigger from somewhere in the public gallery.

'So you went to your office. What happened there?'

'Well, we had sex.'

'And afterwards?'

'Afterwards I called her a taxi and she went home. I sent her some flowers the next day.'

'Very gallant of you,' Mrs Bishop said drily. Another distant snigger. 'How did she respond?'

'She didn't, really. She seemed to lose interest in me completely. If anything, she started to take advantage. As one of the largest advertising agencies in London, we often have to send repre-sentatives to attend consumer focus groups, say, or work late at client functions. If I ever tried to get Jo to do anything like that, she made an excuse.'

'She had stopped taking her work seriously?'

'I got the impression she thought that having had sex with me meant she didn't have to bother with all the boring stuff any more.'

'On the morning of July the eleventh, did you receive a call from Miss McCourt's flatmate, Ros Taylor?'

'I did, yes.'

'What was the nature of that call?'

'She was phoning to tell me that Jo was sick and wouldn't be coming in that day.'

'And what was your reaction?'

'I was a bit sceptical, to be honest. Ros had called in sick for her several times before. I suspected that she was pulling a fast one. Now, of course, I know that she was.'

'Did you confront Miss Taylor with your suspicions?'

'No.'

'Why not?'

'I could hear them laughing at me.' He paused. 'I thought, to be honest, that if she was in that sort of mood I'd rather she stayed away.'

The next person to climb the steps of the witness box was a woman of about thirty or so. She was wearing a beautiful bottle-green jacket that undoubtedly cost more than I earned in a month. Her hands, though, shook uncontrollably as she took the oath in a voice that was little more than a whisper.

'Would you state your name, please?' Mrs Bishop's own voice had dropped to a sympathetic murmur.

'Caroline Henson.'

'And what is your relationship to the defendant?'

'I'm his wife.'

'How long have you been married?'

'Six years.'

'Would you tell the court where you have been staying for the past month?'

'At the Priory, in Roehampton. It's a specialist clinic for treating dependency.'

'Did you refer yourself, or were you referred by someone else?'

'It was my own choice to go there.'

'What was the nature of the problem you were seeking help for?'

Mrs Henson's hands tightened on the wooden rail in front of her. 'I'm an alcoholic,' she said in a tiny voice.

'Has your treatment been successful?'

'So far. I've been dry since I came out.'

'Then you are to be congratulated for addressing a very serious illness,' Mrs Bishop said. 'Did your addiction to alcohol cause problems in your marriage?'

Mrs Henson nodded.

'You have to answer,' Mrs Bishop prompted gently.

'Yes.' Caroline Henson cleared her throat. 'I was very difficult to live with for a long time. Gerry tried to help me, but it's in the nature of alcoholism that you abuse those who love you.'

'Could you be more specific?'

'To be honest, it's all a bit of a blur. I remember rows – throwing things. I was often violent, particularly if he'd tried to hide the bottle. On several occasions I attacked him and scratched his face. Once I smashed a glass and threw it at him. He had to have stitches.'

'And your physical relations?' Mrs Bishop asked delicately. 'Did they suffer?'

'Of course. I was incapable of loving him in any normal way.' She ground to a halt, whispered, 'I'm sorry,' then said in a stronger voice, 'Most of the time I was only really interested in the next drink.'

'How did your husband react to your illness?'

'He was always trying to get me to see a doctor. I'm afraid I ignored him.'

'That must have been difficult for you both.'

'I guessed that he was desperately lonely. I recognized that I might be driving him into having an affair. But by that stage I didn't care. I just wanted him to leave me alone to drink.'

'Are you saying that you feel responsible for his relationship with Jo McCourt?' Mrs Bishop said gently.

'Of course.'

'Was there anything specific, any one event, that made you realize you had to stop drinking?'

'Yes.'

'Would you tell the court what that was?'

'A policeman came to see me one afternoon when Gerry wasn't there. Gerry was at the police station himself, in fact, with our solicitor.'

'Presumably the detective who came to see you must have been aware of that?'

'Yes. He made it clear he'd wanted to see me on my own.'

'What was this policeman's name?'

'I found out later it was Collier. Superintendent Collier. He was the man in charge of the investigation.'

'What were you doing when he came to your house?'

'Just drinking.'

'Were you drunk?'

'Pretty much.'

'Perhaps Superintendent Collier wasn't aware of that.'

'I had a half-bottle of vodka in my hand for the entire interview. When I finished it, he suggested that I find another one. And another glass for him.'

'How much of that second half-bottle did you drink between you?'

'All of it.'

'That must have made it rather hard for him to interview you properly.'

Caroline Henson laughed bitterly. 'He didn't try.'

'Really? Why not?'

'He hadn't come to interview me, not really. He'd come to tell me that my husband had been having an affair.'

'Did he tell you that the girl was dead?'

'No. He said the girl was causing trouble – making accusations. He said the police didn't believe her but they had a duty to investigate.'

'What sort of accusations?'

'He didn't say. I thought it must be something to do with sexual harassment. I wasn't really thinking straight.'

'You must have been upset.'

'Yes. Very.'

'Did he suspend the interview?'

'No. He just poured me another drink.'

'What did he do then?'

'He asked me to sign something. He said it was just a formality to get this girl out of their hair.'

'Did you try to phone your solicitor?'

'My solicitor and my husband were still at the police station. I tried to phone them but their mobile phones weren't working.'

'So you signed the witness form the policeman wrote out for you?'

'Yes.'

'Did you read what you had signed?'

'No. I just wanted him to go away.'

'Are you now aware what that statement purported to say?'

'Yes. It said I had no idea what time my husband came back on the night of the murder, but that it definitely wasn't before I went to bed.'

'Was that true?'

'No. Gerry was back well before midnight.'

'When your husband discovered that you'd been tricked into making this misleading statement, was he angry?'

'No. Gerry doesn't get angry. He said it might cause problems but that we'd get through it.' A tear trembled in one of Caroline Henson's large black-rimmed eyes. 'That was when I started to realize how much I'd let him down.'

'And you subsequently decided to seek treatment.'

'Yes.'

'How is your marriage now?'

She nodded. 'We're going to be all right. What doesn't destroy you makes you strong.'

'Thank you,' Mrs Bishop said gently. She sat down.

'Mrs Henson,' Nick Hawthorne said jocularly. 'This is a pack of lies, isn't it?'

She stared at him frostily. 'Of course not.'

'You had to find some way of casting doubt on an extremely incriminating statement – one that had been made of your own free will.'

'No.'

'Why did you become an alcoholic, Mrs Henson?'

'I suppose I have an addictive personality.'

'You said earlier that your alcoholism caused problems in your marriage. Are you sure it wasn't problems with your marriage that caused your alcoholism?'

'My lord!' Mrs Bishop jumped up. 'This is speculative as well as irrelevant.'

The judge said, 'Is there a valid point to your question, Mr Hawthorne?'

'My lord, I am trying to establish whether Mrs Henson has been under any pressure to deny her own statement.'

'Then I suggest you ask her directly.'

'Mrs Henson, have you at any time been put under any pressure to deny your statement?'

'No,' she whispered.

'Do you really expect the court to believe that the police would jeopardize an important investigation – an investigation in which there was already a wealth of evidence to implicate your husband – in order to get a misleading statement from you?'

She shrugged helplessly.

'In any case, your evidence today changes nothing,' Hawthorne said. 'As you've pointed out yourself, at the time of the events we are discussing you were in the grip of chronic alcoholism. Any alibi you might now provide for your husband is manifestly unreliable.'

'Objection, my lord. My learned friend is commenting.'

'Do you have a question, Mr Hawthorne?'

'My lord, I see no reason to detain the jury further with this witness's testimony,' Hawthorne said. He sat down.

The young man who walked in and took the oath was vaguely familiar, though at first I couldn't place him.

'Would you tell the court your name please?'

He looked nervously at the judge. 'My name's Gary Lewis.'

'Are you employed, Mr Lewis?'

'No, I'm signing on.'

'Would you tell the court where you were on the evening of July the tenth?'

'I went to a party at this place in West Hampstead.'

'That would be at 27 Broadhurst Terrace?'

'Yeah, that's the one.' So that was where I must have seen him before: at the party.

'Were you an invited guest?'

'I went with a couple of mates. One of them knew the girl who was giving it, and he said it would be all right.'

Suddenly I realized exactly where I had seen Gary Lewis before. On the night of the party, he had been asleep in my bed.

'Was it a good party?'

'Yeah, it was sweet.'

'Did you take anything apart from alcohol while you were at the party?'

Gary Lewis said, 'Yeah. I took some E this bloke gave me.'

'You took some ecstasy?'

'Yeah. Only it wasn't a tab, see, it was a popper.'

The courtroom had gone very quiet. Only Gary Lewis seemed unaware of the impact he was having. He rubbed his head nervously and looked around him.

'Are you saying that it was in liquid rather than tablet form?' Mrs Bishop prompted.

'Yeah. I did think it looked a bit dodgy, but by then I'd had a bit to drink so I went ahead and dropped it anyway.'

'You took the liquid ecstasy. What happened after that?'

'I started to feel well rough.'

'You were ill?'

'I felt, you know, really tired. I just wanted to crash. I don't remember much after that. I think I found a bed and tried to sleep it off.'

'When did you wake up?'

'This bird came and started giving me grief, like, that I was in her bed and I had to get out. So I went and slept in my mate's car.'

'The person who gave you this liquid ecstasy. Did he have more?'

'Yeah, he had quite a few.'

'Do you know what happened to them?'

'He said he was going to get rid of them at the party.'

'Did he indeed,' said Mrs Bishop. 'No further questions.'

'Mr Hawthorne?' the judge asked.

'I have no questions for this witness,' Hawthorne said. 'But I should like to consult with my instructing solicitor.'

'Very well. As it is now almost four o'clock, we shall rise and convene again tomorrow morning at ten.'

As soon as the judge had gone an excited buzz wafted up into the gallery from the courtroom.

'You know what that means,' the middle-aged woman in front of me was saying to her companion. 'He thinks the prosecution will want to drop their case.'

'You'd think the police would have learned by now,' the companion said, shaking her head.

'It's all targets,' the first woman said knowledgeably. 'It's like his lawyer said. They've got certain targets and they've got to meet them.'

I felt a flash of pure, boiling anger. Who were these crones, and what gave them the right to come along and watch my case? They knew nothing about it. I pushed past them. As I left I heard one of them say, 'Oh, look. Isn't that the poor girl who gave evidence?'

Bill's mobile was switched off. I discovered later that he'd been in a meeting with Hawthorne and Collier and the CPS solicitors, discussing whether or not to withdraw.

The CPS view was that the police's version of events had been compromised, and that it would inevitably affect the whole case.

Derek Berry asked Bill what the police position was.

'If we pull out now, we'll effectively be branding two people as liars,' Bill said. 'First, my governor has been accused of script-writing Caroline Henson's statement.'

'I'm sure he's been accused of worse in his time,' Berry murmured with a smirk.

'Secondly, we'll be saying that we no longer have any confidence in Ros Taylor's testimony. You know what that means. The papers will massacre her.'

It was Hawthorne who had the final word. Bill told me later that his recommendation had been based entirely on his belief that the jury had found me personally convincing. 'They might not believe the police evidence,' he had argued, 'because the police are hopelessly tainted by association with every miscarriage of justice case they've ever read about in the *Daily Mail*. But equally, they're so accustomed to stories of police incompetence and corruption that they tend not to be too shocked by them. Ros Taylor, on the other hand, has the sort of face juries like to believe.'

And so, ultimately, one convincing lie became more important to the trial than dozens of unconvincing truths.

'Would you tell the court your name and occupation, please?'

'My name is Richard Scott. I am a Professor of Pharmacology at Southampton University.'

'And you are an acknowledged expert in the effects of drugs and toxins on the nervous system?'

'I've published over twenty peer-reviewed articles and studies on the subject, yes.'

'Would you explain for us the effects on the body of gamma-hydroxybutrate, also known as GHB or liquid ecstasy?' Mrs Bishop said.

'A lot would depend on the size and physical condition of the person taking it. Factors like gender would also be relevant, as would whether or not any other intoxicants or medications were already present in the body.'

'If, for example, we were talking about a healthy young woman who had recently ingested cocaine or cannabis and also drunk several glasses of wine, what might the effects be?'

'For a small dose, say one hundred milligrams or less, mild intoxication, sleepiness, a general relaxing of social inhibitions, feelings of well-being and euphoria. A larger dose, say two hundred milligrams, might knock the person out cold. A dose in between the two would have highly unpredictable results.'

'Such as?'

'Well, in a few cases the specific combination of chemicals could result in paranoia, constriction of breathing, hallucinations, psychotic episodes, panic attacks, that sort of thing – what drug abusers refer to as a bad trip.'

'And what form might these hallucinations take?'

'For example, the person who was having these hallucinations might be unable to distinguish between what was real and what was imaginary, or imagine things which weren't really there.'

'And see someone who wasn't actually present, in other words?'

'Yes.'

'Thank you. No further questions.'

Hawthorne got to his feet. 'Professor Scott, did you examine Miss Taylor at the time of the attack?'

'No.'

'When you describe bad trips and hallucinations you are then, I take it, speaking hypothetically?'

'Yes, I am.'

'And there is no evidence which has been brought to your attention which suggests that this hypothetical situation you describe – this bad trip – actually occurred in this specific instance?'

'No.'

'It is, in fact, pure speculation.'

The professor hesitated.

'Thank you,' Hawthorne said, and sat down again.

The defence called Gerry Henson. He walked up to the witness box and read his oath quietly and calmly, the very model of wronged innocence.

'Mr Henson, what is your profession?'

'I'm an art dealer.'

'A successful one?'

'It has given me a very good living, yes.'

'Would you describe for us your relationship with Miss McCourt?'

He said slowly, 'It was a stupid relationship.'

'Why so?'

'Because I was married. I betrayed the woman I love. I should have known better.'

'And why didn't you know better?'

'Well, there were problems at home. My wife and I were going through a difficult patch. And Jo was,' he paused, as if searching for the right phrase, 'seductive, in every sense of the word. Beautiful, young, uninhibited – I'd never met anyone quite like her.'

'Did you lavish gifts on her?'

'Oh yes.' Henson looked shamefaced. 'I happen to have made a good deal of money, and Jo certainly wasn't averse to having me spend some of it on her.'

'What sort of things did you buy her?'

'Champagne, holidays, jewellery. And clothes. I bought her a lot of clothes.'

'Did you ever buy her a raspberry-coloured linen shirt with mother-of-pearl buttons?'

'Yes.'

'Is this it?' Mrs Bishop picked up a cellophane evidence bag. She held the shirt up for Henson to see.

'Yes. I bought that at Ralph Lauren in New Bond Street.'

'It looks like a man's shirt.'

'It is. She liked wearing men's shirts sometimes.'

'This is the shirt which the police took from your house, isn't it?'

'Yes.'

'The shirt on which the forensic laboratory found traces of Miss Taylor's DNA.'

'So I'm told.'

'How did it come to be in your house?'

'About three weeks after Jo died I went to her flat to retrieve some of the things I'd given her. I don't quite know why I did that. I suppose they had sentimental associations for me.'

Mrs Bishop said deliberately, 'So you picked up this shirt when you went back to the flat three weeks *after* Miss McCourt's death?'

'That's right.'

There was an audible intake of breath from the jury box as the quicker ones amongst them worked out the implications of this.

Mrs Bishop continued calmly, 'Yes, that tallies with Miss Taylor's account, doesn't it? She told the court – let's see . . .' She made a show of leafing through her notes. 'She told the court that you came back to get some of your things. She also told the court that she was in the habit of borrowing her flatmate's clothes.'

'Yes. On more than one occasion I saw her wearing things I'd bought for Jo. I never objected. They were very close, and it seemed quite normal.'

'You can explain, then, why the forensic laboratory found Ros Taylor's DNA on a shirt that was in your house?'

'Well, yes. It seems to me to be very simple. I gave the shirt to Jo. At some point her flatmate must have worn it. Much later I retrieved the shirt from the flat, and took it back to my own house.'

The words fell from his beautiful lips like pearls, shiny and indestructible.

'No doubt the jury will remember,' Mrs Bishop said, smiling at them, 'that Miss Taylor and Miss McCourt had both pierced their navels in the week before their holiday.'

'I don't know about Ros – Miss Taylor,' Gerry said, 'but I do remember that Jo's piercing bled occasionally for a few days after she'd had it done.'

'Which would explain the spots of blood the police found on the shirt.'

'Yes.'

Oh, they were clever. They had worked it out together, every detail.

247

'And the other secretions the forensic laboratory found? The ones that matched the swabs from her vagina?'

'Presumably they were something to do with Ros.'

'To put it plainly, she must have made love or masturbated while wearing this shirt?'

'That's the only explanation I can think of,' Henson said, almost apologetically.

'Those residues were nothing to do with you, then?'

'Absolutely not.'

'Mr Henson,' Mrs Bishop said, 'this explanation for the forensic evidence seems so straightforward – and so simple – why did it not occur to the police?'

Gerry shrugged. 'I don't know. I tried to tell them what I thought must have happened, but it was almost as if they weren't interested. I got the impression they'd decided I'd done it and didn't want to hear anything that made life more complicated for them.'

'And how does that make you feel?'

'Well, very angry, obviously. Not because they've accused an innocent man, though that's caused me huge embarrassment. What really upsets me is that while they were wasting time trying to pin her murder on me, the real killer has been walking around scot-free.'

'Mr Henson, I must ask you: did you rape Jo McCourt?'

'No, I didn't.'

'Did you kill Jo McCourt?'

'No, I didn't.'

'Did you rape Ros Taylor?'

'No, I didn't.'

'Did you assault Ros Taylor or Jo McCourt and cut Ros Taylor with a knife?'

'I did not.'

'Yet Ros Taylor has identified you as the man who attacked her.'

'Yes.' Gerry sighed. 'I can only think that Ros is mistaken. She was very close to Jo.'

'Thank you, Mr Henson. Would you remain in the witness box? It may be that my learned friend has some questions for you.'

25

Hawthorne got to his feet slowly. In his hand was a sheaf of notes which he was annotating with a pencil. If he was disturbed by the way the case was going, he didn't show it.

'How do you spell your name?' he murmured, glancing at Henson. 'Is that Gerry with a G or a J? I seem to have both in my papers.'

'With a G.'

'Did you panic when you killed Jo McCourt?'

There was a long, hushed silence. For a moment I thought Hawthorne had caught Gerry off balance. Then he said calmly, 'As I told the court earlier, I didn't kill her.'

'What you told the court was a pack of lies carefully constructed to allow you to evade responsibility for your crimes.'

'No,' Gerry said, smiling faintly.

'An ingenious story, designed to explain away the forensic findings. But it's curious, isn't it, that there is not a single piece of additional evidence to back up your account?'

Henson shrugged. 'I suppose it happens sometimes.'

'It also happens sometimes, Mr Henson, that people come to this court and lie under oath.'

'I'm not lying.'

'That is a matter for the jury to decide.'

'My lord,' Mrs Bishop said wearily, 'my learned friend is commenting.'

The judge said, 'Indeed. Mr Hawthorne, you may make a speech at the appropriate time.'

Hawthorne said, 'Did you tell your wife that you were sleeping with Miss McCourt?'

'Not at the time, no.'

'She must have wondered sometimes where you were. What did you tell her?'

Henson shrugged. 'Various things.'

'Various *lies*.'

'I suppose so, yes.'

'You must be a very accomplished liar.'

Gerry Henson was no fool. He said cautiously, 'No more than most people.'

'No, Mr Henson. You had a passionate sexual affair for – what was it – five months? Complete with long afternoons in bed, trips to foreign parts, purchases of clothes and other presents, and all the time you managed to conceal this from the person closest to you. Could most people do that?'

'I'm not proud of what happened, Mr Hawthorne.'

'Then why didn't you stop? Break the affair off?'

'As I said, it was difficult.'

'You were a man obsessed?'

'Hardly.'

'Ah yes.' Hawthorne consulted his notes. 'You told the court, didn't you, that it was just a casual relationship.'

'Yes.'

'And yet the evidence suggests otherwise. This was no brief fling, was it? This was a reckless affair which you pursued even though it involved you in lie after lie for five months.'

'No.'

'Even three weeks after Jo's death,' Hawthorne persisted, 'you went back to her flat and, according to your own account, you removed items which had what you called "sentimental associations". Is that the action of a man for whom his affair meant nothing?'

Henson opened his mouth, then closed it again. Hawthorne let him struggle. The silence lengthened. 'Well?'

'I was fond of Jo. That's all. I wanted to keep some things to remember her by.'

'Mementos.'

'If you like.'

'As killers are said to keep mementos of their victims.'

Mrs Bishop objected wearily. Hawthorne was hitting his stride, though, and seemed unconcerned. 'When you were at Miss

McCourt's flat, did you take some baby clothes from her wardrobe?'

'Yes. I thought she had bought them for my godson.'

Hawthorne said deliberately, 'You took them because you were the father of her unborn child.'

'At that time I wasn't even aware that she had been pregnant.'

'The court may find that rather unlikely.'

'It's the truth.'

'The truth, Mr Henson, is that you were furious when you discovered that she had aborted your baby.'

'No.'

'You had proposed marriage to her, and she had turned you down.'

'No.'

'It must have been quite a shock to you. There you were, a rich, successful, good-looking man, accustomed to getting exactly what you wanted – whether it was a work of art for your collection, or a young woman for your bed. But Jo McCourt refused to be owned by you. She had an affair with you, but on her own terms, and when she had had enough of you she ended it, a rejection you could not bear, and which tipped you into a jealous rage.'

'No.'

'And it wasn't only her your anger was directed at. Her flatmate and best friend, Ros Taylor, who you knew had been encouraging Jo to break from you – in your eyes she was guilty too, wasn't she?'

'None of that happened.'

'Let me suggest to you what I think was the sequence of events. You had been to that flat on many occasions. You knew the layout, the fact that there was access to the windows from the street. You knew that the two young women often left the windows open and unlocked when they were at home on warm evenings. You stole in and you drugged them with a date rape drug you had brought with you expressly for the purpose. And while they were lying comatose and vulnerable, you raped them both.'

'No.'

Hawthorne ignored him. 'But then something unexpected happened, didn't it? Neither girl was as incapacitated by the drug

251

as you had predicted. Ros Taylor recovered sufficiently during the attack to recognize you as you brutalized her.'

'This is ridiculous,' Gerry said calmly.

'And Jo McCourt actually tried to fight you off. What happened next? You placed your forearm against her neck and you crushed her windpipe.' Hawthorne paused. 'And you dragged Miss McCourt's body – the body which you knew might well bear traces of your own DNA, which the police would undoubtedly identify – you dragged her body into the shower in an attempt to wash off the forensic evidence, before staging the scene to make it look like a burglary. And then you went back to your wife as if nothing had ever happened, didn't you?'

'I've told the court what happened.'

'No, Mr Henson. You've told the court what you want us to believe.' Theatrical pause. 'No further questions.'

Mrs Bishop got to her feet. 'My lord, in the circumstances I would like to ask the prosecution to recall Miss Taylor to the witness box, with your permission of course.'

'I thought you might make such a request. Mr Hawthorne?'

Hawthorne hesitated. 'I have no objection, my lord.'

'Is Miss Taylor present?' the judge asked.

An expectant silence fell. I said reluctantly, 'I'm here.' Sixty pairs of eyes swivelled towards where I sat in the gallery.

'Would you return to the court, please?' the judge said. 'Counsel have some further questions for you.'

Like a child sent out of class I edged past the other seats in the public gallery and made my way down to the courtroom. The usher held the door open for me. I walked towards the witness box.

As I climbed the four steps to the witness box I felt my phone buzz. Under the guise of switching it off I glanced at the text message on the screen. It said: *Whtevr u do dnt chnge yr story.*

'Miss Taylor,' Mrs Bishop began, fixing me with a frosty stare. 'Earlier in this case you told the court that you positively identified my client as the man who attacked you.'

'That's right.'

'We have now established that, at the time of this attack, you were under the influence of a powerful hallucinogenic drug.'

I knew by now to wait for the question.

'We have heard that the drug in question may have been left at your flat after the party the previous night. Do you have any recollection of finding such a drug?'

'No.'

'Might this be due to the memory loss you were suffering from?'

'No.'

'You sound, if I may say so, a little less certain than the last time you were giving evidence.'

'I'm quite certain.'

'We have also heard that this drug, taken in combination with other chemicals, can cause psychotic episodes.' Mrs Bishop paused. The court was deathly quiet. She said, 'In other words, Miss Taylor, it's quite possible that you killed Miss McCourt yourself.'

Everyone was staring at me, waiting for my response. I thought I was going to faint.

'Did the police ever ask you if you killed her?'

'No.'

'How very remiss of them. Well, let me ask you now. Did you kill Miss McCourt?'

I couldn't breathe. 'No,' I gasped.

'It is a hot afternoon and you have both bunked off work. Perhaps your flatmate says, "Look, I've found some funny-looking ecstasy. What a shame to let it go to waste"?'

'No.'

'The drug has a series of unpredictable effects. You become increasingly paranoid. Was there perhaps some sort of struggle, during which Miss McCourt fell, and hit her head on her bedside table?'

'No. Of course not.'

'If so, there would have been copious amounts of blood, which would have made you panic even more. Did you throttle her? We have been told that the mark on her neck was caused by a watch, but it could just as easily have been a bracelet.'

'No. It wasn't me. It's absurd.'

'Then who was it?'

'It could have been anyone.' The words slipped out before I had a chance to think. I started to correct myself but I was too late. Mrs Bishop's eyes had snapped up and locked onto mine. 'It could have been *anyone*?'

'I mean – it was Gerry.'

'Earlier you told the court that you were absolutely sure that you saw my client raping you. Now you say it could have been anyone.'

'I only meant it wasn't me.'

'It wasn't you, and it wasn't the defendant either.'

'It was—'

'The truth is, Miss Taylor, no one knows who killed Jo McCourt. There is no conclusive evidence at all.' She sat down.

Hawthorne got up. 'Miss Taylor, I have just three questions for you. First, when the defendant came to your flat to remove various articles of clothing, did you see what he removed?'

'I saw the bag, yes.'

'Was a red linen shirt amongst the articles he removed?'

'Not that I saw.'

'When the defendant raped you, did you see what was he wearing?'

I instantly saw what he was getting at. With one small embellishment I could undo all the doubt and confusion that Mrs Bishop had managed to sow. I didn't hesitate. 'Yes. He was wearing a red linen shirt.'

'Thank you.'

After the cross-examinations came the final speeches. Hawthorne went first.

'Over the last week you have heard several different versions of what happened,' he said to the jury. 'Let us put those on one side now, and remind ourselves of the facts.

'Some time on the night of July eleventh, two young women were drugged with gamma-hydroxybutrate in sufficient quantities to render them both temporarily unconscious. The police medical examiner who examined Miss Taylor and the pathologist who examined Miss McCourt both agreed that their injuries were consistent with rape. Jo McCourt was murdered. From her wounds we can deduce that she came round for long enough to struggle with her attacker. Her body was then dragged to the shower. Ros Taylor had that day's date carved into her back – a sadistic, cold-blooded injury that immediately marks this crime out as being much more than a commonplace assault by a stranger.' He paused. 'Miss Taylor later identified her attacker as the man you see before you in the dock. Police interviews had already established that he had good cause to be angry with both victims. One of the victims was in the process of breaking off her affair with him, having been encouraged to do so by the other victim. When his house was examined by forensic experts, they found a shirt bearing traces of Miss Taylor's blood and other secretions, as well as a hair that had been torn out by the root. The simple explanation of these facts is that the accused is indeed the man responsible.

'Counsel charged with defending him has, not surprisingly, put forward a different interpretation. They claim that the substance which drugged the two women may have been already present in the flat. The prosecution cannot prove that it wasn't. But the question you will have to ask yourself is this: does it substantially alter the prosecution's case? Is it so very different if the attacker found the drugs in situ, rather than bringing them with him?

'The defence have also suggested a rather different explanation of the forensic evidence. They suggest that the defendant returned to the flat and removed the shirt in question to his own house, despite maintaining that he had no particularly strong feelings for the deceased.

'It is up to you, the jury, to determine which explanation to believe – the simple, obvious one, or the complicated, ingenious one proposed by the defence.' He looked at them for a moment to emphasize his point. 'The key witness in this case, of course, cannot give evidence because she is dead, throttled by the accused with his forearm as she fought for her life. Perhaps it was even as he was raping her. We shall never know, just as we shall never know what else Jo McCourt could have told us.

'We do, however, have the evidence of her flatmate, herself the victim of a despicable and horrific crime. She has come here, bravely facing the stare of the man who raped her, and the hostile questioning of his counsel, for one reason only: to tell you what happened on that terrible night. Everything that Miss Taylor said to you is supported by hard evidence – the individual pieces of which, taken separately, may not be enough to condemn the defendant, but which taken all together are enough to make you believe that the man who committed these atrocious acts is the man standing before you in the dock.'

He sat down.

Mrs Bishop also began calmly.

'Ladies and gentlemen of the jury, it is not your job to decide what actually happened on that tragic night of July the eleventh. We know of course that two young women were drugged, and that one of them was killed, in circumstances that still remain mysterious. But that is not the issue which brings you here. You are here to decide one thing, and one thing only: whether my client, the defendant, has been proved beyond reasonable doubt to be the person responsible.

'Before you reach your decision, I would ask you to consider three things. First, have the police proved that his character is consistent with such an act? Second, do they have any material evidence which establishes that he did it? And thirdly, is there any testimony which points beyond reasonable doubt to his guilt?

'The prosecution have alleged that the possible cooling of a relationship between the defendant and Miss McCourt was enough to make him rape and kill her, and rape the friend who suggested it. There is, of course, no direct evidence that such a cooling-off ever took place. But even if it did, the allegation is an unlikely one. Thousands of relationships come to an end every day, yet thankfully crimes such as this are almost unheard of. Most men – and most women too for that matter – take the break-up of a relationship in their stride. They shrug, they feel a little miserable for a while, and they move on. Where is the evidence that suggests my client is an exception? Where is the proof that he is some kind of deranged sociopath, green-eyed with jealousy, tipped over the edge of reason by the end of a mere extra-marital affair? You have seen none because there *is* none.

'The material evidence, of course, we have discussed at some length in this courtroom. The central plank of the prosecution's case, the forensic evidence linking my client to one of the victims, turns out to be meaningless – the result of tests made on a garment which was lying around Miss McCourt's flat both before and after her death, until my client himself removed it to his house.

'And finally, there is the testimony of the witnesses. Regarding Miss McCourt, they paint a picture of a likeable, adventurous, attractive young woman enjoying to the full her freedom as a career girl in the capital.' Mrs Bishop paused. 'Unfortunately, she also appears to have succumbed to some of the temptations of her lifestyle. She embarked on a series of sexual encounters, including an affair with her boss and also with a married man – the defendant. Both men feel that she was using them at least as much as they were using her. She mixed with a fast set and partied as hard as she was able to. She took drugs. Inevitably, some of the people she mixed with were from the margins of society, people who may have played by a more dangerous set of rules than she did herself.

'And yet the police have chosen to ignore this aspect of Miss McCourt's life. Having failed to trace all of the shadowy figures who attended her final party, a party which took place just twenty-four hours before her death, they seized instead on my client as the most available suspect.'

Mrs Bishop stopped and drank from a glass of water before she went on. 'There is of course another piece of testimony to consider, and that is the evidence given by Miss Taylor. Miss Taylor, we should not forget, has suffered terribly. Her best friend has been killed: she herself has been viciously attacked. She remains adamant that the person who carried out these attacks is the defendant. Yet we should not forget that her identification of the defendant came after, not before, the police arrested him. Was her identification perhaps swayed by that fact? She says not. But she is also, as we have seen, a vulnerable and impressionable young woman who is clearly still deeply traumatized by the events of that terrible night. What she saw, and what she *thought* she saw, may be two entirely different things. She had in her blood a particularly potent combination of cannabis, alcohol and liquid ecstasy. She awoke too incapacitated to move, let alone to fight off her attacker. I suggest to you, members of the jury, that she was therefore also too incapacitated to make a clear and reliable identification of the man who attacked her, let alone of what colour shirt he was wearing.

'This is not a case in which you have to conclude that either the defendant or Miss Taylor must be lying. There are discrepancies between their accounts, certainly. But your job is simply to note that the discrepancies exist, and that the prosecution have not adequately explained them. On that basis, I suggest, you cannot possibly bring in a guilty verdict.'

She sat down. There was a palpable release of tension. I saw the jury shake themselves and look around, like an audience suddenly released from a play. It seemed to me that, of the two counsel, Hawthorne had come across better but Mrs Bishop had actually done a better job for her client.

The judge had begun to speak. Because he was sitting higher than the jury, and at the same time looking at them over his glasses, he had to sink his chin so far into his chest that up in the gallery it was hard to hear what he was saying. Gradually, though, the court quietened down, and I could make out some of the words.

He talked about the issue of identification at length, saying that it was the key to the whole case. He told the jury that the central plank of the identification evidence was my testimony. They would have to decide, first, whether I really did remember accurately what I saw that night, and secondly, whether what I remembered was what actually happened. I thought he meant to imply that I was lying, but in fact he was only leading up to a reminder that Mrs Bishop had suggested that I might have been hallucinating. 'That is precisely why trial by jury exists: so that twelve ordinary members of the public can weigh up the evidence for and against, and use their common sense to tell them what happened. If you believe that a reasonable person would look at this evidence and find the accused guilty, then you must return a guilty verdict. If you believe that the evidence, taken as a whole, is not strong enough to convince a reasonable person such as yourself, then you must find him innocent.'

Bike-riding QC's career hits pothole

Motorbike-riding barrister Elizabeth Bishop, QC (pictured, above, arriving at the Old Bailey on her prized Harley-Davidson) suffered a rare setback yesterday when she failed to persuade a jury that art dealer Gerald Henson was innocent of administering a date rape drug to his former girlfriend and her flatmate, before raping both women in a callous attack which left one woman dead and the other mutilated.

The court heard that married Henson, 36, had carried on a reckless five-month affair with his victim, who cannot be named for legal reasons, frequently taking drugs and indulging in sado-masochistic sex. During the attack both women were cut with a knife.

'This is one of the most unpleasant cases that has ever come before me,' Judge Harold Shaw told the defendant after the jury returned a 10-1 majority verdict following two days of deliberation. 'You are a callous and violent man, who has shown no remorse and who has expertly manipulated those around you into backing up your lies.' During the trial Henson's wife had given evidence suggesting that the police had taken advantage of her alcoholism when gathering evidence.

Neither the defendant nor his counsel showed any emotion at the verdict. Legal sources say, however, that the result is a setback for Mrs Bishop, a flamboyant figure known as much for her frequent accusations of police corruption and evidence-fixing as for her legal expertise. 'Liz Bishop commands higher fees than many barristers fifteen years her senior,' the source commented. 'Clearly, people aren't going to go on paying that sort of money if she can't get them off. And it looks as if juries are increasingly sceptical of the suggestion that police evidence is always suspect. It seems that the excellent job the CPS is doing in preparing these cases is finally bearing fruit.'

Detective Inspector William Thomson told reporters afterwards: 'There was a wealth of evidence, not all of which was presented to the court. Luckily, the testimony of the second victim proved conclusive. She has suffered two ordeals at Henson's hands, once when he raped her and once when his refusal to plead guilty forced her to go through the trauma of giving evidence in court. We very much hope that she'll be able to put this behind her now and get on with rebuilding her life.' Asked whether Mrs Bishop's aggressive questioning of the victim may have cost her client the jury's sympathy, he declined to comment.

Dealer's secret world, page nine.

4

ROS

Nothing is true; everything is permitted.

– Nietzsche

26

There was a party to end all parties, in a strange little pub on the edge of a council estate behind the Edgware Road. Apparently it was equidistant between Paddington Green police station and the ambulance station on the other side of the road, plus it sold curry and chips, so that was where they drank. God, did they drink. Each round involved getting at least two pints for the men, with a chaser for each pint. The female detectives drank almost as much – the pints without the chasers. As well as my old friends from CID, there were endless support staff with gothic-sounding titles: Senior Collator-in-waiting; Holder of the Metropolitan Region Stapler, that sort of thing. Nick Hawthorne came, bringing his own bottle of champagne, and the junior who had cross-examined the pathologist. Alice Turnbull gave me a big hug and shrieked, 'We did it!' It was that 'we' that struck me – these people were a team, the prosecution victory was a victory for all of them, and I was like their centre forward or striker or whatever. I had been passed the ball and I had scored with it. People kept slapping me on the back and congratulating me. Collier was there too, and his 'Well done, darling' had an edge to it, a hint of gratitude that the verdict had probably saved his bacon. 'Thought I was going to come a cropper there,' he added, beaming.

A group of younger detectives who were with him, hanging round him like acolytes, cheered and whooped.

'To Miss Rosalind Taylor,' he said, lifting his glass high. 'May God bless all who sail in her.'

More whooping. Someone stuck a beer bottle under Collier's mouth as if it were a microphone, and said, 'Superintendent, would there be any truth in the allegation that you scripted Mrs Henson while she was taking drink?'

'Mrs Henson is a liar,' Collier said. 'She said we shared the bottle. As a matter of fact, she drank most of it herself.' Roaring and hilarity.

I didn't need to say much. I was whirled from one shouting group to another like the end person in a Scottish reel, buffeted by yelled conversations full of strange acronyms and police jargon – SOACs and PACE, Section Eighteens, cozzers and plonks and grass-eaters.

You could tell who the detectives were – they moved around the room with a swaggering restlessness, slipping from group to group, very conscious of their status. There was one called Micky who decided that he was going to impress me. He pulled out his warrant card. 'See that? We call that the International Disco Card. That gets you into any nightclub in London, that does. Free drinks all night. If you want to go to Annabel's later, just have a word. I'll sort you out.' I could think of nowhere I was less likely to want to go than Annabel's, but I didn't have the heart to tell him so. Unfortunately he took my glassy-eyed smile as a sign that he was doing well, and when he started stroking my back Alice had to come over and rescue me.

'Thanks,' I told her. 'Have you seen Bill?'

'I think he's over there.' She nodded in the direction of a knot of shouting men. She caught my smile and said, 'You like him, don't you?'

I kept smiling. 'Maybe.'

'He certainly sticks out in this lot, I'll give him that.'

'They seem all right.'

'Try working with them.'

I was a bit drunk. 'Have you shagged any of them?' I asked. But she was drunk enough not to take offence.

'Too many.'

'How many's that, then?'

'One.'

We laughed at that, and she said seriously, 'Now it's over, do you think Bill and you might ever – you know?'

My expression must have given me away, because she did a double take. 'Christ. You have already, haven't you?'

I shrugged.

'I never thought he'd ever do that,' she said, almost to herself. 'He must have fallen for you pretty hard.'

Soon afterwards she left, and I allowed Nick Hawthorne's junior to ply me with Bacardi Breezers and courtroom stories, until the room started spinning and I stumbled outside to think very seriously about whether or not I was going to have to throw up. Which was where Bill found me half an hour later, when he came out to track me down. He wrapped his jacket round me and walked me down to Edgware Road to find a cab, and everyone crowded out of the pub to cheer us off, like a wedding party waving off the happy couple.

The next morning I woke up in my own bed, my head throbbing. I staggered into the bathroom on autopilot, and collapsed onto the loo seat.

There was water hissing behind the shower curtain.

I screamed. The shower curtain was pulled back, and Bill's face peered out at me, concerned. 'What's wrong?'

'Nothing.' Then, because he knew something was, I said, 'The last time I felt this bad was when . . . that was where I found Jo, and the shower was on . . .'

I cried then. He came out of the shower to hold me, pulling me tight against his warm wet skin. I lifted my face to his and let him kiss the tears away. Because it was over, and we'd won, and now we were going to be together.

There was a pile of letters on the mat, far more than I ever usually received. I opened one. It was a note of congratulation from Charlotte. I felt bad: she'd wanted to come and sit with me during the trial, and I hadn't let her. I put it on one side as a reminder to call her. The next was a letter on the letterhead of the local paper, the *Ham and High*.

Dear Ros Taylor,

Congratulations on winning your case. If you would be interested in doing a short interview about your experience – without, of course, compromising your anonymity – please get in touch with me as soon as possible on the number below. I think your story will strike a chord with many of our female readers.

Yours sincerely,
Jennie Allen

Features editor

'So much for my right not to be identified,' I said, showing it to Bill. He grunted.

'They have to agree not to publish your name and address. That doesn't mean they can't find it out themselves.'

'Fuck her. It's over.' I threw it in the bin.

I picked up the next letter. It had been delivered by hand – there was no stamp or address, and my name had been typed on the envelope with an old-fashioned manual typewriter. Inside was a postcard, a black and white picture of a woman's face, photographed through a glass of water so that half her face was distorted by the curvature of the glass. I half recognized the picture – it was a Man Ray, or someone like that.

I turned the card over. Typed on the back were two words.
Thank you.
'Here's an odd one,' I said, passing it to Bill.

'Probably just some loony. Art Lovers Against Rape or whatever.' He took the pile of post from me and put it to one side. 'What about some breakfast?'

There was an estate agent's just round the corner in Canfield Place that had a sort of touch-screen computer in the window. You entered all your requirements and your price range and the computer showed you what was available.

'God, it's all so expensive.'

'Much better to move to Stoke Newington,' Bill suggested. 'I know a place out there that's really cheap.'

'Don't tell me. I'd have to give the landlord regular blow jobs in lieu of rent.'

'Sounds like a pretty good deal to me.'

I put my arm round him. 'I think I need my own place. Just for a while. Then if I do decide to move in with you . . .'

'You'll be able to move out again when we argue?'

'I was going to say, you'll know it's not just because I need somewhere to stay.'

'Can I help?' One of the estate agents had come to the door.

'We're just looking.'

'Fair enough.' He glanced at the screen. 'Though if that's your price range, I've just had a new instruction you might be interested in. One large bedroom in Belsize Park.'

Belsize Park was just up the road. 'Can I see the details?'

''Fraid not. This has literally just come in. Tell you what, I'm on my way there now, to measure up. You can come with me if you like.'

I hesitated.

'In the current climate, it'll be sold by the end of the week,' the estate agent said mildly.

'Go on, Ros,' Bill urged. 'You said yourself, you've got to move.'

So we all piled into the estate agent's car and drove up the hill to Belsize Park. And the flat, just as he'd said, was very nice: light and reasonably spacious, with a view over Regent's Park in the distance.

'What do you think?' I asked Bill.

'Mmm. First floor, so good security. Seems to have everything. We'd have to check out the local pub, of course.'

I sighed. 'That's all that matters, is it?'

'Are you part of a chain?' the estate agent wanted to know.

'It's a bit complicated.'

'Not necessarily,' Bill said. 'Probate's all finished. Jo's family will be happy for you to sell.'

'If you want to put it on the market,' the agent said, 'I'd be very happy to come round and value it for you. With no obligation, of course.'

I shrugged, suddenly absurdly happy. 'Well, why not?'

We had lunch in the local pub, which got a thumbs-up from Bill as it sold London Pride, served Thai food and had Sky Sports. 'That's me happy,' he said.

I looked around. I liked it too. The area was nice, and it would be easy to get to work. What else mattered?

'I'll wait and see what I get for my half of the old flat,' I said.

'OK. Shall we get back? Now that beer's taken the edge off my hangover, I quite fancy a shag.'

When we got back there was another pile of letters waiting. I picked them up and flicked through them.

'Don't bother with those now,' Bill said. 'Let's go to bed.'

'There's another one,' I said slowly.

'Another what?'

I showed him. 'Hand delivered.' As before, the front of the envelope just bore my name. I opened it.

Another card – the same photograph. I turned it over. On the back was typed:

Any fool can love a beautiful woman. He's simply showing off his good taste when it comes to the female form.

How much better to love an ugly woman because you have seen in her something that is beautiful.

And to love a beautiful woman because of the one tiny ugliness or flaw she keeps hidden from the rest of the world – surely that's the greatest love of all?

M.A.

PS: I love you, Ros. I won't stop loving you because of what you did.

'How very odd,' I said.

Bill said, 'Don't open them in future. Throw them away.'

I looked at the card more closely. 'It *is* Man Ray.'

'Who is?'

'The card. It's a Man Ray. They sell these at work, in the gift shop.'

'So? They probably sell them everywhere.'

I allowed him to take the card from me, and I didn't see what he did with it.

Bill had to get up to go in to work. I dozed sleepily for an hour or so in bed. The weekend stretched in front of me. I had no commitments, no worries. The phone rang but I couldn't be bothered to get out of bed to answer it. After a minute the answer machine cut in, but whoever it was didn't leave a message.

I could hear music coming from outside, or maybe from the flat above. Rock music, nothing I recognized. I lay in bed listening to it idly. The volume increased. Perhaps Ian from upstairs was getting carried away.

Then I suddenly knew that the music wasn't muffled enough to be coming from upstairs. I pushed myself upright and listened.

The music was coming from inside my own flat, from the stereo in the living room. And it was getting louder and louder – deafeningly loud – as if someone was standing on the other side of the closed living room door and slowly cranking the volume control up to maximum.

'Bill?' I called. But I knew that if Bill had come back he'd have come straight into the bedroom. And he never listened to deafeningly loud rock music.

I stood up and pulled on a dressing gown. I was going to have to go and see who was playing the music.

I thought: maybe Bill left the door unlocked when he went out.

The music was so loud now it was distorted as well as deafening, fizzing and sizzling, with a flatulent rattle of bass in the lower register. 'Turn it down,' I shouted. My voice was barely audible over the din.

Blindly I pushed open the living room door.

There was no one there. The speakers were shaking and sliding on their shelves. I crossed to the stereo and turned the volume all the way down.

The windows were closed, as were the window grilles.

I went and checked the front door. It was closed, the latch fastened.

I was alone.

I phoned Bill.

'When you left earlier, did you close the door properly?'

'Yes, of course. Why?'

'Are you sure?'

I heard him say, 'Just put it over there, will you? I'll be two minutes.' To me he said, 'Yes, positive. Have a look if you're bothered.'

'I *have* looked. It's closed now. What I want to know is, was it closed when you left?'

'Whoa. Just a minute. What's happened?'

'I heard music.'

'Music?'

'Really loud – I mean painfully loud. Someone was in here playing music.'

'You saw this person?'

'No. The door was closed. I heard them.'

'Heard what, exactly?'

'I told you. The music.'

He said cautiously, 'So you didn't actually hear a person moving around?'

'Stop talking like a fucking policeman. I'm telling you, there was someone in here.'

There was a moment's silence. I could tell he didn't believe me. 'Shall I come back?' he said at last.

I said, 'Do you believe in ghosts?'

'Ghosts? Jesus, Ros. Where did that come from?'

'That note, remember? "Thank you." What if . . .' I hesitated. 'What if it's Jo – oh, I don't know, that sounds crazy, but what if someone's trying to make me think it's Jo?'

'But the other note was signed M.A.,' he objected. 'Why M.A.?'

'I don't know.'

'Look, I'll come back. Wait there, will you?'

'I'm hardly likely to go for a fucking stroll,' I snapped, but he had already put down the phone.

'Jo?' I whispered.

The LED lights on the stereo began to flicker and dance. I'd turned it off, hadn't I? Or, at the very least, turned it right down.

Music filled the room. Thumping rock music. I sleepwalked over to the volume control and turned it down all the way.

A moment later, the sound was once again at full volume.

Perhaps it's just a faulty stereo, I thought. And then a terrible thought struck me.

I took my keys and went up to the front hall, locking the door behind me. There, on the mat, was another note. The same typewritten name. Ros Taylor. No address, no stamp. I tore it open.

The ninth commandment, Ros. Thou shalt not bear false witness.

I carried it back downstairs and placed it on the table. *Get a grip on yourself.* I went to the bookshelf and found a dictionary of quotations. I looked through the As. As I thought, the second card had been a quotation too: M.A. stood for Marcus Aurelius.

The entryphone buzzed, and I jumped. But it was only Bill.

'Are you all right?' he said as I let him in.

'Yes. But look. There's been another one.' I showed him the card.

'I thought we agreed to throw those away?' he said gently.

'No. You agreed,' I said angrily.

He sighed. 'Where's this stereo?'

I pointed. 'Over there.'

He went over and examined it. Then he stood up and said, 'Do you know where the remote control is?'

'Um. No. It's around somewhere. It always is.'

He fished down the back of the sofa. 'This it?' I nodded.

'Wait here, will you?'

He went outside. Thirty seconds later, the CD player turned itself on and began to play. The volume went up, then down.

Bill knocked on the door again. I let him in. 'Anything happen?' he asked.

'Yes. It started doing it again.'

'That was me, out in the street.' He tossed the remote back onto the sofa. 'Most likely one of your neighbours has just bought himself a similar system. He turns up his TV, you get Pink Floyd or whatever. He tries to record *Match of the Day*, you get the *Phantom of the Opera*. Let's move the hi-fi over to the other side of the room, away from the window. That should sort it.'

I had started to cry.

'And no more crap about ghosts,' he added gently.

'God, Bill. I'm so sorry.'

'That's all right. I wanted to come back, actually. I've had some good news. I've been asked to apply for the AMIT – the area major incident team.'

'That's good, is it?'

'As good as it gets.'

'And it's all down to winning that case?'

'Sort of.' He hesitated. 'It's also to do with how we won it.'

'Meaning what?'

'I think my superiors suspect that we – that I had to get my hands dirty. I think in a funny sort of way it helped.'

'Collier and his pals think you're one of them now.'

'I guess so, yes.'

'And are you?'

He laughed. 'We're all on the same side, if that's what you mean.'

Something occurred to me. 'Bill, did you ever sleep with Alice Turnbull?'

He shrugged. 'Once. A very long time ago, when we were both probationers. Why? Did she say something? I'm surprised she even remembers.'

'She said she'd slept with one detective, and that was one too many.'

'Ouch. Not very flattering.'

'I don't think she meant it like that. I think you broke her heart, Bill.'

'Not Alice. She's a cozzer. Tough as old boots, like the rest of us. Why do you ask, anyway?'

I pushed the eject button on the CD player. 'She said she thought you were different.' I picked up the disc and looked around for the box.

It was a strange thing, but I couldn't recall either myself or Jo ever having bought an album by Fleetwood Mac. The song that had been playing was called 'Tell Me Lies'.

27

By Monday I'd convinced myself I'd been over-reacting after the stress of the last few weeks. That morning I went back to work. Most of them knew about the trial, of course, and there was a little impromptu gathering in the lab, with champagne being drunk out of distilling beakers and Barry Powell, the director himself, coming to make a speech welcoming me back.

'I have doubly good news,' he said. 'As a direct result of Ros's investigations, the painting *Polynesian Woman* – oil on canvas, attributed to Gauguin – has now been reclassified as *Polyfibre Woman* – Dulux emulsion on oily rag, attributed to Dodgy Bloke in Pub.' He paused for the laughter to subside. 'As the culprits are already detained at Her Majesty's pleasure, there seems little point in bothering with another prosecution. We have therefore decided to make a presentation of the evidence to our favourite scientific assistant. Ros, would you please step forward.' He beckoned to a packer, who came in carrying the little painting I had spent so much time poring over. 'And just in case you are ever tempted down the path of criminality yourself, Ros, we have taken the precaution of inscribing it with a warning that not even a Cork Street dealer could ignore.' He swivelled the painting round to show us all the back. Across it was written in large, cartoon letters THIS IS A FAKE. There was a ripple of laughter and applause as I went up to collect it.

'Of course, I always knew there was something wrong with it,' he added, to jeers and catcalls.

'Thank you,' I said. I looked at the friendly faces. 'It's good to be back.'

*   *   *

'Of course,' Alex said gloomily when everyone had gone, 'it's blood money.'

'What is?'

'Giving you that trinket. They feel guilty because it was the gallery who introduced you to Henson.'

'I'd forgotten that.' I touched the surface of the painting. 'And I don't think it's a trinket. It's beautiful.'

'Beautiful but worthless. I'd sooner have had a cheque.'

I booted up my computer. Having been away for the whole duration of the trial, I had over a hundred emails to wade through.

The phone rang. 'Ros Taylor,' I said.

'Hi, Ros,' a voice said hesitantly. 'Remember me?'

I clicked on an email offering me larger breasts or my money back, sending it to the deleted folder. Somehow I seemed to have got my email address onto yet another junk-mail list. 'Probably, but you'll need to remind me.'

'It's Nathan.'

'Nathan.' The boy who had called me a bitch because I wouldn't go out with him. 'What do you want?'

'You said to call back later in the year. So I'm calling back.'

'Nathan.' I struggled to find the words. 'Look, I've been away. All sorts of things have been going on—'

'I know. Jo and all that.' He paused. 'You sent the police round to see me, remember?'

'Did I? No, hang on a minute. The police interviewed everyone I'd had contact with. You'd called me the day I – the day it happened, that's all.' I didn't like the implication that I somehow owed him a favour, just because he'd had to give the police an alibi.

'Well, it's water under the bridge as far as I'm concerned. I'm calling because you're probably feeling lonely now, without Jo around, I mean. I'd like to take you to a film. I think that's better than dinner, for a first meeting, but we can always—'

'Look, Nathan,' I said, 'I'm not feeling much like going out at the moment. It's nothing personal but I just don't want to see anyone.' I am being calm and courteous and clear, I thought. The three Cs. I waited. I thought, if he calls me a bitch, I'll call him a deformed little wanker.

But Nathan just said meekly, 'It's OK. I understand. But if you change your mind or – or maybe just want to chat, let me know.'

'Thanks. Bye, Nathan.'

I returned to my emails. I was still going through them half an hour later when the packer came up again, this time carrying a huge bunch of roses wrapped in cellophane.

'That's more like it,' Alex said approvingly.

'Just arrived,' the packer said with a smile.

My first thought was, *oh no, Nathan*. Then I went cold. There was a note. My name, typed on the envelope. Ros Taylor.

I opened it.

Roses for Ros.

And a different picture. This is 'Leda and the Swan'. Presumably you know where to find it. Go and look at it in your lunch break – you usually stop around 1.20, don't you? I suggest 1.40 in front of the picture. You'll have time to get one of those wrap things you like from Pret a Manger first.

Please understand – you are quite safe from me. I just want to see you looking at the picture. If you hold the flowers while you are looking at it, so much the better.

You can't really refuse me, can you?

I turned the card over. A pale neo-classical maiden was swooning in the embrace of a giant swan. I knew the picture, of course. It was one of the jewels of the gallery's collection.

'Is something wrong?' Alex said.

'No. I'm fine.'

I went over to the computer and logged on to the directory of the gallery's works.

Leda and the Swan – attr. Michelangelo.
C212

Leda was a beautiful mortal who was secretly beloved by Jupiter. In order to consummate his feelings for her, he crept up on her in the form of a giant swan while she slept beside a river. She awoke to find the swan already mounting her but, according to Ovid, 'her disquiet quickly turned to love'. As a result of the rape she became pregnant with Helen, whose beauty maddened men such as Theseus and whose own abduction caused the Trojan War.

The original painting was commissioned by the Duke of Ferrara, but was given by Michelangelo to the model after an argument with the Duke's representative, who was unhappy with the overtly erotic treatment. It was subsequently lost. This copy is believed to be by either Michelangelo himself or his student Rosso.

I looked at my watch. Ten past one. I lifted the phone.
'Police, Paddington Green, how may we help you?'
'Detective Inspector Thomson, please.' There was a long wait. Christ, even the police were now playing tinny classical music while they put you on hold.
'Incident room.'
'Is DI Thomson there, please?'
'Sorry, that case is finished. Have you tried CID?'
'Could you transfer me?'
'Hang on.' The phone went dead. I tried again, but this time it was engaged. I looked at my watch again: 1.20.

I thought: if the man who's writing these notes is really going to show up, he'll be there already. But he won't be expecting me for another twenty minutes. I could get a look at him.

The galleries would be crowded with tourists, and each room had a security guard on duty. There was no way he could try anything with so many people around.

I looked around to see if there was anyone else in the lab I could ask to come with me. But everyone had drifted out to lunch.

The *Leda* was in Room 8, in the furthest reaches of the West Wing. To get to it I had to make my way through a labyrinth of echoing galleries, full of jabbering foreign schoolkids wearing guided-tour headphones. The picture had been hung in the centre of one wall, so that it dominated your view if you approached it from the main doorway. I had deliberately approached from one of the side galleries, hoping to slip into the room unnoticed. There was a crowd of maybe twenty or thirty people, but no one I recognized. I did spot a slightly seedy-looking middle-aged man, but after a few minutes it became apparent he was with his wife, who returned to his side briefly to chivvy him along. There was a knot of students surrounding a tour guide, but she was talking in German and it seemed unlikely it could be any of them. A good-looking unshaven young man who flicked his eyes at me was joined a few moments later by a beautiful willowy girl with her sunglasses perched on top of her head.

Then the crowd shifted, and I saw a man standing directly in front of the *Leda*, listening to the commentary coming through his headphones. He was about thirty, shaven-headed. As the voice in his ear spoke, he moved his eyes to different parts of the painting in response to what it was saying. There was something obscene about it: the huge white swan triumphantly positioned between the girl's naked thighs, one of which was twisted sideways in sleepy erotic abandon; the bird's writhing neck, coiled languorously along her breasts, a sharp contrast to the flailing wings as it used them to force itself deeper inside her, and then this man peering at it all in close-up, his eyes swivelling from feather to flesh as a disembodied voice told him what to look at.

All his attention was on the picture. I edged closer, and closer still, until I was close enough to touch him, poised all the time for flight.

The voice coming from his headphones was Italian. The cadences were unmistakable. As I stood there, he moved smartly on to the next picture, again positioning himself directly in front of it and examining it in the same minute detail.

I went over to the security guard. 'Thomas, there hasn't been anyone in here acting strangely, has there?'

'They're all pretty strange. Especially the Germans.'

'But nothing unusual?'

He shook his head and said regretfully, ''Fraid not.' I saw his point: when you spent your whole working day staring at a room full of tourists, you weren't likely to forget if something unusual had happened.

'Thanks.' I turned away. Just for a second, I thought I saw a head I recognized as it moved away from me at the far end of the gallery.

I set off after it. Whoever it was had turned into a side gallery.

There were people in the way, and I had had no more than a glimpse, a tiny flash of some familiar black-grey hair. I broke into a run. As I turned the corner I almost collided with him.

Alex.

'Hello,' he said.

'What are you doing here?' I blurted.

'Holbein.' He gestured at the painting in front of him. 'One of my favourites. What about you?'

I said something noncommittal. It couldn't be Alex. Lots of the staff liked to have a look at the pictures in their lunch breaks. I often did it myself. It was a coincidence, nothing more.

That afternoon I got a call from Nicholas Spence, one of the curators, asking me to come down and see him. When I got to his office he had a painting on his desk, which he was examining with white-gloved hands.

'Ah, Ros,' he said, taking off one of the gloves to shake my hand. 'Please come in. Would you like a cup of tea?'

'I'm fine, thanks.' There was a story that someone had once asked Dr Spence for Earl Grey instead of lapsang souchong and had been treated to a twenty-minute lecture on the folly of their choice.

'I just wanted to say well done. I'm so glad you're . . . but you really must tell us if there's anything we can do . . .' He took off his glasses and chewed one earpiece furiously while he waited for my response.

'Really, I'm fine.'

'Good, good,' he said, relieved. 'Now, what about these chaps?' He indicated the painting. 'What do we think? Are *they* fine?'

It was an altarpiece; very old, even to my untutored eye, and very much of the pre-Renaissance period, when paintings were more like religious icons than realistic tableaux. It showed a crucifixion, with a figure obviously meant to represent Christ hovering over a stable scene in which Mary was suckling the infant at her breast. Although the draughtsmanship was crude, the painting had been recently cleaned and the colours – the pinks and blues of the fabrics, and the gold leaf which represented the sky – were gorgeous.

'I wouldn't know,' I said truthfully.

'The thing is, we're not sure either. We used to be sure, and now we're not.'

'What's the problem?'

'How much do you know about, ah, perspective?'

'Not a great deal,' I confessed.

'Before the Renaissance, perspective was based on guesswork, not mathematics. Then in the early fifteenth two of our old Florentine chums, Leon Alberti and Filippo Brunelleschi' – he pronounced both names in perfect Italian – 'stumbled on the secret. The key was realizing that, from the spectator's viewpoint, the picture has to stretch away to an infinite point in the distance – what Alberti called the vanishing point.' He had grabbed some paper and was sketching a crude diagram as he spoke. 'Once you know that a picture should have a vanishing point, everything makes perfect geometric sense.'

'I see.'

'Now, what's interesting about our stable here is that, although it's very crude, it has a vanishing point.' He glanced at me to see if I understood. 'The thing is, once you know perspective, it becomes intuitive. It's like knowing a secret – it's remarkably hard to make yourself forget it and paint, as it were, from inside the mind of someone who doesn't have the secret.'

'So if there is a vanishing point, this picture's a forgery?'

'Perhaps. There is another possibility.'

I could see that he was hoping I'd guess for myself what that was, but I had to ask, 'What's that?'

'There's always a chance that the gentleman who painted this picture,' he indicated the altarpiece, 'might have worked out the geometry of the vanishing point by himself, back in the fourteenth century, more than a hundred years before either Alberti or Brunelleschi. In which case, this little piece might be rather important.' He smiled. 'In fact, I've written an essay about it.'

'Ah.'

'It would, of course, be somewhat embarrassing if, having published an article claiming that this was an undiscovered gem, it turns out to be as bent as a ten-bob note. Which, thanks to Mr Drewe and pals, the international art world will be inclined to think it is.'

'But Drewe didn't do old masters. So far as we know, he only faked modern works.'

'So far as we know. But pre-Renaissance artists are an easy target for any forger. By and large, it doesn't take huge talent, just an ability to make it look old.'

I looked at the altarpiece again. 'What's its provenance?'

'Murky. But I've got a couple of people working on that. Your task, as you can probably imagine, is to see whether the bright light of science can shed any answers.'

'Shouldn't it go to a specialist? Or one of our outside consultants?'

'We're all very impressed with the work you've been doing, Ros. Alex specifically suggested you for this.'

'I'll need a budget to run some speculative investigations – carbon dating, X-rays and so on.'

'Whatever you feel is necessary.' The curator smiled happily. 'If I'm right, it will be money well spent.' He indicated the picture. 'I'll get one of the packers to bring it up, shall I?'

'Thanks. Presumably it needs to be kept very secure.'

'God, yes. This is a disaster check, nothing more. I'm afraid we'll have to take it away from you at the end of every day. And you'll have to wear a mask, of course – mustn't have it breathed on.'

I was so excited about working on a project as important as the altarpiece that I managed to forget all about the notes until I left the building. When I got home, though, there was another envelope waiting.

Dear Ros,

So you stood me up. That was stupid of you. Please understand, we can do this the easy way or the hard way – the choice is yours. But do it we will. The one thing you cannot do is ignore me.

Do I have to spell it out? You lied to the court. A man is in prison because of that lie. If the lie is ever revealed, you will go to prison yourself. Judges don't take a very lenient view of perjury, apparently – it's one of the few crimes that affects them personally.

I'm going to give you one single chance to stop this. If tomorrow you wear the tight white T-shirt with no bra, the one you wore the Tuesday before last, I'll accept it as a message that you want to be left alone, and I will respect your wishes.

An interesting dilemma, isn't it? To stop me playing this game, you have to play the game. In chess this is called a zugzwang – a forced move.

Ah, you are saying, but how do I know I can trust this person? After all, he's writing me anonymous notes, which is not a very nice or trustworthy thing to do. And he cut me. (I'm sorry I cut you, actually. I just wanted you to know I'd been there. Like signing my handiwork.)

The answer, Ros, is that you have no choice. You have to trust me. Your trust is all I want or ask. I don't want to hurt you again.

I called Bill. I had to leave three messages on his mobile before he called me back. I read him the note.

'Don't handle it,' he told me. 'Leave it on one side. I'll bring an evidence bag.'

'Don't be crazy. We can't let anyone else see this.'

'Wait there,' he said quietly. 'We need to talk about this face to face.'

By the time he arrived, though, he had decided I was over-reacting.

'This letter doesn't prove anything, Ros. It could just be a hoax – it probably is just a hoax. There's no reason why we shouldn't hand it to the police.'

'If the police had this, they'd have to investigate the allegations he makes, wouldn't they? Face it, Bill. Henson didn't do it. This guy did. We've made a terrible mistake.'

'Now wait a minute—'

'I said what I did because you told me that forensic evidence proved beyond doubt that Henson was guilty. But it didn't, did it? Henson's defence came up with a perfectly reasonable explanation for the forensic evidence. The jury didn't convict because of the forensic, they convicted because I stood up in court and said that

Henson was wearing that red shirt when he raped me. What if Henson's lawyer was telling the truth?'

'It wasn't only your testimony that convicted him. His wife lied—'

'She was a drunk, for God's sake. Your boss bullied her into making a statement.'

'There was other evidence that didn't come to court. Remember the other woman he attacked? The man who saw him walking away from here carrying a black bag at three o'clock in the morning?'

'I don't know. Maybe there's a good reason why evidence like that is inadmissible. Maybe it *is* too flimsy to rely on.'

'So you'd rather believe a few lines scribbled by some loony?' He was getting angry now. We both were.

'He says, "I don't want to hurt you again," Bill. What does that sound like to you? It's a threat.'

'It could be speculative.' Bill waved at the letter. 'It could be someone who suspects you lied, but doesn't have any proof. If you respond in any way, you'll be saying he's right. You'll have admitted that you're guilty.'

'It's *we*, remember? *We're* guilty. I may have lied on oath, but you fucked a witness, remember?'

'Oh, Ros.' He held open his arms. 'Ros, don't be like that. Whatever happens, of course we're in this together. Whatever happens, I love you.'

Before the trial, when we'd been mucking about with the lie detector, I'd tried to make him say those words into the microphone. And he'd refused. He said it wasn't because it wasn't true, but because it was too important.

'Then I'll say it,' I'd said. 'I love you.' The screen display had scribbled its wriggling lines of stress and intonation and so on and had decided I was, mostly, telling the truth. Mostly, but not completely.

'Hang on,' I said. 'I'm just not saying it the right way.' I picked up the microphone and said, very calmly, 'I. Love. You.' That was truer, apparently. 'I lurve you.' Not bad. I tried one like Donald Duck. 'I love you, Daffy.' That was truer still. But the truest one of all was when you said it so often the words just ran into each other and meant nothing at all: 'IloveyouIloveyouIloveyou.' The less it meant, the more certain the machine became.

'If we hadn't done the things we've done – if I just walked off the street with a letter like that – what would the police advise me to do?'

'Well, the Protection From Harassment Act means that stalking is an offence. But you still have to prove that the stalker's intention is malicious and that he has acted unreasonably and threateningly over a long period of time. We'd probably just give you a copy of our leaflet telling you how to make yourself less of a target.'

'What does it say about things like this?' I pointed to the letter.

'Don't react, don't respond, don't get angry. Stalkers are like bullies. The more you show them you're scared, the more excited they get.'

'So I shouldn't do it? I shouldn't wear a white T-shirt tomorrow?'

'Christ, no. You can't let this guy think he's got to you.'

28

The next morning I got up, showered, and put on the white T-shirt. I stood looking at myself in the mirror. It was my favourite T-shirt.

I thought, perhaps *not* wearing this T-shirt is reacting too. Or what if I wore it but put a shirt on top?

And then I thought, what in God's name am I doing? I'm trying to negotiate in my head with a man who has no right to ask anything of me at all.

I took it off and put on a blue sweatshirt instead. I thought, I'll never wear that white one again.

No notes that morning. Nothing at work. The only thing delivered to my desk was the altarpiece. Everyone clustered round to admire it. Tricia said, 'Oh, it's really sweet.' I knew what she meant – there was something about the combination of blue and gold and the pious, crudely drawn faces that gave the picture a kind of naive innocence.

'This picture I like,' Alex said decisively. 'If it is a fake I shall be very disappointed.'

'And if it isn't, Ros'll be disappointed,' Tricia pointed out.

'Me? I don't care either way,' I said. But of course she was right: although my job was simply to discover the truth, it would be fantastic if I personally found the evidence which showed the art world it was a forgery.

I had a job convincing St Thomas's hospital that I wanted to book their ultrasound scanner for a painting. 'Could I have the patient's name?' the receptionist kept wanting to know.

'It's an altarpiece. We'll pay the usual rate, of course.'

'Does the patient have BUPA?'

'No. Look, we've done this before. Maybe you should check with your consultant. Say that it's the National Gallery.'

A pause. 'Would that be employer's medical cover, then?'

I sighed. 'If you like.'

'And the patient's name again?'

If I said Madonna, she'd probably think I meant the singer. 'Mary Joseph.'

'Is that Mrs or Miss?'

It was hard not to giggle. 'I'm not sure. But she does have a son from a previous relationship. He'll be coming along too.'

'And the nature of her condition?'

'She's been seeing seraphim and cherubim.'

'That's an eye complaint, is it?'

'More likely neurological.'

'Thank you,' the receptionist said, with the triumphant weariness of a person who'd always known she'd get there in the end. 'I'll book you in for Friday morning.'

'One other thing. She'll have some security guards with her. Will that be all right?'

'If she's going private she can bring whoever she likes.'

There was a ping as an email hit my in-box. I looked at the sender ID, and froze. It was from Jo.

But Jo was dead.

I clicked on it.

From: Jo McCourt (joMcC@burnett.co.uk)
Subject: Today's dress choice

Hi Ros,
Greetings from paradise! I am having a great time up here and working on my tan. Thanks for standing up for me in court. Only problem is, though, Gerry Henson didn't do it. And now you've gone and pissed off the person who did.

That was really, really stupid, Ros. Can I make a suggestion? If he gets in touch with you and offers you a chance to make amends, do whatever he asks you to do. It's not worth playing games with him - after all, look what happened to me.

Love and all that,
Jo (or what's left of her)

I felt as if I had just walked into a wall. I picked up the phone and called IT.

'Simon, is it possible to trace the source of an email I've just received?'

'Does it have a sender ID?'

'Yes, but it's not one that makes sense.'

'Was it sent from an office or home?'

'An office, supposedly.'

'It could be someone who knew that person's log-in and password, then. But even if they didn't, there's an easy way to make it look as if an email comes from someone else. All you'd have to do is change the header preferences on your outbox for a few minutes. You could put MarilynMonroe@WhiteHouse.com if you wanted to.'

'But surely it's possible to find out who really sent it?'

'No,' he said apologetically. 'It's a complete myth that emails can always be traced back.'

I forwarded the email to Bill, with a note that said: *I think this constitutes a threat, don't you?*

There was no answer. I tried his mobile, but it was switched off. Eventually, just as I was about to go home, he replied:

To:	RosTaylor@nationalgallery.org
From:	ThomsonW@metpolice.org
Subject:	Re: Today's dress choice

Ros,
Yes, this probably constitutes a threat but you'd have
to prove that a) it was from the same person who sent
the other notes and b) that it's the same person
referred to as 'he' in the email - a confession made
in the third person doesn't count, and a court would
probably say that this is just a sick joke.

I can't call now - something big is kicking off at
this end and I need to jump on it right away.

B.

Thanks a lot, I thought.

To: ThomsonW@metpolice.org
From: RosTaylor@nationalgallery.org
Subject: Re: Re: Today's dress choice

Will you be coming round tonight?

To: RosTaylor@nationalgallery.org
From: ThomsonW@metpolice.org
Subject: Re: Re: Re: Today's dress choice

Don't think so. Sorry.

To: ThomsonW@metpolice.org
From: RosTaylor@nationalgallery.org
Subject: Re: Re: Re: Re: Today's dress choice

I think I need you to. I'm scared. Sorry to be a
hopeless girlie but there it is.

To: RosTaylor@nationalgallery.org
From: ThomsonW@metpolice.org
Subject: Re: Re: Re: Re: Re: Today's dress
              choice

I've just been put on a big murder investigation. I've
got to go to a briefing now, then an autopsy that'll
probably take all night.

Let's talk tomorrow. In the meantime, don't panic. It's
almost certainly a sick joke.

*   *   *

I ordered a taxi by phone. When I got to Broadhurst Terrace I asked the driver to wait a couple of minutes until he'd seen me go in through my door.

'No problem, love,' he said cheerfully. 'Can't be too careful, can you? A girl got done in round here, it was in the paper. Want a receipt?'

I unlocked the front door. Immediately my eyes went to the table where the post was put.

There was nothing for me.

Thank God. I went downstairs and let myself into the flat. Before I did anything else I checked to make sure there was no one else there.

There was a knock on the door. My heart jumped into my throat.

'Who is it?' I called cautiously.

'It's Ian. From upstairs.'

I opened the door, but left the chain on. 'Hello.'

'It's Ian,' he said again.

'Yes.'

When he realized I wasn't going to take the chain off he looked embarrassed and said, 'Um, this was with my letters. Must have got put in the wrong pile.' He handed me a letter through the crack.

'And I – I just wanted to say how sorry I am about Jo,' he began.

'Yes?'

He paused. I still didn't take the chain off. He said, 'Perhaps now's a bad time.'

'Yes.'

Fuck him, I thought as he turned and headed back up the stairs. When he'd gone I ripped the envelope open.

Ros,

I'm not angry.

I *was* angry, but on reflection I'm pleased. I'm pleased because you've made your choice, and it's one which will give me infinitely more pleasure than leaving you alone.

Talking of pleasure – did you know that you came when I raped you? Did they tell you that, the doctors, or can't their scientific tests see that far? It's true, though. You were unconscious, but your body responded to me when I went down on you.

I felt like Ali Baba kneeling before the cave of wonders. Open sesame. It took a long time but I was patient.

Did you know that your insides have the same salt ratio as sea water? It's because we came from the sea, long ago. You tasted of cooped-up oceans, Ros, and your little clitoris went hard when I chewed on it. And though you were unconscious I felt the little shakes and twitches when you came, like a dog chasing rabbits in its sleep. So you see, your body is a lot less choosy than you think.

Ros, what's going to happen will be unpleasant for you. But it's nothing compared to the pain I've experienced – the pain of wanting you. All I'm doing is spreading that pain around a bit. A little more for you, a little less for me. What can I say? I'm sorry, I really am.

You will say, 'How can he hurt me if he claims he loves me?' Because like all women you have an idea that love is something nice. If only you knew what really goes on inside our heads.

Love is selfish. Sometimes people get lucky, and get to be selfish in pairs. You do me and I'll do you. I don't think that would ever happen between you and me – no: let's be honest and say I *know* it wouldn't. So I'm taking second best. If I can't have your love, I'll have your fear. If I can't have your body willingly pressed against mine, I'll put it there by force. Of course it isn't perfect. But it's what I can get.

You are the custodian of your beauty – a strange phrase, but I find myself saying it to myself over and over again. You don't own your body, Ros. You inherited it, and you will pass it on to the next generation, and in the meantime you hold it in trust, making sure that none of it gets spilt on people like me, the revolutionaries who cut off the aristocrats' heads and tear down their palaces, taking by force what we were denied by birth.

You've probably guessed by now that I killed Jo. But I didn't rape her. When they said at the trial she'd been raped, that upset me. I could have fucked her but I didn't. It was only ever you. And it will only be you again.

I'm still going to give you a choice.

The first choice is this: leave your door unlocked so that I can get in. Have a bath, wash your hair and brush it, dab on a little scent (but not too much), take a sleeping drug and go to bed, naked, in fresh white sheets. If you do this, I will make love to you but I will not kill you. It will be no worse than having an operation, and when it's over, it will be done with.

Or you can lock the door against me, in which case I will still rape you, but it will be a different sort of rape. For a start, you'll be awake, or awake enough to know what's happening. By the end of it, though, you will be dead. I will look into your eyes and you will beg me to kill you, and I will. But not until then.

You have a third choice, of course, which is that you can go straight to the police and ask them to protect you. You'll have to explain who I am – *what* I am – and why I am still free. You'll go to prison. But I will still come for you eventually, when you get out. By then, as an ex-convict, the police won't be interested in protecting you any more. (If, indeed, they will be now. You've seen the police at work. They don't exactly fill you with confidence, do they?)

Anyway, you have a couple of days to think about this. If you decide to take the sensible course, email me. I've set up a Hotmail account – Custodian@hotmail.com.

If I haven't heard from you by Sunday, I'll assume that you would rather be my victim than my lover.

29

I felt as if someone had hit me. I staggered around the flat, double-checking all the windows, making sure there wasn't a single crack of light through which anyone could see me while I wept and shrieked and swore. Then I curled up on the sofa in a state of numb catatonia. I stayed on that sofa all night.

Next day I called another taxi to take me to work. Putting on my white lab coat no longer made me feel safe. The feeling of detachment and normality it had given me had only been an illusion.

I couldn't work. I stared at the image of Christ on his golden cross blindly. I think I would have prayed to him, too, if there hadn't been the possibility that the fucking thing was another fake.

Alex came over to talk about the altarpiece. He wanted to check what investigations I'd be running. Somehow I managed to snap into autopilot.

'I'm going to order a total ion chromatogram,' I said. 'I want to check the varnish composition.'

Alex nodded. Pre-twentieth-century varnish was different from modern, synthetic varnishes. You could fake old varnish, by mixing larch resin with mastic and turpentine, but most forgers were unlikely to bother. Discovering that the panel was coated in synthetic varnish would be a big clue that it was a forgery.

'I've already booked a basic ultrasound and a scan for diffraction analysis. If that's inconclusive, I think we should get an XRF done.' An energy-dispersive X-ray with fluorescent spectroscopy, to give it its full name, was the biggest gun in our investigative armoury. It could generate a computer print-out of every single chemical element in the paint. Clever forgers, of course, used pigments that matched those available at the time the picture was meant to have been painted. But even clever forgers sometimes made mistakes.

'Then there's carbon dating of the wood – if we get it done at the Freer it'll only mean removing a tiny sample. And if they can analyse a few fragments of paint for, say, acid and protein, that might be handy too. I was going to phone them this afternoon, when the States have woken up, and see what they suggest.'

'Good,' he said approvingly. 'That's exactly what I would have done.' He glanced at my face. 'Are you all right?'

'Fine,' I said brightly.

'You seem a bit distracted.'

'I'm just tired, that's all.'

'It must be hard, coming back to work after all you've been through. That's why I thought—' He indicated the painting. 'Something to get your teeth into. But if it gets too much, you will tell me, won't you?'

'Of course.'

'Remember it's only a painting. People are more important. Well, some people, anyway.' Just for a moment, he took my hand in both of his and squeezed it.

'I'll be fine,' I said again.

At ten Tricia took a phone call from the front desk.

'Ros, there's a policeman to see you downstairs.'

Thank God. I took the letter and ran down to the foyer. But it wasn't Bill. A thin, short man in a dark suit and a taller woman were waiting for me. The man was carrying a briefcase. The desk guard said something to him as I came down the stairs and he turned towards me.

'Ros Taylor?'

'Yes?'

The man produced a card. 'My name is Detective Superintendent Scratton, and this is Detective Sergeant Hill. Can we have a word in private, please?'

We went to one of the meeting rooms. I watched while Scratton got some papers out of his case. Then he took an old-fashioned ink pen from his inside pocket and uncapped it. I used the time to try to pull myself together.

'I represent a department of the Metropolitan Police called Internal Investigations,' he began. 'Essentially, we investigate complaints about, and allegations against, individual police officers. I'm here because we've had a complaint about one of the officers involved in your case.'

'Who from?' I managed to say.

'The complaint was anonymous.' He gave me a brief, professional smile that didn't reach his eyes. 'Which, of course, makes it extremely hard to assess whether or not there's any truth in it. Nevertheless, we have to take all allegations against our officers very seriously.'

'Yes. I suppose you do. May I see it?'

'See what?'

'The complaint.'

'Not at this stage. May I ask, what makes you think it was a letter?'

I shrugged.

'The allegation concerns the conduct of Detective Inspector Thomson.' He gave me a hard look and I realized that I shouldn't have said 'who from?' but 'who about?' 'You know the officer I'm referring to.'

'Of course. Bill was in charge of the investigation.'

'So you know him in a professional context.'

'Yes.'

'Have you had any contact with him apart from that?'

'What sort of contact?' I heard myself say.

'Have you met him anywhere outside of a police station?'

'We sometimes met in coffee shops. When he was updating me about the case. I didn't like going to the station.'

'But those were meetings related to the investigation.'

'Yes.'

'Was his conduct always completely professional?'

'Yes. Always.'

'Did you ever see him in the evenings, for example?'

'Um.' I tried to think. We had been together so often. Other policemen would be able to tell Scratton that. Or would they lie about it? I decided to play for time. 'Well, I went to the party after the trial finished. All the detectives were there.'

'What about before the trial finished?'

'Once or twice. Just casually.'

'Did you have any kind of relationship with him?'

I glanced at the woman but there was nothing in her eyes that could help me. She was only there to provide the necessary X chromosomes so that the interview could take place. I looked at Scratton again. 'Only a professional one.'

'Did he ever ask you out?'

'No,' I said truthfully.

'Did he ever proposition you in any way, either verbally or non-verbally?'

'No.' That was also true, as it happened. It had been me who had propositioned him.

'Have you ever had sexual relations with him?' His eyes were as expressionless as the woman's.

'Don't be ridiculous,' I said.

'Do you know where he lives?'

'I haven't a clue.'

He reached into his briefcase and pulled out a glossy ten-by-six photograph in a plastic wallet. 'I'm showing you a photograph that was sent to us. Can you identify yourself?'

The photo showed me walking away from Bill's flat. It must have been taken during the court case. I recognized the suit I'd worn in court.

'It certainly looks like me,' I said weakly.

'Would you have any reason to be in Stoke Newington?'

I said, 'Well, one of my friends, Tricia Mills, lives in that area. I stay with her sometimes.'

Scratton's gaze didn't leave my face. 'What's her address?'

'Fernley Road. Um, number thirty-nine.'

'When you go to see her, how do you get there?'

'Tube, usually. I don't have a car. And then I walk from the tube.' I tapped the photo. 'This is probably just me walking back to the tube station. I must have passed your detective's house and not even realized it.'

He nodded, but it was more the kind of nod that acknowledges a good move by an opponent than a nod of agreement. 'Have you ever noticed anyone taking pictures of you?'

'No. But – it's strange, but several times over the last few months I've had the feeling someone was following me. And once I found that all my rubbish had been opened, but no one else's in the street had been touched.'

Another nod, more thoughtful this time.

'Is Bill in trouble?' I asked.

Scratton replaced the top of his fountain pen. 'Not if his account matches yours. It's probably just a mischief-maker, or possibly even some unscrupulous friend of Mr Henson's trying to stir up grounds for an appeal.' He began to gather his notes together. 'You'll have to come in to Scotland Yard later to sign the record of interview, if that's all right. Just give me a couple of hours to get it typed up and shipshape.'

'No problem.'

'And we'll need to talk to your friend Tricia Mills. Can you tell me where I can find her?'

'She works here, in the Science and Conservation Department.'

'Oh.' The fountain pen came out again. 'Well, in that case we might as well have a word with her now.'

I desperately tried to think of some way of stopping them from talking to Tricia before I'd explained to her what she'd have to say. I opened my mouth. Nothing came out.

The policewoman said, 'Sir, you've got the Commissioner at eleven thirty.'

'Christ. So I have. Well, it'll have to wait until tomorrow, then.'

I ran upstairs and explained to a completely uncomprehending Tricia why she had to say that I'd come to stay with her sometimes during the trial.

'It makes sense. I didn't want to be alone. Please, Trish. It's nothing dodgy, it's just that he's not meant to be going out with me and he'll get into trouble if they know.'

Put like that, it was young love versus faceless bureaucrats. I knew Tricia was no lover of authority. Every time there was any kind of protest in Trafalgar Square she was always out there, shouting and whistling with the rest of them.

'Well, go on then,' she said reluctantly.

'You're an angel.'

I ran out into Trafalgar Square and jumped in a taxi. 'St Mary's, Paddington,' I told the driver.

I've got to go to an autopsy that'll probably take all night. Please let him still be there, I prayed. I had to get to him before Scratton did.

At the hospital I retraced the route I took with Bill and Charlotte all those millennia ago, down to the pathology suites. The same receptionist was presiding over the same empty waiting room, littered with the same magazines.

'Is Detective Inspector Thomson here?'

'Is that Mr Harkur's autopsy?'

'Probably.'

She ran her finger down a list. 'Yes, I think he's still there. Do you want to wait?'

I waited forty-five minutes before a grey-looking Bill came out. With him was another man I didn't recognize. I recognized the notebook he was carrying, though, which was standard-issue Met.

Bill glanced at me and said to the other man, 'I'll meet you by the car.'

He waited until he was out of earshot, then turned to me. 'Shit, Ros, this really isn't a good idea.'

'A man called Scratton from Internal Investigations is investigating us. Someone sent him a photo. And I got this last night. I tried to reach you but your phone's been off.' I pushed the letter at him. 'It's all right about Scratton, I've got my friend Tricia to lie for us. But you're going to have to get rid of all those emails I sent you. And the text messages on your phone.'

'Whoa. Whoa. Calm down. One thing at a time.' He glanced at the letter, then said, 'No, tell me about Scratton first. What did he want?'

'I told you, he's got a photograph.' I took a breath, counted to three, and then explained again about the interview and what I'd said.

'And this girl Tricia. How reliable is she?'

'She'll be fine.'

'If she isn't, if they suspect anything at all, they'll suspend me and carry out a proper, detailed investigation. If they do that they'll find evidence. Too many people have seen us together.'

'Coppers. They won't tell on us, will they?'

'I don't know.' Bill looked worried. 'Ros, a long time ago, just before I met you, I told an Incident Review Board that I'd overheard a policeman making a racist remark. I didn't name him, because I couldn't, but some of my fellow officers thought I should have kept my mouth shut anyway. Some of them might quite like to see me in trouble.'

'None of them can prove we slept together.' A thought struck me. 'Except I did tell Alice Turnbull. But she won't tell anyone, will she?'

'Alice won't lie. If she's asked, she'll tell the truth.'

'Not if it gets you into trouble. She's in love with you, Bill. Well, maybe not in love, but she definitely has a thing for you.'

'She won't lie,' he repeated. 'I know. She's like I used to be.' He sighed and looked at the letter. 'OK. Let me read this.'

As he read his face hardened even further. 'Oh, Christ,' he muttered. Then: 'We've got to go to Scratton and tell him everything.'

There was nothing I could say.

'I'll go to them right away,' he said. 'Oh, shit. What a mess.'

'I can't, Bill. I can't go to prison. Isn't there anything else we can do?'

'I don't know.' All the fight seemed to have drained from him. 'I just don't know.'

He had been strong for me during the investigation. Now I had to be strong for him. I said, 'Right. Let's not rush anything. We've got until the weekend to decide what to do about this.' I pointed to the letter. 'And Tricia will keep Scratton at bay, for a little while at least. Let me think. There has to be a way out of this.'

I thought, I will not be that man's victim all over again.

Suddenly all my panic had evaporated, replaced by a calm anger. I was not going to be destroyed. I was going to win this fight, no matter what it took.

I went back to the office and put on my white coat again. I was a scientist. There was a logical, rational plan somewhere that would resolve everything. I just had to find it.

30

'This came for you.'

Another envelope, in the gallery's internal mail system this time. *Ros Taylor, Science and Conservation Department.* But this time my hands, as I opened it, weren't shaking.

Inside was another of the gallery's postcards. *The Rape of Europa*, by Guido Reni. This time the inevitable unclothed podgy maiden was being rogered by a bull – all very beautifully, of course, but that was undoubtedly what was going on. An even podgier Cupid peeked at them from behind laced fingers.

I turned it over. On the back was a drawing of a loveheart. Around it, in very small letters, it said:

My sweet darling Ros,

Have you listened to the gallery's guided audio tour recently? I did, the other day. It had something very interesting to say about the inclusion of Cupid in this picture.

It set me thinking, actually. Why do we draw a loveheart to signify that we're in love? It looks nothing like a heart, after all. And then it struck me – of course, it's not a heart at all, it's a *yoni*, that Cavern of Wonders whose entrance lies between your legs.

Before I send this I am going to kiss my drawing, as I hope soon to kiss the real thing. Just to reassure you again – you will feel nothing. There will be no lasting marks. Except, perhaps, a faint half-memory, transparent like a ghost, that imprints itself on your heart – not to mention on that other place –

The text ended abruptly where it reached the bottom of the card. I logged on to the gallery's intranet and called up the part of the audio tour relating to the Guido Reni. A chirpy voice issued from my iMac:

'*The Rape of Europa*, by Guido Reni, is dated approximately 1620. It tells the story of the beautiful Europa, with whom the pagan god Jupiter fell in love. Transforming himself into a bull, he ravished her and bore her away to Crete, where their story becomes entwined with another myth, that of the Minotaur. The inclusion of Cupid is unusual in portrayals of this story. Reni seems to be suggesting that Jupiter was motivated by love, not lust. The painting may have been a commission by a patron who wished Reni to emphasize this interpretation. The painting is on loan from the collection of Sir Denis Mahon . . .'

I clicked it off. Whoever was sending these notes knew the gallery's collection very well. But that didn't necessarily mean anything. All the information was readily accessible.

If only, I thought, we could get the police to investigate properly.

The phone rang. It was Julia Pressburg, my contact at the Freer lab in New York, returning my call about the altarpiece. We chatted about science stuff – the difference between XRF and XRD; whether chromatographs or spectrographs would ultimately prove more useful. I asked her if there were any other investigations she'd recommend.

'We've got some great new toys over here,' she enthused. 'We've just taken delivery of a new electron microscope from Japan that can pick fingerprints off of varnish, and we have a laser diffractor and a Polymarker in addition to the carbon-dating facilities . . .'

Something prickled at the back of my mind. Polymarker. Where had I heard that name before?

Then it came to me. At the trial. The forensic scientist droning on. '*Polymarker is less informationally rich than STR but more accurate when the amounts to be tested are very small . . .*'

I said, 'Julie, Polymarker tests for DNA, doesn't it?'

'That's correct.'

Before I send this I am going to kiss my drawing . . .

'And it works with very small amounts of material?'

'Minuscule. We've had good results from as little as five cells.'

I picked up the envelope. 'Could you isolate DNA from a piece of card that someone had touched against their lips? I mean, that they'd kissed?'

'Possibly.'

'What about the gum on the back of an envelope? You know, if someone had licked it to seal it?'

'Depends. But yeah, we'd have a pretty good shot.'

'How quickly could you do that? If I sent some samples over by FedEx tonight?'

'Say a week. But for that kind of timescale it's gonna cost you.'

'That's no problem,' I heard myself saying. 'There'll be some material with you tomorrow morning. Then another batch in a few days' time, for matching.'

'Sure, honey. You send me whatever you want.'

I isolated the envelope flap and the loveheart into half a dozen dry mounts and sent it over. But that was only one half of the equation. I would need a DNA sample from the killer to match to. And before I could even think about getting that, I had to generate a pool of suspects.

You're a scientist, I reminded myself. Forget your emotions. Just write down who it *could* be.

I pulled a piece of paper towards me. I thought, it could be anyone.

Correction: anyone I know. This man writes me intimate letters. He describes my clothing. This man thinks he knows me.

It's someone I've met.

I could send over maybe a dozen samples for matching, no more. These tests would cost tens of thousands of dollars. Too many samples, and it would occur to Julie to ring someone more senior than me for authorization. I needed to find a way of keeping down the number of suspects.

If I were a policeman, I'd commission a psychological profile, and prioritize the suspects who matched it.

Then I thought: I already have a profile. Dr Griffin wrote one. It was part of the evidence bundle presented in court.

I still had all the papers at the flat. I called myself a taxi and got back there as fast as I could. The profile was in the middle of the bundle. *Profile of an Unknown Offender*, Dr Stephen Griffin MA, DPhil, CPsychol, AFBPsS.

As I read it, several things became clear. Dr Griffin had based his opinion on various pieces of information that were now out of date. He'd assumed, for example, that the rapist had been the same person who had administered the drugs. But if you assumed that Jo and I could have found the drugs after the party and taken them ourselves, a very different picture emerged.

What really made me sit up, though, was a section about DNA testing:

6.3 It is significant, in my opinion, that expert examination of the crime scene has not yet turned up any DNA evidence which can be said with any certainty to be the offender's. Either the offender's DNA is there, but impossible to isolate because there is a valid reason for its presence, or else the offender took extraordinary precautions against leaving any. This might be because his DNA is already on file somewhere, as is the case with all offenders on the Sexual Offences Register, many police officers, and people with genetic conditions such as haemophilia or Huntington's Disease. Alternatively, it might simply be because he envisages a long criminal career and wishes to take every possible precaution against being caught. A third possibility is that he considers himself an obvious suspect who would be included in any DNA screening activity by the police.

An obvious suspect, I thought. Again, someone who knows me.

Griffin had referred to the cutting as the killer's 'signature'. That was absolutely right, of course. He'd left me on my bed, posed like a tableau. Like a piece of art, and then he'd signed his handiwork.

Art. *Art.* The Michelangelo, the Guido Reni, the references to the gallery's tour. Everything came back to art.

I took a clean piece of paper and wrote: *The offender is knowledgeable about art.*

But he also knew about science. He had left no DNA trace at the crime scene. He had changed the header on an email to obscure its origins.

I wrote: *The offender is competent, if not skilled, at scientific and technical matters.*

I stared at what I'd just written. I only knew one person who fitted both categories, and that was my boss, Alex.

Alex, who had been near Room 8 when I'd been told to go and stand by the Michelangelo.

Alex, who had given me the afternoon off on the day of the rape. Who had known, therefore, that I'd be at home.

Alex, who told me that I was far too young and beautiful to be stuck in a museum.

People are more important than paintings, Ros. You look upset. Is there anything you want to tell me?

Don't jump to conclusions, I told myself. He's on the list, that's all.

Carl Howell was out, of course. There was no way a jobless black sex offender had written those notes. The two teenagers who'd jacked my phone were out for the same reason.

The most technically savvy person I knew was Simon, the IT guy.

He's on the list too, I thought.

I wrote: *The offender is obsessed with me. Therefore, the chances are he's not in a relationship. He doesn't think he'd be able to attract me in the normal way. He is unlikely to appear confident or successful.*

I wouldn't have said Alex was shy or unconfident. However, so far as I knew, he was single. And he might well assume that he was way too old for me, quite apart from being my boss.

Simon, of course, was cripplingly shy. And now that I thought about it, there was something faintly creepy about the way he'd pushed himself forward as my confidant and shoulder to cry on.

Alternatively, maybe he was just a nice guy.

I shook my head. All this was speculation to which I'd never get any answers. The DNA was the crucial thing. Simon was already on the list. But who else?

Nathan, I thought. There was definitely something obsessive about Nathan. But the police had interviewed him, early on in the investigation. He'd been using the internet, and had been able to prove it.

The internet. Computers again. Coincidence? I put him down with a question mark.

Next I wrote: *The offender has good access to my flat and the gallery.*

All the names I'd got so far had access to the gallery. My flat was more out of the way – but that might simply indicate how obsessional this person was. On the other hand, there were also people around me in the flat – people like Ian.

By now I had four names:

1. Alex.
2. Simon
3. Nathan?
4. Ian from upstairs??

I sat back and sighed. Now that it was written down, my little list seemed childish and amateur, a pathetic attempt to play detective.

But, I reminded myself, even the police didn't catch people by working out who did it. They caught people by working out who *hadn't* done it. 'Like the varnish,' I said aloud. 'Modern varnish doesn't prove a painting's fake, but medieval varnish proves it isn't.'

By six o'clock I had fourteen names.

Bill studied my list in silence. I tried to explain how I'd got to it. I wasn't sure if he thought I was just kidding myself, but he did eventually say, 'It can't harm to check them out. If you really think you can get hold of their DNA.'

'I haven't thought about the how yet. Only the what.'

'You sound like Collier,' he muttered.

'Speaking of which, when you eliminated Nathan from the original inquiry because he said he was using the internet, how did you know he was telling the truth?'

'If I remember rightly, his home phone records tallied with what he said.'

'Oh. But hang on. That doesn't prove anything, does it?' I objected. 'His computer might have been connected to the internet, but how do we know he was sitting at the computer? I'm no expert, but it would be easy enough to dial up and then go out, leaving your computer still connected.'

Bill nodded reluctantly. 'I suppose so. There's very rarely absolute proof, you know. If he was interviewed and his story seemed to check out all right, my officers wouldn't have had any reason to follow it up any further. That's just the way it goes.'

I crossed out the question mark next to Nathan's name. 'Bill, there's something else that's puzzling me. Dr Griffin says the killer didn't leave any DNA.'

'That's right.'

'But in his note, he specifically says he went down on me.' Bill winced. I said impatiently, 'Forget that it's me we're talking about here. What I'm wondering is, when I had my examination at the rape suite, Dr Matthiesson took a swab. Why didn't they find his DNA then?'

'Because they didn't test the genital swabs.'

I stared at him. 'What? Why not?'

'Because at that stage it didn't look as if we were dealing with the sort of rapist who would do that,' he said wearily. 'Ros, there are over a hundred different tests that can be done on the material gathered by a rape kit protocol. We don't have the resources to do all of them for every single rape. Running any investigation is a series of financial compromises. You just have to hope that you're making ones that don't matter.'

I said quietly, 'What about the internal swabs? Did you use those?'

'I can't remember,' he muttered. 'Probably not.'

'So I lay on a trolley and let some stranger – a perfectly pleasant and professional stranger, but a stranger nevertheless – shove her hand up me, without the benefit of lubricants, as she told the court in graphic detail, when it was of no relevance to the investigation?'

'The doctor was following standard procedure. At that stage, she couldn't have known which tests would become necessary. No one could.'

'Let me tell you something, Bill. I'm glad I'm not relying on the police any more. Because you're fucking useless, you know that?'

'Yes,' he said quietly. 'I do.'

31

Ian from upstairs was the lowest on my list but the easiest to get DNA from. I simply invited myself in for a cup of coffee. While he was making it I asked if I could use his bathroom. Then I locked the door and crouched down to investigate the floor of the shower.

There was a hank of wet hair trapped by the cross-wires of the drain. I had brought tweezers, plastic gloves and a supply of envelopes. As I fished it out, damp and glistening, I remembered Dr Matthiesson saying the hair needed to have roots. I peered closely at the soggy mass. It looked smelly and decayed and suspect. There had to be something better.

I peered up the side of the cubicle. Stuck to one of the tiles was a tiny, perfect treble clef of red hair. I plucked it with the tweezers and placed it in an envelope. Then, to be on the safe side, I sealed the envelope straight away and wrote Ian's name on the front.

Alex, too, was reasonably straightforward. When he was working in the lightbox I went to the cupboard where we kept our coats. Because we wore lab coats while we were working, all of us kept our jackets and coats on hangers in the cupboard. Alex's black leather coat was at one side. I switched on an ultraviolet torch I'd brought with me and directed the purple beam at the collar. Under the UV half a dozen white flakes of dead skin appeared, like a constellation of stars. I pulled a strip of sterile surgical tape from a roll, placed it firmly across the collar, and pulled it off again. The flakes of skin came with it. I took the strip of tape to my bench, isolated a cluster and dry-mounted it onto a slide, just as Alex emerged, blinking, from the lightbox.

Two down, twelve to go.

* * *

Simon was more difficult. In the end I decided the simplest thing was to deliberately crash my computer, then feed him cups of coffee and biscuits until I spotted something with DNA on.

Unfortunately Simon didn't seem to be thirsty or hungry. Nor did he bring a jacket with him. He did pick up my computer screen and move it around to try to see what was wrong with it, but even I could see that it wasn't very practical to ship a whole computer monitor over to the States.

Then I saw, sticking out of his pocket, the edge of a paper tissue. It was a pretty good bet that he'd used it at some point. It was the best I was going to get. I leaned over the keyboard shamelessly, ostensibly to look at what he was doing on the monitor but actually to distract Simon while I hooked the tissue out of his pocket with my left hand. It fell to the floor. I kicked it under my desk, and retrieved it when he'd gone.

Over the next few days I scrabbled around after half-eaten biscuits and licked forks. I snaffled up clipped crescent moons of nail. I pounced on cigarette ends, their stubbed front ends crumpled as car wrecks. My hoard included a piece of grey, hardened chewing gum, a licked stamp intercepted in the post-room, and a used sticking plaster. On the floor under the curator's desk I found a single extravagantly long pubic hair, crooked as an unravelled coathanger. Every single fragment of humanity went into a separate envelope, and every single envelope went straight to Julia in New York.

That still left Nathan. I was reluctant to phone him and say that I'd like to meet up after all, but I couldn't think of any other way of getting to him. I took care to suggest somewhere very public, though. The crypt of St Martin-in-the-Fields had been turned into a café, and it was often full of people who had just been to a service or a Bible-reading class in the church above. If I wasn't safe there, I reasoned, I wasn't safe anywhere.

If Nathan was surprised I had finally decided to see him, he didn't show it. In fact, I got the impression he was actually so arrogant that he accepted it as no more than his due. Unfortunately, he was also too arrogant to do small talk. Long, intense silences were left, into which I was clearly meant to drop sentences of great significance. Except that I couldn't think of any.

My plan had been to get him to eat something with a spoon, or at least a frothy cappuccino, and hope that there would be enough material on that to do a test. But all he wanted was a glass of red wine. I wasn't sure, but I imagined that a glass, while good for fingerprints, might not be much good at retaining organic tissue. As the minutes stretched into an hour, and an hour into two hours, I had a sudden vision of myself having to sleep with him in order to get some DNA, tiptoeing away from his bed with a used condom in my hands like some rare species of fish. Gross. I shook my head to clear the image away.

Leaning forward, I said, 'Do you know what I'd really like now?'

'What?'

'A cigarette. Will you have one with me?'

'I don't smoke.'

Fuck.

'I'm going to the gents,' he said abruptly.

Plenty of DNA there, but I could hardly follow him.

At the table next to me a waitress, trying to make space for a tray, knocked a wine glass onto the floor. It shattered, and she turned to me with a horrified gasp of apology.

'Don't worry,' I assured her. 'Look, I'm fine.' The glass had been half empty, and none of it had hit me.

'I'll get a pan,' she said. She had a pleasant Australian voice. 'Just be careful where you put your feet, eh?'

'Don't worry. I'll be careful.'

She had already rushed off, almost colliding with Nathan, who was coming out of the gents. I thought: it's now or never. I bent down and carefully picked a long sliver of glass off the floor. Putting my hand casually over Nathan's wine as if I was just making a bit more space, I dropped the shard into his drink.

'Where were we?' he asked, settling himself in his chair.

'Having a great time,' I said. 'Cheers.' I raised my own glass to my lips. Automatically he did the same. A split second later there was a muffled '*Fuck!*' as he bent forward to spit the glass out. He put the back of his hand to his mouth. When he took it away it was red with blood. 'Fuck!' he repeated. A drop of blood fell onto the paper tablecloth. He got up, his face flushed and angry. 'What have you done?' he hissed. 'You fucking cow. I saw you—'

'It was me,' the waitress said, coming back with a dustpan and brush. 'Oh, Jesus. Did that go in your drink? That was my fault, I am *so* sorry. Hey, are you OK?'

Nathan was staring at me, his eyes blazing. 'It was her. I saw her playing with my drink.'

I said calmly, 'She broke a glass. A bit must have gone in your wine.'

'Here.' The waitress handed him a glass of water. When he drank, a skein of red blood twisted through the clear liquid. He said to me, 'I suppose you think this is funny.'

'I'm not laughing.'

'You've been laughing at me all night. But you won't go on laughing much longer.' He put his hand to his mouth and stalked out.

'Jeez, I am *so* sorry your boyfriend's pissed with you,' the waitress said.

'He's not my boyfriend.'

'Thank God, eh?' the waitress said, and we shared a smile. When she had gone I carefully tore off the part of the paper tablecloth spotted with Nathan's blood.

That night there was another note. It said:

Don't hate me, Ros. Hate will eat you up inside and make you ugly.
I couldn't bear to be the one who wiped that beautiful smile from
your eyes.

It was Friday night, forty-eight hours before the deadline.

I went to see the estate agent. I sat down in his cramped little office and told him that I needed to get away from someone.

'If I buy this flat, how can I make sure that no one – I mean absolutely no one – could find out I was living there?'

If he thought it was a strange request, he didn't show it. 'You'll be on the electoral register. That's the first place anyone would look.'

'Can I get myself off it?'

'If you don't mind not having a vote.'

'Believe me,' I told him, 'that's the least of my worries. What else?'

He thought. 'Phone records are the next most obvious thing.'

'Fine. I don't need a phone, I'll use my mobile.'

'They'll need an address to send the bill to.'

'Can they use a PO box?'

'I suppose so. You'll need to put your name on your mortgage deeds, of course, although under the data protection act you can ask that it be kept confidential. But you'll need an address for your credit card, your bank, utility bills . . . the truth is, if someone's determined to find you, they probably will.'

At a strange shop off Baker Street that sold equipment for would-be spies I tried to buy a can of mace.

'We're not allowed to sell that any more,' the smooth assistant told me. 'I can sell you a pepper spray, though.' He opened up one of the cabinets and brought out a tiny silver canister, a bit like a trendy perfume bottle.

'That looks a bit lightweight,' I said dubiously. 'Will it actually stop someone?'

'It takes a whole bottle of Tabasco and explodes it into someone's face,' he said calmly. 'It would certainly stop me.'

'Oh. Put like that, I can see it wouldn't be very pleasant.'

'Handy for making bloody Marys, too,' he said. 'Do I take it you're looking for enhanced personal security?'

'Well, yes.'

He pulled something else out of the cabinet. It looked like a very fat, bulbous pen. At one end there was a metal tip, like a bullet, with three metal rings set into the circumference of the pen higher up. 'This is the most effective thing we've got.' He placed it in my hand. It was surprisingly heavy.

'What on earth is it?'

'It's a stun gun. Well, technically it's a cattle prod, but believe me, if you get prodded with this you're not going anywhere except down on the floor.'

'God. Is it safe?'

'Don't worry. You have to turn on the power, there, and then keep your thumb on the button. Then you touch the tip against the person who's attacking you. The current will go through fabric, leather, and so on.'

'I'll take it.'

I walked out into the glare of the street with the prod heavy in my pocket. It was almost funny how much reassurance it gave me. I felt like a gunslinger. All the men walking down Baker Street with their eager little cocks flapping around inside their trousers and the sex thoughts buzzing around inside their heads had better look out now. I had what they had. I was tooled up. The feeling lasted exactly ten seconds, until some swaggering Arab youth turned his head to leer at me and I averted my gaze, just as I always did.

On Sunday, the last day before the killer's deadline, I made Bill take me out. We did normal, couple things around Stoke Newington – went to the cinema, where we watched a children's film because all the adult offerings were about people doing nasty things to each other, got a takeaway, walked in the park.

He tried to explain about the case he was on. 'This man we're about to arrest, his name is Sammy Harkur and he's one of the biggest crack dealers in North London. I've been after him, one way and another, for about three years.'

'I thought you only investigated a case for thirty-one days.'

'This is different. This isn't one case, it's dozens. He's murdered, pimped, pushed, bribed, you name it, all on an industrial scale. It's probably the most important case of my career.'

I thought, and you don't want to blow it by giving yourself up. What happened in that courtroom is over. Just another nasty little secret, to be pushed into its own compartment and then locked away.

Which was unfair of me, I know, because Bill was just as worried as I was. He just couldn't think of any answers.

That night, he couldn't get hard.

'I'm sorry,' he said, rolling away from me. 'I don't know what—'

'Shh,' I said. 'Don't worry. I'll take care of it. Lie back and close your eyes.'

I wriggled on top of him and kissed him, slowly. I brushed his face with my hair, swinging my head so that it stroked him, lightly, all the way down his chest, his hard stomach. I washed his cock with my tongue and I sucked each of his balls into my mouth, one by one.

After a few minutes he said, 'Maybe I'd better get hold of some Viagra.'

'It doesn't matter,' I lied. 'It's just the stress.'

I thought of the rapist. Somewhere, at that moment, he could be thinking of me, his erection stiff as a spike as he contemplated what he would like to do to me.

It was so unfair. Why me, why us, why any of it?

Bill came with me back to the flat on Monday morning to see whether there had been any response to the missed deadline. There hadn't, but I knew the letter-writer too well by now to get my hopes up.

I was right, of course. He had saved it for the gallery. The personnel director, Kate, was standing by my desk with Simon from IT when I got in.

'Ros, have you read your emails yet?' she asked carefully.

'No. I've just got here.' One look at her face told me that it wasn't good news. 'Is it something unpleasant?'

'Yes. Very.'

I pressed the power button and heard my computer chime as it booted up.

'Actually, I don't think you should look at it,' she said. 'We've sent another email telling everyone to delete it without opening it.'

That should ensure that everyone read it. 'You mean it's gone all round the gallery? To everyone?'

'I'm afraid so. Ros, do you know who might have sent it?'

'No,' I said shortly. 'Just some nutter. Because of the trial.'

'I'm going to call the police—'

'There's no point, Kate, honestly. I'm already in touch with the police and they know what's going on.' I entered my password and scrolled through my emails. There was only one with an attachment. I clicked on it.

A picture of me being fucked by a dog. Only it wasn't me, of course. It was someone else's body, and my head. You couldn't see the join, but if you looked carefully you could tell that my face was slightly grainier than the rest of the picture. Not that anyone would be looking carefully at my face. At the bottom it said:

Hmm - she's nice. But is she for real?

I said to Simon, 'Can you block any more emails from this creep?'

He looked worried. 'Well, there's software that can filter out all attachments with pornographic photographs. But it may be difficult – it can't tell the difference between this sort of thing and a Rembrandt.'

'Are you all right, Ros?' Kate said anxiously.

'I'm fine,' I said. And it was true. I wasn't frightened any more. I felt disgusted and angry and also strangely excited. The guy wanted a fight. I was going to fight him. I didn't know how or where yet, but I was going to fight him.

Half an hour later the phone rang. When I picked it up a polite voice said, 'May I speak to Miss Taylor?'

'Speaking.'

'Miss Taylor, it's Edward Mills from Mills and White, the funeral directors.'

'Yes?'

'I had a message to call you. Is now a good time, or shall I call back?'

'What message?'

'I'm sorry?'

'This message to call me. What exactly did it say?'

'I understood that you had a deceased person you wanted us to collect.'

'Who left the message?'

He sounded puzzled. 'My understanding is that you did, Miss

Taylor.' I heard the sound of rustling paper. 'That's right. It says here Ros Taylor, and the number I've just called.'

'It's a practical joke,' I said shortly. I cut off his grovelling apologies with a curt, 'Don't worry about it,' before I put the phone down on him.

Then there was the phone call from Julia in New York, and that was a different matter altogether.

'Good morning, Ros,' she said, and I said 'Good morning' back although it was two o'clock in London.

'Well, I've got the results from the Polymarker.'

'Great. That was quicker than I thought it would be.'

'Yes. The way the machine works is that negatives come through pretty quickly. It's matching a positive that takes the computer a little time.'

'Hang on.' I was trying to get my brain round this. 'Are you telling me that none of the samples I sent over are a match?'

'That's correct. Is that good news or not?'

Presumably I thanked her, enquired after the weather in New York, told her that I'd be sure to look her up next time I was over. I can't remember any of the rest of the conversation. I remember putting the phone down and staring at it numbly. It was good that it wasn't Alex, of course, or Simon, or any of the other men whose DNA I'd sent over. But that meant I had absolutely no idea who it could be. I was no nearer working out who my stalker was than I had been six months ago. Science had failed me. Once again I was on my own.

No notes that night. But someone had carefully and painstakingly removed the nameplate from my doorbell and replaced my name with the word 'liar'.

'Will he give up?'

Bill stroked my hair. 'I wish I could say yes. But I spoke to a detective who's dealt with several cases like this and she seemed to think that he won't. These activities are what the shrinks call self-reinforcing. He's getting off on the idea of scaring you. That alone motivates him to go on doing it. If he starts to get bored he'll escalate it, not walk away.'

We were in bed. His libido still wasn't functioning.

I said, 'Sometimes I think about having him killed. Maybe I should hire a hitman.'

'Who would you hit? Besides, you'd just get ripped off.'

'You must know hundreds of killers.'

'Strangely enough, they're not my biggest fans.'

'I could get the money. I could add it to the mortgage when I move.'

'Are you serious?'

'I don't know,' I admitted. 'But when I think about killing him – when I imagine just wiping him out – I don't feel that it's wrong. I just think what a relief it would be if it was really all over.'

He said, 'Sometimes I think about killing him too. It's like an instinct, a male thing. Wanting to protect you.'

'I know. Sometimes I want you to forget your scruples and say, just let me tear the bastard limb from limb. Only for a second, mind. I mean, I know it's not really feasible. But when I think of you killing him, it feels so good. So inevitable. Because I know you want to protect me and I don't want to be scared any more.'

It was dark. These conversations are easier in the dark.

'Killing someone isn't easy. It's not like TV. No one ever dies that quickly.'

'I've got something that would knock him out. A stun gun.'

More silence.

I said, 'Could you?'

'Could I what?'

'Could you kill someone?'

We were so close that I could hear his breath catching. 'I already have.'

'When?'

'Last year. It was a hostage situation. A man had gone into his ex-wife's home with a gun. I was outside. We were all spread out, waiting for the negotiators to try to resolve it peacefully. I was on the immediate left-hand side of the door. Eventually he came out, pushing her in front of him. We told him to throw down his weapon but he didn't. She lay down, so he was just standing there with the gun in his hand. He was smiling. I saw him bring his gun up – two-handed, like he meant business, but quite slowly and calmly. Then he pointed it at her. In those situations the orders are very precise. If you've got a clear shot and you can take it, you do. So I shot him.'

'Jesus.'

'I don't think he was going to kill her, actually. I think it was a kind of death wish on his part. Suicide by cop, they call it.'

'How did you feel?'

'I felt fine. I got a commendation.'

'How did you really feel?'

He exhaled slowly. 'I thought – is that it? Taking someone's life, this big taboo, this thing we put criminals in jail for the rest of their lives for – and it was as easy as shooting a paper target on the practice range.'

I ran my hand over his chest. 'Did you shoot to kill?'

He grunted. 'You always do that, whatever the politicians say. There is absolutely no difference between shoot-to-stop and shoot-to-kill. You just do what you have to do.'

I whispered, 'Could you do it again?'

He didn't reply.

'It's just that I can't think of any other way out.'

'Ros. I'm a policeman. This is England. We don't execute people.'

'OK. Sorry. Are you cross?'

'Of course not.'

'It was just a fantasy.'

I reached down and cupped his cock and testicles in my hand. They felt so fragile, so limp, like a bird with a broken neck. There had been a time when just the touch of my hand had been enough to make him harden, but not now.

He said harshly, 'Do you want to come?'

'No. Go to sleep. I like holding you like this.'

32

Ros,

I have been reading about rapists. According to the *British Journal of Psychiatry*, 2001, volume three, I am an extreme narcissist. My desire for you is actually a desire for myself.

Crap.

When Mike Tyson – a convicted rapist – assaulted Lennox Lewis at a televised pre-match press conference he was reported by several eyewitnesses to have snarled, 'I'm gonna fuck you till you love me.'

Rape is better than love – because even if you love someone, you won't let them possess you. You won't give them the power of life and death over you. But you give that power to a rapist, which is why you can't help loving the man who violates you.

I'm going to fuck you till you love me. And then I might kill you, or I might not.

Stop fighting me, Ros. Let it happen.

You can still choose the easy way out.

'The board is made of oak, which carbon dating places at round about fifteen hundred. This is unusual, if the altarpiece is genuine, since Renaissance artists usually preferred poplar.'

I paused and looked at my audience to make sure they weren't bored. But in fact Dr Spence and his assistant curators seemed riveted.

'XRF analysis shows that the pigments used are mainly gold, verdigris and cobalt, fixed with tempera. This is consistent with the pigments in use at the time – no zinc white or Prussian blue. But – and this is the big but – the tempera has also been carbon dated, and is of more recent origin: about nineteen fifty.'

Dr Spence sighed. He could see where this was heading.

'The final piece of evidence is the radiograph. This shows quite clearly that the wooden base once contained wormholes, which have been filled with lead paint. In other words, whoever painted this picture used a piece of wood that was already old when he got hold of it. The most likely scenario is that he bought an old oak cabinet at an auction, pulled it apart, and used the panels as the basis for a number of forgeries. The wormholes are the clincher. No self-respecting Italian painter would have painted on a worm-eaten bit of oak, much less filled in the wormholes with a kind of paint that hadn't even been invented yet.'

'So it's a fake.' Dr Spence looked at his desk, where the altarpiece lay in a perspex case.

'Yes. Not Drewe, of course – he wasn't active in the fifties, and even if he had been, there's no record of him going to the trouble of finding old pieces of wood to paint on. I'd say we're looking at another copyist altogether.'

'Well, it doesn't matter who the prick was.' Dr Spence closed the case. 'We'd better let the insurers know.'

'Of course. I'll prepare a written report.'

'And thank you, Ros. Another excellent piece of work, even if you are the bearer of bad tidings.'

At that moment the gallery's security alarms went off – a cacophony of bells, all at slightly different pitches. Dr Spence looked at his senior assistant. 'Is that a drill?'

'I don't think so.'

'Oh, gracious. I suppose we'd better do what we're meant to do.' Wearily he got up and began locking his safe.

When the scare was over, it turned out that it had been caused by a vandal attack in one of the galleries. Someone had taken a marker pen and scrawled the word 'liar' on one of the paintings when the security guard's back was turned.

'Which painting was it?' I asked with a sense of dread.

'Only a bloody Michelangelo,' Alex said, outraged. '*Leda and the Swan.*'

*   *   *

317

That night's note:

Ros,

Think of this as foreplay.

Fear is a strange emotion. Normally it comes in flashes: the sudden heart-in-mouth moment when you realize a car is pulling out and hasn't seen you; the jolt as a ladder tips under your feet; a phone ringing in the middle of the night. Unpleasant though it may be, it is at least energizing, in a brutal sort of way.

But there is another sort of fear, the sort that is not about adrenalin but survival: a constant, seeping state of terror. In the news just then there was a lot of coverage of the conflict between the Palestinians and the Israelis, both groups trying to live their lives normally but constantly wondering whether they would be the next victim of a soldier's bullet or a suicide bomb. That was how I felt: under siege. Life staggered on as normally as possible under the circumstances, but I was a walking zombie. All my fighting spirit had evaporated. I felt lethargic and washed out and – sometimes – so tired that the idea of dying was becoming almost welcome.

Sometimes I thought there was almost nothing left between Bill and me. Perhaps Griffin had been right and I had always been attracted to him because of his badge, the illusion of protection that it seemed to offer. Because now he couldn't protect me, I no longer loved him. Or rather, I no longer had the energy to love him. Like a pregnant mother saving all her strength for the approaching birth I had turned inward, away from him.

I read somewhere that the terminally ill go through various stages: first shock, then anger, and then denial. After that comes despair, and after that, finally, acceptance – the state of resignation that obituary writers like to call bravery.

I was very close to bravery.

Bill said, 'We can't go on like this.'
   'No. We can't.'
   'We're not even talking any more.'
   'Do you want to leave?'

'Do you want me to?'
'I don't know. It's up to you.'
'Christ, Ros.'

I stopped washing my hair or wearing make-up. I thought that perhaps if I smelt, and made myself look spotty and ugly, whoever it was might lose interest. I was very careful not to smile. My face was a mask. I had switched off all the muscles that responded to what others did or said, turning my impassive statue's gaze on everything around me.

Bill said, 'We can't go on like this.'
'We've already had this conversation.'
'I can't let you do this to yourself.'
'It's not me who's doing anything. It's him.'
'I'm going to turn myself in.'
'We've had this conversation, too.'
Suddenly, we had run out of things to say to each other.

It was a great honour. Of all the technicians in the Science and Conservation Department, I had been selected to assess the damage to the priceless *Leda and the Swan*.

I was given my own office. The security guards were told to include me on their patrols. There had been a time when this would have made me feel more secure.

I propped the painting on the workbench and examined it with a magnifying glass. The word LIAR had been scrawled with black marker ink in letters about four inches high, over the white feathers of the swan and Leda's pale skin. Although it had been done hastily – the cross of the A went right across the I and the R – the letters were all the same size. The writing didn't slant to one side as you'd expect if someone was writing on an upright surface with one eye on the guard and escape.

Like the numbers on my back, I thought. Controlled, relatively small, neat. Organized.

I opened a tub of cotton ear buds and moistened one in water, one in a mild acetone solution and one in an even milder solution of pure alcohol. I was going to try what was, by the standards of our department, a fairly high-risk manoeuvre. I was hoping to

319

dissolve the pen ink but not the layers of paint underneath it, relying on a few microns of varnish, and my own delicacy, to prevent me from smearing one of the gallery's undoubted masterpieces into a muddy pulp.

I tried the water first. To my astonishment, the lettering came away immediately. The stalker had used a water-based pen.

Most marker pens contain permanent ink, or at least are oil-based. The exception is a pen made for use with whiteboards, which has to brush off easily and thus contains a very large-chain polymer which doesn't bond with the smooth surface of the whiteboard. It looked as if that was what had been used here.

In other words, the stalker had gone to considerable lengths not to damage the masterpiece.

I sat back and thought about this. It didn't square with what I knew of the lunatics who usually deface paintings. But it was clear that the man who was after me considered himself an art lover.

I thought how ironic it was that Michelangelo himself had probably only contributed a few brushstrokes to his pupil's work, yet it was considered a masterpiece, while John Drewe's efforts were dismissed as forgeries.

I wiped the rest of the lettering off with a tissue, then buffed the surface with a blast of compressed air and a final wipe with synthetic polish. The *Leda* was literally as good as new. There were going to be some very relieved people amongst the gallery's management.

Then I saw it. On the very edge of the frame, caught in a tiny crack where it had splintered slightly, was a single blue thread. I examined it with the magnifier. It was on the lower right-hand edge, just where a man turning away from the picture at close quarters might brush against it with his arm.

I photographed its location, in case it was ever needed for evidence, then removed it and placed it on a dry mount.

I went and found one of the security guards. 'I need a thread from your jacket,' I told her. She seemed to take this odd request in her stride, holding out her arm for me to draw a thread from the cloth with tweezers. I took it to the microscope and made a second mount. Even under the 200x lens, the two threads were identical. I could get an electron magnification to prove it, but I didn't need to. The guard's uniforms were made of a rough, cheap serge that wasn't likely to be worn by any of the gallery's usual visitors.

You are the custodian of your beauty. I find myself saying it to myself over and over again . . .

I've set up a Hotmail account – Custodian@hotmail.com . . .

The vandal – my stalker – was one of the guards who stood in the galleries all day, mindlessly staring at the stream of visitors who in turn mindlessly stared at the art on the walls.

Then I remembered. I had invited the guard in the Michelangelo's gallery to our party. His name was Thomas Fraser. He was young and good-looking and friendly and he'd once bought me a chocolate muffin in the gallery café. I'd been in front of him in the queue and I'd been looking at the muffins but decided against it when he'd reached out from behind me, picked one up, and said, 'Here. On me.' After that we'd chatted occasionally whenever we passed each other in the corridors. I had probably spoken no more than a dozen sentences to him in my life.

Thomas Fraser's shift finished at two thirty, more or less the same time that I'd left the gallery on the day of the murder. He must have followed me then. But today I was following him.

He took the tube to Queens Park. I followed him to a block of flats. He went in, and I waited. According to the list by the entryphone, Thomas Fraser lived in Flat 5. An hour later he came out again. He'd changed out of his uniform. I waited until he was safely out of the way, then went to the low covered enclosure where the dustbins were kept. I was lucky. Each bin was marked with the number of the flat it was for. I reached into Number 5's bin and pulled out a sack of rubbish. I ripped it open and tipped it on the ground, releasing an avalanche of stinking stale curry-flavoured refuse.

'What are you doing?'

The question had come from a young woman who was about to put her own rubbish into one of the other bins. I looked at the number on it. Nine. Not one of Thomas's immediate neighbours.

'I've lost something,' I said. 'An earring. You know how it is. I need to check we didn't throw it away.'

321

'You are going to clean that lot up, aren't you?' she said suspiciously.

'Of course.'

She sniffed, as if to imply that she didn't necessarily believe me. I squatted down to examine my booty.

A number of supermarket Green Thai Curry cartons. An empty bottle of whisky. An empty box of computer discs. A butter wrapper, thick with rancid globs of butter. Carrier bags, newspapers, sandwich packets. The usual detritus of a life.

Something glinted. A disposable twin-blade razor cartridge. I picked it up by the edges and examined it. The blade had an encrusted ridge of dried shaving foam. Stuck to the foam were dozens of black bristles, like those tiny little decorations you sprinkle on cakes. Each one was a capsule of Thomas Fraser's DNA.

I picked it up and put it into a bag I'd brought with me. There was a sheaf of papers in the rubbish as well, half covered in curry sauce. I pulled at them. Photographs.

Photographs of me, dozens of them. Or rather, one photograph, reprinted dozens of times, all slightly different. Sometimes it was the crop, sometimes the zoom, sometimes the colours that were different. Sometimes he'd even digitally altered my hair, or my neck, or retouched my eyes to make them bigger. In one I appeared to be naked, my face spliced onto another photograph just as he'd done with the email he'd sent round the gallery. There were a whole series of my lips, redrawn on a computer in a dozen different ways.

I gagged. Then I cleared the rubbish up with my hands. There was always a chance that the nosy neighbour would mention me to Thomas Fraser, and I thought he'd be less likely to worry if there was no sign that I'd ever been there. He might even convince himself that she'd mistaken the number on the bin.

I sent the DNA sample to New York. I knew I had found my man but I wanted to have proof, the sort of proof that Bill would understand.

It occurred to me that Thomas Fraser himself had told me where to find out more about him. *According to the* British Journal of Psychiatry, *2001, volume three, I am an extreme narcissist . . .*

I went to the British Library and ordered it from the stacks. It took a bit of time as I didn't have a card, but I used the gallery's name and eventually a bored-looking librarian handed me a magazine.

The psychopathology of violent sex offenders: some diagnostic issues.
Robson, S.J.; Forman, T.; Healey, G.H.

A detailed review of the literature concerning one hundred and twelve sexual assaults. The authors propose that rapists should be allocated to one of five diagnostic categories, each with its own distinct pathology. These are the 'sadistic rapist', the 'anger rapist', the 'predatory rapist', the 'reassurance rapist' and the 'stalker-rapist'.

Sadistic rapists

The 'sadistic rapist' combines aggression with sexual fantasy. The more aggressive the attack becomes, the greater his arousal. He is likely to appear calm and even bored – fear and emotion are for the victims, not the victor. He tends to use knives and other implements on sexually significant parts of the body. He may carry a torture kit consisting of knives, whips, different forms of restraint and other implements such as pliers. He will be a dominant personality, possibly with an interest in fringe philosophies such as survivalism, the Nazi party or the occult. Like the reassurance rapist (see below), he may well ask the victim if he is hurting her – but unlike the reassurance rapist, he is seeking the answer 'yes'. He may well force his victim to co-operate in speaking various 'scripts', such as:

'Do you like the pain?'
'Yes, I like the pain.'
'Tell me how much you like it.'
'I like it a lot.'
'Tell me you love it.'
'I love it.'

– the element of control being as important as the script itself.

Sadistic rapists typically commit highly idiosyncratic, even ritualized offences. They often travel large distances looking for suitable victims. They may not ejaculate at the time of the offence, preferring to exercise self-restraint at the scene and to relive it later in privacy. They may kill their victims when they have finished with them, although it should be noted that this is a strategy to avoid capture – the actual killing holds no pleasure for this type of rapist. They will typically also have acted out their 'scripts' with prostitutes or wives, gradually moving from fantasy, to the borderlands of fantasy/acting out, and thus to the offence itself.

Sadistic rapists account for only 4% of rapes, although the damage they do makes them disproportionately dangerous.

That wasn't the sort of person I was dealing with, I thought. Although I had been cut, a sadistic rapist would have wanted me to be awake and aware of what was happening.

Anger rapists
'Anger rapists' choose victims who represent a group the offender bears a grudge against – mother, wife, girlfriend, teacher. Their rage tends to spill over into uncontrolled violence. But the anger rapist rarely kills once his anger is sated. He prefers humiliating acts, such as anal sex followed by oral sex. He rarely ejaculates internally. He may carry a knife, although his use of it will typically be disorganized and inconsistent. He takes few precautions. Attacks are often preceded by precipitating stressors – events or pressures which trigger the impulse to rape. The rapes typically take place in a geographic comfort zone immediately around the offender's own home.

Anger rapists represent about 5% of all rapes.

Predatory rapists
The 'exploitative' or 'predatory' rapist is the second most common type. These rapists are opportunists, although they may increase the likelihood of finding a suitable victim by going out 'hunting' in likely environments such as bars and clubs. They prefer strangers, although they may well have raped acquaintances, colleagues or even family members early in their 'career'. This kind of rapist considers seduction and rape as interchangeable strategies. His goal is to force submission or humiliation, considering that by doing so he has won a 'game' or competition – though it should be noted that the perceived competition is as much with other men as it is with the woman.

The predatory rapist uses drugs, alcohol, charm or trickery to overcome initial resistance. The assault will typically include anal and oral penetration and may also include spitting or urination. It rarely involves paraphilia, other than mild domination. He will be sexually selfish, understanding that the rape holds no pleasure for the victim. He will take care to minimize the risk of capture, both by telling the victim that no one will take her word against his and by eliminating forensic evidence. He may make the victim swallow his semen for this reason, though he may prefer to ejaculate on the victim's face. He is unlikely to return to his victim. Mementos taken from the victim will remind him – and her – that he now 'owns' her. He may well collect trophies of various kinds in other aspects of his life – cups, awards, photographs, souvenirs etc.

Predatory rapists account for 20% of all rapes.

Neither of those categories described my rapist either, though I could see now why Griffin's profile had allowed the police to get it so wrong. He had been assuming that the use of drugs had been a typical strategy by a predatory rapist to overcome resistance. He had no way of knowing that we might have taken the drugs voluntarily.

Reassurance rapists

The most common type of rapist, however, is the 'reassurance' or 'power assertive' rapist. In general this rapist feels inadequate and sexually unsuccessful. He believes himself incapable of attracting women like the victim in the normal way, and rapes in order to reassure himself of his masculinity. If he carries a knife, he is unlikely to use it. He may fantasize a relationship with his victim, asking her to kiss him, talk to him, tell him that she loves him etc. He may apologize to her after the attack, walk her to her home, or give her gifts or 'life advice' (such as telling her that she mustn't allow being raped to destroy her life) – hence the term that is sometimes used to describe this category, 'gentleman rapists'.

Reassurance rapists are likely to kiss and fondle their victims, shifting positions frequently during intercourse. They may attempt cunnilingus, ask the victim to masturbate, or attempt to make the victim climax. Reassurance rapists are unlikely to attempt anal penetration or wear a condom and typically ejaculate inside the victim. They may demand that she swallow the ejaculate as a demonstration of her feelings for her attacker. (If semen has been swallowed, forensic traces of male-specific antigen may still be present when an oropharyngeal sample is taken.) If reassurance rapists have a paraphilia it is likely to be a fetish, such as an obsessive interest in one part of the body.

Reassurance rapists may spend several weeks planning an assault. They often contact the victim after the attack, to see whether she has been 'persuaded' by the rape to start a relationship with the attacker. There is a strong cognitive dissonance between their image of themselves and the victim's actual experience – they often claim in interviews that they are 'not really rapists'.

Reassurance rapists account for 70% of all attacks, although they vary greatly in the intensity of their obsession.

That was much more like it. The stuff about fantasizing a relationship, the life advice, the pretence that it wasn't really rape – all that was very close to my own situation.

It was when I started to read the final part of the article, though, that my blood really ran cold.

Stalker-rapists

Reassurance rapists who fixate on one victim are rare but extremely dangerous. These 'stalker-rapists' are unable to let go of their belief that the victim 'belongs' to, or is somehow 'meant to be with' the offender. They may believe that they have shown considerable restraint in the past and that the victim should reciprocate with displays of love or sexual favours. Obsessive accumulation of knowledge of the victim's private life – reading mail, going through clothing, accessing private emails and so on – fuels the illusion of an intimate relationship (some stalker-rapists compare their relation-ship with their victim as being like the arguments between an old married couple: one even suggested to his victim that they should go to marriage guidance to resolve their difficulties). What the victim thinks doesn't matter – in the extremely narcissistic mindset of the stalker-rapist, she has forfeited her right to say no by her persistent refusal to say yes. The victim becomes, in fact, little more than a projection of the offender's own obsession. 'You don't seem to appreciate how nice I'm being at the moment,' one stalker-rapist wrote, 'so I've decided it's time to change the rules.'

Stalker-rapists tend to discount the danger they pose to the object of their obsession, but once a threat has been made they consider it a point of honour or a test of their love that they carry it out to the letter. They are meticulous and organized in the way in which they do so, remaining remarkably flexible in the execution of the plan whilst completely inflexible about its objective. At some point the desire to be feared by the victim replaces or supplants the desire to be loved by her. Once this threshold is reached, the reassurance rapist effectively becomes a sadistic rapist, but without the sadist's desire to avoid capture.

Stalker-rapists are the least common type of rapist, representing only about 1% of all rapes.

There was absolutely no doubt about it. Thomas Fraser belonged to the category of rapist which the authors considered to be the most dangerous of all. At the moment he was still deluding himself that I might return his affection, or at least agree to sleep with him. Once he realized that wasn't going to happen, he'd turn from a stalker into a sadist. And there seemed to be absolutely nothing I could do about it.

33

It was, of course, through no great skill on my part that I had managed to clean the graffiti off the Michelangelo: it had required hardly any more expertise than a mother wiping chocolate off a baby's bib. But the importance of the outcome had blinded my superiors to the straightforwardness of the method, and once again I found myself being fêted for my brilliance. Almost immediately I was asked to help out on another major project, this time an Oudry that had supposedly surfaced after many years on the missing list. Opinion was divided as to whether the recovered painting was genuine or a cynical attempt to deliver a 'lost' masterpiece. The new owner, a private collector, was prepared to pay handsomely for our advice.

'It's like a production line in here,' Alex cried happily as the Michelangelo was replaced by the still life. 'Next!'

I said nothing. I had just seen Thomas Fraser. He was part of a group of security guards who had been sent to remove the Michelangelo. I managed to keep well out of his way, but I saw him glancing around and realized that he was looking for me. Through the glass wall of the office I saw him touching the chair I'd been sitting in with the back of his finger. He inhaled deeply. God, I must have left a scent in there without even realizing it.

It was as if he knew that I was looking at him. He turned his head towards me, and for the briefest of moments our eyes met.

It can't have lasted longer than half a second.

He smiled.

I read somewhere that when spies are in the field and they want to transmit coded information back to base, they have special transmitters that compress their messages into tiny split-second bursts, to minimize the time they spend on air.

I barely reacted to his smile – in fact, I think I froze. But something in my reaction must have sent a burst of data, a sudden cascade of information back and forth between us. We both knew.

That afternoon Julia called from New York to say that there was a more than ninety-five per cent chance that the DNA from the razor blade was the same as the DNA from the letter. The machine was still crunching the numbers, but the match probability could only go up, not down.

He was waiting for me.

I left the gallery at six. I had a taxi waiting in Orange Street. It was pouring with rain, but as I hurried with my head down to the driver's window I looked up and saw him standing by the side of the gallery, watching me. He was drenched. He looked as if he could have been there for hours, impervious to the deluge.

I jumped into the back of the taxi and slammed the door. At the last moment, just as the driver released the clutch, Thomas stepped forward and placed something under the windscreen wiper, where it flapped around damply. The cab driver swore, pushed his window down, and reached round to pull it free.

'It's for me,' I told him. He passed it over his shoulder, muttering something about idiot pedestrians.

Ros,

I must do this. Just once. That's all I ask. I must have you. An exorcism. After that I'll disappear. On my life.

Thomas.

I lay in my bath, staring at the ceiling, hands crossed on my chest like a carving on a tomb.

So now I knew who it was. I had been so focused on that objective that I had never stopped to ask myself what I would do when I found out. Like the good scientist I was, I had assumed that with knowledge would come the understanding of how to use it.

But the simple fact remained: I couldn't go to the police. I had made a stupid, terrible, criminal mistake. If I confessed to it now, both Bill and I were finished.

I called Derek Berry, the CPS lawyer. It probably wasn't a clever thing to do but I didn't know many solicitors.

'Derek, it's Ros Taylor.'

'Miss Taylor. I trust you're well?'

'Yes, very well. I just wanted to ask you a hypothetical question.'

'Yes?'

'If someone perjured themselves in court, and someone else got sent to prison as a result, what would the sentence be?'

'Hmm.' I could hear his slimy little mind thinking, wondering whether there could be an excuse to ask me out to dinner in this. 'It would depend on the circumstances,' he decided at last. 'May I ask why you want to know?'

'It's for a book I'm writing.'

'Ah. Well, if you could tell me a bit more of the plot . . .'

'It's not really relevant. It's just a minor point.'

'Perhaps over a drink, then.'

'If you don't know, don't worry. I can always ask someone else.'

'No, no,' he said quickly. 'I could probably look it up while you wait – hang on.' I heard the sound of pages being riffled. 'Well, the maximum sentence is seven years,' he said at last. 'Though if my memory serves, around four or five is more usual. Jeffrey Archer got four years for his perjury, Jonathan Aitken got eighteen months. But those were libel trials. For perjury in a criminal trial you could probably expect five or six.'

I noted that 'you'.

'And of course there might well be a civil claim for compensation from the perjured party,' he added helpfully. 'That could be millions.'

'Thank you,' I said. I put the phone down before he could say any more.

Five years. When I got out I would be in my thirties. My career, it went without saying, would be over. I would be old, and an ex-convict. My life would be nothing.

*   *   *

According to the article in the psychiatric journal, following his threats and promises to the letter was a point of honour for Thomas, a test of love.

He had promised that if I did it, that would be the end of it.

The horrible truth was that I had no alternative but to trust him.

I sent an email to the Hotmail account.

From: RosTaylor@nationalgallery.org
To: Custodian@hotmail.com
Subject:

All right. You win. If you really do swear to leave me
alone afterwards, I'll do what you want.

The reply was swift.

From: Custodian@hotmail.com
To: RosTaylor@nationalgallery.org
Subject: You

You don't sound very enthusiastic, Ros. Yes, I swear.
But are you sure this is what you want? If so, you
have to ask me nicely.

From: RosTaylor@nationalgallery.org
To: Custodian@hotmail.com
Subject: Re: You

Please. Please do what you want to do. I want this to
be over.

From: Custodian@hotmail.com
To: RosTaylor@nationalgallery.org
Subject: Re: Re: You

In the circumstances, I suppose that's as positive as
you're likely to be.

Here are my instructions. Follow them exactly, or all
assurances are off.

There are two parts to this. First, if I am going to
disappear I will need money.

Recently you took delivery of a painting, an Oudry
called 'The White Duck'. You have been asked to
authenticate it by carrying out some scientific tests.

Carry out the tests as per your instructions, but
substitute modern materials so that the test results
will make it look as if the painting is a fake. I
leave the details to you. When this has been done,
get back in touch with me.

I told myself I had no choice.

I sat at my lab bench and stared at the Oudry. So far as I could
tell, it was completely genuine. The initial chromatograph and
the pigment spectrograph had both come back normal. It had
superficial damage where it had been cut out of its frame and
restretched onto a fresh canvas, but it could easily be repaired.

I was going to allow Thomas Fraser to steal *The White Duck* as
effectively as if I'd walked out of the gallery with it under my arm
and handed it to him. In fact, this theft was going to be even more
effective than that, because a famous painting known to have
been stolen is often unsaleable, whereas I was simply going to
render it temporarily worthless. Once it had been reclassified as a
fake by an institution as respected as the National Gallery, Fraser
would be able to pick it up at an auction for a few thousand
pounds. Then it would be a simple matter to re-run the tests,
announce that it was genuine after all, and sell it for something
closer to its true value.

On the other hand, I wasn't hurting anybody. In fact, the
present owner would probably be delighted when it was classified
as a fake – if we said it was genuine, he'd have to reimburse the
insurers for what they'd paid out when it was first stolen, and
he'd almost certainly have spent the money by now. The insurers

332

wouldn't care much either. They'd have written off the loss years ago, and bumped up the premiums to their other customers to cover it.

I went to a drawer where I kept old slides and found one I'd made from the nylon brush fibres caught in the so-called Gauguin. There had been so many of them, it hadn't been necessary to send them all off for analysis. I peeled off the label, scrubbed the slide with lighter fluid to remove all traces of the label gum, and stuck a fresh label on with today's date and the Oudry's catalogue number. I waited until Alex left the lab before taking a tiny sliver of the Calder he had been working on. That was also genuine, but an XRF would show that the pigments were modern. For a Calder, that was fine, but for an Oudry it meant a fake. Again, I labelled the evidence with the Oudry's catalogue number. Finally, I isolated a fragment of white paint for carbon dating. The paint came from the corner of the office, where the wall had been scratched by workmen moving heavy furniture. I stuck a scalpel under a tiny loose flap of paint, lifted it away on the tip of the blade, and transferred it to another slide. When the sample came back from New York, the beautiful white duck in the Oudry would appear to have been created from household emulsion.

```
From:      RosTaylor@nationalgallery.org
To:        Custodian@hotmail.com
Subject:
```

It's done. The results will take a few days to come through but there won't be any doubt.

```
From:      Custodian@hotmail.com
To:        RosTaylor@nationalgallery.org
Subject:
```

Good.

Tomorrow night, unlock the security grilles on your window and leave the window ajar. Take two doses of GHB or a strong sleeping pill - I assume you have

this? If not, let me know and I will send you some.
While you are waiting for it to take effect, bathe and
wash your hair. A little scent would be nice but be
careful not to use too much. There should be fresh
linen on your bed - proper linen: Morrows in Jermyn
Street have some wonderful thick French sheets.
Purchase eight large candles and place them around
your bed. Be careful not to put them near anything
that might catch fire. Obtain the CD of Rachmaninov's
Vespers sung by the Ensemble Gilles Binchois and have
it playing on the CD player on repeat, quite low.
Light the candles. Lie on the bed. Do not wear
anything, but cover yourself with one white sheet. Go
to sleep. I know it will be hard because you will be
nervous but do not be tempted to take any extra pills.
Think of yourself as a child waiting for Christmas
morning, knowing that unless you close your eyes
Santa won't come.

That's all. When you wake up it will be over. Perhaps
the memory of what we have done will somehow linger in
your body - not in your brain of course, which will
have known nothing of all this, but in your skin, your
joints, your muscle memory. Go to work. Smile at the
world. Take your beauty to others and let them see it.
I'll never trouble you again.

I went to Dr Griffin. I hadn't seen him since the trial. His
secretary didn't want to let me see him but I had learned that if
you simply repeated what you wanted enough times people like
that eventually gave in. I was told that I could see him for five
minutes between two other appointments.

I was calm and fluent. I told him that I was having trouble
sleeping. I needed a prescription for sleeping pills.

'Have you tried homoeopathic remedies?' he wanted to know.
'Relaxation techniques, aromatherapy, vitamin E?'

It was almost funny, the idea of my facing Thomas with
nothing stronger than a few essential oils. 'I need something
that'll knock me out when all else fails,' I told him firmly.

'Well, all right. It's a last resort, mind. You don't want to get into the habit of using this stuff.' He wrote me a prescription. 'If I may say so, you don't seem to be recovering as well as I'd have hoped,' he said, handing it to me. 'Is there anything you want to talk about?'

I shrugged.

'Still a few gaps in the memory?' he asked.

'Not really. The odd bit of white mist here and there. I remembered most of it before the trial.'

'Yes, of course.' For a moment I thought he was going to say something else. Then a buzzer on his desk sounded. He seemed distracted.

'Look, take this for now, and come back for a proper talk when we've both got more time,' he said, handing me the prescription. 'Make an appointment on your way out.'

'All right,' I said. I walked out of his office and straight past the reception desk. I had no intention of seeing Dr Griffin ever again.

I didn't buy the French linen sheets. I did buy the candles, though, and the CD. I didn't want to give him any excuse to say that I hadn't kept my part of the bargain.

I lay in the bath. I left the lights off. Everything was happening in the dark, where nothing is real. I took two sleeping pills out of the blister pack and slid down so that my face was under the surface. I opened my mouth. As it filled with water, I dropped them in and swallowed.

It's done, I thought numbly.

After that, it was just like getting ready for a night out. Like an automaton I brushed my wet hair. I put a tiny dab of scent behind my ears. I put on lip gloss and a tiny amount of mascara. I drew a tiny highlight in the corner of my eyes. I knew it was illogical but I felt less naked with my make-up on and the familiar ritual replaced the need for thought. I didn't want to think any more about whether I was doing the right thing. I just wanted to get it over with. I put on the music – creepy, ethereal singing, like a state funeral. I lit the candles. I took my towel off and got into bed. I had placed a condom conspicuously on the table, just in case he hadn't thought of bringing one. I had also poured myself a drink and now I sipped it slowly, just for the alcohol, while I waited for sleep to come. While I waited for death to come, and breathe on me with his rough breath, and then go away again. I felt dizzy. It's started, I thought. I felt the way I felt when I was rushed into hospital to have my appendix out – terrified but resigned. There was no way out but this. The walls bulged. The room was collapsing slowly all around me. My skin felt numb and my face belonged to someone else. I couldn't move my hands. Here it comes, I thought. My eyes closed. Darkness rushed in like a torrent of black water and swept me away.

5

BILL

Beware of the half-truth: you may have the wrong half.

– unknown

34

I sat opposite Lenny Scharf and looked into his eyes.

'This is how it is, Lenny. Sammy Harkur has given us a statement saying that it was you who killed Joshua. He's also told us that it was you who silenced little Danny Mazola in the van. He's given you up. The investigation is now closed. We have our murder, and we have our murderer. End of story.'

Lenny returned my stare. 'He never said anything of the sort and you know it.'

'Want to see the statement?'

His eyes widened. I reached into my briefcase, leafed through my papers, and casually tossed a statement across the table at him. 'Have a read of that. You can read, I take it?'

It was very quiet in the interview room. Not even the whirr of the tape recorder, for the simple reason that the tape recorder had been turned off a long time ago.

Before he reached the end I said, 'After all, a man who could kill his own brother is perfectly capable of stitching up his number two. Not that he did kill his brother, of course. According to that statement, you had been sampling the merchandise and flew into a violent and unprovoked rage.'

I was talking quickly so that he wouldn't spend too much time examining Sammy Harkur's signature. It was good, but it wasn't that good.

'You've got to admire him, really,' I said. 'I thought it was a nice touch, throwing in Danny. Sammy's thinking ahead, as usual. One murder, you'd be out in twelve years, you might come looking for him. Add the child as well, and you're looking at – what? Twenty? Twenty-five? Sammy will have retired to his own little Caribbean island by then.'

Lenny swallowed. I could see a twitch pulsing in his lip. 'I never touched Danny,' he said.

'Really? Somewhere else, were you? Because if you were there, then you were part of it.'

'I was the driver. I was driving the fucking van. I saw it in the mirror.'

'You weren't the driver, Lenny. Chris Patts does Sammy's driving.'

'He got lost. He couldn't find the fucking motorway. Sammy lost his rag. Told Chris to get in the back and me to drive.'

I took the statement and slipped it, unnoticed, back into my case. I reached out and turned the tape recorder on.

'Well, I'm listening,' I said.

After we brought Sammy Harkur in, there was the obligatory piss-up. For some reason, though, on the way to the pub I stopped by my desk. The computer was covered in Post-it notes. I ignored them. But as I pulled my jacket off my chair one of them fluttered to the floor.

Call Dr Griffin. Urgent.

I looked at the other messages. There was another from him, as well. *Steve Griffin. Says it's urgent.*

I sat down and dialled the number. His secretary said he was with a patient and would call back when he was free.

I put my jacket on, then sat down again. Might as well hang on. The pub could wait.

Eventually he called back. 'Bill, I'm glad I got you. It may be nothing, but I'm worried about Ros Taylor.'

'Why?'

'She came to see me earlier for some sleeping pills. I thought at the time she looked a bit rough, but I was in a rush so I asked her to make an appointment. I checked with my receptionist. She didn't.'

'Meaning what?'

'She hasn't shown any signs of being suicidal, has she?' he asked bluntly.

He didn't bother with the charade of pretending that I hadn't been seeing her, so I didn't either. 'Not that I've noticed. I mean, she's been depressed, but she seemed to me to be getting over it.'

'OK. It's probably nothing. But it might be an idea to get one of the SOOFs to drop in on her on Monday, just in case.'

'I'll do that,' I said. 'Alice Turnbull has a good relationship with her. I'll see if she's free.'

I went to the pub but my heart wasn't in it. Eventually I slipped away without drawing attention to the fact that I was going and got a taxi up to Broadhurst Terrace. On the way I made the cabbie pull over at the all-night grocery on the Finchley Road, where I bought her one of those silly bunches of flowers, the ones that are so perfect they look artificial.

I stood outside her flat, thinking.

I knew she couldn't be suicidal. Ros wouldn't do that. But I knew that I hadn't been much good to her recently and I didn't know how I was going to bridge the distance between us.

I didn't want to talk to her just yet. I simply wanted to see if she was there. It was very late now. I went and looked over the railings into the basement where her flat was, to see if the lights were still on.

Candlelight flickered from behind the curtains. That was odd. Why candles?

I climbed over the railings and dropped quietly to the ground. The security grille was pushed back and the window to the sitting room was ajar. That was strange too. Since the murder, Ros had been paranoid about making sure the window and grille were closed and locked.

I pushed the window open.

I thought, I shouldn't be doing this. If she sees me coming through the window, she'll freak.

I wanted to watch her, to see her without being seen. I pushed the curtain aside.

Candles. Lots of them, in the bedroom. Music playing. I could just see her bare legs, stretched out on the bed. And the sound of someone in the shower.

It could just be a friend, I thought. Not a lover. Just a friend.

I swung my legs over the window ledge. The door to the bathroom was open. In the bedroom Ros was asleep, curled up on the bed naked with one arm thrown up in post-coital abandon.

341

The shower was turned off. I waited. A man came out of the bathroom. He turned. His eyes widened. He said, 'So she—'

I lunged at him. His hand, when it came up, had a knife in it. I didn't understand that. I didn't understand where the knife had come from.

And then I thought, *Oh Christ, no. Sleeping pills – a knife –*

I got hold of the hand with the knife and twisted it back on itself. My instructors at Hendon would have been proud of me. They would not have been so proud, though, of what happened next. There is a very controversial choke hold that involves getting onto someone's back and wrapping your right arm round their neck whilst pulling their right arm up and backwards. It has been banned, now, because there were too many deaths in custody as a result of its use.

I used it.

He didn't look very dead. He was jerking and break-dancing on the floor like a fish out of water. But I knew that what I was seeing was air hunger, that stage of dying from a broken neck in which the lungs are still trying to fill themselves through the collapsed airways and the body is still fighting to get itself upright.

It takes around three minutes for a person with a broken neck to turn into a corpse. I stood and watched. Dialling 999, for a variety of reasons, was never an option.

35

I went to check on Ros. She was deeply asleep but her pupils responded sluggishly to light. I kissed her, put her in the recovery position and sat down to watch her.

I didn't turn the music off or blow the candles out. Not at first. Because it was good, watching over her like that. I had just killed a man but I wasn't horrified by what I'd done. I felt quite calm.

After a while I got up, pulled the sheet from her body and inspected her minutely. I told myself that I was checking for injuries but the truth was a little more complex than that.

She seemed fine. On the table beside the bed was a condom, still in its wrapper. I thought that I had probably interrupted the attacker before, not after, he did what he came to do. But I had to know.

I inspected the sheets and between her legs. I had to know. Dear God. Like some crazed jealous husband I crouched between her legs and I actually sniffed her. Killing makes you do strange things.

I rolled her back into the recovery position. Light was beginning to seep through the curtains. And now, finally, I blew out the candles and I watched her beautiful face as the heaviness of the drugs slowly left it and she became Ros again.

At around 8 a.m. I kissed her again. She looked at me, quite unsurprised, and said, 'Is it over?'

'Yes,' I said. 'It's over.' She smiled at me radiantly, turned over and went back to sleep.

*   *   *

I took her breakfast in bed, fresh coffee and toast and orange juice. I said, 'There's no easy way to tell you this. There's a dead body in the other bedroom.'

She looked at me with her big eyes and said nothing.

'It seemed like the only solution.'

She nodded, slowly, and went on eating toast.

Later, she said calmly, 'We're going to have to cut him up. That way we can dispose of the pieces separately.'

I said, 'That's crazy. It'll get traced back to us sooner or later. You of all people know how it works. It's Locard's principle – every contact leaves a forensic trace.'

'Yes. That's my point. I do understand exactly how forensic evidence is collected. So we'll be able to make sure we don't leave any.'

I went out and bought things from a list she gave me. I got a cleaver from a hardware shop. I bought a whole bunch of other things too, to avoid drawing attention to myself – a salt grinder, a steel colander, six plates, a wooden spoon, some Marigold gloves. I also bought ten rolls of dustbin bags, black tape and a roll of Clingfilm. Then I went to a barber's and had my hair cut just as she'd told me, a number two, right down to the skull.

I stood in the shower and she soaped me all over. I waited, quite still, while she snicked the hair from my body with a razor. Gradually I emerged from the white cocoon of foam, sleek and gleaming.

'Now I need to oil you. There mustn't be any dead skin.'

When she had finished she told me to clip my fingernails very short.

While I was out she'd taken the dustbin bags and coated Jo's bedroom with them, layer upon layer, until the inside of the room was a just a black, shining cube that sent distorted reflections receding on all sides to infinity.

I went through his clothes for personal effects. There wasn't much, just a set of house keys, a packet of condoms, a small digital camera and a letter addressed to Ros. I put them on one side without opening the letter. Then I stripped the clothes off the body. It was hard work. I put them into a dustbin bag, which I took through to the other room.

'Bill,' she said, 'you're sweating.'

'Is that a problem?'

'Yes. Low-count machines can trace DNA from anything organic. Even a drop of sweat.' She came and wiped my face with a tissue. 'I'd better help you.'

'You can't. Your hair—'

'I'll wear a shower cap.'

'I've been to a lot of autopsies. I know what to do.'

'I'm a scientist,' she said. 'I've done dissections. This is no different.'

When I was a kid my father used to come back sometimes from the pub with a brace of pheasants, a brightly coloured cock and a smaller brown hen, their heads tied together with a loop of baler twine as if they were kissing. They would be hung up by the twine from a hook in the larder ceiling for a week or even more. Then it would be time to pluck them, or, if it was the end of the season and the birds were tough and only fit for the pot, skin them instead. We'd do both birds at once, my father working on the cock, me the hen. First you chopped off the neck with a cleaver. Sometimes there would still be grain in the bird's crop, the undigested remains of its last meal. Two more blows, and the black scaly feet were off too. Then you fanned out each wing and chopped them off with a blow through the joint nearest the body. After that, the top layer of skin came away, feathers and all, like a fur coat being peeled off. Finally, under a running tap, a cut was made under the tailbone and someone with a small hand – i.e. me – had to reach inside and tug out everything that was inside the chest cavity: the tiny hard pieces of the heart and liver, the soft, knobbly guts, the collapsed sack of the lungs.

You always thought it was going to be worse than it was. And you couldn't back out, not with your father watching.

She made us aprons and gloves out of the dustbin bags.

I rested the cleaver on the soft skin of the neck, just below the

Adam's apple. I could see bristles poking through the skin. 'Tilt his head back,' I said.

She knelt above the body and took the head in two hands, one on each side. When she tilted his chin up the neck rose and tightened.

'Now,' I said. I lifted the cleaver and brought it down hard. There was a sound like a groan from the mouth as the neck parted effortlessly, the cleaver slicing through the white tube of the thorax and burying itself in the vertebrae. Blood gushed from the severed veins. In cross section, they were as thick as worms.

'Keep pulling,' I said. I worked the blade free of the bone and hacked once, twice, three times. Each time blood arced up and splattered us. Then the vertebrae gave way. Now there were only two thin threads of skin holding the head in place. A final blow with the cleaver, and they were gone.

She got a bin bag and, turning it inside out, bagged the head up.

'Wrap it in paper. Anything to disguise its shape.'

'Hang on,' she said. She left, and came back with a pot of Sainsbury's yoghurt. 'It'll decompose quicker if we add live bacteria,' she said matter-of-factly. She poured the yoghurt into the bag all over the head and rubbed it into the head though the plastic. There was a smear of yoghurt on the back of her hand and she licked it off absentmindedly. 'What about dental records?'

'What about them?'

'We have to break his teeth.'

'If we break his teeth there'll be tooth fragments everywhere.'

'We could smash them through the bag,' she pointed out.

I used the end of the cleaver handle to smash at the mouth. The bag started to lacerate, and we had to wrap it in several more layers before we were finished. Then, while she got to work wrapping up the head in dozens of layers of newspaper, like a pass-the-parcel, I hacked off the hands. We slashed the end of each finger to make fingerprint ID difficult, and then we dropped the hands into another bin bag and began the same process of bagging up.

'Now what?'

'The legs, I suppose.'

I looked at his legs. They were more daunting than the hands.

'You're sweating again,' she said. 'Let me.'

'I don't want you to get involved.'

'It's a bit late for that.' She caught my eye. Suddenly, what I'd just said seemed hilariously funny. There we were, in our home-made blood-spattered noddy suits, dismembering a human body, and I didn't want her to get involved.

It was no time to laugh, but we laughed. We laughed until the tears came, and she said, 'Careful. DNA,' and wiped the liquid gently from my eyes with a tissue.

She turned the body over and hacked off the legs below the knees. Where I had used brute force, she used intelligence, putting the cleaver into the joints and prising them apart. We wrapped the torso in the bloodied bags it lay on and sealed it. Then we took turns to shower the blood off ourselves. We were left with three sealed packages, one large and two small.

While Ros rinsed down the flat, I took the bags outside and placed them with the other rubbish bags outside three different houses. It wasn't ideal, but I knew from a case I'd worked on the previous year that it was as safe a way of disposing of a body as any of the more complicated methods. When I came back she was lying on the bed. I went and lay next to her.

'How do you feel?' she asked.

'Better than I suppose I ought to.'

'Me too.'

My hairless chest felt strange when she rubbed it. 'You must be tired, though.'

'I ache all over,' I admitted.

She sat astride me, kneading the knots in my shoulders and arms. I closed my eyes. 'That's nice,' I said.

As she worked her way down my stomach I felt myself thickening.

'I love you,' she whispered.

347

36

Dearest Ros,

By the time you read this it will all be over. I hope you're all right – no headache or anything like that.

It occurred to me that you might like to know exactly what happened on the night of the eleventh of July. Perhaps you have already remembered – I was never sure how much of your so-called amnesia was faked and how much was real. But for what it's worth, this is what I saw.

Do you remember how hot it was that night? It was one of those sweltering nights you get in London sometimes, in the summer, when the evening seems barely cooler than the day. You had been away on holiday, I remember, and I had been waiting eagerly for you to get back so that I could resume my role as your invisible watcher. That's right – I had already been following you around for several months by then. Ever since you walked into my gallery one afternoon in April with your white coat on, talking earnestly to the curator about some conservation issue or other, touching your neck with one finger, which is what you always do when you are being serious.

There was nothing else to think about, all those hours sitting in that gallery like some art world equivalent of the guards outside Buckingham Palace, my brain buzzing with thoughts of you . . . I used to imagine your face, your body, hanging on the wall, a dozen giant Ros's everywhere I looked. And then I started following you home, hoping to get a glimpse of what I had only imagined. That was how I came to discover that your flatmate and her boyfriend were not always very thorough about drawing the curtains. But believe me, they were only ever a sideshow. I would rather have watched you brush your hair just once than see your flatmate fingering herself a dozen times.

That day you had your phone stolen. I was distraught when I heard. What use is a guardian angel if he doesn't guard? I went looking for the culprits but of course I didn't find them. As I was coming back, though, I saw you, leaving the gallery early, going home. So I followed you. And I watched.

To begin with it was just you and Jo. Then Henson came back. Slimy Henson. He'd been out to get cigarettes. I watched, but it was boring for a while, and people were coming home from work. I had to move. I came back later, though. I saw the three of you together. That was what made me angry. I knew about Jo and the slimy man but I couldn't bear to think of you being part of it as well. And then I almost got caught by the boy delivering pizza when he parked his moped against the railings. So I went away again, and came back much later, but I was still angry. It looked as if the slime had gone home. Everything was quiet. I crept inside and that's when I found you. The slime hadn't gone, he was asleep, you were all asleep.

I wasn't interested in Jo. But she started to wake up and I had to shut her up before she woke the slime.

So you see, it was quite understandable, what happened. If you hadn't done what you did, I wouldn't have done what I did either.

Goodbye, Ros. I am sorry that this was the only way I could get to be near you. If in some other universe we had met differently, and you had loved me back, you would have found that my love was something quite wonderful. But it's too late for all that now.

Thomas

37

She said, 'I've got to tell you something.'

'What?'

'I've remembered what happened. All of it. Somehow all this has shaken it loose.'

'You don't have to talk about it if you don't want to.'

'I do. I want you to know the truth.'

She came back from work early that day, because her phone had been stolen. Jo had already taken the day off, originally to tidy up after the party, but then Henson had phoned Ros and discovered that Jo was at home. He'd gone round to see her.

Ros had walked in and found Jo sprawled across the sofa, wearing nothing but a dressing gown. The belt from the dressing gown was tied round one of her wrists.

Ros stopped dead. 'Jesus, Jo.'

'Oh, it's you. I thought it was Gerry. He's just popped out to get some fags.'

'I thought you were going to dump him.'

She sighed. 'So did I. But Gerry had other ideas. Lots of other ideas. I'm pathetic, aren't I? I just can't give it up. Did you get the photos?'

'No, I forgot. I came home early because my phone got stolen.'

Ros told Jo about the phone, by which time Gerry had returned with wine and cigarettes. They opened the wine, and one thing led to another. At some point Ros went out to pick up the photos and to buy more wine. And at some point Jo suggested that they take the liquid ecstasy she'd found when she was clearing up after the party. They put it in the wine. It made them mellow. All three of them had collapsed onto the sofa, a triangular tangle of arms and legs, with Gerry openly running his hand inside Jo's dressing gown, flirting with her in front of Ros.

'Did that make you jealous?'

She thought about it. 'Not jealous of her, no. Jealous of *them*. Of what they had – of what Jo said they had.'

'Go on.'

Jo had looked up at Ros and smiled. Gerry's hand was inside her robe, cupping her breast, the thumb moving rhythmically under the cotton. 'We're not embarrassing you, are we?'

'Course not. You've got no secrets from me, remember?'

Gerry laughed. 'You tell her all about it, do you?'

'Ros and I share everything,' Jo said.

'Everything?'

'Why not?'

Jo slid her hand into his trousers. The drug was making Ros dizzy. She closed her eyes, but when she did that she seemed to be floating away. From a long way away she heard Gerry say, 'I'm not sure there's enough of me to be shared by both of you.'

Jo laughed. 'Not the impression I'm getting.'

Ros felt nervous and mellow and daring all at once. She opened her eyes and took another sip of the drugged wine. She said, 'What makes you think I want him?'

Jo said, 'Don't knock it till you've tried it.' And then someone's hands were on her shirt, undoing her buttons, and there were other hands pulling at her waist, and she was full of excitement and trepidation and chemically processed love.

'And?'

'And nothing. That's it. A drunken, E'd-up, three-way shag. I remember thinking even as he did it that she'd have to dump him after that. There was no way their relationship could survive the embarrassment.' She sighed. 'I suppose I'd always fancied him, you see. Fancied him and found him a little bit repulsive at the same time, if that makes sense. And the fancying bit was mainly because of Jo. Because of wanting to see him through her eyes. And Henson – he'd always flirted with me, when Jo wasn't around. That was our little secret. I think that was one reason I blocked it all out, because I felt guilty about flirting with him behind her back.'

'Did you enjoy it? The sex, I mean.'

'Not really. It wasn't anything like the fireworks she'd been talking about. Mind you, nothing ever is when you've taken drugs.'

I said, 'You don't strike me as the sort of person who would enjoy something like that.'

'Jesus, Bill.' She laughed mirthlessly. 'I'm a criminal. A perjurer. An accessary to murder. What difference does it make that I once let my best friend's boyfriend get inside my knickers?'

But it did make a difference. A lot of difference. To Thomas, at any rate, watching outside the window.

She said, 'I still don't see why Gerry didn't call the police when he came round.'

'Neither do I. Unless he'd been so out of it he really thought he'd killed her himself. But probably it was just panic. He didn't want his wife or anyone to find out he'd been there. So he pulled her body under the shower and tried to make it look like a burglary. He probably assumed you were dead too.'

She sighed. 'Thomas was right. He was a slime.'

'A slime who's in prison for something he didn't do.'

We lay on our backs in the dark.

'Ros, what I'm about to tell you is very important. When you said in court that you remembered Henson raping you, that wasn't a lie. That was a confabulation – your mind playing tricks on you. You thought it was the truth. It was only after the trial that you realized about Thomas, and then you came to me right away to make a statement. As for Thomas, you didn't read his letters. You passed them straight on to me. You've done nothing wrong. Nothing.'

'But why should anyone ask me about that?'

'Just in case.'

When Dr Griffin accused her of falling in love with my uniform, with a symbol of something that could protect her, he was only seeing half the picture. Because there was also the fact that I had fallen in love with a uniform as well, although in my case it was the shapeless tracksuit trousers and Gap T-shirts provided by the rape suite. She had been someone, finally, I could protect.

She still was.

She said, 'When I went through his rubbish, I found some photographs he'd taken of me. I think they'd been printed off a computer.'

'Did anyone see you there?'

'One woman. A neighbour. Do you think it matters?'

I felt very tired, so tired it was actually remarkable I couldn't sleep. I said, 'We've got his keys. We'd better go round there.'

I drove her to his flat. I was worried about leaving forensic traces in my car but it couldn't be helped. I needed someone with me in case anything happened. I made her tie her hair back and keep her head off the head support. It was all we could do.

She directed me to the block of flats where he lived. It seemed pretty straightforward. There were only four keys on his keyring, so we didn't have to spend a long time trying different keys at the front door, which might have attracted suspicion.

We let ourselves into his flat. Thomas Fraser had been a smoker. The place stank of stale cigarette smoke. Books about art lay scattered everywhere. There were paintings, too, stacked against the walls, huge canvases with garish modern portraits on them, presumably his own work.

'Oh Christ,' Ros said. 'That's me.' She reached out to the stack of canvases.

'Don't touch anything.'

She pulled her hand back. 'What do we do about these?'

'They're too big to take with us.'

'I'll get some bleach,' she said. She went into the kitchen. I looked round for his computer. I'd been hoping for a laptop, but Fraser had a large, old-fashioned Apple, the type of thing I'd seen designers and people who worked with graphics using. I picked it up. It weighed a ton. I unplugged the monitor. We wouldn't need that. Then I thought: but leaving the monitor will prove that someone's stolen the base unit. I had to take them both.

Ros was working through the canvases one by one, quickly scouring the surface of each picture with bleach. 'There.' She looked round and saw me struggling with the computer. 'I'll get the door.'

I managed to get it as far as the stairs. I rested it on the banister and paused, panting. Ros pressed the button for the lift.

'Not the lift,' I managed to say.

'I'll take the keyboard.'

We were almost at the bottom when we heard voices. We waited until they'd gone, then resumed our progress towards the front door. 'I'll get the car,' Ros said. Someone was coming in through the door. A woman. Ros gave her one quick glance and kept walking.

'What are you doing?' The woman's voice was shrill.

Ros said smoothly, 'We're taking this to be repaired.'

'You were here before. You were going through the rubbish. I asked Thomas about you.' She stared at us accusingly. 'You said you'd lost an earring. Thomas didn't know anything about it.'

'We're friends of his.'

'Then you won't mind if I ask him.' She pressed a button on the entryphone.

Ros said, 'Actually, we're police officers. We're removing this equipment for examination.'

'Do you have identification?'

I put the computer down and got my warrant card out. She looked at it. 'Oh. I see. What's happened?'

'I'm afraid we can't discuss that. The investigation is still ongoing.'

'We've had a lot of burglaries, you see. And you can't be too careful, can you?'

'That's all right. It's good to be cautious.' Ros held the door open for me and I picked up the computer.

We stopped the car near some waste ground and threw the computer out of the window. We reckoned kids would find it and take it apart for spares. Within a few hours there wouldn't be anything left.

She said, 'That woman. I made a stupid mistake, didn't I?'

'It was fine.'

'I shouldn't have said we were police. I never thought she'd ask for ID.'

'It shut her up.'

'But they'll knock on her door, won't they? Sooner or later, when they've realized Thomas Fraser has gone missing. She'll remember it, and tell them then.'

I said, 'Maybe she'll be out. Maybe she lives on the top floor and the plonk responsible for taking statements won't bother to walk that far. Maybe she won't even mention it.'

'Maybe.'

We drove on in silence for a while. Then she said, 'But we can't be sure. If we wanted to be sure—'

I said angrily, 'I'm not killing anybody else, Ros. Certainly not some innocent bystander who might or might not be able to say that she saw us taking a computer from Fraser's flat.'

'Of course not,' she said quickly. 'That wasn't what I meant.'

We drove on. I didn't ask her what she had meant, and she didn't tell me. And I didn't tell her the reason I'd reacted so angrily was that it had crossed my own mind first.

6

ROS

Whoever fears no truth need fear no lies.

– Thomas Jefferson

38

I went back to work. I'd like to say that I was racked by guilt but I wasn't. It was over. Bill had saved me. I found myself humming as I worked on my latest project.

Alex walked into the lab and stopped short. 'My God, Ros. What happened to you?'

'I decided I was fed up with being a brunette, that's all.' I touched my hair, a short blonde bob, self-consciously. 'What do you think?'

'It's – well, it's different. But it suits you.'

'Thank you.'

'And the lips, too. Christ. What's brought this on?'

'I decided it was time to move on, that's all.'

'Aha. The girl's in love.'

I gave him a kiss on his grizzled cheek. 'Just happy.'

That afternoon I got a call from Kate, the personnel director. She wanted me to come and see her. I went down to her office, where I found Simon from IT and another man who was introduced as Peter Thorpe, a policeman.

'Is there a problem?' I said. I was thinking that this couldn't be anything serious, not with just a single detective.

'Simon has been trying to find out where that revolting email came from,' Kate said. 'I'm afraid we've got some very worrying news. It seems possible that it was sent by one of the gallery's own employees.'

I wondered why she thought that made it worse than if it was sent by someone who knew me from outside. She was saying, 'As you know, it's a clear breach of our email policy to distribute anything which is indecent or offensive. Our disciplinary procedures allow us to suspend the person responsible immediately, and if necessary turn the matter over to the police.'

'So have you done that? Suspended him, I mean?'

'The problem we're having is that the employee in question hasn't turned up for work this week.'

'It's a man by the name of Thomas Fraser,' the policeman added. 'I've been to his address myself and there doesn't seem to be anybody there.'

'Has he hassled you in any other way?' Kate asked me. 'Made a nuisance of himself, or given you any unwanted attention?'

I did my best to look baffled. 'No,' I said. 'He always seemed very polite.'

'Well, I'm sure he'll turn up,' the policeman said. 'I'll leave it for a while before we call the search parties out. If he gets in touch, though, will you let me know?'

'Of course,' I said.

Days passed, then weeks. We heard nothing, and I almost let myself believe that we had got away with it. But there was still one thing we had to get right.

At 7 a.m. one Friday morning in December Bill walked into Paddington Green police station and went up to the front desk. Ignoring the greeting from the desk sergeant, he said, 'I am here to make a formal statement about a sexual relationship between myself and a witness who appeared for the prosecution in the trial of Gerry Henson.'

I am in the lab, working on a nice little Bulleid, when through the glass walls I see two uniformed policemen and a policewoman heading towards me. With them is another man, the plainclothes detective from Internal Investigations. Scratton.

I stay calm. It's important to finish writing the address and get these samples in the post.

He opens the door to the lab and walks in. 'Miss Taylor.'

'One moment,' I say coolly. I lick the label and stand up to put the envelope into the outgoing post tray. 'Yes?'

'We need to talk to you at a police station.'

'What about?' I gesture at the painting. 'I'm very busy.'

'Ros Taylor, I am arresting you . . .'

He is still talking, reciting the caution at me in a sing-song voice like a dirty limerick. I am being arrested. Not charged, arrested. I know the difference now. But the people who have come in and are watching us – Alex, Tricia, one of the curators standing open-mouthed – don't know that. Alex, bless him, gets angry. One of the policemen has to hold him back; there's even talk of arresting him, too, for obstruction.

'Oh, for God's sake,' I say. 'Let's get this over with.'

The doctor takes three blood samples. I feel the tiny sting as the needle pushes into the soft white skin in the crook of my elbow, the tiny rip of muscle as it slithers inside the vein. The tubes into which she syringes the blood are colour coded, purple, grey and red, just as I remember them. On the red-topped tube are the words: 'ATTENTION. Serological samples only. This tube contains no anticoagulants. For DNA use purple jar.'

I sign the form that says I give my consent. I hold out my hand for the fingernail examination, the short wooden toothpicks that are scraped under each nail and then carefully bagged up in a paper evidence envelope. The doctor is not as gentle as Dr Matthiesson, or perhaps she knows why I am here, what I am suspected of, and murder suspects are not treated as gently as rape victims.

It is not only fragments of Thomas Fraser's DNA they are looking for. I am made to give them six pubic hairs, to spit into a jar, to blow my nose into a sterile tissue, to pop up on the couch while the doctor inserts into me a narrow Pedersen speculum moistened only with saline solution because lubricant can contaminate the swabs. The fact that they are performing so many tests is good. It means that they're not quite sure what I'm guilty of, whether I slept with Bill or Thomas or both, whether I'm a killer or an accomplice or even just a victim.

They say the first lie is the hardest, but it isn't true. It's the very last lie that's the tricky one, the one you tell to protect all the other lies, the lies you've told to other people and the lies you've told to yourself. Particularly the lies you've told to yourself. They're the dangerous ones, the ones you barely notice until it's far too late.

I am taken to an interview room.

'I want to ask you first about your relationship with Detective Inspector Thomson,' Scratton says when the tapes are rolling.

I say, 'I had a sexual relationship with Detective Inspector Thomson for over three months. It began before the trial and ended soon afterwards.'

Scratton receives this information with a stony glare. I get the impression this was meant to be his trump card. 'Are you aware that you should have made this relationship known, both to the judge and to Mr Henson's defence team?'

'Yes.'

'And that had you done so, your evidence would have been ruled inadmissible?'

'Yes.'

'Did you at any time discuss your evidence with Detective Inspector Thomson?'

'No,' I say calmly. 'We never discussed my evidence. My evidence was, to the best of my knowledge, entirely accurate.'

'And truthful?' he says sardonically.

I look him in the eye. 'And truthful.'

'Where's Thomas Fraser, Ros?'

'I've no idea.'

'He hasn't been at work. No one's seen him at his home. He hasn't used his credit cards. We're treating that as very suspicious.'

'I'm glad you're taking it so seriously. But I haven't seen Thomas for weeks.'

'What did Thomas Fraser have to do with the death of Jo McCourt?' This is the nub of it, and we both know it. If they can prove that he killed Jo, they'll have a motive for Bill and me to have wanted him dead.

'Gerry Henson killed Jo. Your own officers gave evidence to that effect.'

His eyes are cold. 'We've got a warrant to search your flat. Would you give us your keys, please?'

I hand them over. 'Let's hope they do a better job than last time.'

'They'll do an excellent job, believe me.' He chews at a nail. 'We're charging Bill Thomson with murder,' he says, almost as an afterthought.

For several hours I am left alone. I suppose they are waiting to see what the search team finds. I am fairly sure there will be nothing. But I know – we all know – that it will only take a hair, a drop of blood invisible to the naked eye, a drop of sweat, a tear.

So we wait.

We've made a promise to each other, Bill and I. If we get through this, we will always tell each other honestly what we're thinking, no matter how hurtful it is or what kind of light it puts us in.

For both of us, it seems a more important vow than any of the ones that other people make in church.

I am very cold in the paper suit I have been given to wear. Again, there seems to be some distinction between rape victims and murderers at work here. I have been offered no Gap tracksuit, no hot shower, no free toiletries. Scratton comes in and sits down. He stares at my nipples through the thin white paper. Good, I think. Perhaps it'll put him off his stride.

'Bill Thomson has confessed,' he says without preamble.

'Confessed to what?'

'Everything. Perverting the course of justice, conspiracy to murder, disposing of the body.'

I know their tricks. I smile and say nothing. I know very well that Bill has done nothing of the sort.

The hours tick by. Scratton leaves and comes back again. He is holding something in a transparent evidence folder. He grins at me. I don't like that grin. He shouldn't be happy. He should be hostile and angry and frustrated.

'Well, we've searched your flat,' he says.

'And you didn't find anything.'

'No,' he agrees, 'we haven't. So far. Although we still have,' he consults his watch, 'eighteen hours before we need to let you go.' He sits down and looks at the evidence folder. 'What I have, Ros, are a series of emails between yourself and Thomas Fraser. They were on the computer server at your gallery. You can't delete emails, you see. They get stored automatically.'

'Yes, I know. Thomas sent me emails. So?'

'These aren't just the emails he sent you. These are the emails you sent *him*. And what they show, quite clearly, is that two weeks ago you invited him to your flat for sex.' He looks at me triumphantly. 'Now why did you do that?'

'Inviting your boyfriend to have sex with you is hardly a crime.'

'Fraser was your *boyfriend*?'

'Well – my lover. For a while.'

He blinks. 'Was this before, after or during your relationship with DI Thomson?'

'After, of course.'

'You didn't mention this earlier,' he says accusingly.

'You didn't ask.'

He shakes his head. 'This won't wash, Ros. This email describes sleeping pills, candles, windows left unlocked. It isn't the sort of note you write to a lover.'

'It wasn't a conventional relationship. To put it bluntly, Mr Scratton, Thomas and I have a shared interest in sadomasochism. What you're looking at there,' I nod at the file, 'is just a fantasy. A game.'

'You're seriously telling me,' Scratton says disbelievingly, 'that having been raped yourself you find the idea a turn-on?'

'I believe it happens sometimes. Ask Dr Griffin. It's called acting out. Or something.'

He shakes his head. 'And the pornographic email he sent round your workplace? The anonymous notes?'

'All part of the same game.'

'No,' he says. 'You never had any intention of sleeping with Fraser that night. It was a trap. You lured him to your flat, where DI Thomson was waiting. You killed him there together and you disposed of the body afterwards.'

'There isn't a scrap of evidence to support that suggestion and you know it. Whereas,' I say, 'as you've searched my flat, you'll have found the diary Dr Griffin asked me to keep. You'll find that the daily entries support everything I've been saying.'

'How very convenient,' he sneers. I stare back. He drops his gaze first, flicking through the papers in the file.

'Then there's another email,' he says at last, 'in which he tells you to falsify evidence relating to a picture.'

'Is there?'

'Yes. Now, how do you explain that, Miss Taylor?'

'All part of the same game, obviously.'

'Except there'll be evidence.' He looks almost eager. He thinks he's got me now. 'Yes. That's your mistake, right there. You've made it look as if this picture, this Oudry, is a fake. We'll get you for conspiracy to defraud.'

'And when you find that there's no such evidence, you'll have to drop this nonsense, won't you?'

'We will check, you know.'

'Be my guest. As a matter of fact, you'll find the papers all to hand in the top drawer of my desk. I was looking at them just the other day. There was a problem with some of the results.'

'What sort of problem?'

'A false negative. Funnily enough,' I say, 'it did look as if that painting might be a forgery, for a while. But when I got the tests redone it became clear that it was perfectly genuine.'

Scratton looks as if he's bitten a lemon. 'You were seen removing a computer from Thomas Fraser's flat.'

'Not me.'

'We'll do an ID parade.' His eyes go up to my blonde hair. 'We can make you wear a wig, you know.'

'Go ahead,' I tell him. 'Do whatever you like.'

Suddenly he snaps. He reaches out and yanks off the tape. He grabs the jumpsuit just below my throat and uses it to pull me forward across the table, so hard the material rips. He locks eyes with me. There is real anger there, and I'm frightened, unsure of what he might do.

'Do you know what I really fucking loathe about you?' he hisses.

'I have a feeling you're about to tell me.'

'I knew Bill Thomson before he met you. He had the makings of a good policeman. A little naive, maybe, a little too fond of doing things the hard way. But a good man. And you, you little bitch, you've turned him into a lying toerag.' He releases me. He punches his fist into his palm, hard. Then, abruptly, he gets up and walks to the door.

I call after him, 'No. You're wrong. It was you who did that.'

Fourteen hours to go. They keep coming back. They take it in turns to bully and prompt and cajole. They work on Bill, to see if they can get anything from him to use on me, and then they come back to see if I'll give them anything they can use on him. And when that doesn't happen they get vindictive. Since there's nothing to charge us with, they start trying to destroy us. They tell me things Bill has supposedly said about me, things he's meant to have done, prostitutes he's taken freebies from, suspects he's beaten up, a whole string of women he's meant to have shagged and then abandoned. They even bring some poor little policewoman in who tells me that he's been screwing her for months and didn't he tell me? My only worry is whether he's able to cope with them doing the same to him.

And then, abruptly, it is over. I am free to go. 'For the moment,' Scratton says churlishly, salvaging a little menace from his defeat.

I walk out of there. On the Edgware Road it is dark. Traffic has built up, above us, on the Westway; an ambulance turns its siren on as it tries to shoulder its way through.

He's waiting by the underpass, his face dark with stubble and fatigue. As I run across the road towards him he opens his arms wide and takes a step off the pavement, ready to hold me. And I know that whatever happens, wherever this takes us, I'll always remember him at this moment, just as he is now, standing there with his arms outstretched, like a man stepping down off a cross.

He wraps his arms round me and says, 'Are you all right?'

'I will be,' I say. I slip my own arm round his waist. Drunks are spilling out onto the street, staggering onto the road. Leaning against each other, we attract no attention as we stumble quietly up the street.

Afterword

As I said earlier, *Tell Me Lies* is based on a true story, elements of which have been reported in various newspapers over the last two years without a connection ever being made between them, although it was widely gossiped about in legal circles. I did consider writing it as a true crime book, initially, but after a series of consultations with lawyers I decided that a fictionalized account would serve my purposes just as well and avoid the possibility of litigation. It also allowed me to fill in several gaps in my knowledge with my own suppositions.

The character I have called 'Gerry Henson' spent several months in Her Majesty's Prison Wandsworth, first as a remand prisoner and then while awaiting appeal. His verdict was declared unsafe soon after the revelation that crucial identification evidence presented at his trial had been compromised by a relationship between the witness concerned and a senior detective. He was released soon afterwards and is believed to have come to an arrangement with the CPS regarding compensation.

'Bill Thomson' was dismissed from the police for gross misconduct, although he was never charged with any criminal offence. 'Ros Taylor' left her job soon afterwards. Their current whereabouts is unknown. However, a few months ago I was intrigued to be sent a press cutting from *The Burlington Magazine*, forwarded to me by one of my contacts at the National Gallery, which reported that a small painting by Bulleid had just been sold at Sotheby's for over one and a half million pounds. The article noted that the painting had last changed hands for only four thousand pounds, having been classified as a forgery after extensive scientific tests by no less an authority than the National Gallery's Science and Conservation Department. The

367

new owners had then commissioned a new set of tests from an equally prestigious laboratory in the United States which comprehensively demonstrated the picture's authenticity. As the piece in *The Burlington* wryly pointed out, the whole episode highlighted 'that scientists are on occasion almost as fallible as art historians when it comes to spotting fakes'. The fortunate owners were not identified in the article, other than saying that they were believed to live in Cyprus. Turkish Cyprus, interestingly, does not have any extradition arrangements with the UK.

The forger John Drewe was sentenced to six years' imprisonment in 1998 and was released two years later. Police estimate that at least 140 fakes sold by him are still in circulation. So far as I am aware, however, none of them has ever passed through the National Gallery.

'Alice Turnbull' is still working as a sexual offences officer. She married last year and is currently on maternity leave. I am very grateful for her help in writing this account.

I am also grateful to Jill Robertson, who first told me about Ros; to the Recorder of London, His Honour Judge Michael Hyam, who kindly looked at my courtroom scenes and explained some of my procedural errors – there will be many that remain, but they are the fault of the pupil and not the teacher; to Ros's friends, Cecile Beaufils and Bobby Thomson, who read the manuscript and made many helpful comments; and to the brave survivors on www.aftertherain.com